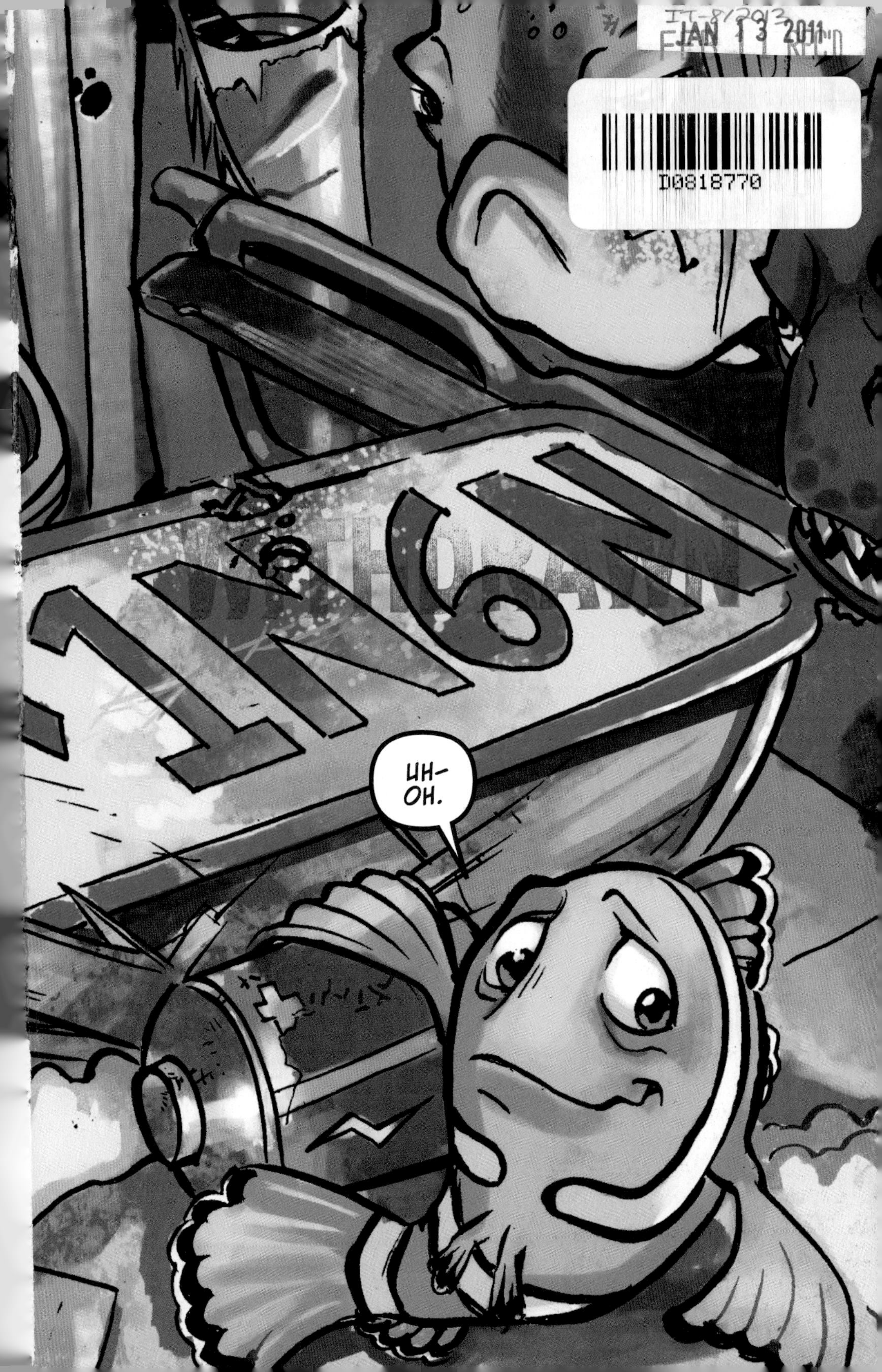
UH-OH.

# DISNEY · PIXAR
# FINDING NEMO

Ross Richie - Chief Executive Officer
Mark Waid - Chief Creative Officer
Matt Gagnon - Editor-in-Chief
Adam Fortier - VP-New Business
Wes Harris - VP-Publishing
Lance Kreiter - VP-Licensing & Merchandising
Chip Mosher - Marketing Director

Bryce Carlson - Managing Editor
Ian Brill - Editor
Dafna Pleban - Editor
Christopher Burns - Editor
Christopher Meyer - Editor
Shannon Watters - Assistant Editor
Eric Harburn - Assistant Editor

Neil Loughrie - Publishing Coordinator
Travis Beaty - Traffic Coordinator
Ivan Salazar - Marketing Assistant
Kate Hayden - Executive Assistant
Brian Latimer - Lead Graphic Designer
Erika Terriquez - Graphic Designer

FIRST EDITION: DECEMBER 2010
10 9 8 7 6 5 4 3 2 1

# LOSING DORY

WRITTEN BY
## MICHAEL RAICHT AND BRIAN SMITH

ART
## JAKE MYLER

### COLORS
**JAKE MYLER**
CHAPTERS 1-2

### RACHELLE ROSENBERG
CHAPTERS 3-4

COVER
**JAKE MYLER**

LETTERER
**DERON BENNETT**

ASSISTANT EDITOR
**JASON LONG**

EDITOR
**CHRISTOPHER MEYER**

DESIGNER
**ERIKA TERRIQUEZ**

SPECIAL THANKS
JESSE POST, STEVE BEHLING, ROB TOKAR, BRYCE VANKOOTEN
AND KELLY BONBRIGHT.

# CHAPTER ONE

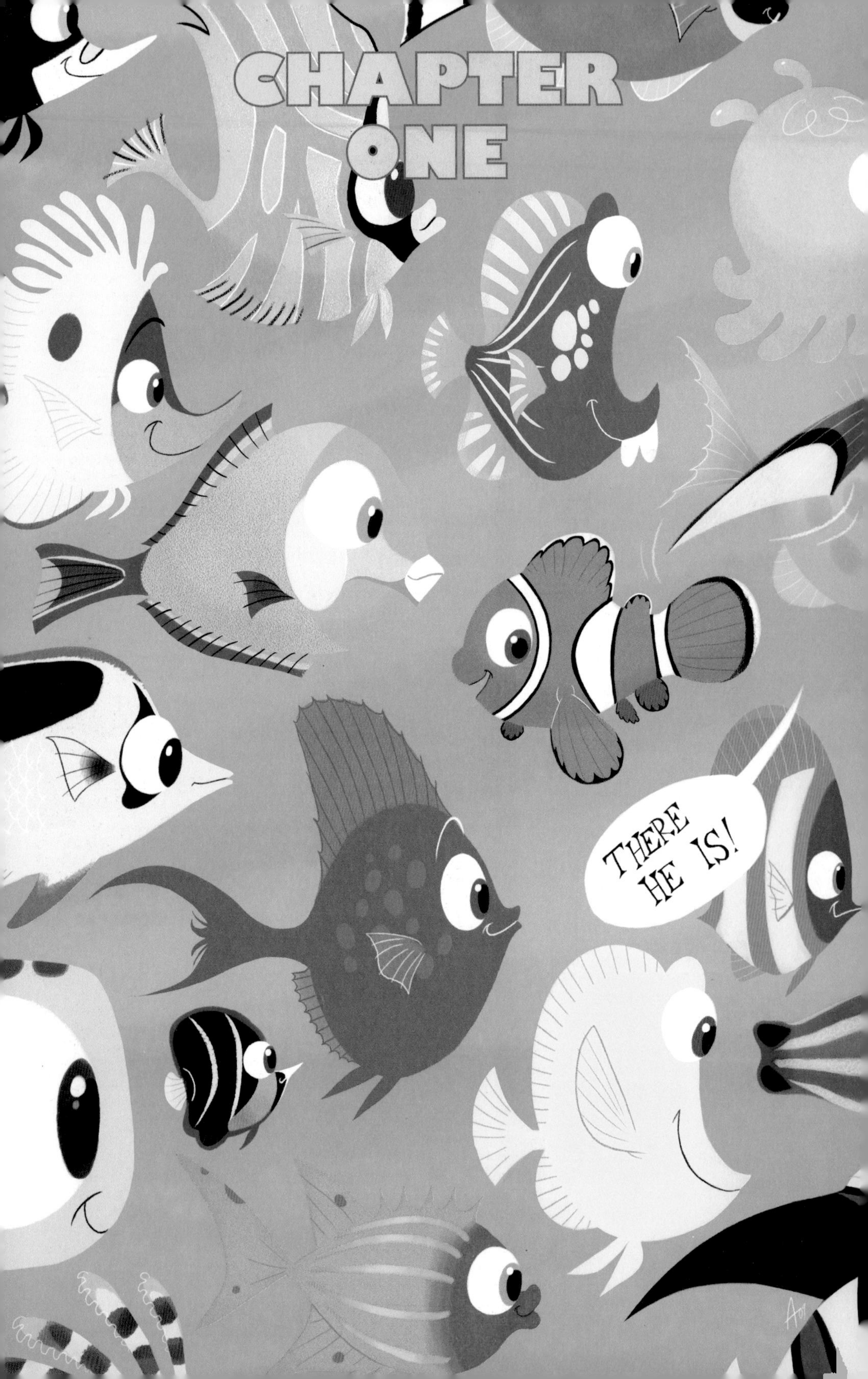
THERE HE IS!

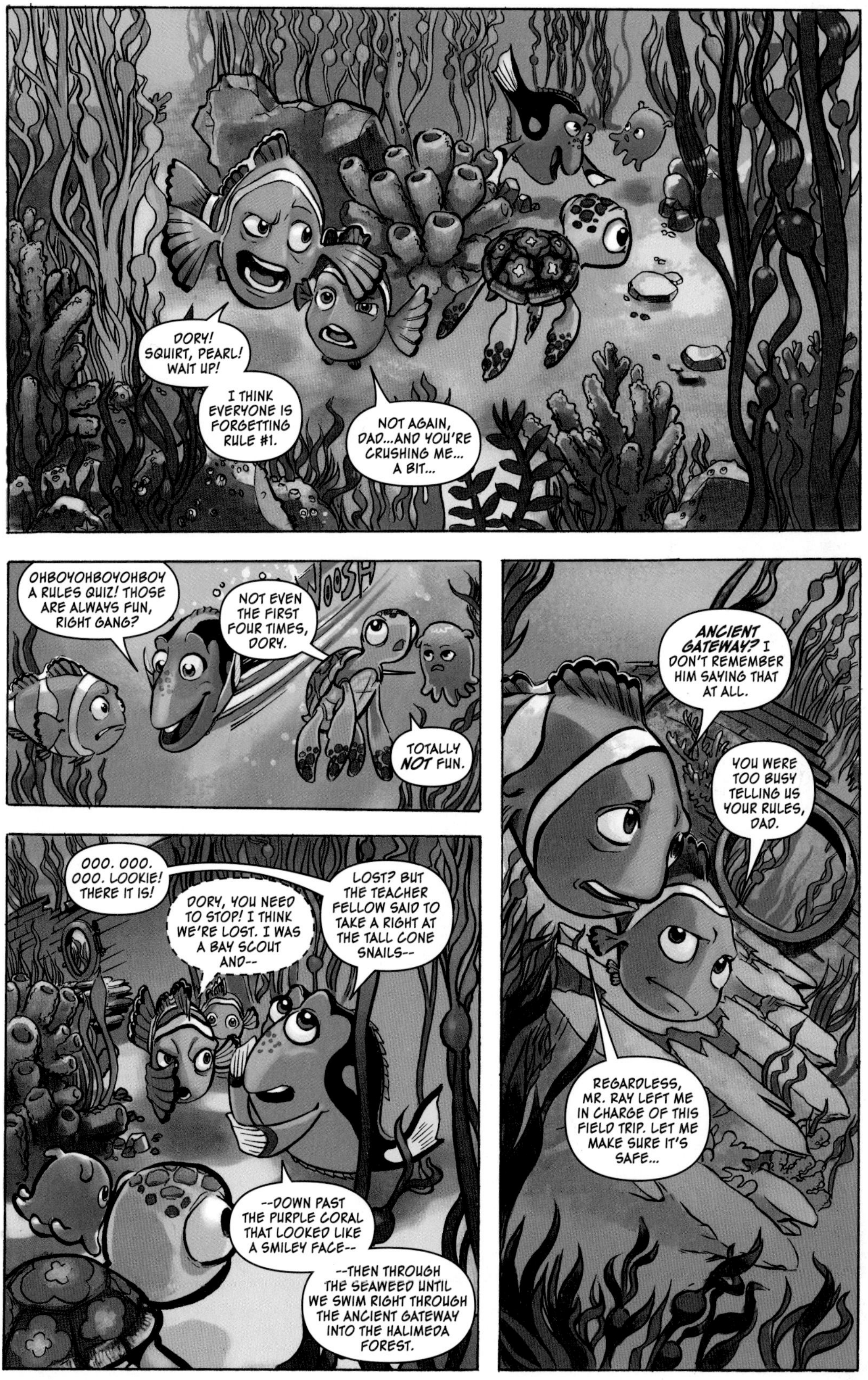
DORY! SQUIRT, PEARL! WAIT UP!
I THINK EVERYONE IS FORGETTING RULE #1.
NOT AGAIN, DAD...AND YOU'RE CRUSHING ME... A BIT...
OHBOYOHBOYOHBOY A RULES QUIZ! THOSE ARE ALWAYS FUN, RIGHT GANG?
NOT EVEN THE FIRST FOUR TIMES, DORY.
TOTALLY NOT FUN.
OOO. OOO. OOO. LOOKIE! THERE IT IS!
DORY, YOU NEED TO STOP! I THINK WE'RE LOST. I WAS A BAY SCOUT AND--
LOST? BUT THE TEACHER FELLOW SAID TO TAKE A RIGHT AT THE TALL CONE SNAILS--
--DOWN PAST THE PURPLE CORAL THAT LOOKED LIKE A SMILEY FACE--
--THEN THROUGH THE SEAWEED UNTIL WE SWIM RIGHT THROUGH THE ANCIENT GATEWAY INTO THE HALIMEDA FOREST.
ANCIENT GATEWAY? I DON'T REMEMBER HIM SAYING THAT AT ALL.
YOU WERE TOO BUSY TELLING US YOUR RULES, DAD.
REGARDLESS, MR. RAY LEFT ME IN CHARGE OF THIS FIELD TRIP. LET ME MAKE SURE IT'S SAFE...

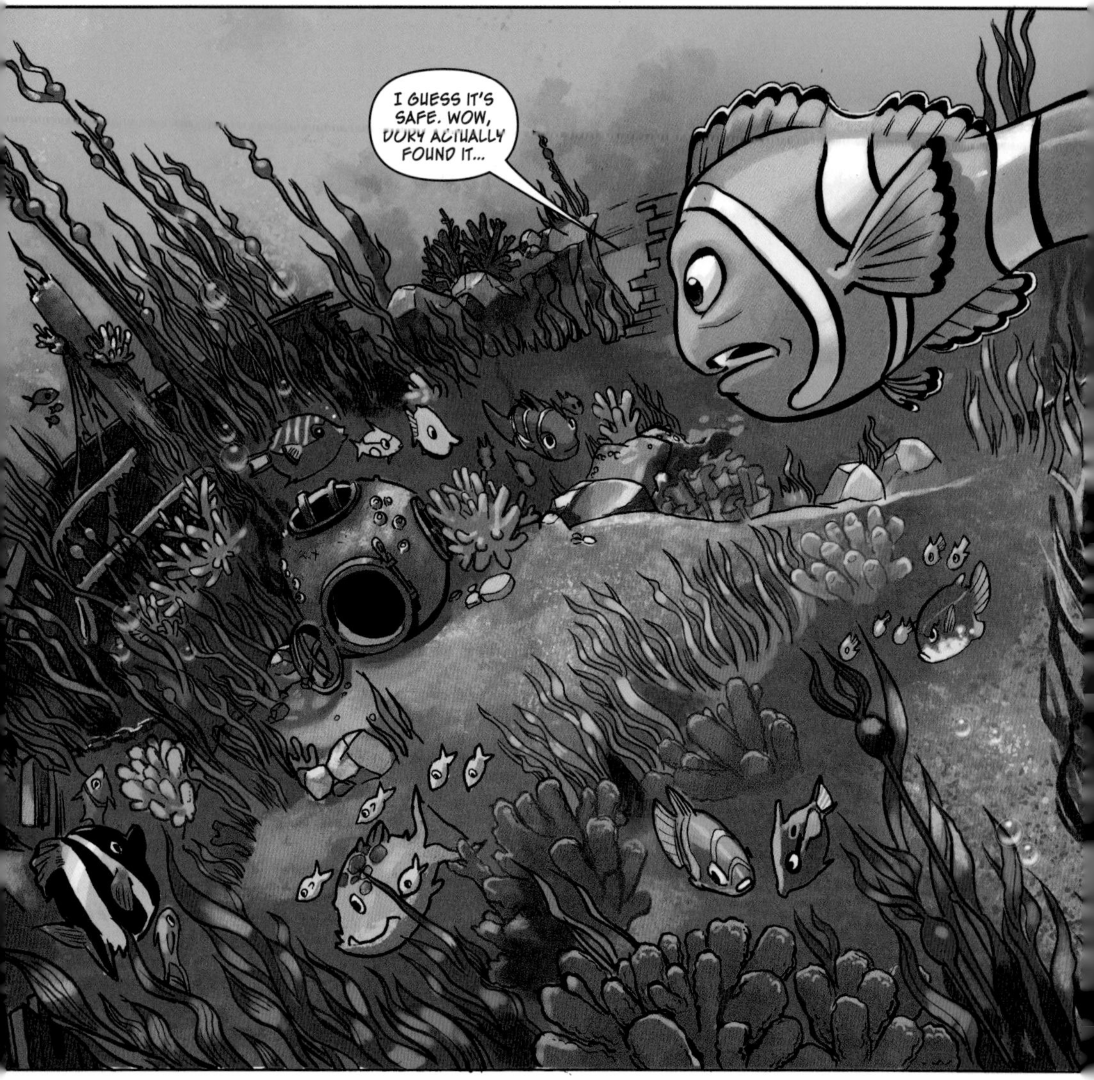

I GUESS IT'S SAFE. WOW, DORY ACTUALLY FOUND IT...


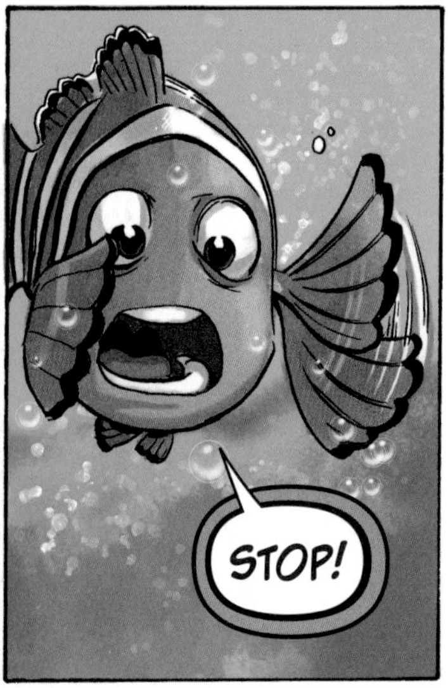

STOP!


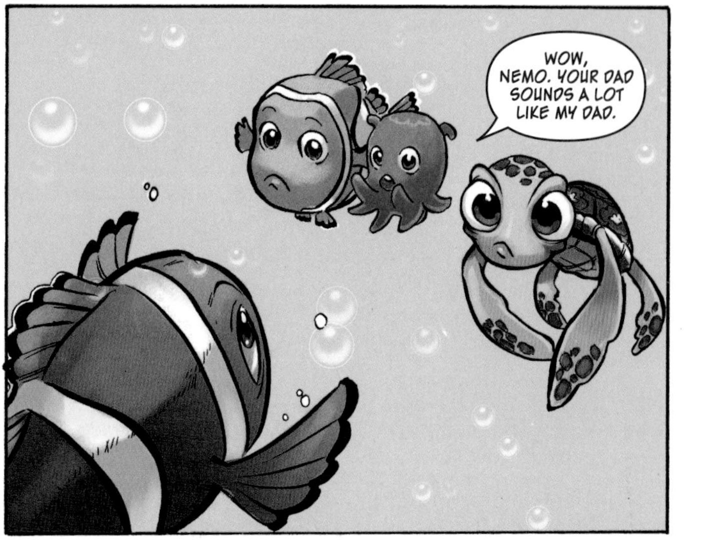

WOW, NEMO. YOUR DAD SOUNDS A LOT LIKE MY DAD.

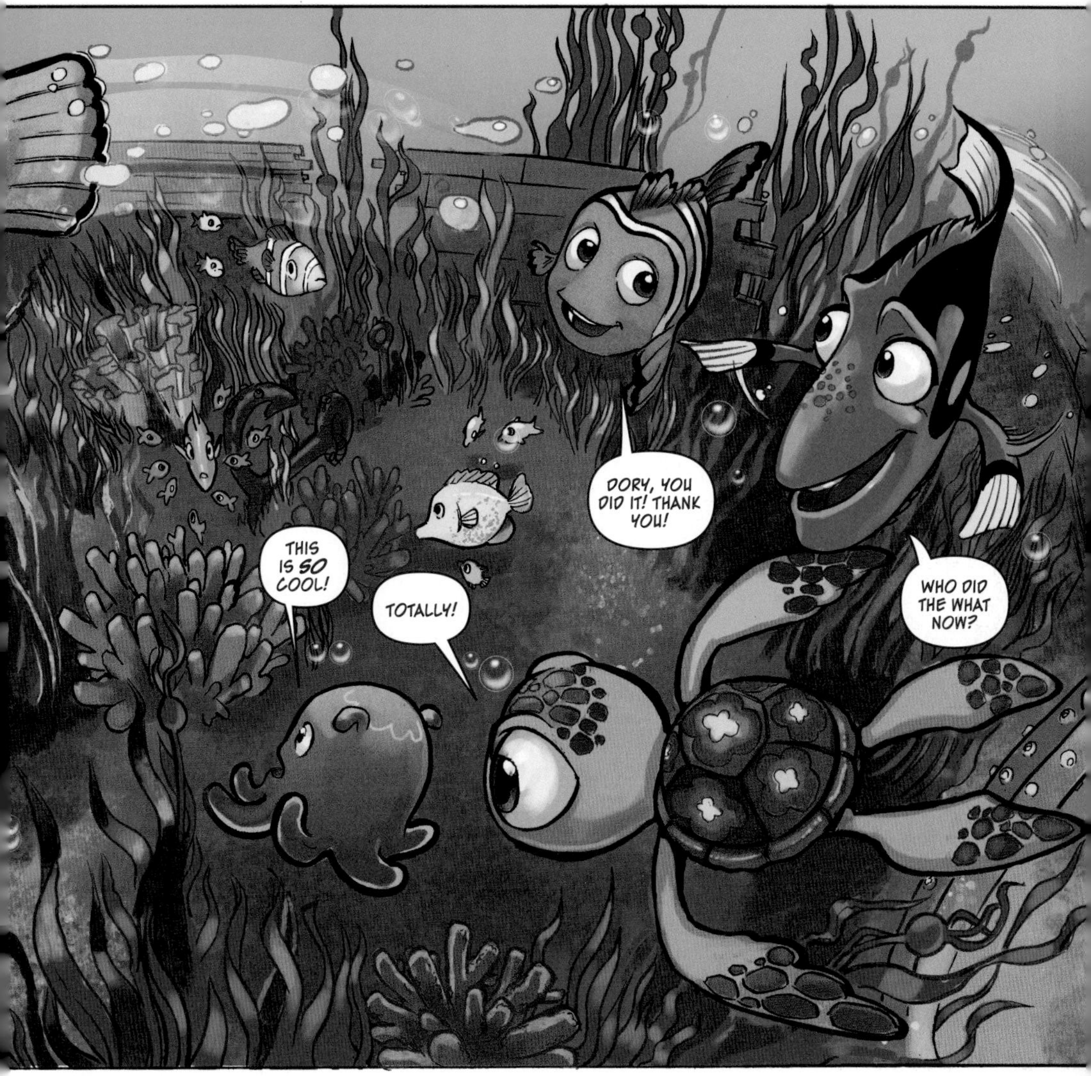
DORY, YOU DID IT! THANK YOU!
WHO DID THE WHAT NOW?
THIS IS SO COOL!
TOTALLY!

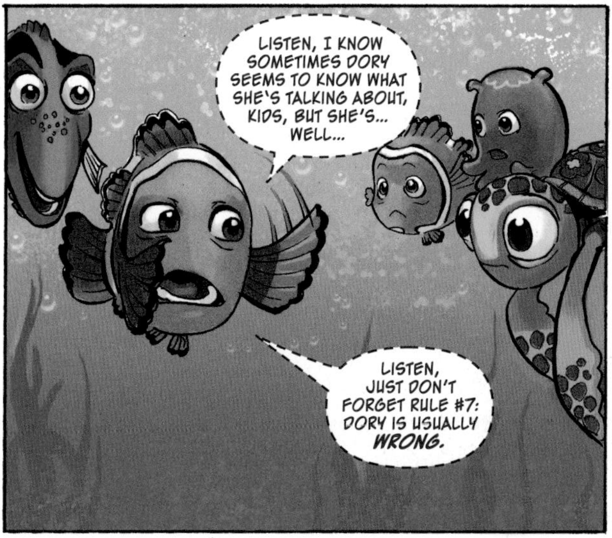
LISTEN, I KNOW SOMETIMES DORY SEEMS TO KNOW WHAT SHE'S TALKING ABOUT, KIDS, BUT SHE'S... WELL...
LISTEN, JUST DON'T FORGET RULE #7: DORY IS USUALLY WRONG.

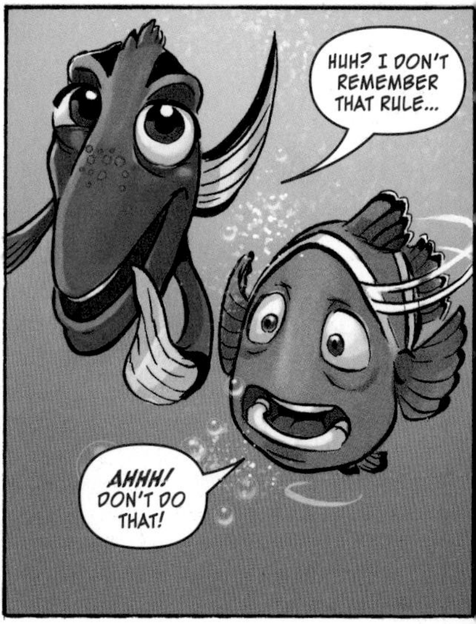
HUH? I DON'T REMEMBER THAT RULE...
AHHH! DON'T DO THAT!

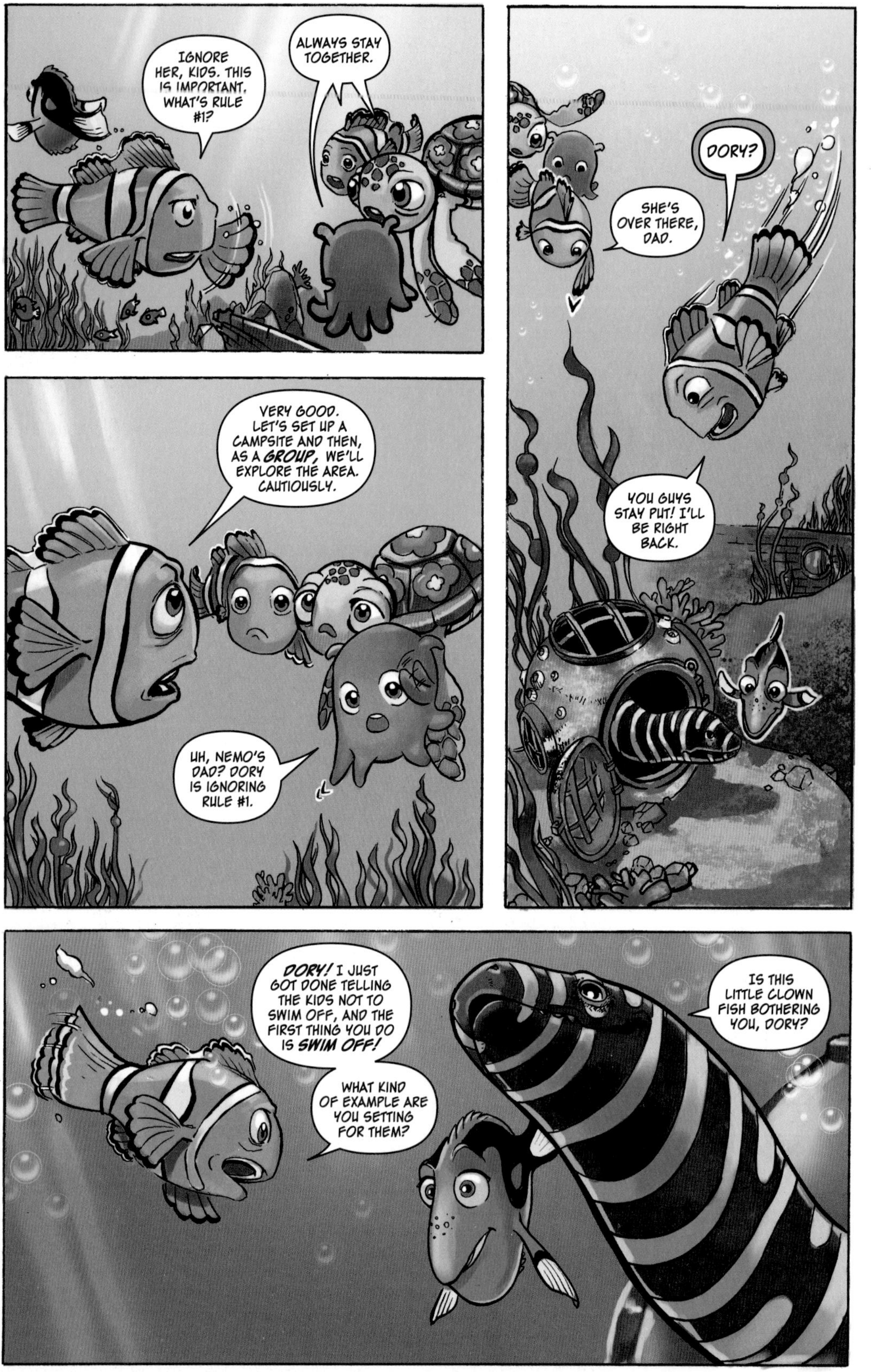
IGNORE HER, KIDS. THIS IS IMPORTANT. WHAT'S RULE #1?
ALWAYS STAY TOGETHER.
DORY?
SHE'S OVER THERE, DAD.
VERY GOOD. LET'S SET UP A CAMPSITE AND THEN, AS A GROUP, WE'LL EXPLORE THE AREA. CAUTIOUSLY.
UH, NEMO'S DAD? DORY IS IGNORING RULE #1.
YOU GUYS STAY PUT! I'LL BE RIGHT BACK.
DORY! I JUST GOT DONE TELLING THE KIDS NOT TO SWIM OFF, AND THE FIRST THING YOU DO IS SWIM OFF!
WHAT KIND OF EXAMPLE ARE YOU SETTING FOR THEM?
IS THIS LITTLE CLOWN FISH BOTHERING YOU, DORY?

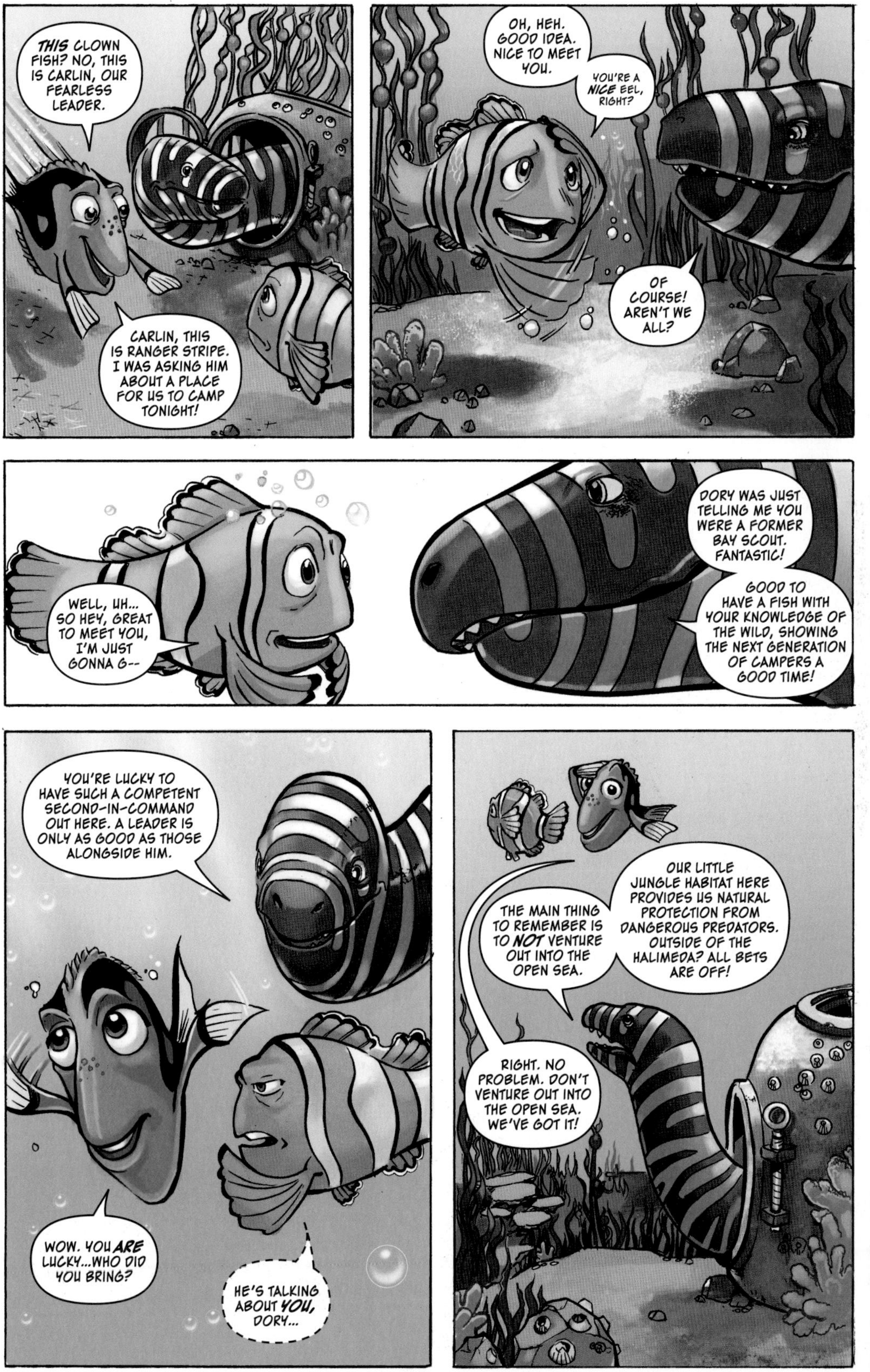
THIS CLOWN FISH? NO, THIS IS CARLIN, OUR FEARLESS LEADER.
CARLIN, THIS IS RANGER STRIPE. I WAS ASKING HIM ABOUT A PLACE FOR US TO CAMP TONIGHT!
OH, HEH. GOOD IDEA. NICE TO MEET YOU.
YOU'RE A NICE EEL, RIGHT?
OF COURSE! AREN'T WE ALL?
WELL, UH... SO HEY, GREAT TO MEET YOU, I'M JUST GONNA G--
DORY WAS JUST TELLING ME YOU WERE A FORMER BAY SCOUT. FANTASTIC!
GOOD TO HAVE A FISH WITH YOUR KNOWLEDGE OF THE WILD, SHOWING THE NEXT GENERATION OF CAMPERS A GOOD TIME!
YOU'RE LUCKY TO HAVE SUCH A COMPETENT SECOND-IN-COMMAND OUT HERE. A LEADER IS ONLY AS GOOD AS THOSE ALONGSIDE HIM.
WOW. YOU ARE LUCKY...WHO DID YOU BRING?
HE'S TALKING ABOUT YOU, DORY...
OUR LITTLE JUNGLE HABITAT HERE PROVIDES US NATURAL PROTECTION FROM DANGEROUS PREDATORS. OUTSIDE OF THE HALIMEDA? ALL BETS ARE OFF!
THE MAIN THING TO REMEMBER IS TO NOT VENTURE OUT INTO THE OPEN SEA.
RIGHT. NO PROBLEM. DON'T VENTURE OUT INTO THE OPEN SEA. WE'VE GOT IT!

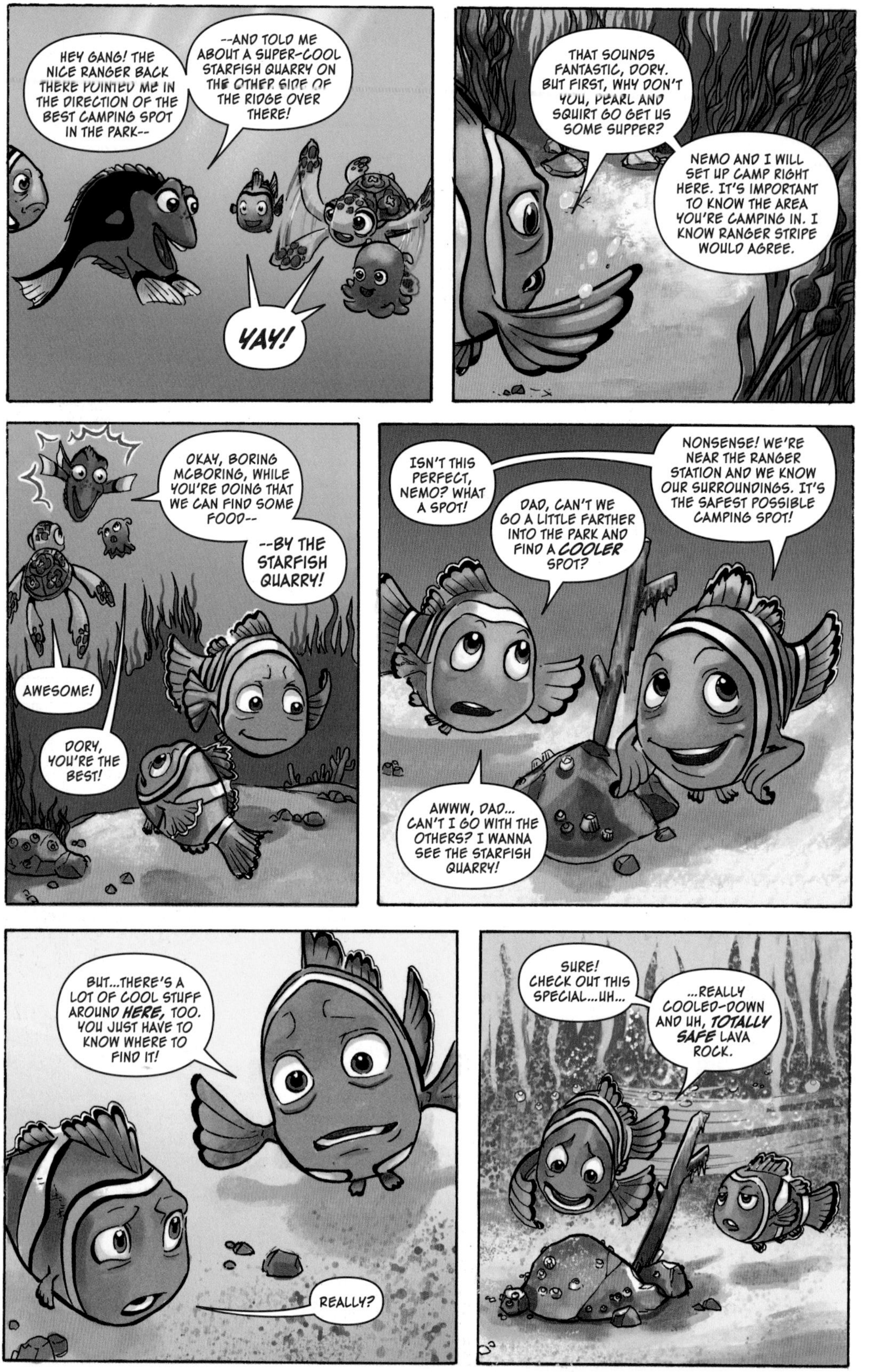
HEY GANG! THE NICE RANGER BACK THERE POINTED ME IN THE DIRECTION OF THE BEST CAMPING SPOT IN THE PARK--
--AND TOLD ME ABOUT A SUPER-COOL STARFISH QUARRY ON THE OTHER SIDE OF THE RIDGE OVER THERE!
YAY!
THAT SOUNDS FANTASTIC, DORY. BUT FIRST, WHY DON'T YOU, PEARL AND SQUIRT GO GET US SOME SUPPER?
NEMO AND I WILL SET UP CAMP RIGHT HERE. IT'S IMPORTANT TO KNOW THE AREA YOU'RE CAMPING IN. I KNOW RANGER STRIPE WOULD AGREE.
OKAY, BORING MCBORING, WHILE YOU'RE DOING THAT WE CAN FIND SOME FOOD--
--BY THE STARFISH QUARRY!
AWESOME!
DORY, YOU'RE THE BEST!
ISN'T THIS PERFECT, NEMO? WHAT A SPOT!
DAD, CAN'T WE GO A LITTLE FARTHER INTO THE PARK AND FIND A COOLER SPOT?
NONSENSE! WE'RE NEAR THE RANGER STATION AND WE KNOW OUR SURROUNDINGS. IT'S THE SAFEST POSSIBLE CAMPING SPOT!
AWWW, DAD... CAN'T I GO WITH THE OTHERS? I WANNA SEE THE STARFISH QUARRY!
BUT...THERE'S A LOT OF COOL STUFF AROUND HERE, TOO. YOU JUST HAVE TO KNOW WHERE TO FIND IT!
REALLY?
SURE! CHECK OUT THIS SPECIAL...UH...
...REALLY COOLED-DOWN AND UH, TOTALLY SAFE LAVA ROCK.

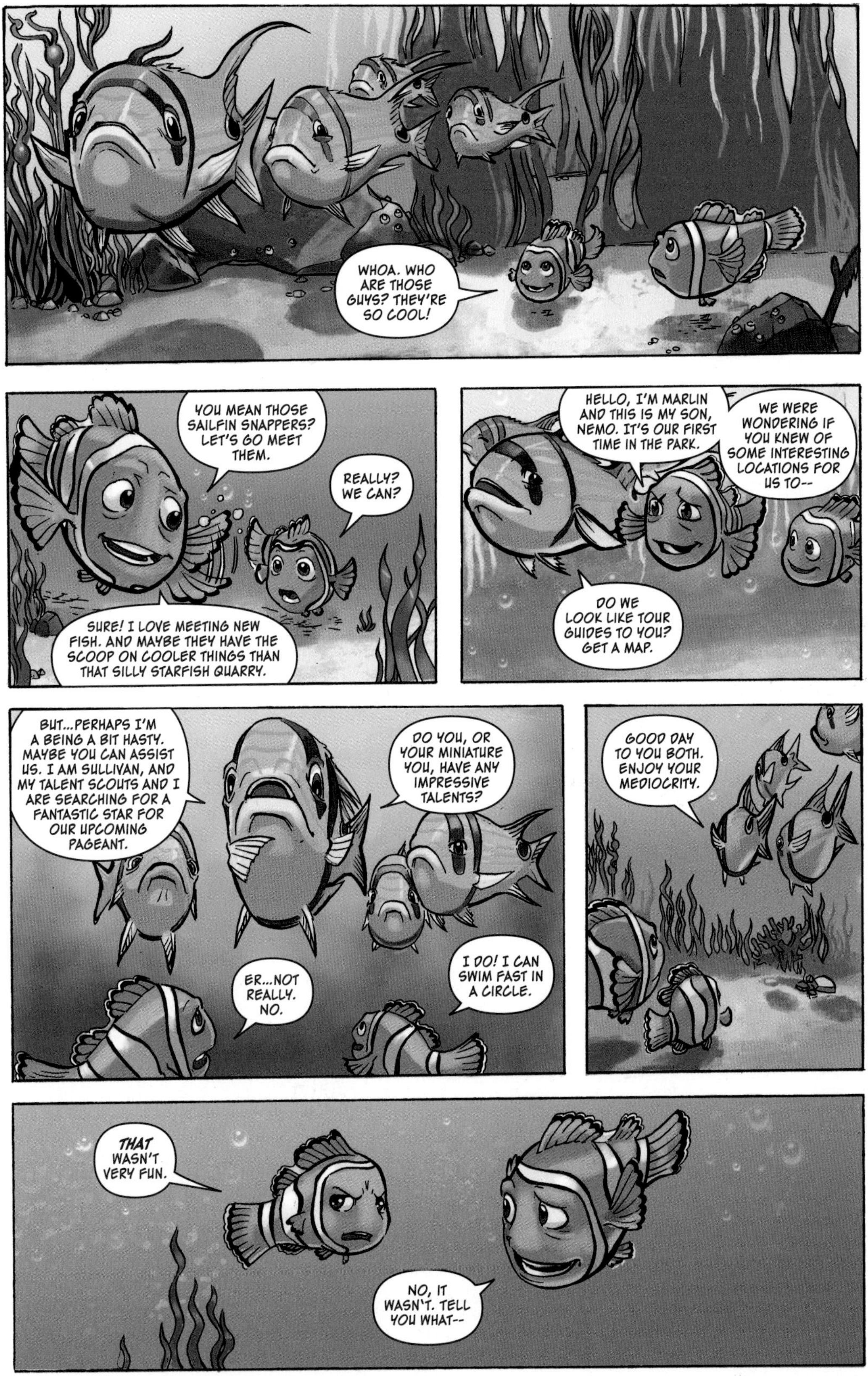

WHOA. WHO ARE THOSE GUYS? THEY'RE SO COOL!
YOU MEAN THOSE SAILFIN SNAPPERS? LET'S GO MEET THEM.
REALLY? WE CAN?
SURE! I LOVE MEETING NEW FISH. AND MAYBE THEY HAVE THE SCOOP ON COOLER THINGS THAN THAT SILLY STARFISH QUARRY.
HELLO, I'M MARLIN AND THIS IS MY SON, NEMO. IT'S OUR FIRST TIME IN THE PARK.
WE WERE WONDERING IF YOU KNEW OF SOME INTERESTING LOCATIONS FOR US TO--
DO WE LOOK LIKE TOUR GUIDES TO YOU? GET A MAP.
BUT...PERHAPS I'M A BEING A BIT HASTY. MAYBE YOU CAN ASSIST US. I AM SULLIVAN, AND MY TALENT SCOUTS AND I ARE SEARCHING FOR A FANTASTIC STAR FOR OUR UPCOMING PAGEANT.
DO YOU, OR YOUR MINIATURE YOU, HAVE ANY IMPRESSIVE TALENTS?
ER...NOT REALLY. NO.
I DO! I CAN SWIM FAST IN A CIRCLE.
GOOD DAY TO YOU BOTH. ENJOY YOUR MEDIOCRITY.
*THAT* WASN'T VERY FUN.
NO, IT WASN'T. TELL YOU WHAT--

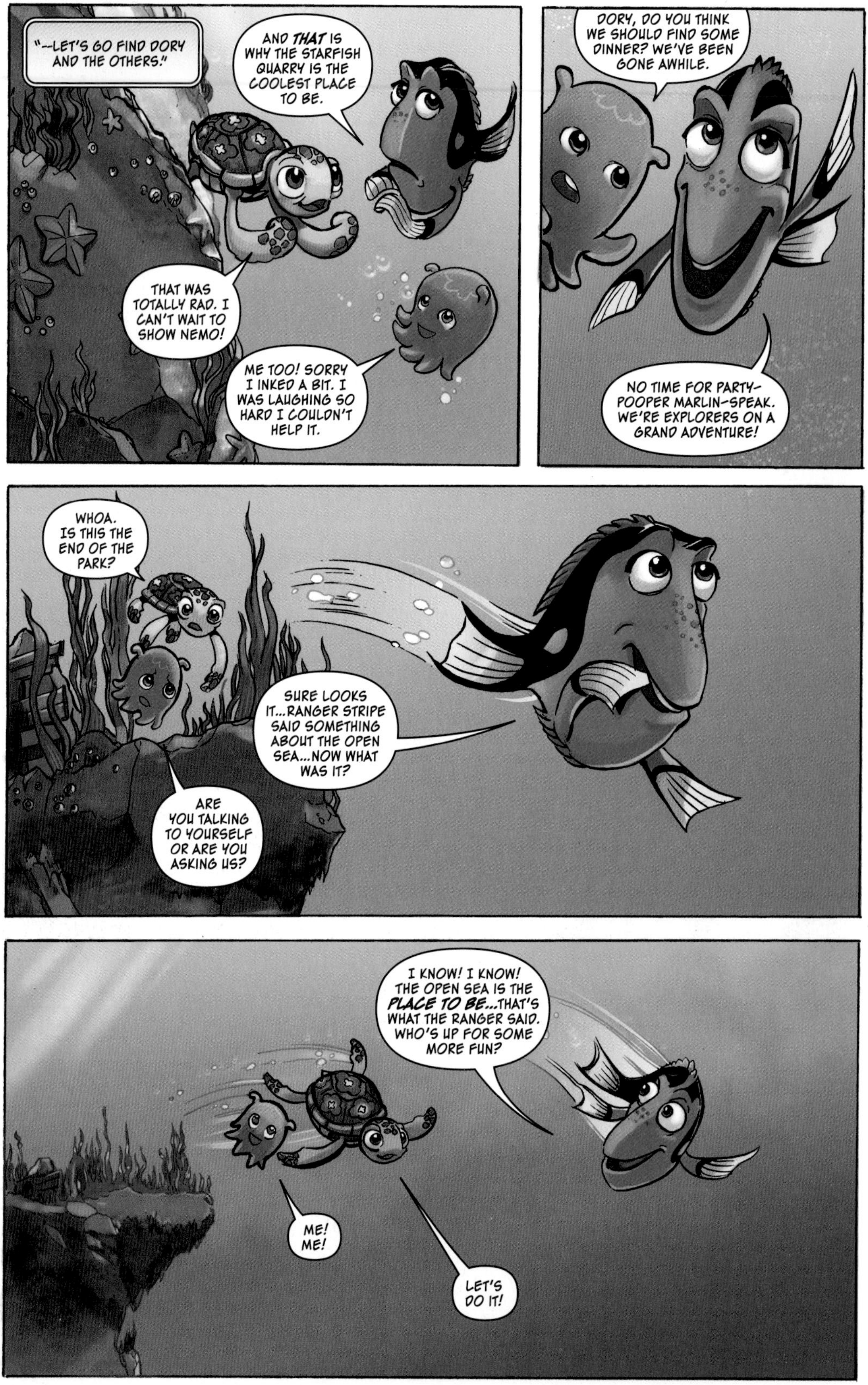
"--LET'S GO FIND DORY AND THE OTHERS."
AND THAT IS WHY THE STARFISH QUARRY IS THE COOLEST PLACE TO BE.
THAT WAS TOTALLY RAD. I CAN'T WAIT TO SHOW NEMO!
ME TOO! SORRY I INKED A BIT. I WAS LAUGHING SO HARD I COULDN'T HELP IT.
DORY, DO YOU THINK WE SHOULD FIND SOME DINNER? WE'VE BEEN GONE AWHILE.
NO TIME FOR PARTY-POOPER MARLIN-SPEAK. WE'RE EXPLORERS ON A GRAND ADVENTURE!
WHOA. IS THIS THE END OF THE PARK?
SURE LOOKS IT...RANGER STRIPE SAID SOMETHING ABOUT THE OPEN SEA...NOW WHAT WAS IT?
ARE YOU TALKING TO YOURSELF OR ARE YOU ASKING US?
I KNOW! I KNOW! THE OPEN SEA IS THE PLACE TO BE...THAT'S WHAT THE RANGER SAID. WHO'S UP FOR SOME MORE FUN?
ME! ME!
LET'S DO IT!

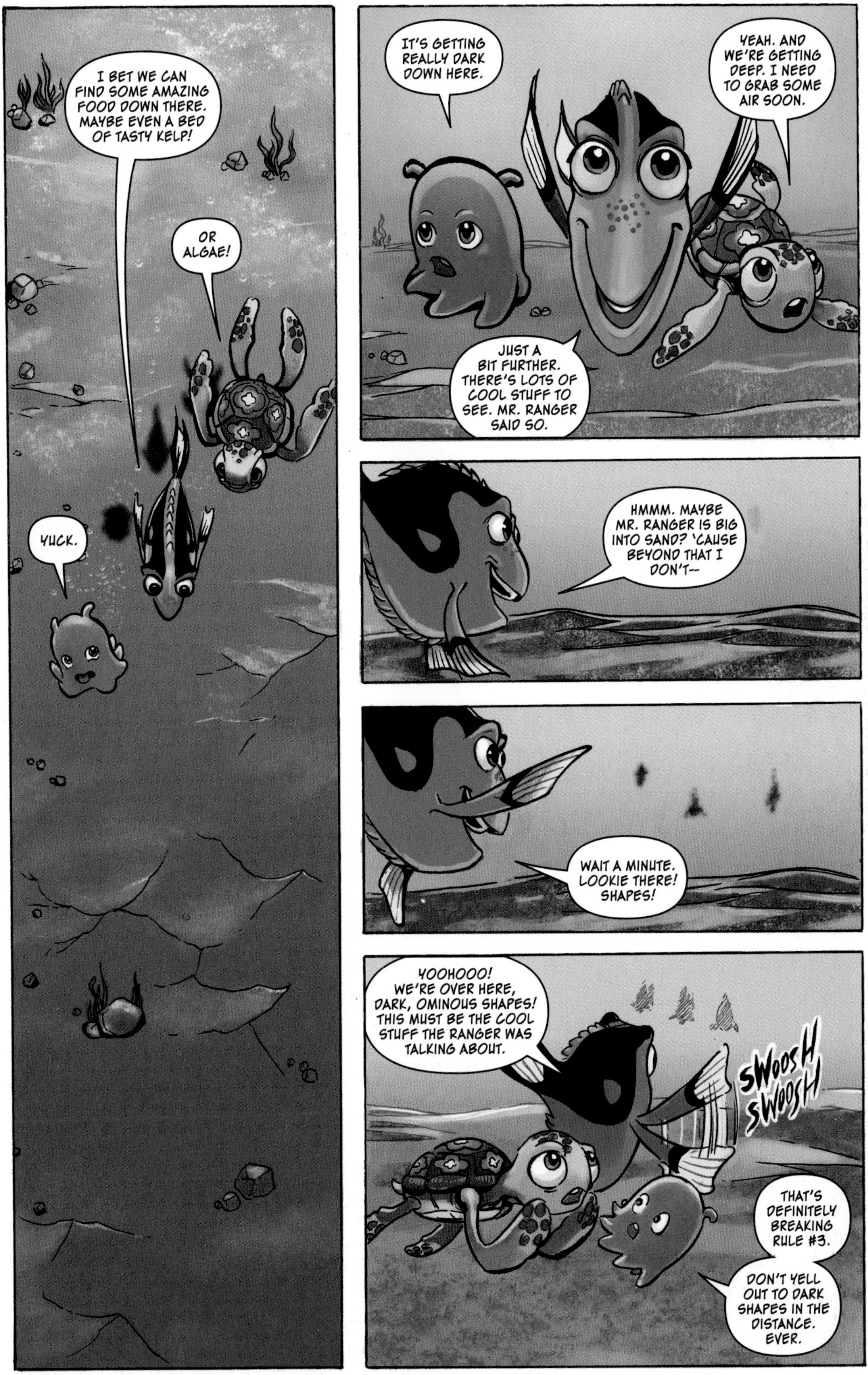
I BET WE CAN FIND SOME AMAZING FOOD DOWN THERE. MAYBE EVEN A BED OF TASTY KELP!
OR ALGAE!
YUCK.
IT'S GETTING REALLY DARK DOWN HERE.
YEAH. AND WE'RE GETTING DEEP. I NEED TO GRAB SOME AIR SOON.
JUST A BIT FURTHER. THERE'S LOTS OF COOL STUFF TO SEE. MR. RANGER SAID SO.
HMMM. MAYBE MR. RANGER IS BIG INTO SAND? 'CAUSE BEYOND THAT I DON'T--
WAIT A MINUTE. LOOKIE THERE! SHAPES!
YOOHOOO! WE'RE OVER HERE, DARK, OMINOUS SHAPES! THIS MUST BE THE COOL STUFF THE RANGER WAS TALKING ABOUT.
SWOOSH
SWOOSH
THAT'S DEFINITELY BREAKING RULE #3.
DON'T YELL OUT TO DARK SHAPES IN THE DISTANCE. EVER.

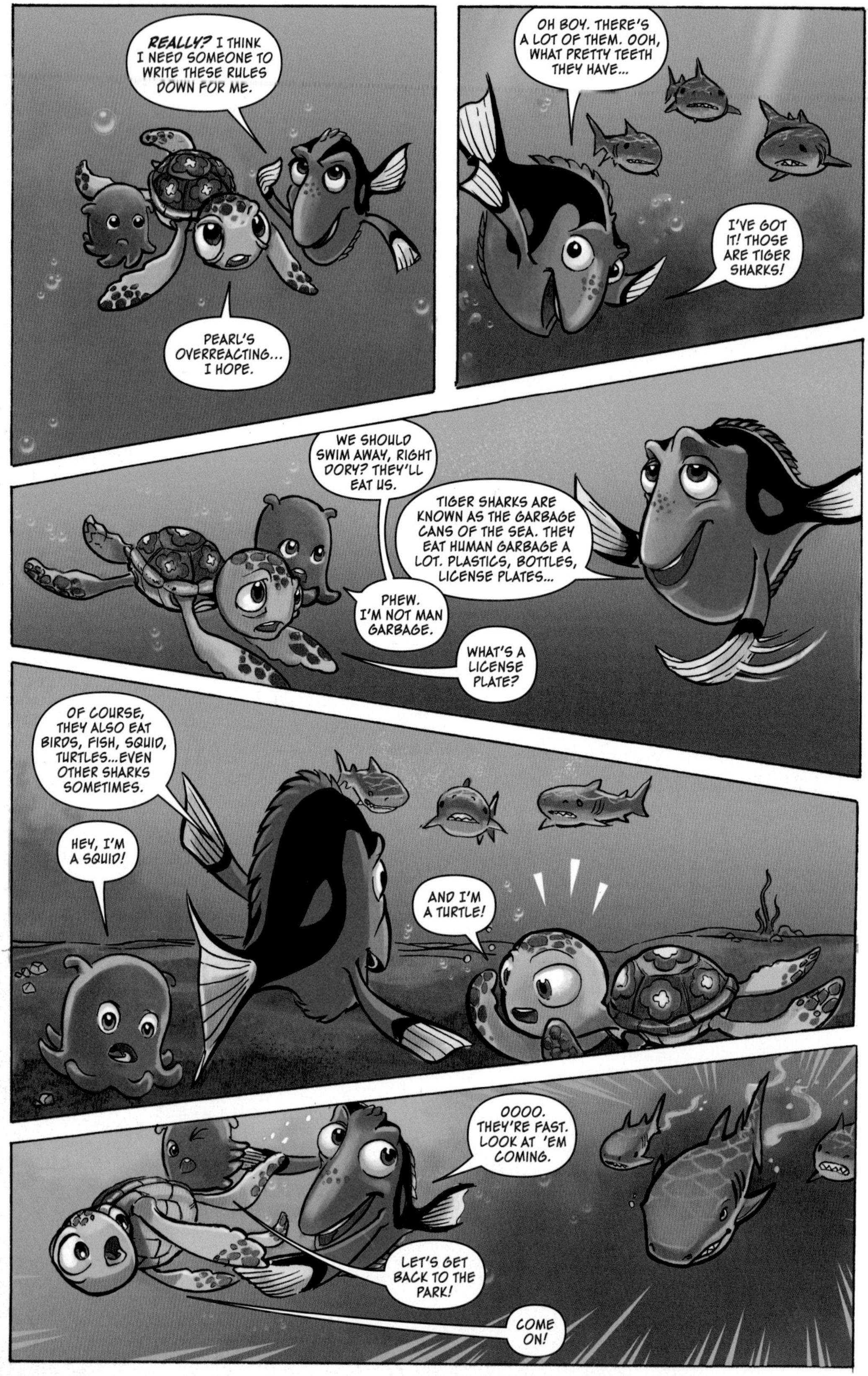
REALLY? I THINK I NEED SOMEONE TO WRITE THESE RULES DOWN FOR ME.
PEARL'S OVERREACTING... I HOPE.
OH BOY. THERE'S A LOT OF THEM. OOH, WHAT PRETTY TEETH THEY HAVE...
I'VE GOT IT! THOSE ARE TIGER SHARKS!
WE SHOULD SWIM AWAY, RIGHT DORY? THEY'LL EAT US.
TIGER SHARKS ARE KNOWN AS THE GARBAGE CANS OF THE SEA. THEY EAT HUMAN GARBAGE A LOT. PLASTICS, BOTTLES, LICENSE PLATES...
PHEW. I'M NOT MAN GARBAGE.
WHAT'S A LICENSE PLATE?
OF COURSE, THEY ALSO EAT BIRDS, FISH, SQUID, TURTLES...EVEN OTHER SHARKS SOMETIMES.
HEY, I'M A SQUID!
AND I'M A TURTLE!
OOOO. THEY'RE FAST. LOOK AT 'EM COMING.
LET'S GET BACK TO THE PARK!
COME ON!

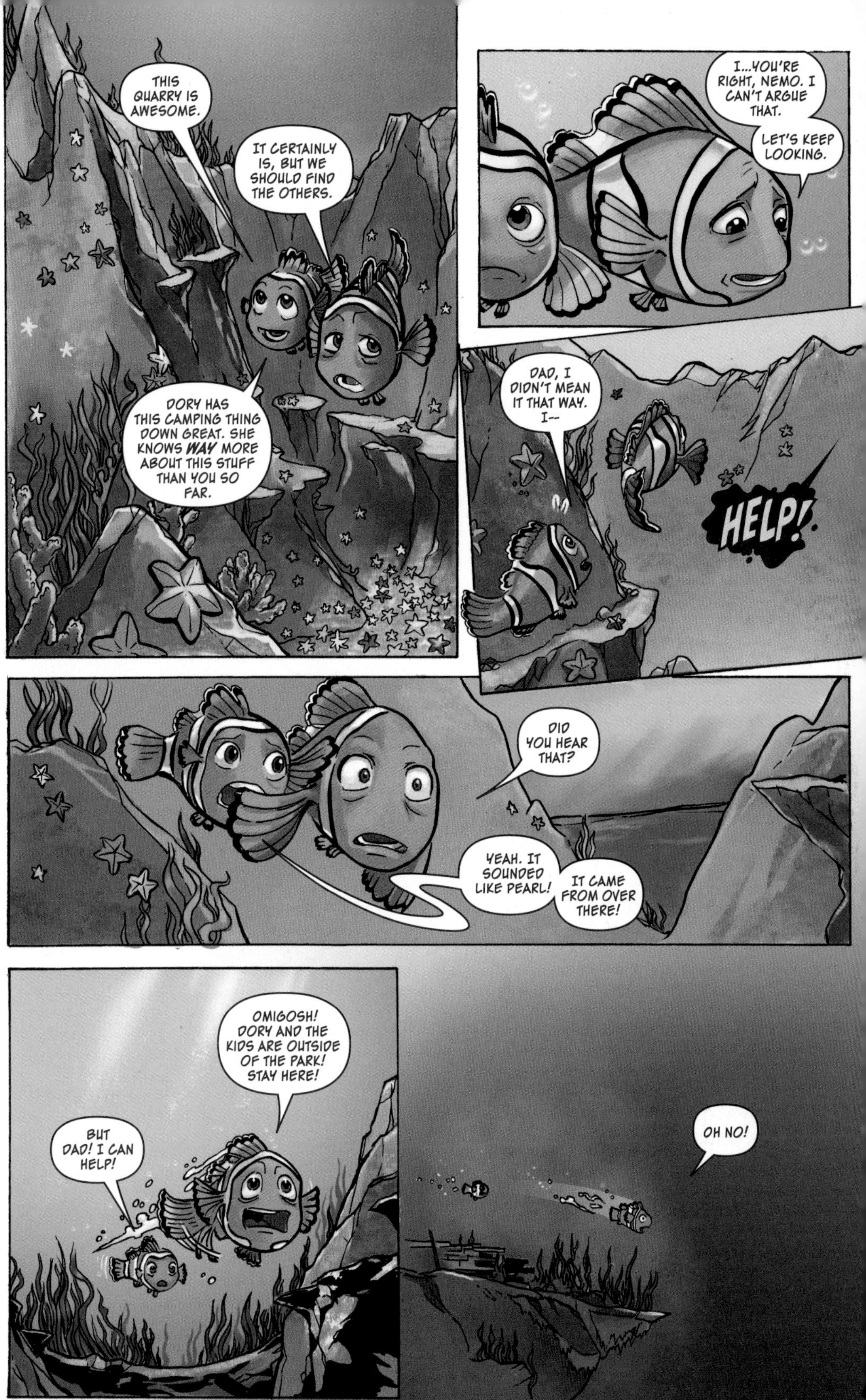
THIS QUARRY IS AWESOME.
IT CERTAINLY IS, BUT WE SHOULD FIND THE OTHERS.
DORY HAS THIS CAMPING THING DOWN GREAT. SHE KNOWS WAY MORE ABOUT THIS STUFF THAN YOU SO FAR.
I...YOU'RE RIGHT, NEMO. I CAN'T ARGUE THAT.
LET'S KEEP LOOKING.
DAD, I DIDN'T MEAN IT THAT WAY. I--
HELP!
DID YOU HEAR THAT?
YEAH. IT SOUNDED LIKE PEARL!
IT CAME FROM OVER THERE!
OMIGOSH! DORY AND THE KIDS ARE OUTSIDE OF THE PARK! STAY HERE!
BUT DAD! I CAN HELP!
OH NO!

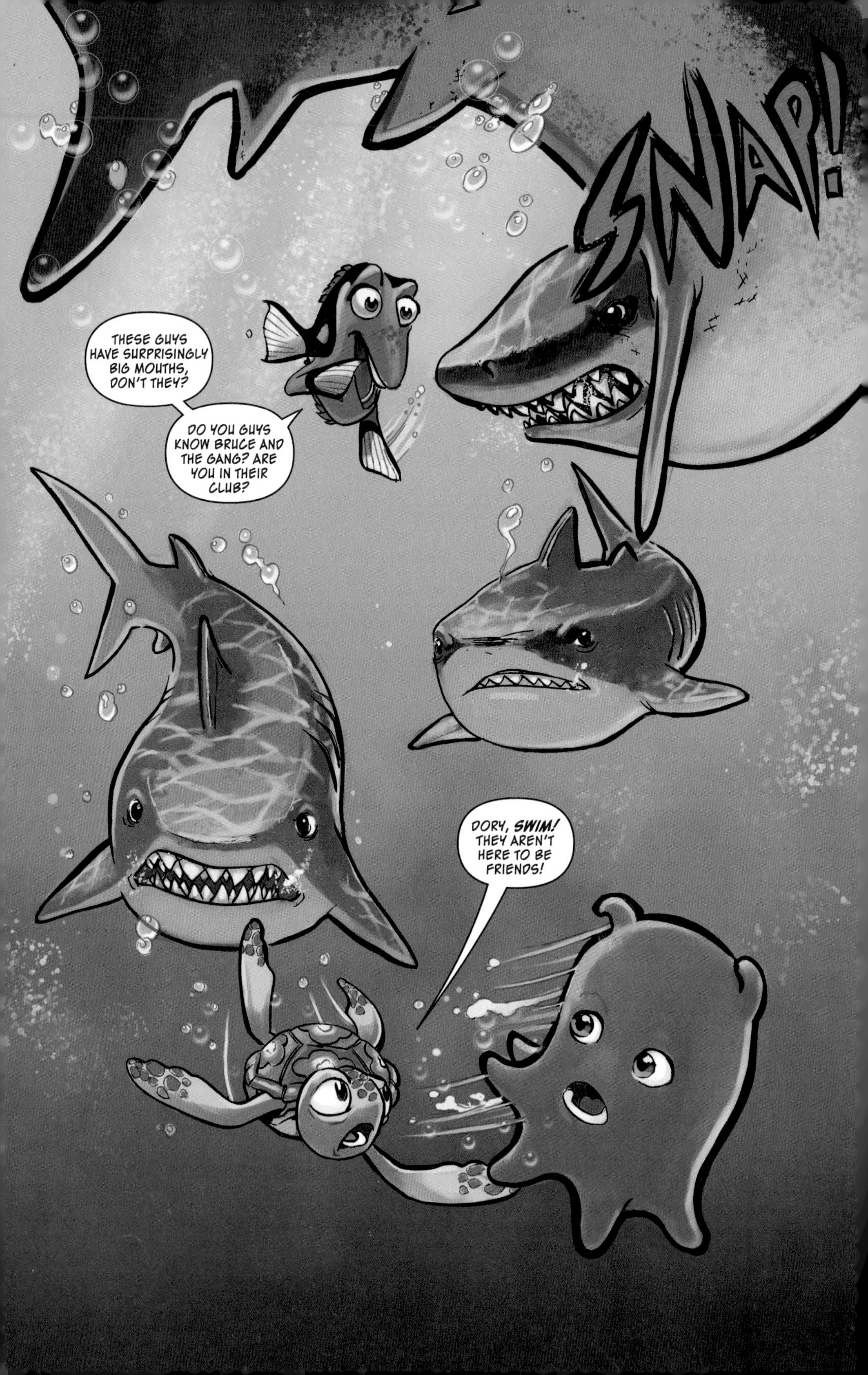
SNAP!
THESE GUYS HAVE SURPRISINGLY BIG MOUTHS, DON'T THEY?
DO YOU GUYS KNOW BRUCE AND THE GANG? ARE YOU IN THEIR CLUB?
DORY, **SWIM!** THEY AREN'T HERE TO BE FRIENDS!

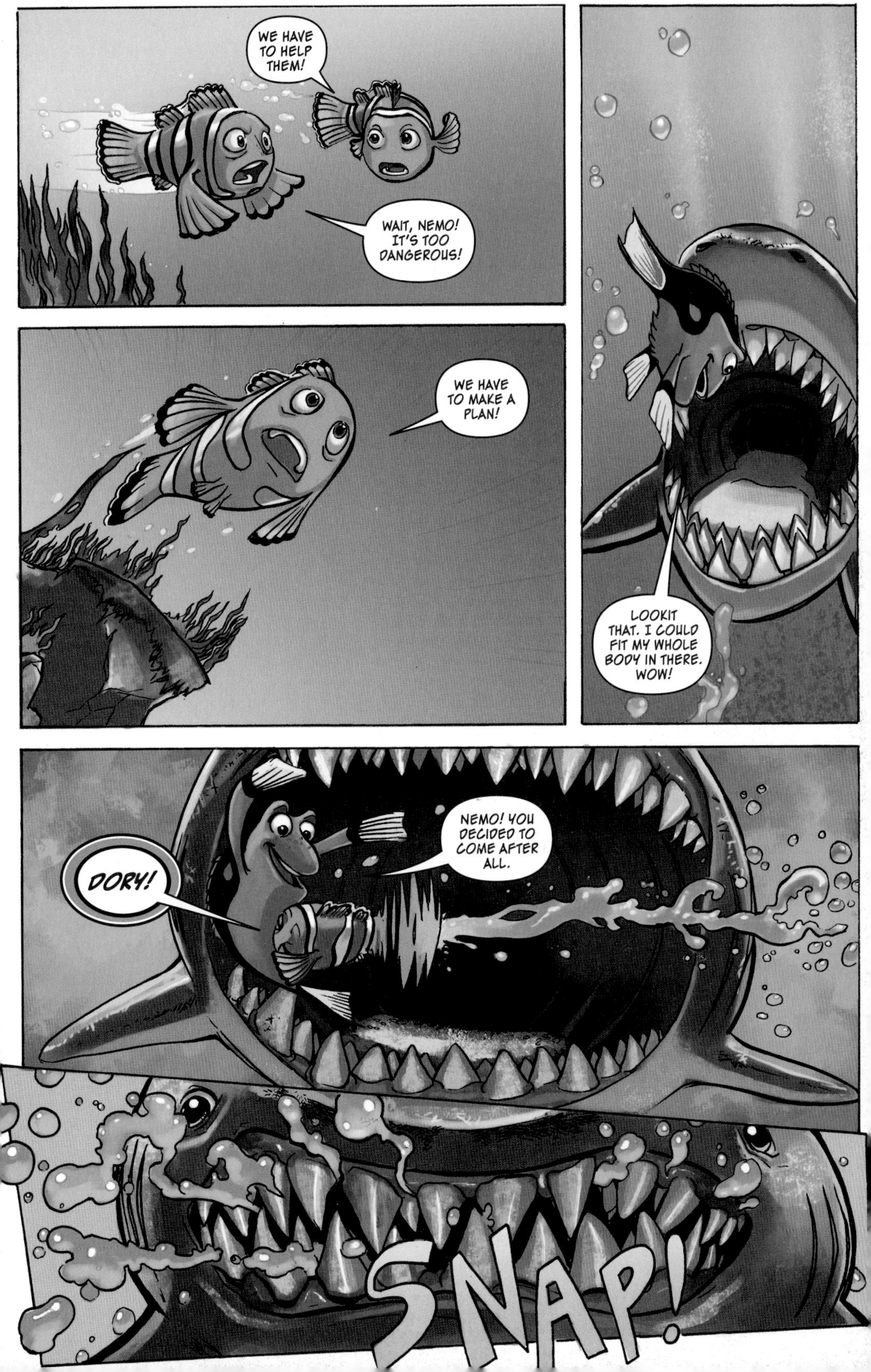
WE HAVE TO HELP THEM!
WAIT, NEMO! IT'S TOO DANGEROUS!
WE HAVE TO MAKE A PLAN!
LOOKIT THAT. I COULD FIT MY WHOLE BODY IN THERE. WOW!
DORY!
NEMO! YOU DECIDED TO COME AFTER ALL.
SNAP!

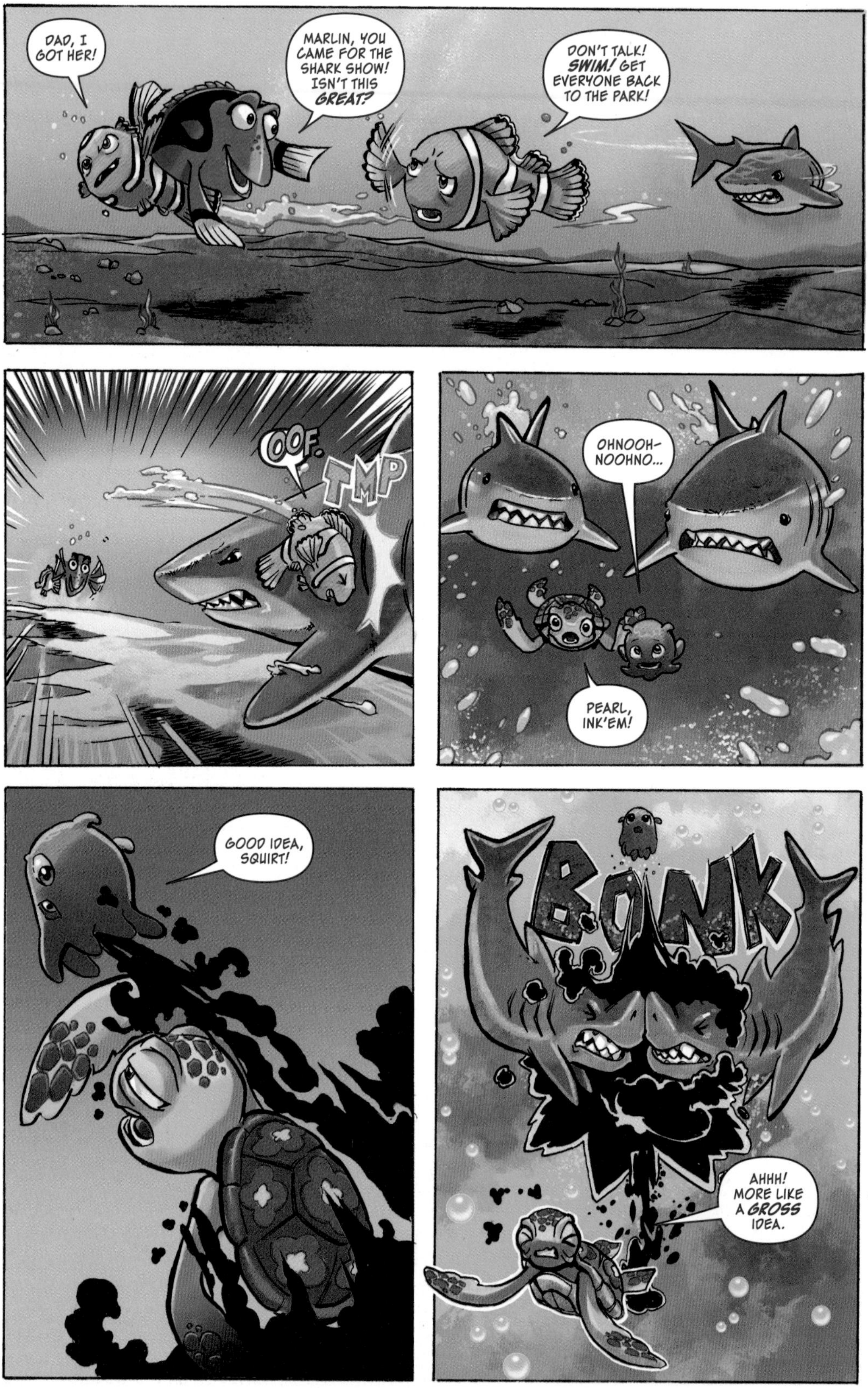
DAD, I GOT HER!
MARLIN, YOU CAME FOR THE SHARK SHOW! ISN'T THIS GREAT?
DON'T TALK! SWIM! GET EVERYONE BACK TO THE PARK!
OOF.
TMP
OHNOOH-NOOHNO...
PEARL, INK'EM!
GOOD IDEA, SQUIRT!
BONK
AHHH! MORE LIKE A GROSS IDEA.

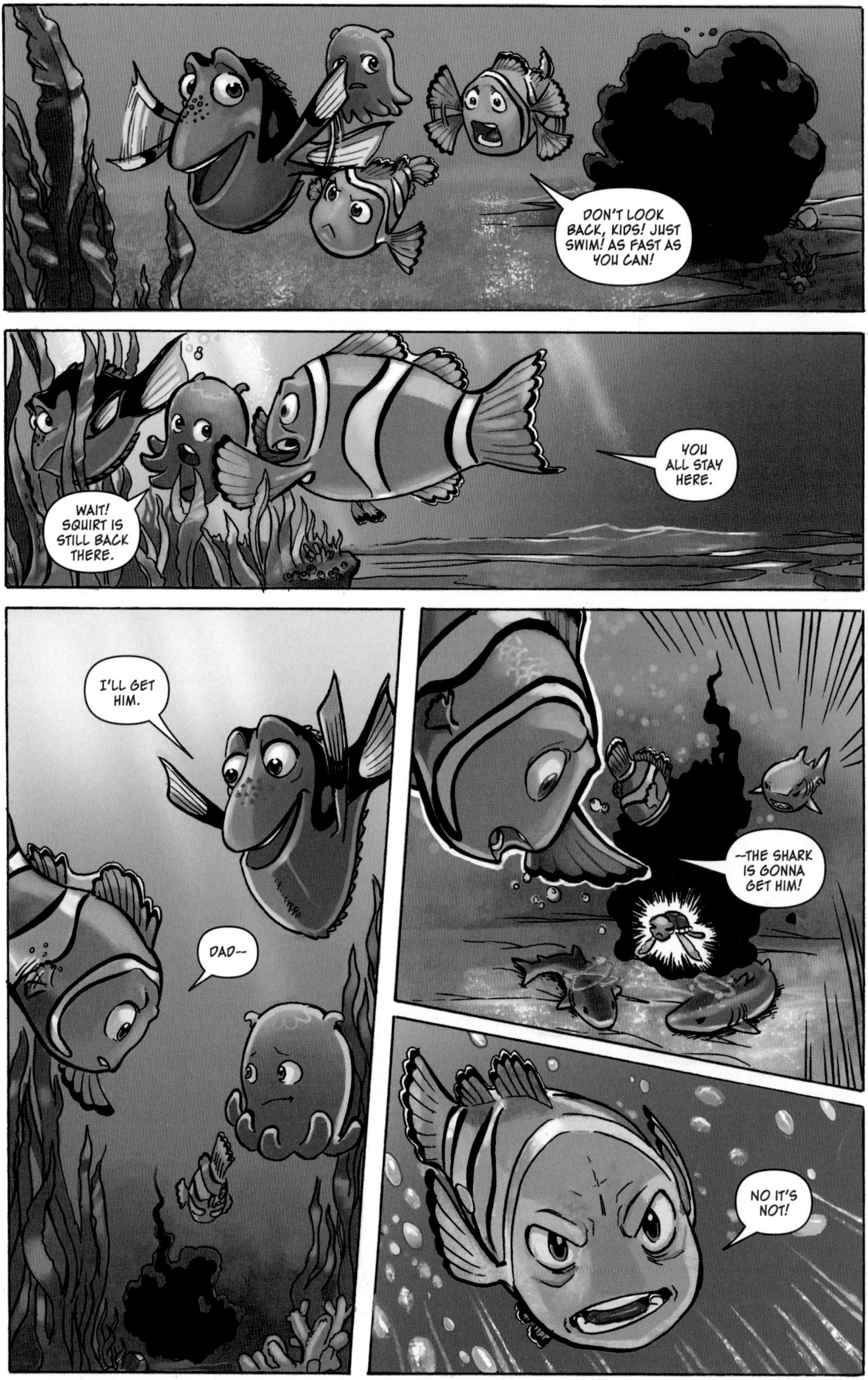
DON'T LOOK BACK, KIDS! JUST SWIM! AS FAST AS YOU CAN!
YOU ALL STAY HERE.
WAIT! SQUIRT IS STILL BACK THERE.
I'LL GET HIM.
DAD--
--THE SHARK IS GONNA GET HIM!
NO IT'S NOT!

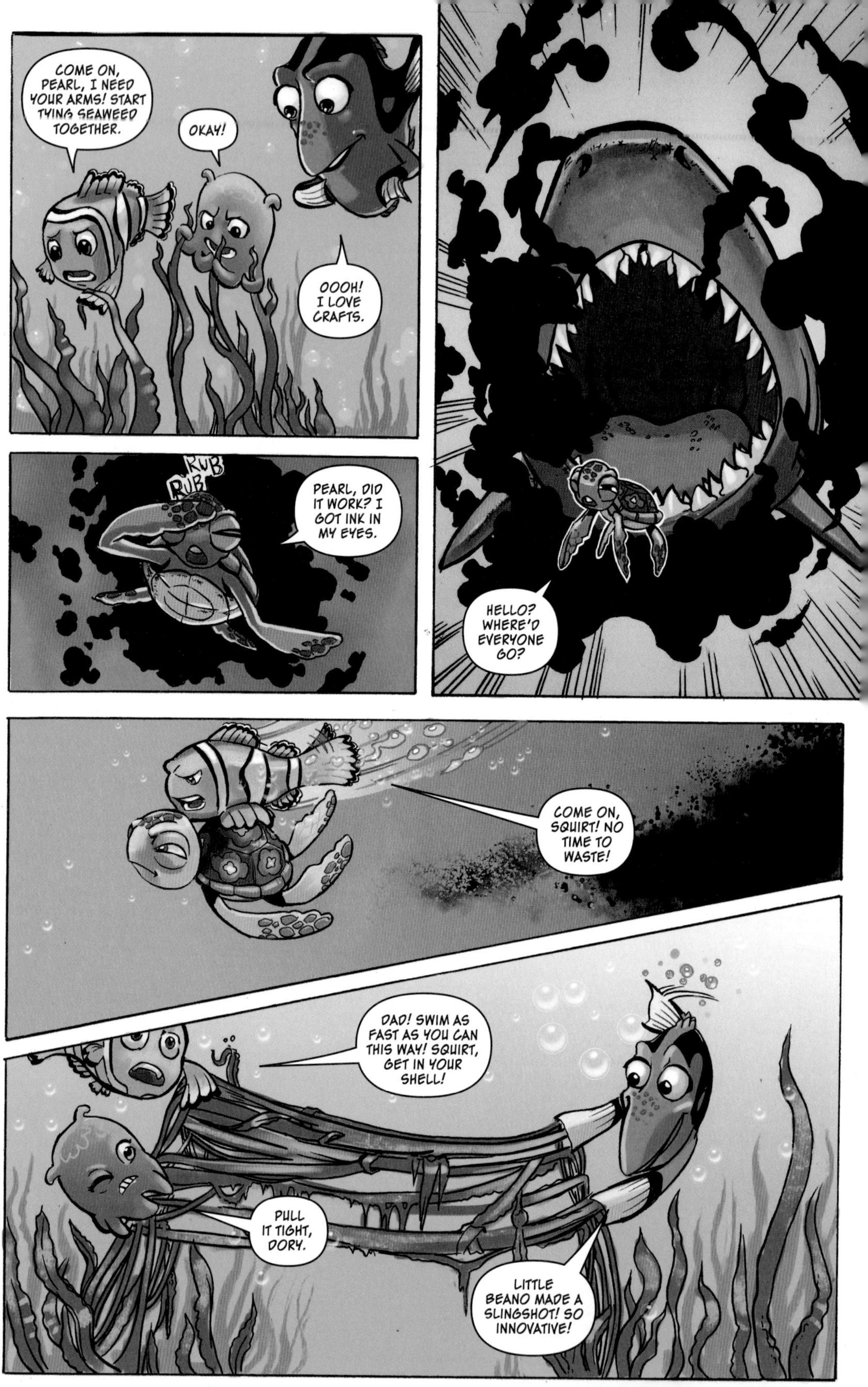
COME ON, PEARL, I NEED YOUR ARMS! START TYING SEAWEED TOGETHER.
OKAY!
OOOH! I LOVE CRAFTS.
RUB RUB
PEARL, DID IT WORK? I GOT INK IN MY EYES.
HELLO? WHERE'D EVERYONE GO?
COME ON, SQUIRT! NO TIME TO WASTE!
DAD! SWIM AS FAST AS YOU CAN THIS WAY! SQUIRT, GET IN YOUR SHELL!
PULL IT TIGHT, DORY.
LITTLE BEANO MADE A SLINGSHOT! SO INNOVATIVE!

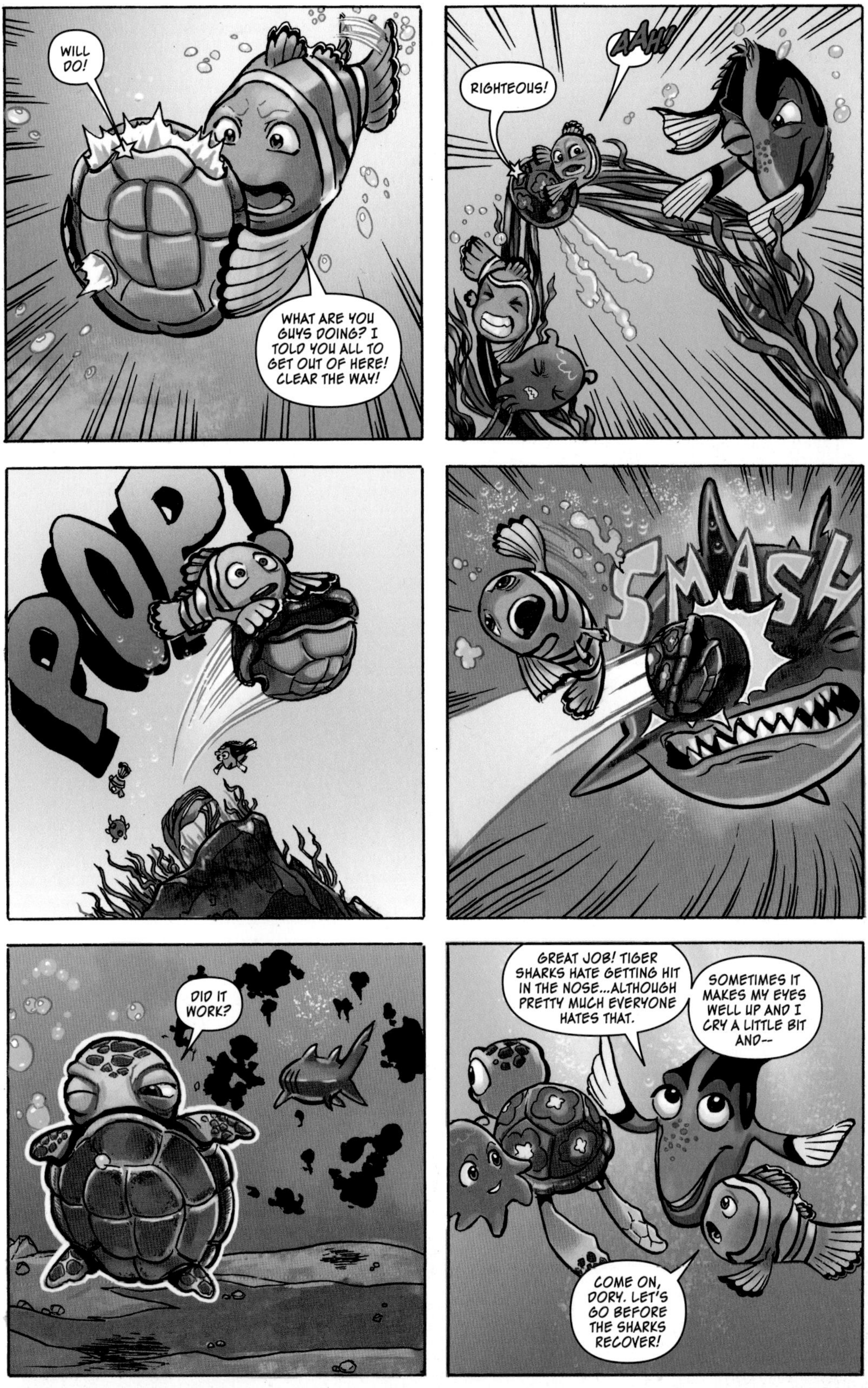
WILL DO!
WHAT ARE YOU GUYS DOING? I TOLD YOU ALL TO GET OUT OF HERE! CLEAR THE WAY!
AAH!
RIGHTEOUS!
POP!
SMASH
DID IT WORK?
GREAT JOB! TIGER SHARKS HATE GETTING HIT IN THE NOSE...ALTHOUGH PRETTY MUCH EVERYONE HATES THAT.
SOMETIMES IT MAKES MY EYES WELL UP AND I CRY A LITTLE BIT AND--
COME ON, DORY. LET'S GO BEFORE THE SHARKS RECOVER!

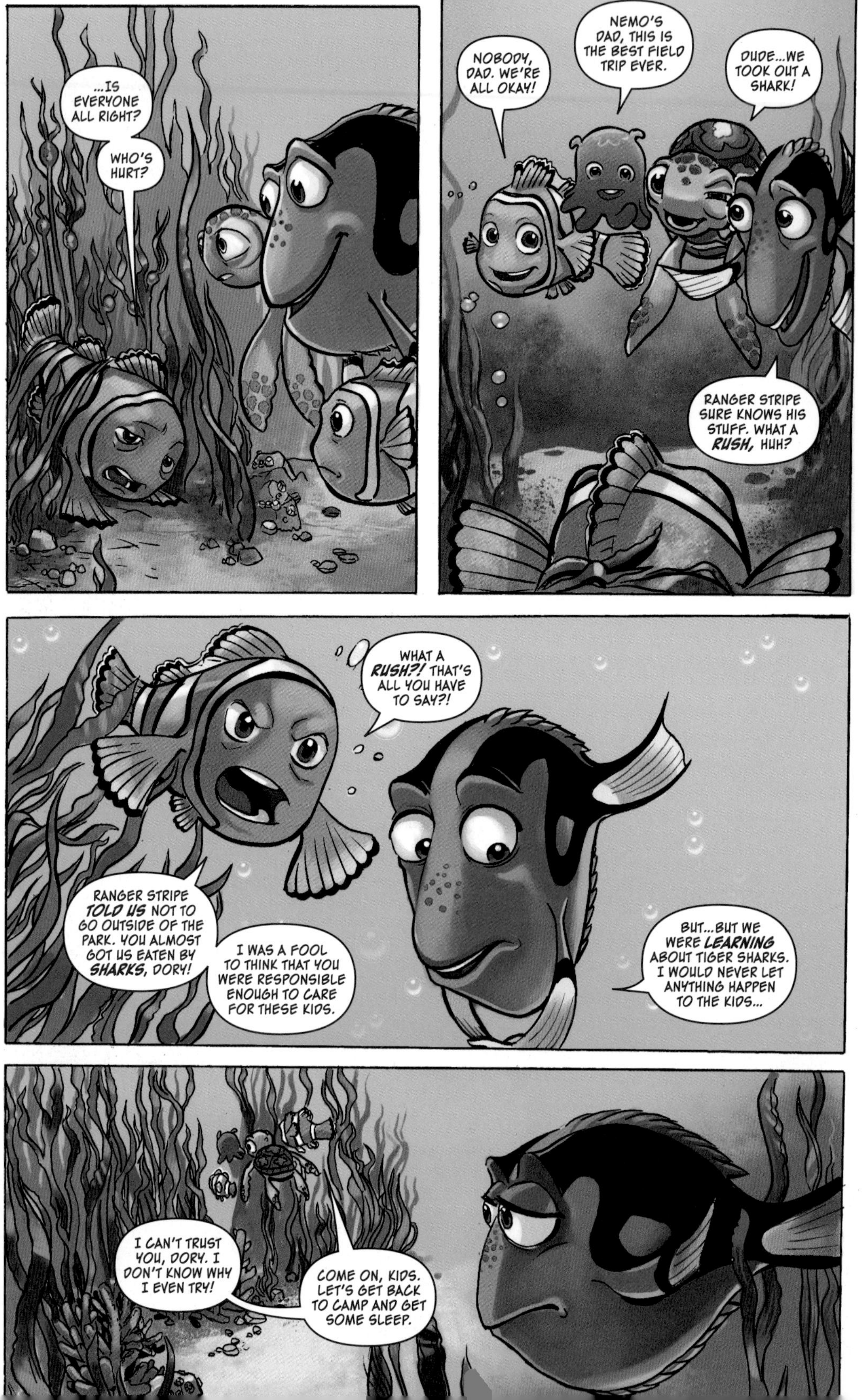
...IS EVERYONE ALL RIGHT?
WHO'S HURT?
NOBODY, DAD. WE'RE ALL OKAY!
NEMO'S DAD, THIS IS THE BEST FIELD TRIP EVER.
DUDE...WE TOOK OUT A SHARK!
RANGER STRIPE SURE KNOWS HIS STUFF. WHAT A RUSH, HUH?
WHAT A RUSH?! THAT'S ALL YOU HAVE TO SAY?!
RANGER STRIPE TOLD US NOT TO GO OUTSIDE OF THE PARK. YOU ALMOST GOT US EATEN BY SHARKS, DORY!
I WAS A FOOL TO THINK THAT YOU WERE RESPONSIBLE ENOUGH TO CARE FOR THESE KIDS.
BUT...BUT WE WERE LEARNING ABOUT TIGER SHARKS. I WOULD NEVER LET ANYTHING HAPPEN TO THE KIDS...
I CAN'T TRUST YOU, DORY. I DON'T KNOW WHY I EVEN TRY!
COME ON, KIDS. LET'S GET BACK TO CAMP AND GET SOME SLEEP.

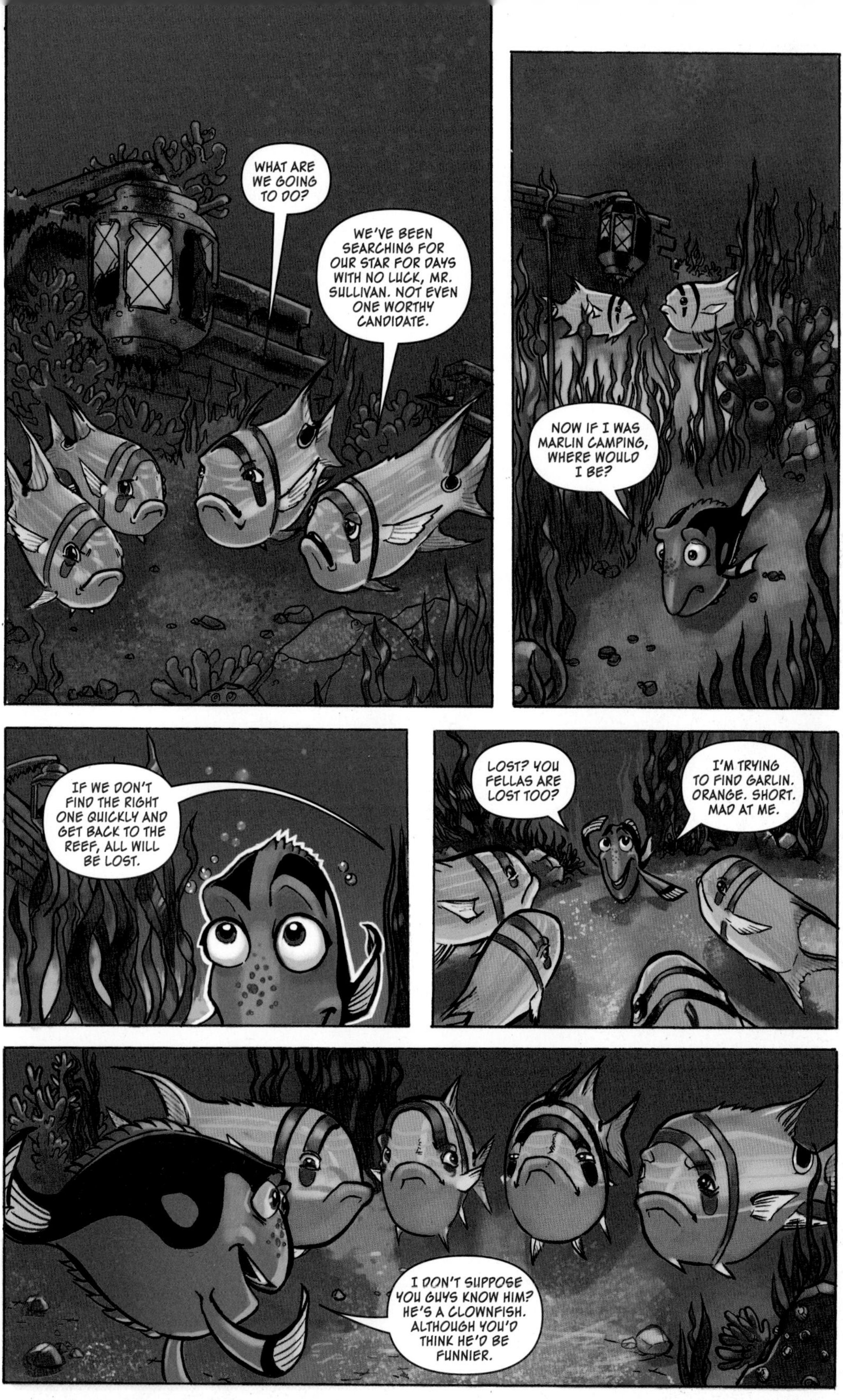
WHAT ARE WE GOING TO DO?
WE'VE BEEN SEARCHING FOR OUR STAR FOR DAYS WITH NO LUCK, MR. SULLIVAN. NOT EVEN ONE WORTHY CANDIDATE.
NOW IF I WAS MARLIN CAMPING, WHERE WOULD I BE?
IF WE DON'T FIND THE RIGHT ONE QUICKLY AND GET BACK TO THE REEF, ALL WILL BE LOST.
LOST? YOU FELLAS ARE LOST TOO?
I'M TRYING TO FIND GARLIN. ORANGE. SHORT. MAD AT ME.
I DON'T SUPPOSE YOU GUYS KNOW HIM? HE'S A CLOWNFISH. ALTHOUGH YOU'D THINK HE'D BE FUNNIER.

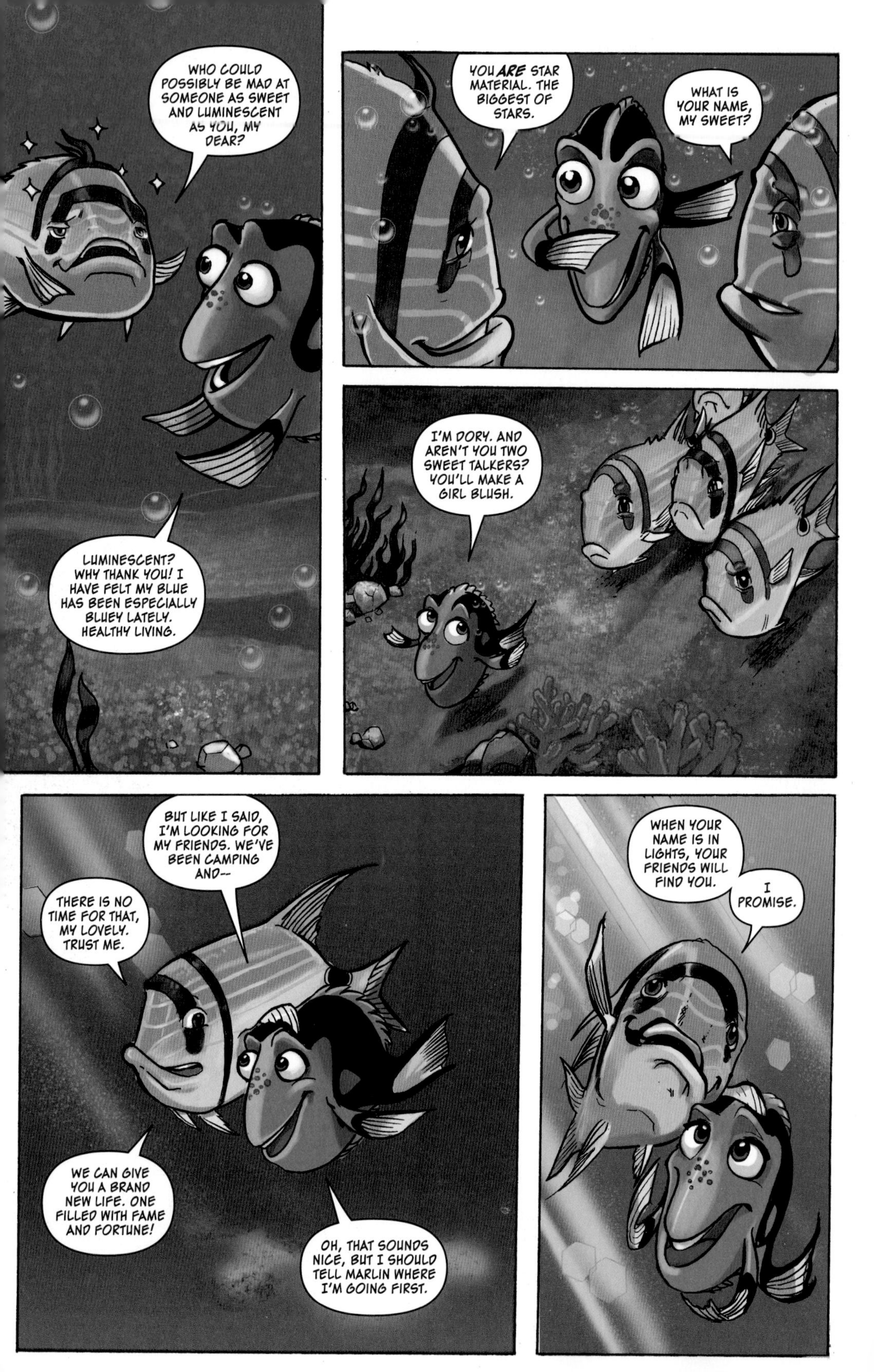
WHO COULD POSSIBLY BE MAD AT SOMEONE AS SWEET AND LUMINESCENT AS YOU, MY DEAR?
LUMINESCENT? WHY THANK YOU! I HAVE FELT MY BLUE HAS BEEN ESPECIALLY BLUEY LATELY. HEALTHY LIVING.
YOU ARE STAR MATERIAL. THE BIGGEST OF STARS.
WHAT IS YOUR NAME, MY SWEET?
I'M DORY. AND AREN'T YOU TWO SWEET TALKERS? YOU'LL MAKE A GIRL BLUSH.
BUT LIKE I SAID, I'M LOOKING FOR MY FRIENDS. WE'VE BEEN CAMPING AND--
THERE IS NO TIME FOR THAT, MY LOVELY. TRUST ME.
WE CAN GIVE YOU A BRAND NEW LIFE. ONE FILLED WITH FAME AND FORTUNE!
OH, THAT SOUNDS NICE, BUT I SHOULD TELL MARLIN WHERE I'M GOING FIRST.
WHEN YOUR NAME IS IN LIGHTS, YOUR FRIENDS WILL FIND YOU.
I PROMISE.

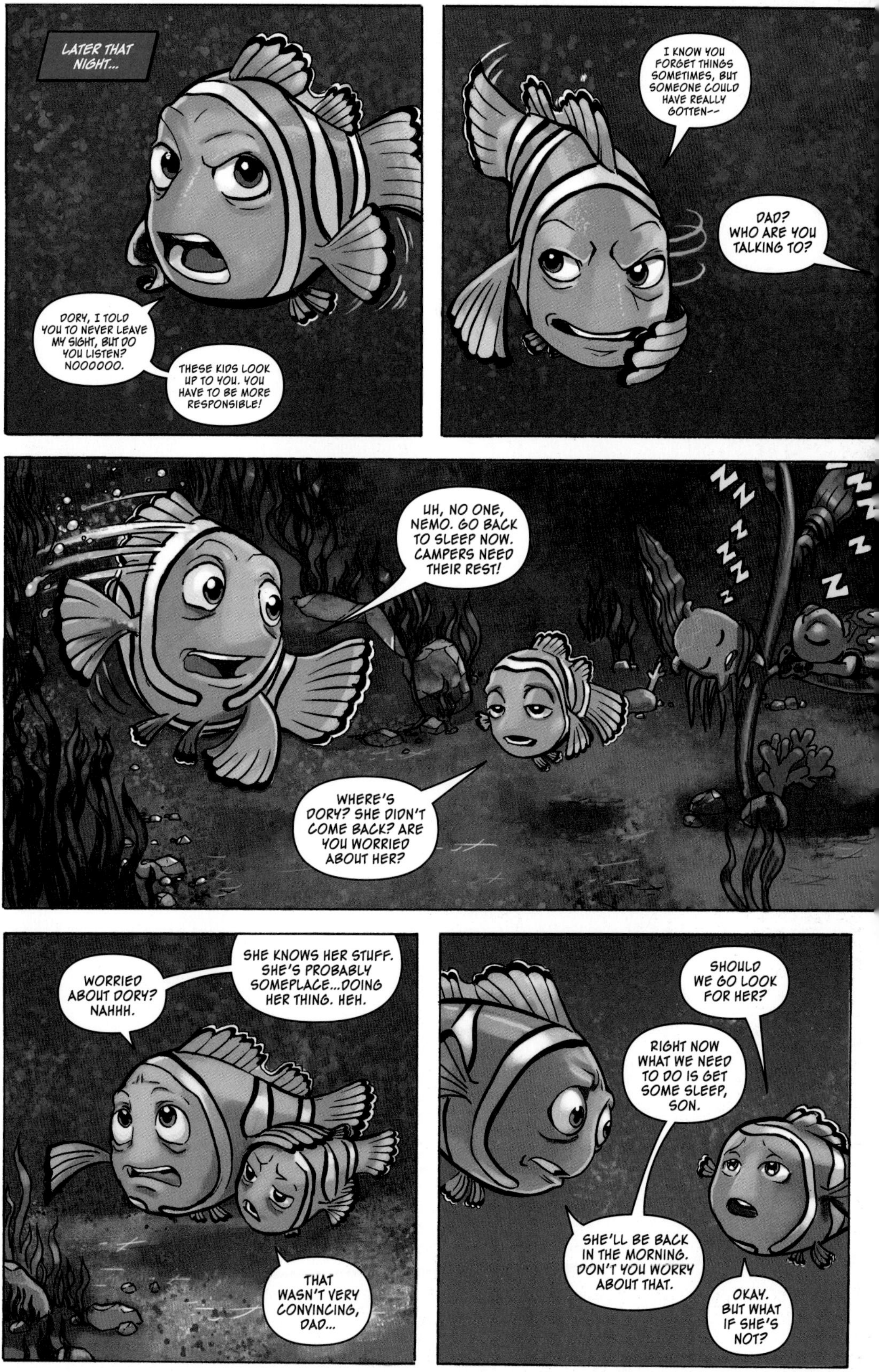
LATER THAT NIGHT...
DORY, I TOLD YOU TO NEVER LEAVE MY SIGHT, BUT DO YOU LISTEN? NOOOOOO.
THESE KIDS LOOK UP TO YOU. YOU HAVE TO BE MORE RESPONSIBLE!
I KNOW YOU FORGET THINGS SOMETIMES, BUT SOMEONE COULD HAVE REALLY GOTTEN--
DAD? WHO ARE YOU TALKING TO?
UH, NO ONE, NEMO. GO BACK TO SLEEP NOW. CAMPERS NEED THEIR REST!
Z Z Z Z Z
Z Z Z Z
WHERE'S DORY? SHE DIDN'T COME BACK? ARE YOU WORRIED ABOUT HER?
WORRIED ABOUT DORY? NAHHH.
SHE KNOWS HER STUFF. SHE'S PROBABLY SOMEPLACE...DOING HER THING. HEH.
THAT WASN'T VERY CONVINCING, DAD...
SHOULD WE GO LOOK FOR HER?
RIGHT NOW WHAT WE NEED TO DO IS GET SOME SLEEP, SON.
SHE'LL BE BACK IN THE MORNING. DON'T YOU WORRY ABOUT THAT.
OKAY. BUT WHAT IF SHE'S NOT?

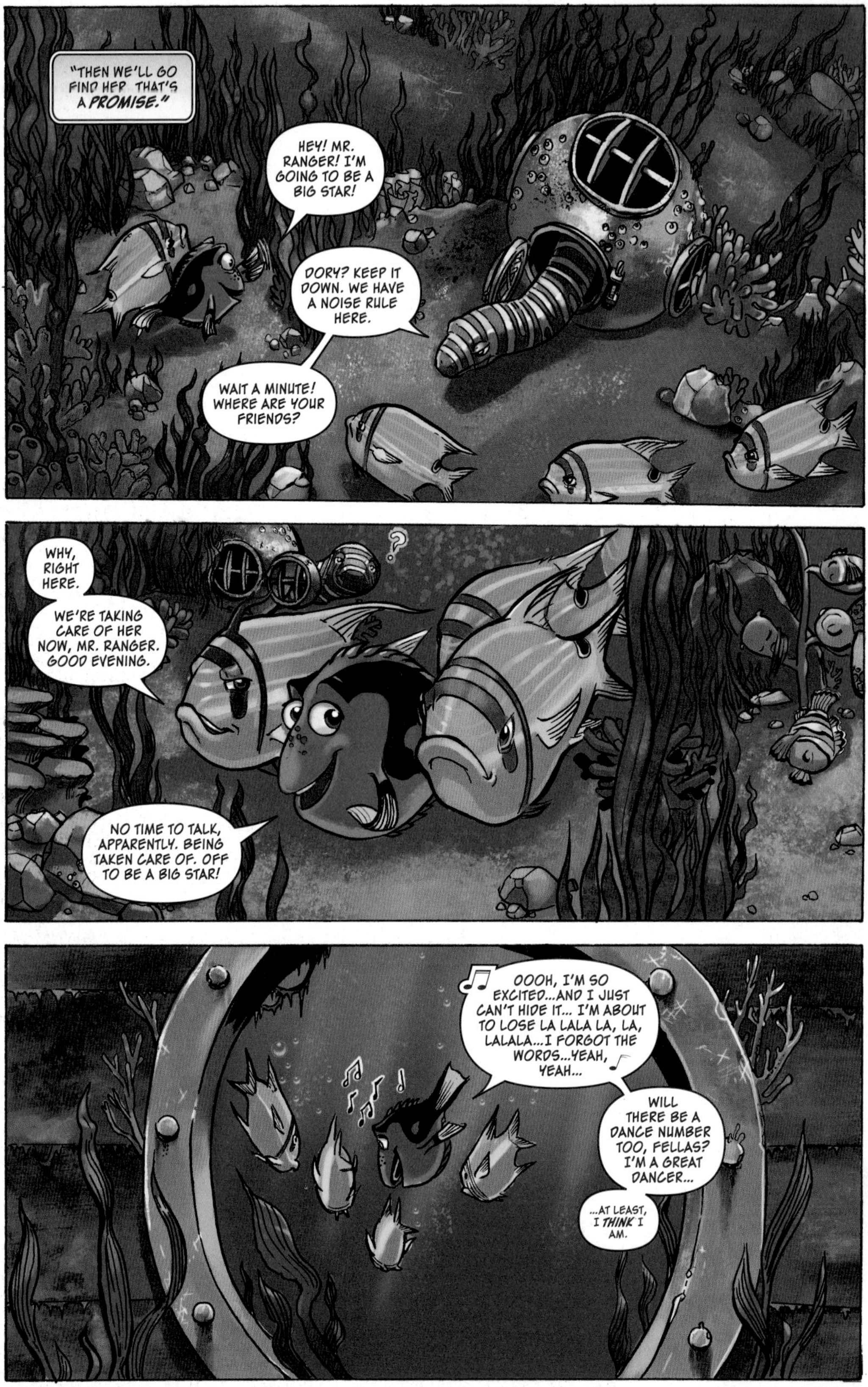
"THEN WE'LL GO FIND HER. THAT'S A PROMISE."
HEY! MR. RANGER! I'M GOING TO BE A BIG STAR!
DORY? KEEP IT DOWN. WE HAVE A NOISE RULE HERE.
WAIT A MINUTE! WHERE ARE YOUR FRIENDS?
WHY, RIGHT HERE.
WE'RE TAKING CARE OF HER NOW, MR. RANGER. GOOD EVENING.
NO TIME TO TALK, APPARENTLY. BEING TAKEN CARE OF. OFF TO BE A BIG STAR!
OOOH, I'M SO EXCITED...AND I JUST CAN'T HIDE IT... I'M ABOUT TO LOSE LA LALA LA, LA, LALALA...I FORGOT THE WORDS...YEAH, YEAH...
WILL THERE BE A DANCE NUMBER TOO, FELLAS? I'M A GREAT DANCER...
...AT LEAST, I THINK I AM.

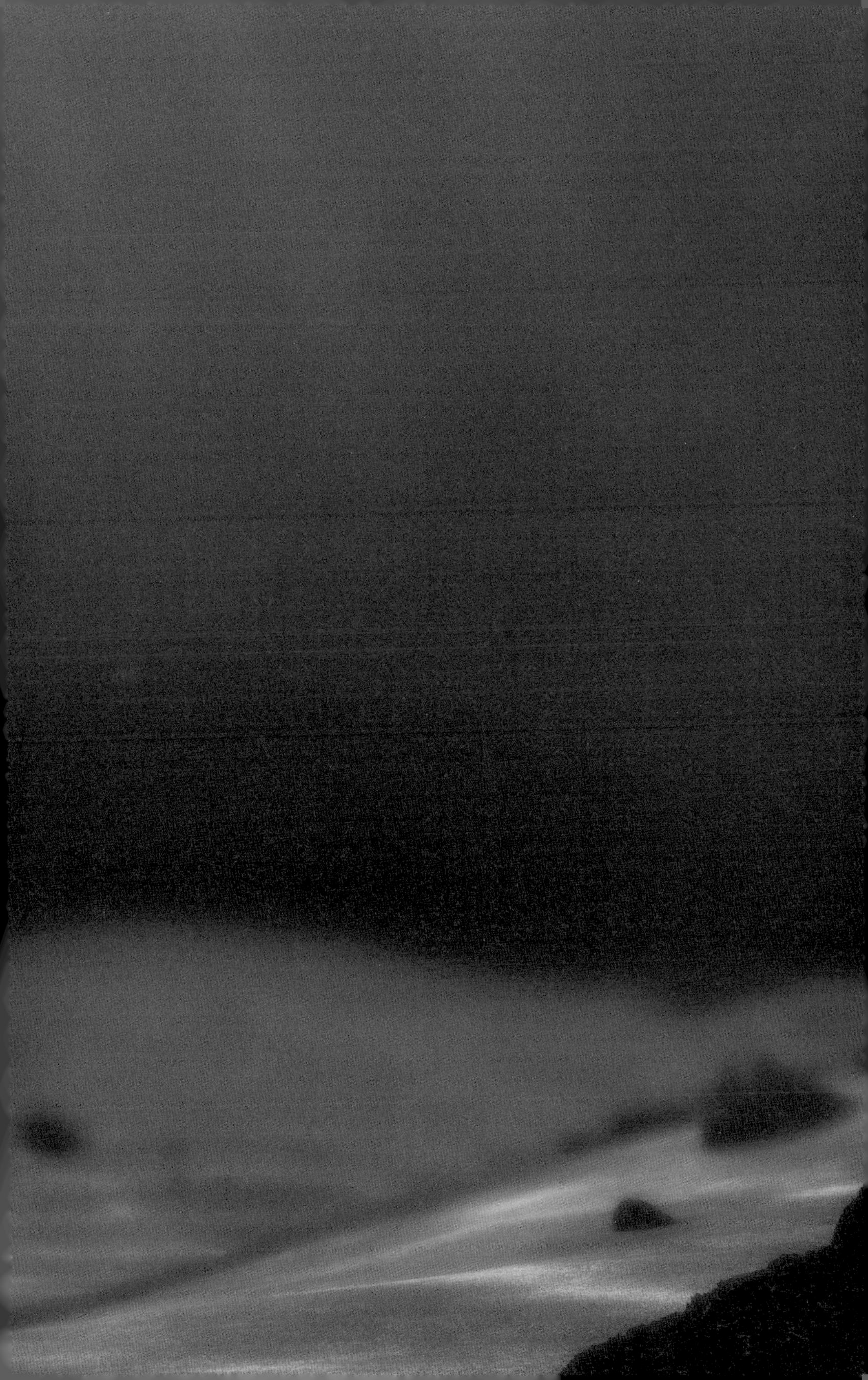

# CHAPTER TWO

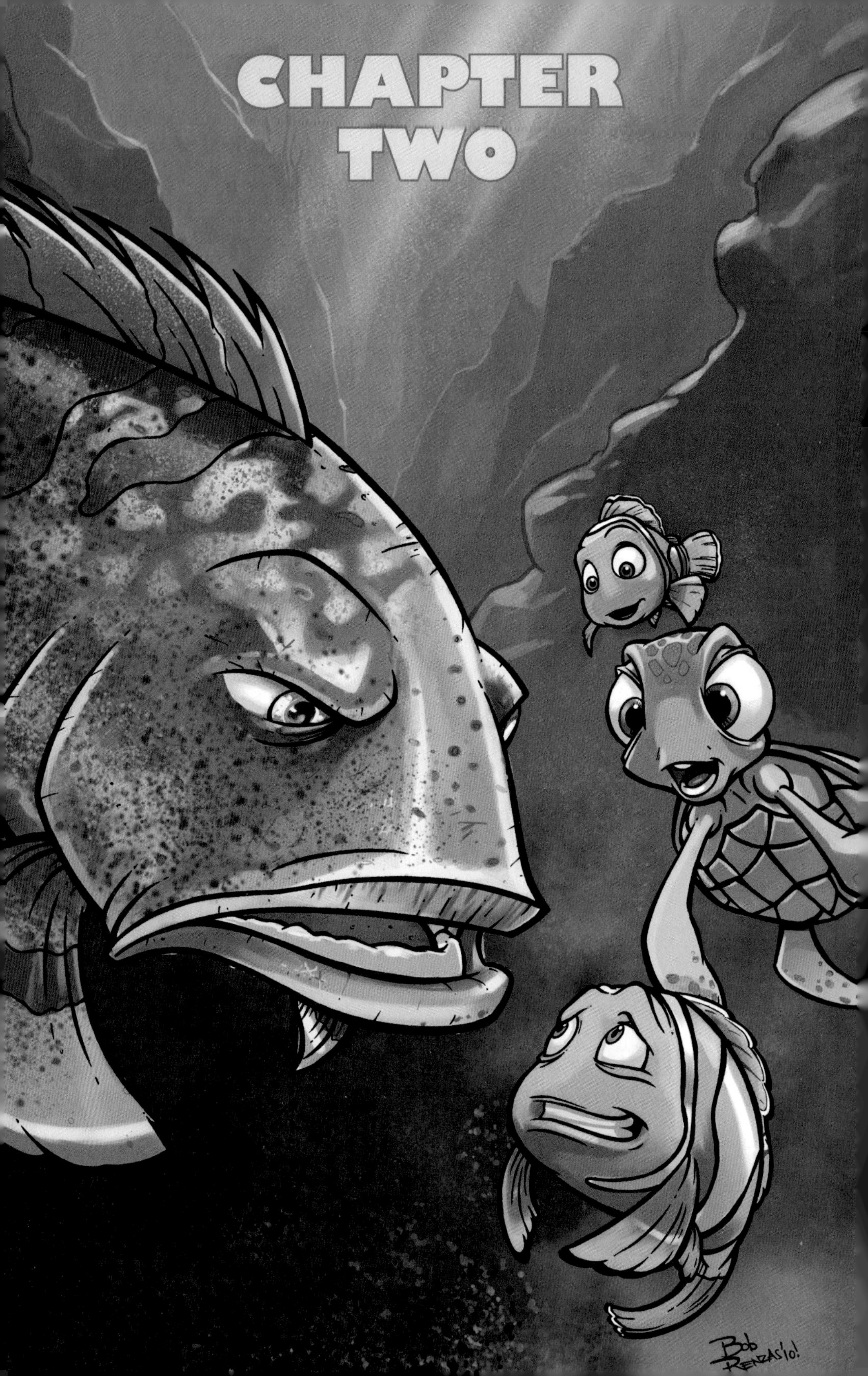

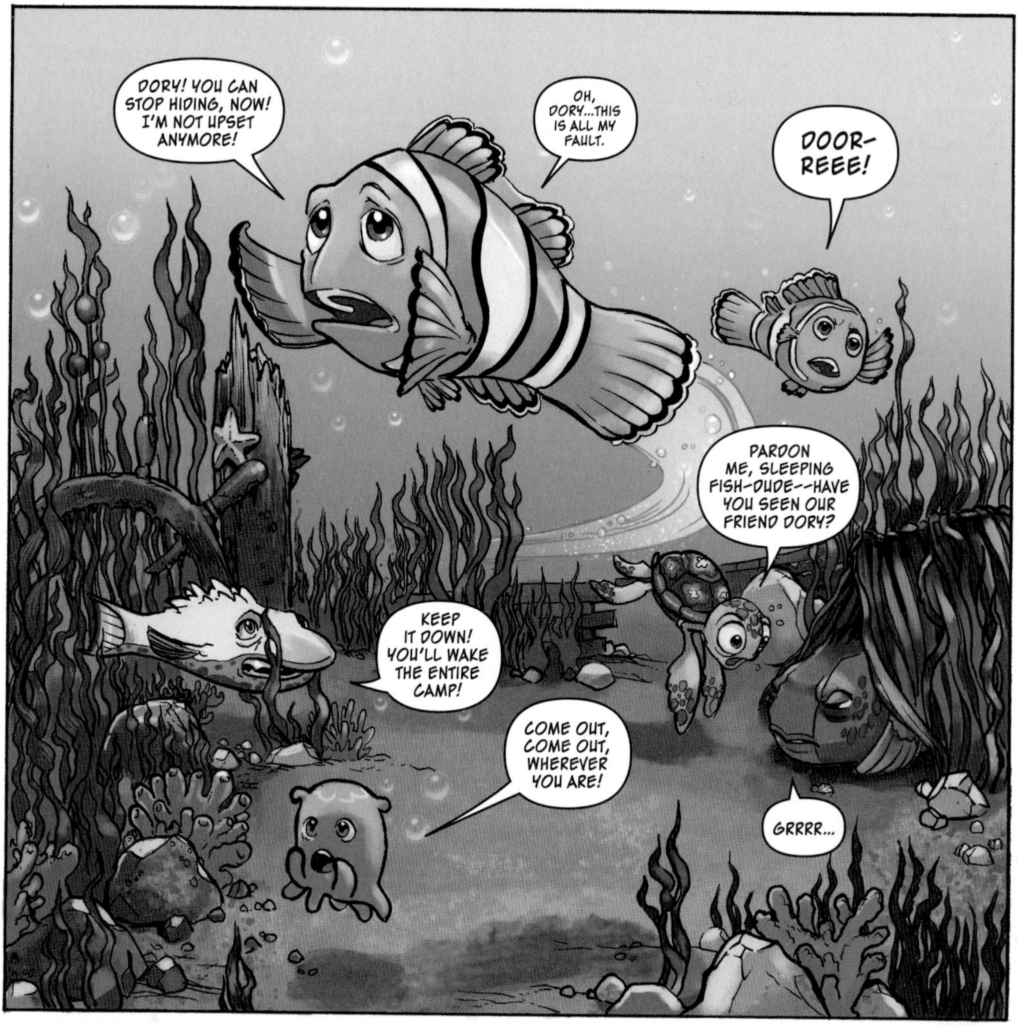
DORY! YOU CAN STOP HIDING, NOW! I'M NOT UPSET ANYMORE!
OH, DORY...THIS IS ALL MY FAULT.
DOOR-REEE!
PARDON ME, SLEEPING FISH-DUDE--HAVE YOU SEEN OUR FRIEND DORY?
KEEP IT DOWN! YOU'LL WAKE THE ENTIRE CAMP!
COME OUT, COME OUT, WHEREVER YOU ARE!
GRRRR...

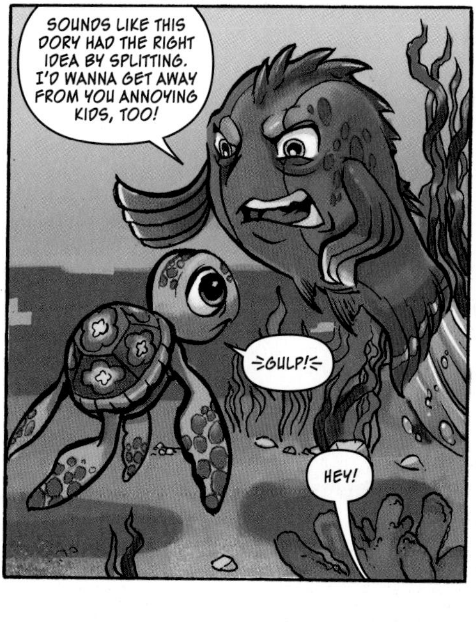
SOUNDS LIKE THIS DORY HAD THE RIGHT IDEA BY SPLITTING. I'D WANNA GET AWAY FROM YOU ANNOYING KIDS, TOO!
GULP!
HEY!

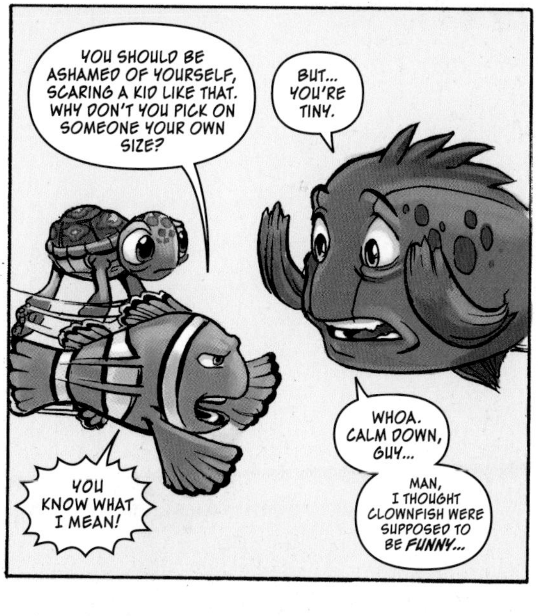
YOU SHOULD BE ASHAMED OF YOURSELF, SCARING A KID LIKE THAT. WHY DON'T YOU PICK ON SOMEONE YOUR OWN SIZE?
BUT... YOU'RE TINY.
YOU KNOW WHAT I MEAN!
WHOA. CALM DOWN, GUY...
MAN, I THOUGHT CLOWNFISH WERE SUPPOSED TO BE FUNNY...

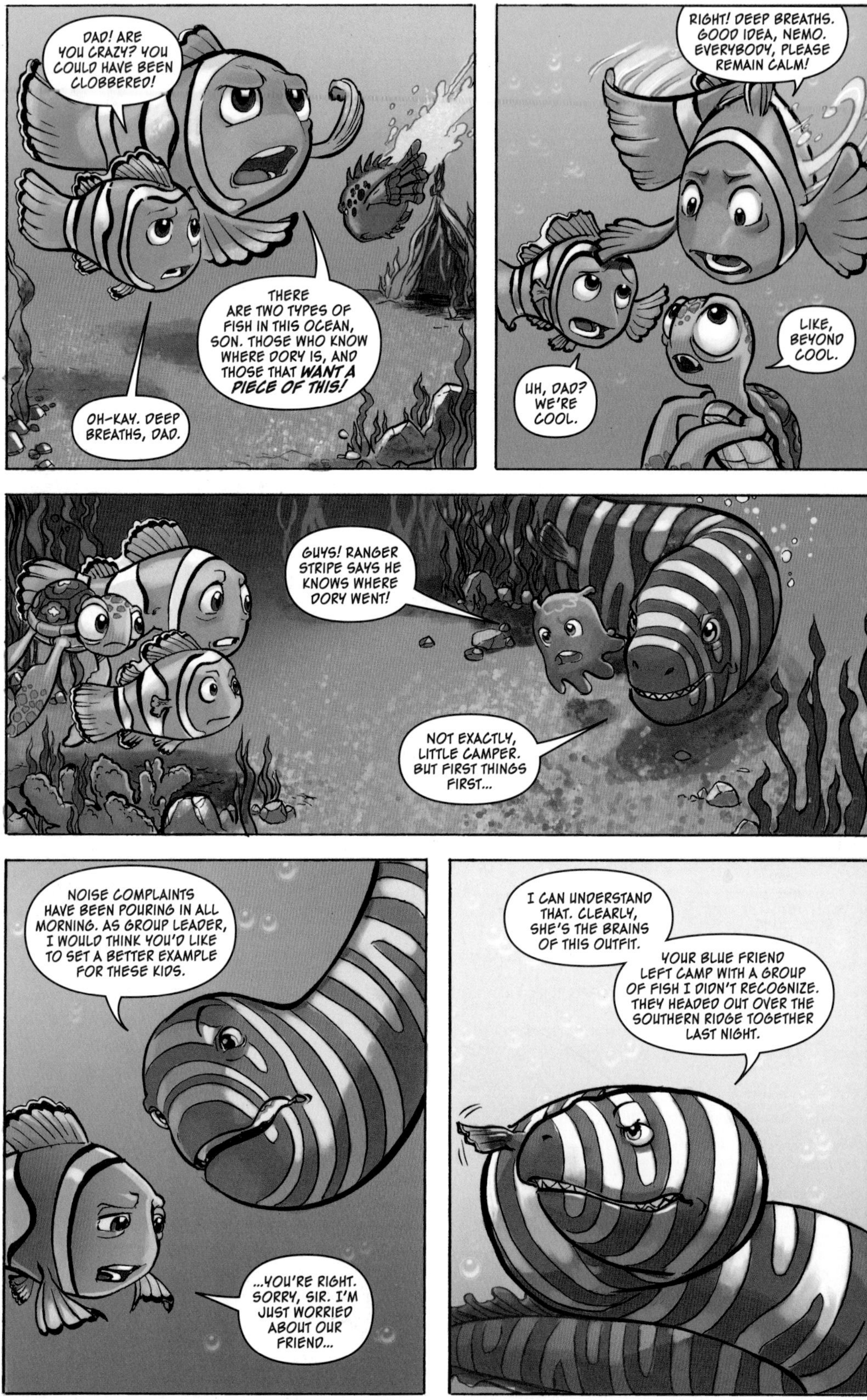
DAD! ARE YOU CRAZY? YOU COULD HAVE BEEN CLOBBERED!
THERE ARE TWO TYPES OF FISH IN THIS OCEAN, SON. THOSE WHO KNOW WHERE DORY IS, AND THOSE THAT WANT A PIECE OF THIS!
OH-KAY. DEEP BREATHS, DAD.
RIGHT! DEEP BREATHS. GOOD IDEA, NEMO. EVERYBODY, PLEASE REMAIN CALM!
UH, DAD? WE'RE COOL.
LIKE, BEYOND COOL.
GUYS! RANGER STRIPE SAYS HE KNOWS WHERE DORY WENT!
NOT EXACTLY, LITTLE CAMPER. BUT FIRST THINGS FIRST...
NOISE COMPLAINTS HAVE BEEN POURING IN ALL MORNING. AS GROUP LEADER, I WOULD THINK YOU'D LIKE TO SET A BETTER EXAMPLE FOR THESE KIDS.
...YOU'RE RIGHT. SORRY, SIR. I'M JUST WORRIED ABOUT OUR FRIEND...
I CAN UNDERSTAND THAT. CLEARLY, SHE'S THE BRAINS OF THIS OUTFIT.
YOUR BLUE FRIEND LEFT CAMP WITH A GROUP OF FISH I DIDN'T RECOGNIZE. THEY HEADED OUT OVER THE SOUTHERN RIDGE TOGETHER LAST NIGHT.

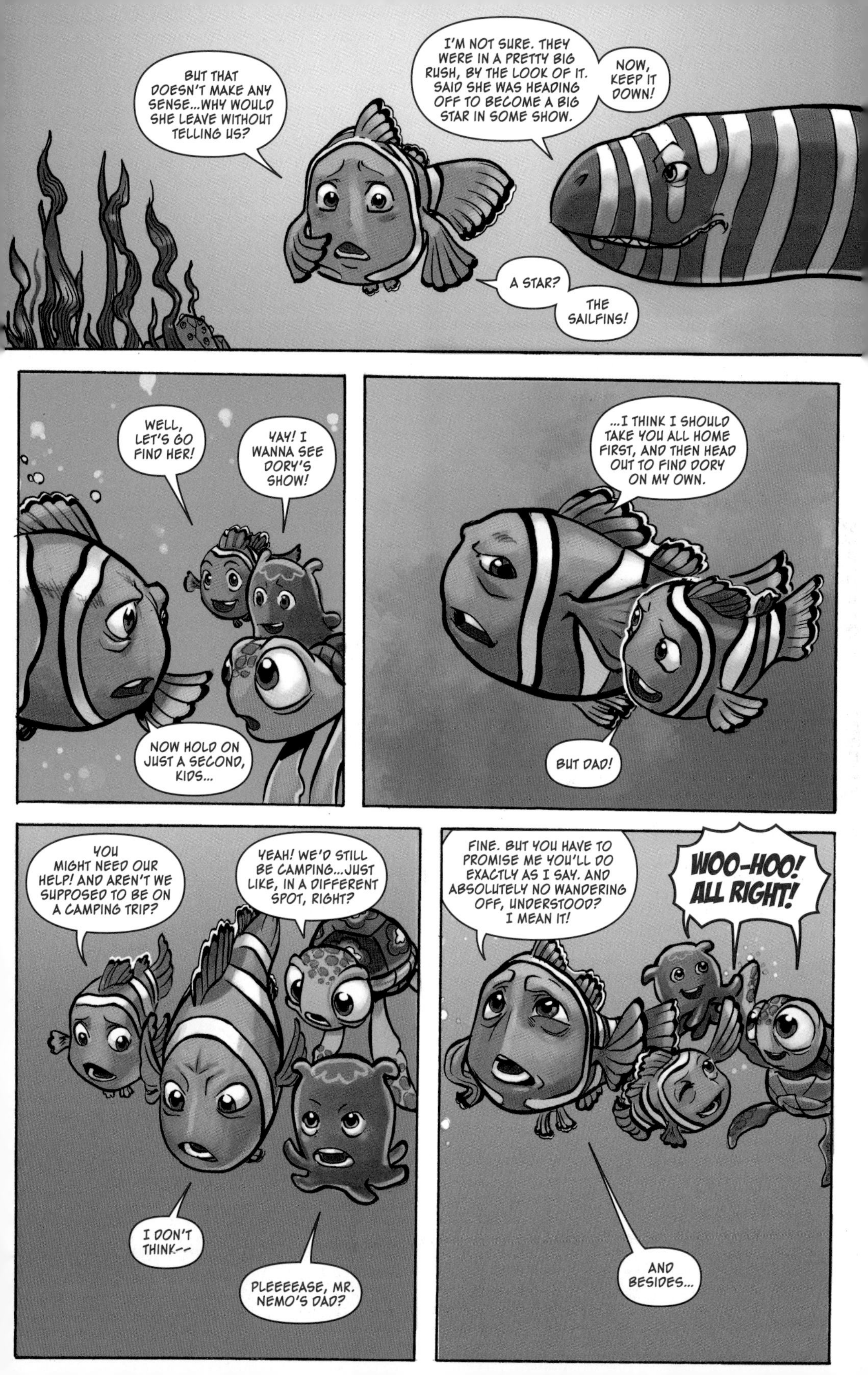
BUT THAT DOESN'T MAKE ANY SENSE...WHY WOULD SHE LEAVE WITHOUT TELLING US?
I'M NOT SURE. THEY WERE IN A PRETTY BIG RUSH, BY THE LOOK OF IT. SAID SHE WAS HEADING OFF TO BECOME A BIG STAR IN SOME SHOW.
NOW, KEEP IT DOWN!
A STAR?
THE SAILFINS!
WELL, LET'S GO FIND HER!
YAY! I WANNA SEE DORY'S SHOW!
NOW HOLD ON JUST A SECOND, KIDS...
...I THINK I SHOULD TAKE YOU ALL HOME FIRST, AND THEN HEAD OUT TO FIND DORY ON MY OWN.
BUT DAD!
YOU MIGHT NEED OUR HELP! AND AREN'T WE SUPPOSED TO BE ON A CAMPING TRIP?
YEAH! WE'D STILL BE CAMPING...JUST LIKE, IN A DIFFERENT SPOT, RIGHT?
I DON'T THINK--
PLEEEEASE, MR. NEMO'S DAD?
AND BESIDES...
FINE. BUT YOU HAVE TO PROMISE ME YOU'LL DO EXACTLY AS I SAY. AND ABSOLUTELY NO WANDERING OFF, UNDERSTOOD? I MEAN IT!
WOO-HOO! ALL RIGHT!

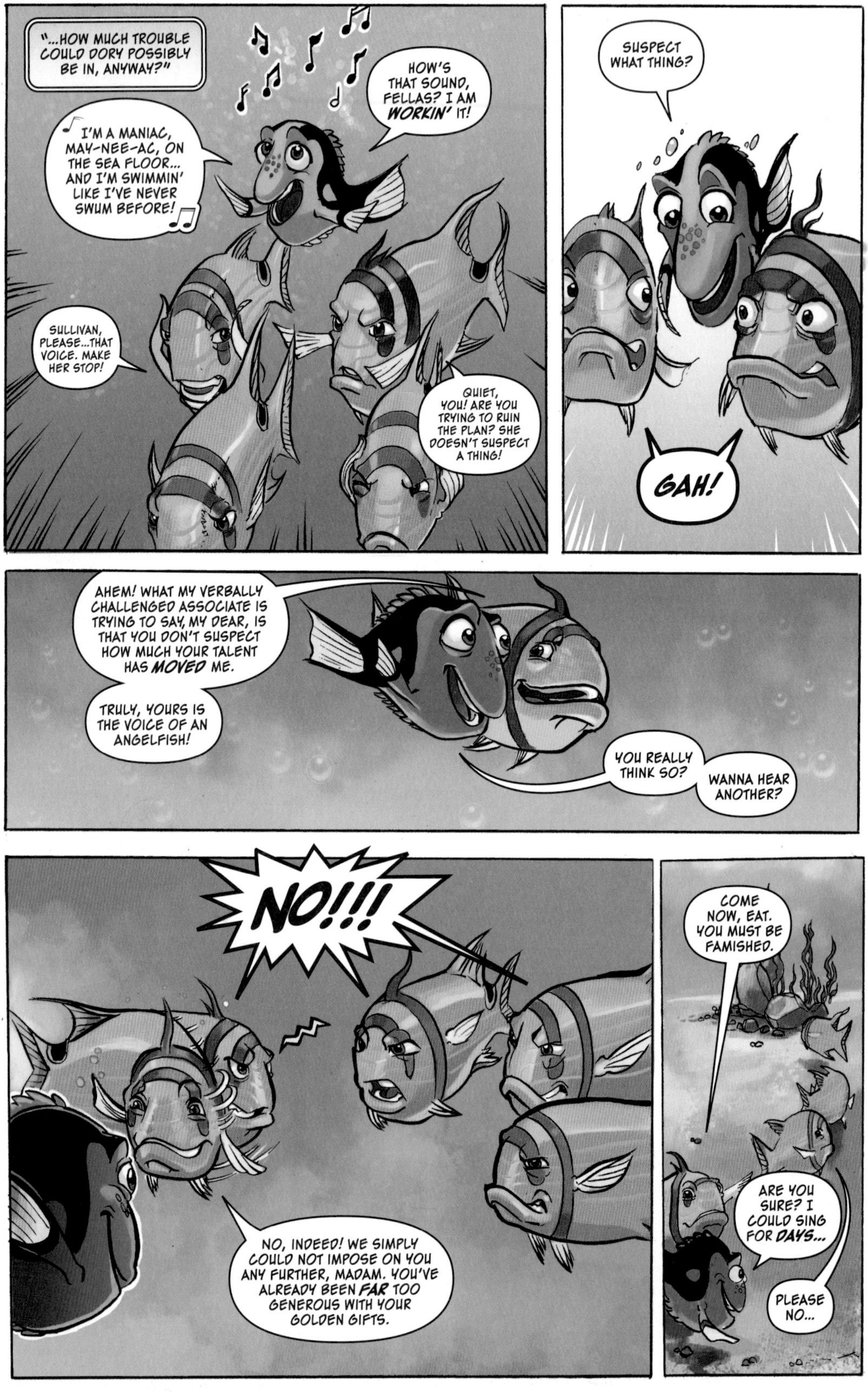
"...HOW MUCH TROUBLE COULD DORY POSSIBLY BE IN, ANYWAY?"
I'M A MANIAC, MAY-NEE-AC, ON THE SEA FLOOR... AND I'M SWIMMIN' LIKE I'VE NEVER SWUM BEFORE!
HOW'S THAT SOUND, FELLAS? I AM WORKIN' IT!
SULLIVAN, PLEASE...THAT VOICE. MAKE HER STOP!
QUIET, YOU! ARE YOU TRYING TO RUIN THE PLAN? SHE DOESN'T SUSPECT A THING!
SUSPECT WHAT THING?
GAH!
AHEM! WHAT MY VERBALLY CHALLENGED ASSOCIATE IS TRYING TO SAY, MY DEAR, IS THAT YOU DON'T SUSPECT HOW MUCH YOUR TALENT HAS MOVED ME.
TRULY, YOURS IS THE VOICE OF AN ANGELFISH!
YOU REALLY THINK SO?
WANNA HEAR ANOTHER?
NO!!!
NO, INDEED! WE SIMPLY COULD NOT IMPOSE ON YOU ANY FURTHER, MADAM. YOU'VE ALREADY BEEN FAR TOO GENEROUS WITH YOUR GOLDEN GIFTS.
COME NOW, EAT. YOU MUST BE FAMISHED.
ARE YOU SURE? I COULD SING FOR DAYS...
PLEASE NO...

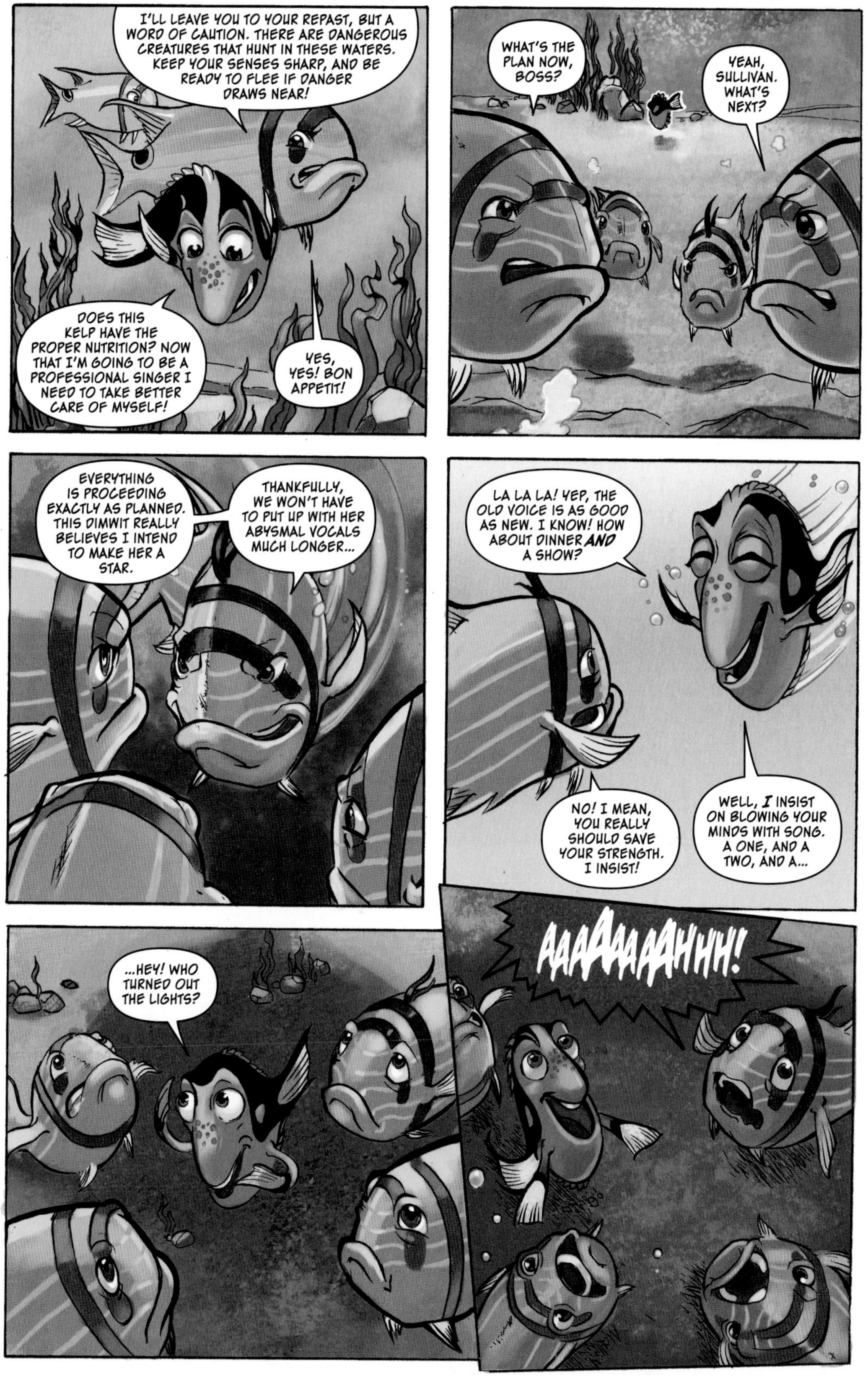
I'LL LEAVE YOU TO YOUR REPAST, BUT A WORD OF CAUTION. THERE ARE DANGEROUS CREATURES THAT HUNT IN THESE WATERS. KEEP YOUR SENSES SHARP, AND BE READY TO FLEE IF DANGER DRAWS NEAR!
DOES THIS KELP HAVE THE PROPER NUTRITION? NOW THAT I'M GOING TO BE A PROFESSIONAL SINGER I NEED TO TAKE BETTER CARE OF MYSELF!
YES, YES! BON APPETIT!
WHAT'S THE PLAN NOW, BOSS?
YEAH, SULLIVAN. WHAT'S NEXT?
EVERYTHING IS PROCEEDING EXACTLY AS PLANNED. THIS DIMWIT REALLY BELIEVES I INTEND TO MAKE HER A STAR.
THANKFULLY, WE WON'T HAVE TO PUT UP WITH HER ABYSMAL VOCALS MUCH LONGER...
LA LA LA! YEP, THE OLD VOICE IS AS GOOD AS NEW. I KNOW! HOW ABOUT DINNER AND A SHOW?
NO! I MEAN, YOU REALLY SHOULD SAVE YOUR STRENGTH. I INSIST!
WELL, I INSIST ON BLOWING YOUR MINDS WITH SONG. A ONE, AND A TWO, AND A...
...HEY! WHO TURNED OUT THE LIGHTS?
AAAAAAAAAHHH!

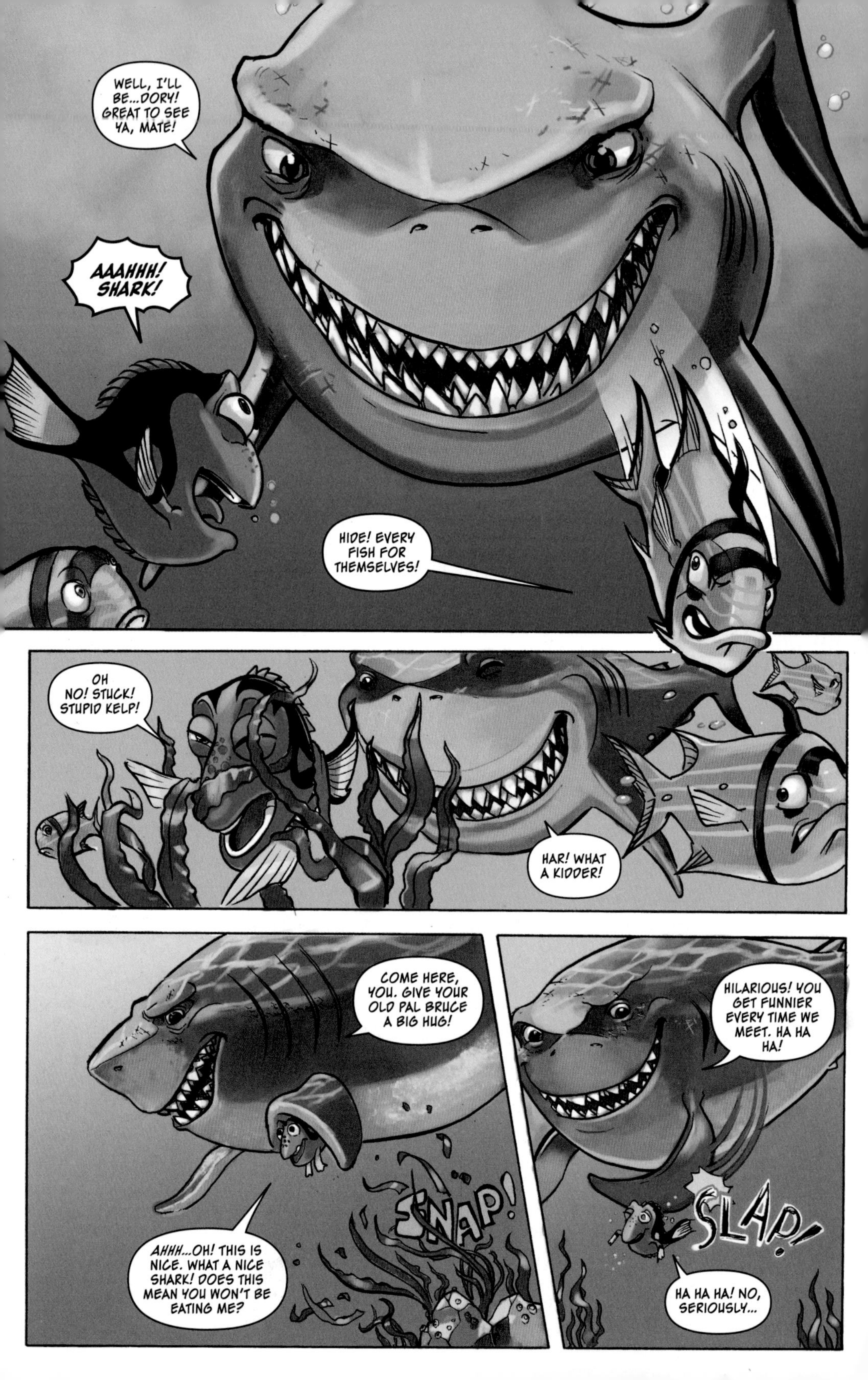
WELL, I'LL BE...DORY! GREAT TO SEE YA, MATE!
AAAHHH! SHARK!
HIDE! EVERY FISH FOR THEMSELVES!
OH NO! STUCK! STUPID KELP!
HAR! WHAT A KIDDER!
COME HERE, YOU. GIVE YOUR OLD PAL BRUCE A BIG HUG!
SNAP!
AHHH...OH! THIS IS NICE. WHAT A NICE SHARK! DOES THIS MEAN YOU WON'T BE EATING ME?
HILARIOUS! YOU GET FUNNIER EVERY TIME WE MEET. HA HA HA!
SLAP!
HA HA HA! NO, SERIOUSLY...

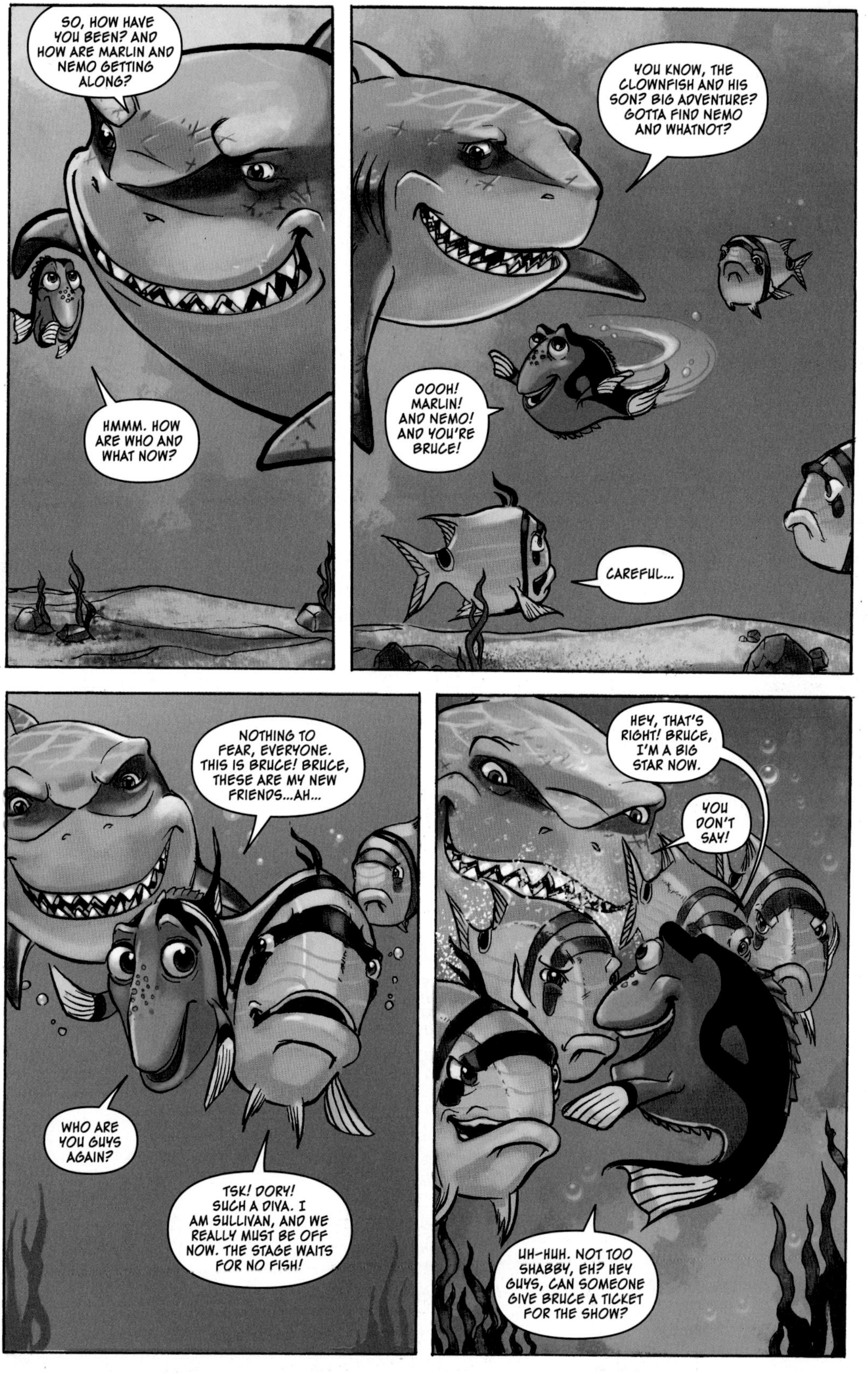
SO, HOW HAVE YOU BEEN? AND HOW ARE MARLIN AND NEMO GETTING ALONG?
HMMM. HOW ARE WHO AND WHAT NOW?
YOU KNOW, THE CLOWNFISH AND HIS SON? BIG ADVENTURE? GOTTA FIND NEMO AND WHATNOT?
OOOH! MARLIN! AND NEMO! AND YOU'RE BRUCE!
CAREFUL...
NOTHING TO FEAR, EVERYONE. THIS IS BRUCE! BRUCE, THESE ARE MY NEW FRIENDS...AH...
WHO ARE YOU GUYS AGAIN?
TSK! DORY! SUCH A DIVA. I AM SULLIVAN, AND WE REALLY MUST BE OFF NOW. THE STAGE WAITS FOR NO FISH!
HEY, THAT'S RIGHT! BRUCE, I'M A BIG STAR NOW.
YOU DON'T SAY!
UH-HUH. NOT TOO SHABBY, EH? HEY GUYS, CAN SOMEONE GIVE BRUCE A TICKET FOR THE SHOW?

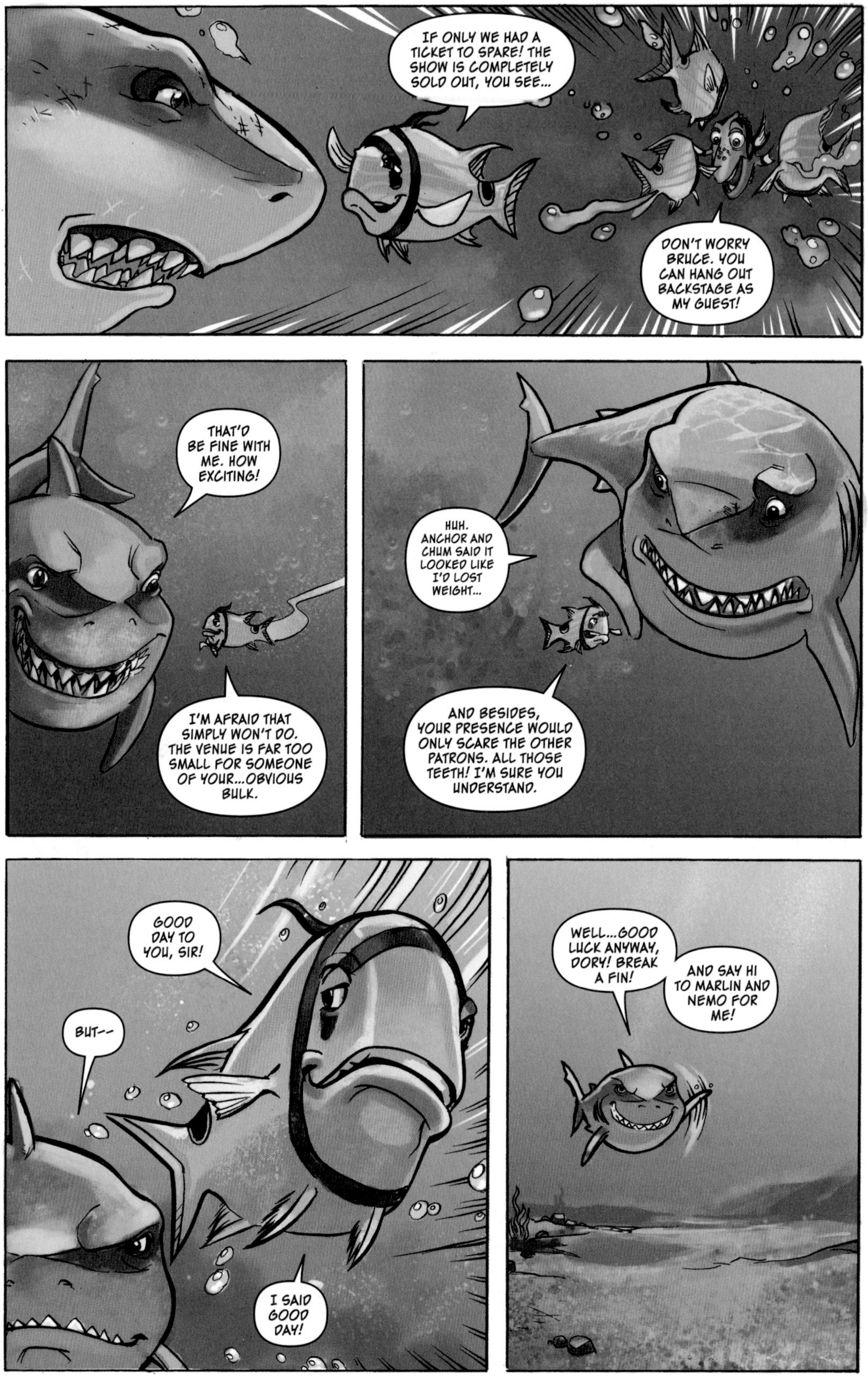
IF ONLY WE HAD A TICKET TO SPARE! THE SHOW IS COMPLETELY SOLD OUT, YOU SEE...
DON'T WORRY BRUCE. YOU CAN HANG OUT BACKSTAGE AS MY GUEST!
THAT'D BE FINE WITH ME. HOW EXCITING!
I'M AFRAID THAT SIMPLY WON'T DO. THE VENUE IS FAR TOO SMALL FOR SOMEONE OF YOUR...OBVIOUS BULK.
HUH. ANCHOR AND CHUM SAID IT LOOKED LIKE I'D LOST WEIGHT...
AND BESIDES, YOUR PRESENCE WOULD ONLY SCARE THE OTHER PATRONS. ALL THOSE TEETH! I'M SURE YOU UNDERSTAND.
GOOD DAY TO YOU, SIR!
BUT--
I SAID GOOD DAY!
WELL...GOOD LUCK ANYWAY, DORY! BREAK A FIN!
AND SAY HI TO MARLIN AND NEMO FOR ME!

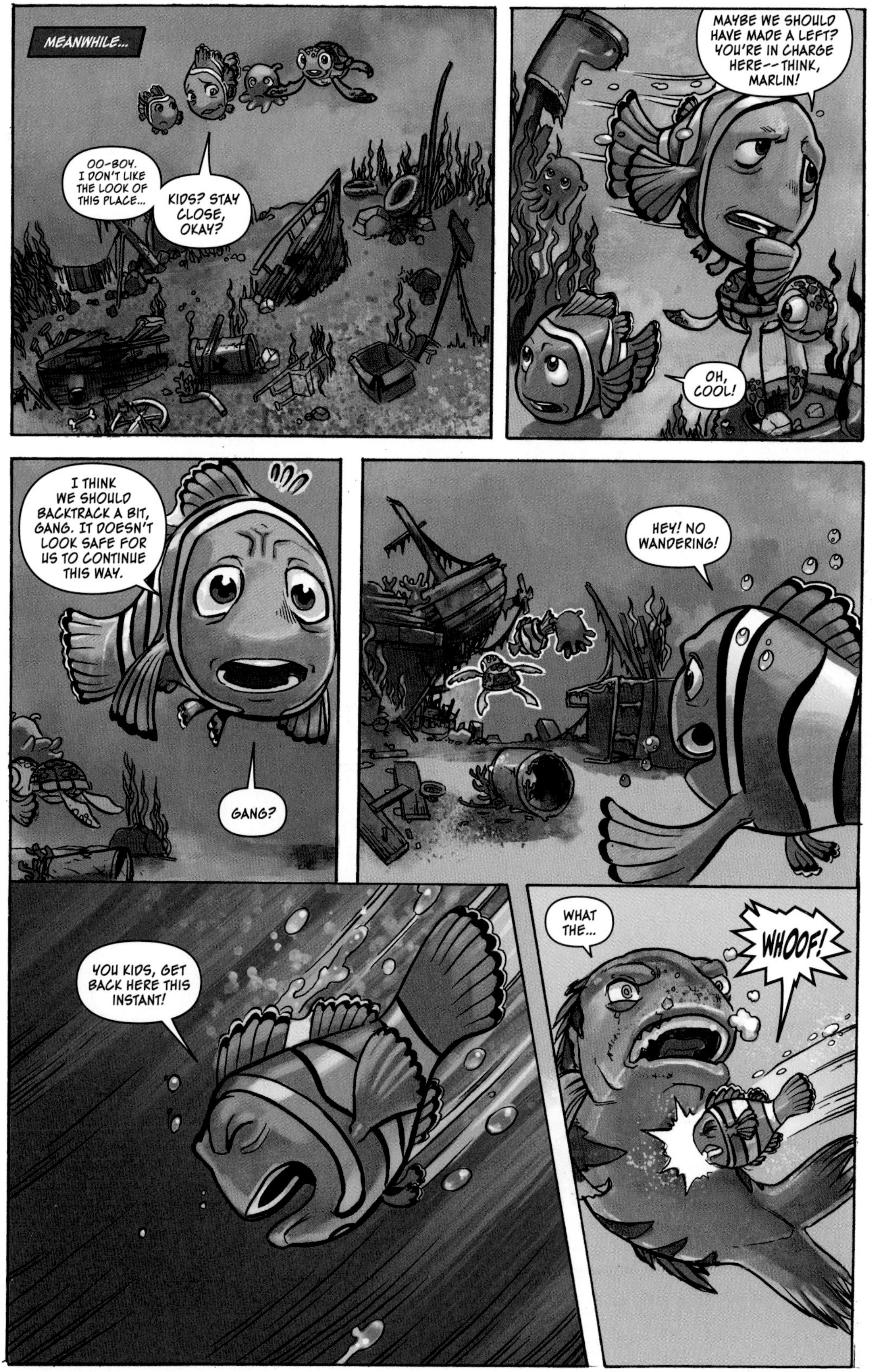
MEANWHILE...
OO-BOY. I DON'T LIKE THE LOOK OF THIS PLACE...
KIDS? STAY CLOSE, OKAY?
MAYBE WE SHOULD HAVE MADE A LEFT? YOU'RE IN CHARGE HERE--THINK, MARLIN!
OH, COOL!
I THINK WE SHOULD BACKTRACK A BIT, GANG. IT DOESN'T LOOK SAFE FOR US TO CONTINUE THIS WAY.
GANG?
HEY! NO WANDERING!
YOU KIDS, GET BACK HERE THIS INSTANT!
WHAT THE...
WHOOF!

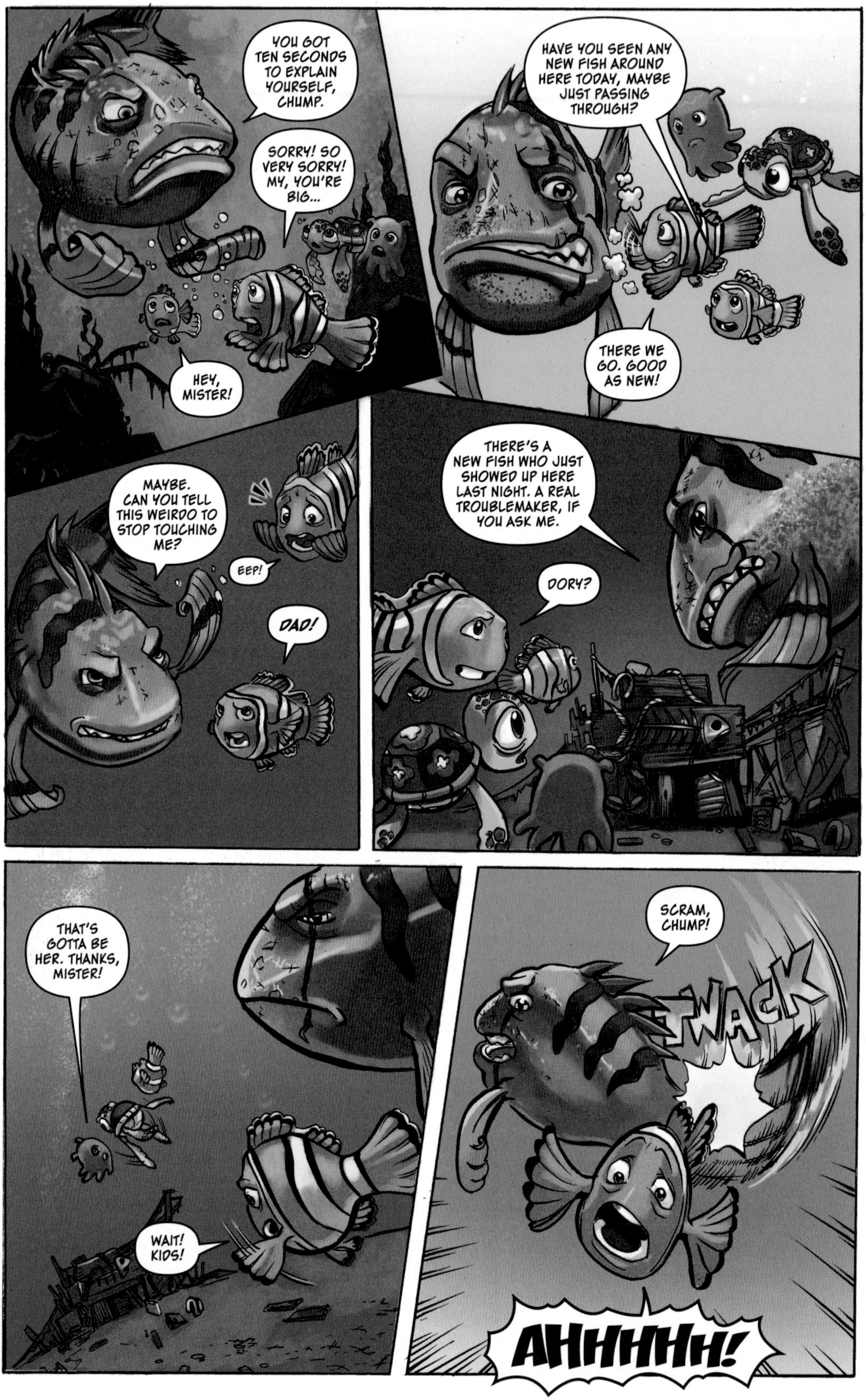
YOU GOT TEN SECONDS TO EXPLAIN YOURSELF, CHUMP.
SORRY! SO VERY SORRY! MY, YOU'RE BIG...
HEY, MISTER!
HAVE YOU SEEN ANY NEW FISH AROUND HERE TODAY, MAYBE JUST PASSING THROUGH?
THERE WE GO. GOOD AS NEW!
MAYBE. CAN YOU TELL THIS WEIRDO TO STOP TOUCHING ME?
EEP!
DAD!
THERE'S A NEW FISH WHO JUST SHOWED UP HERE LAST NIGHT. A REAL TROUBLEMAKER, IF YOU ASK ME.
DORY?
THAT'S GOTTA BE HER. THANKS, MISTER!
WAIT! KIDS!
SCRAM, CHUMP!
TWACK
AHHHHH!

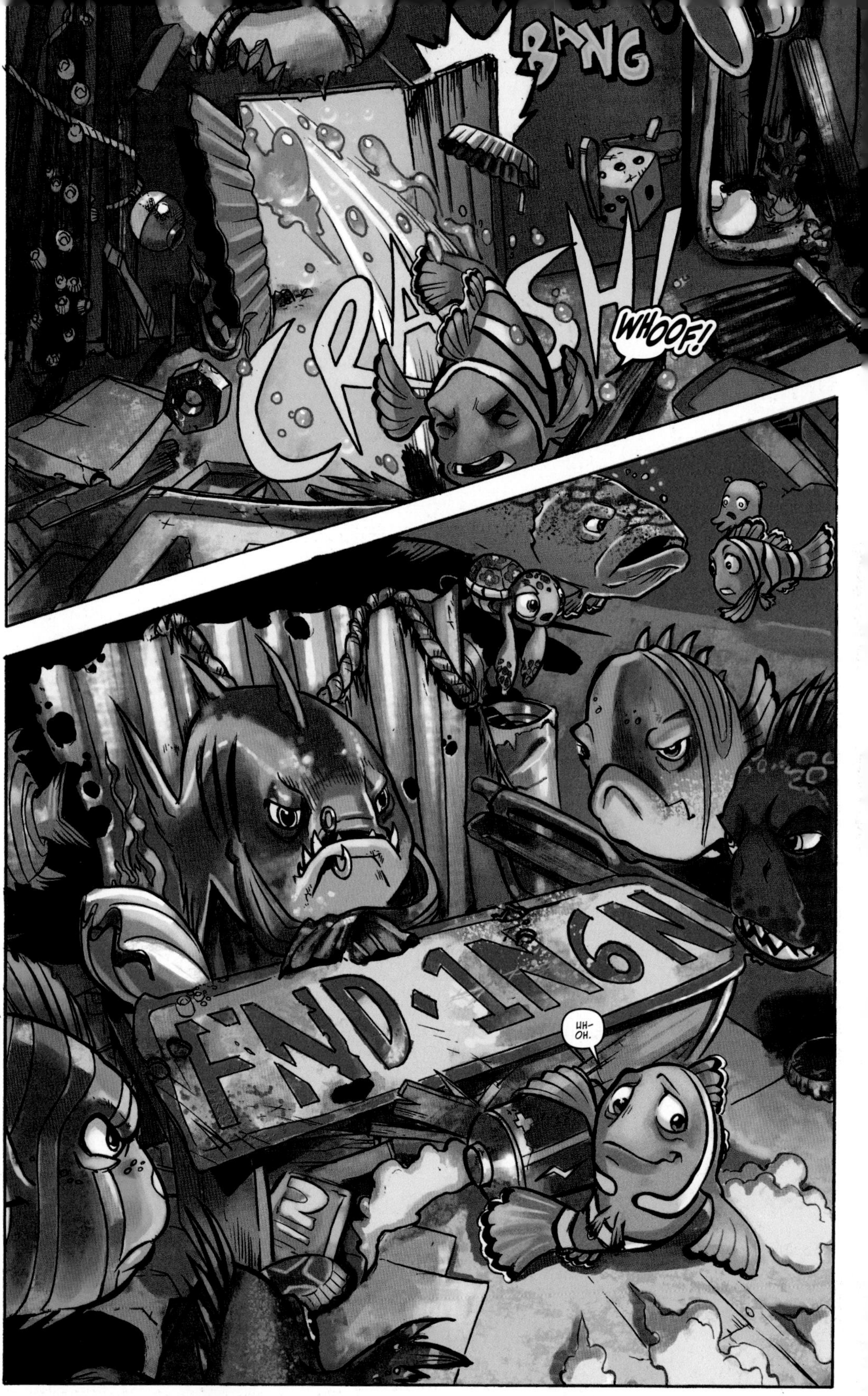
BANG
CRASH!
WHOOF!
UH-OH.

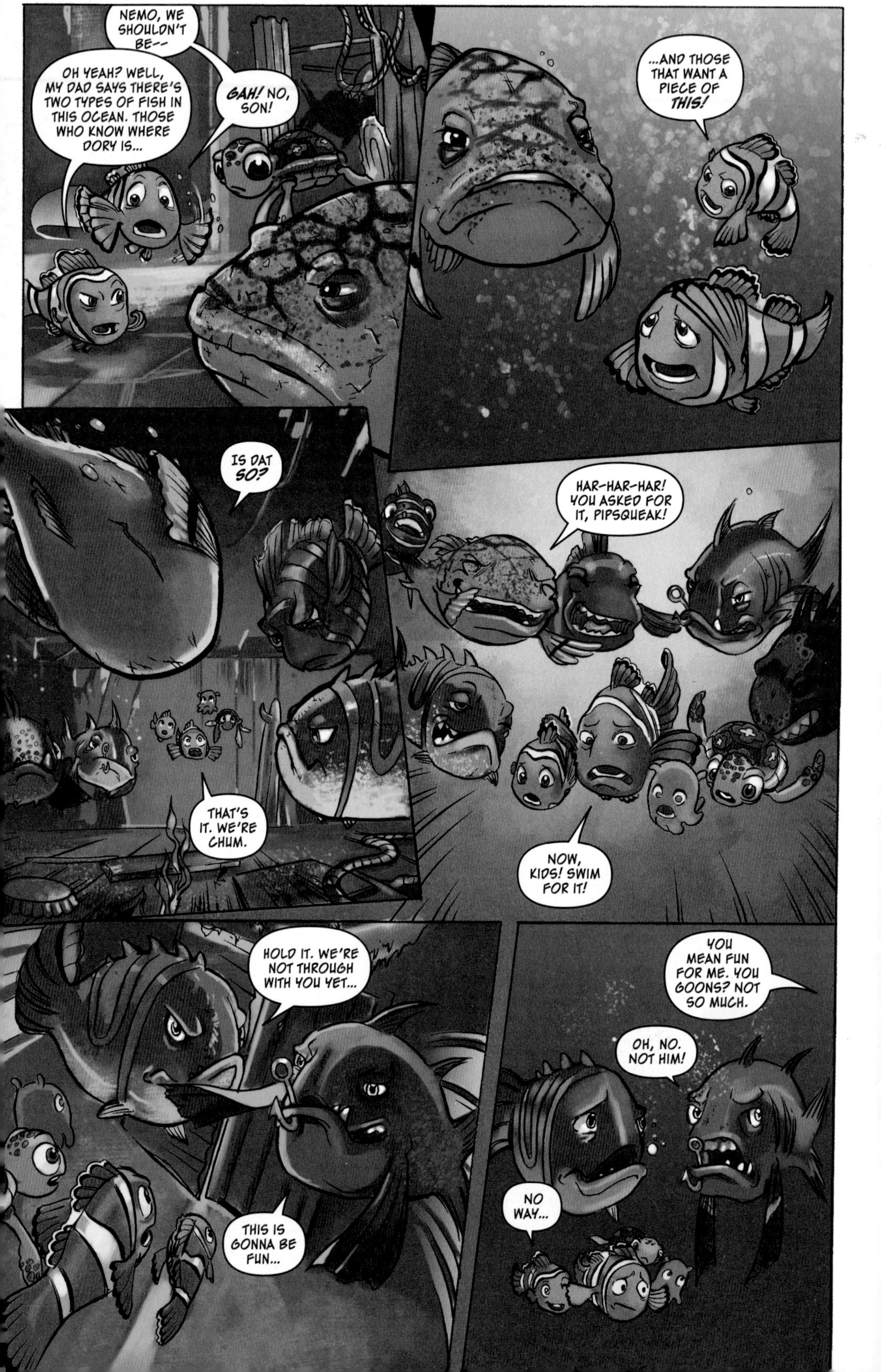
NEMO, WE SHOULDN'T BE--
OH YEAH? WELL, MY DAD SAYS THERE'S TWO TYPES OF FISH IN THIS OCEAN. THOSE WHO KNOW WHERE DORY IS...
GAH! NO, SON!
...AND THOSE THAT WANT A PIECE OF THIS!
IS DAT SO?
THAT'S IT. WE'RE CHUM.
HAR-HAR-HAR! YOU ASKED FOR IT, PIPSQUEAK!
NOW, KIDS! SWIM FOR IT!
HOLD IT. WE'RE NOT THROUGH WITH YOU YET...
THIS IS GONNA BE FUN...
YOU MEAN FUN FOR ME. YOU GOONS? NOT SO MUCH.
OH, NO. NOT HIM!
NO WAY...

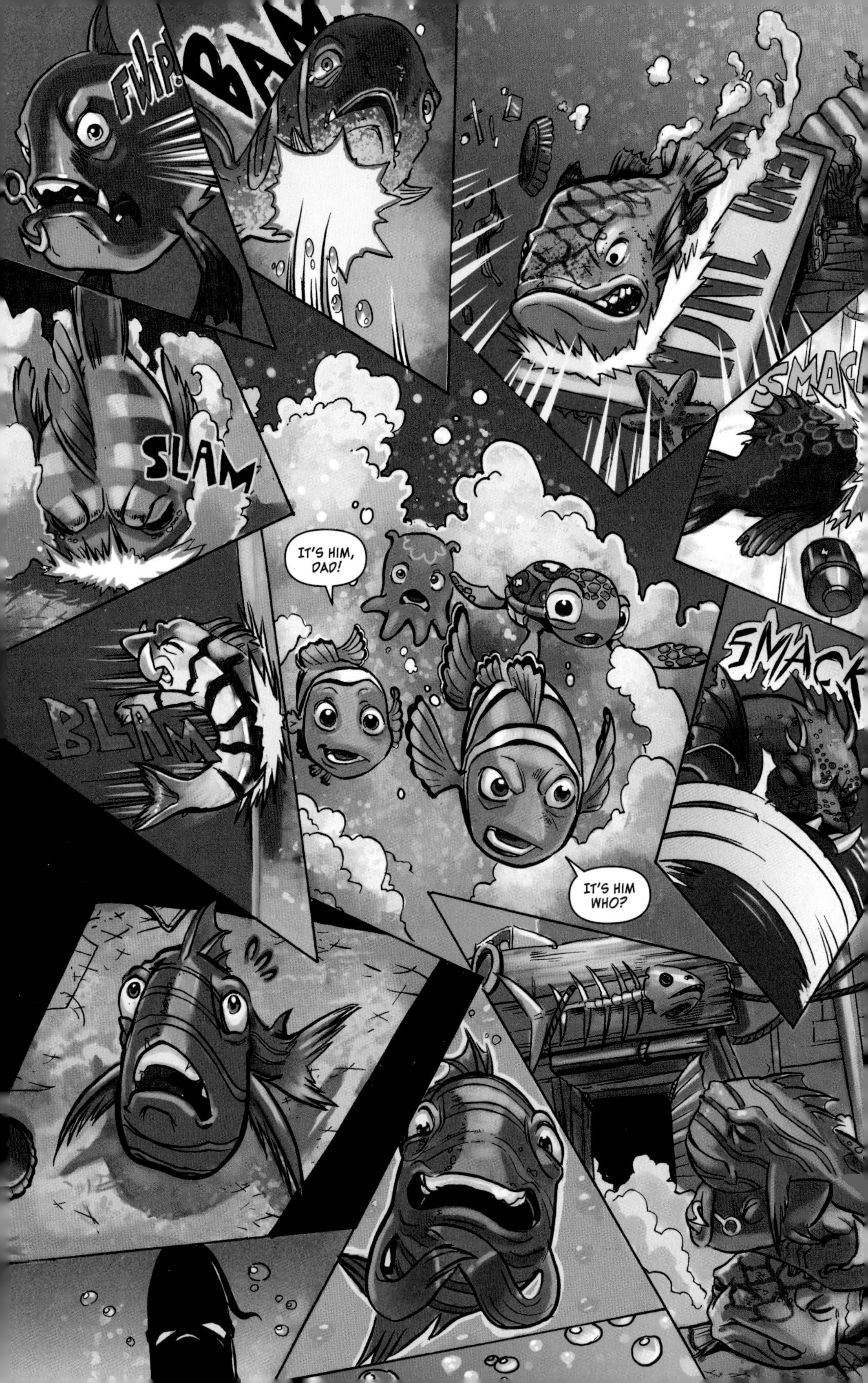
FWIP!
BAM
SLAM
SMACK
BLAM
IT'S HIM, DAD!
SMACK
IT'S HIM WHO?

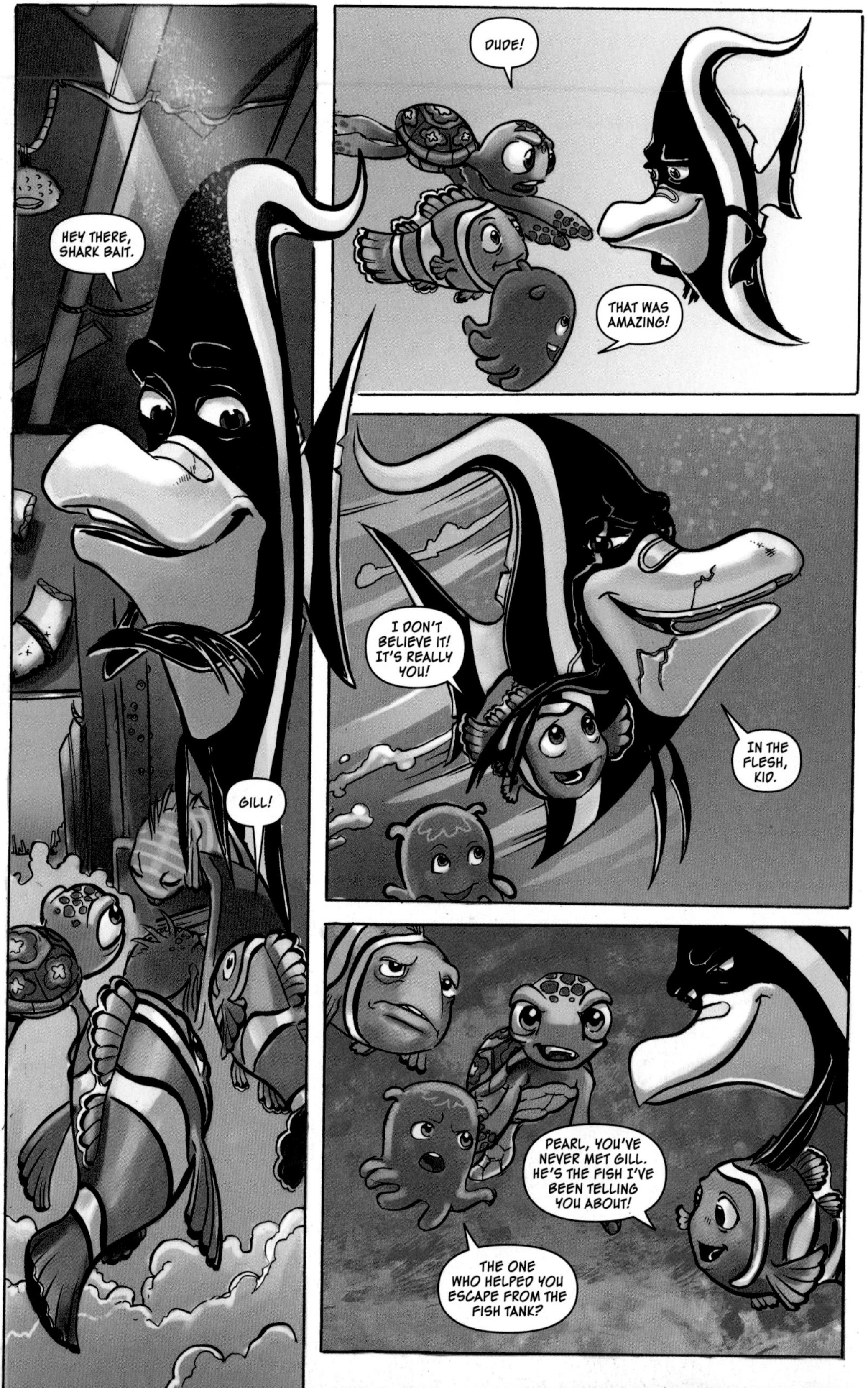
HEY THERE, SHARK BAIT.
GILL!
DUDE!
THAT WAS AMAZING!
I DON'T BELIEVE IT! IT'S REALLY YOU!
IN THE FLESH, KID.
PEARL, YOU'VE NEVER MET GILL. HE'S THE FISH I'VE BEEN TELLING YOU ABOUT!
THE ONE WHO HELPED YOU ESCAPE FROM THE FISH TANK?

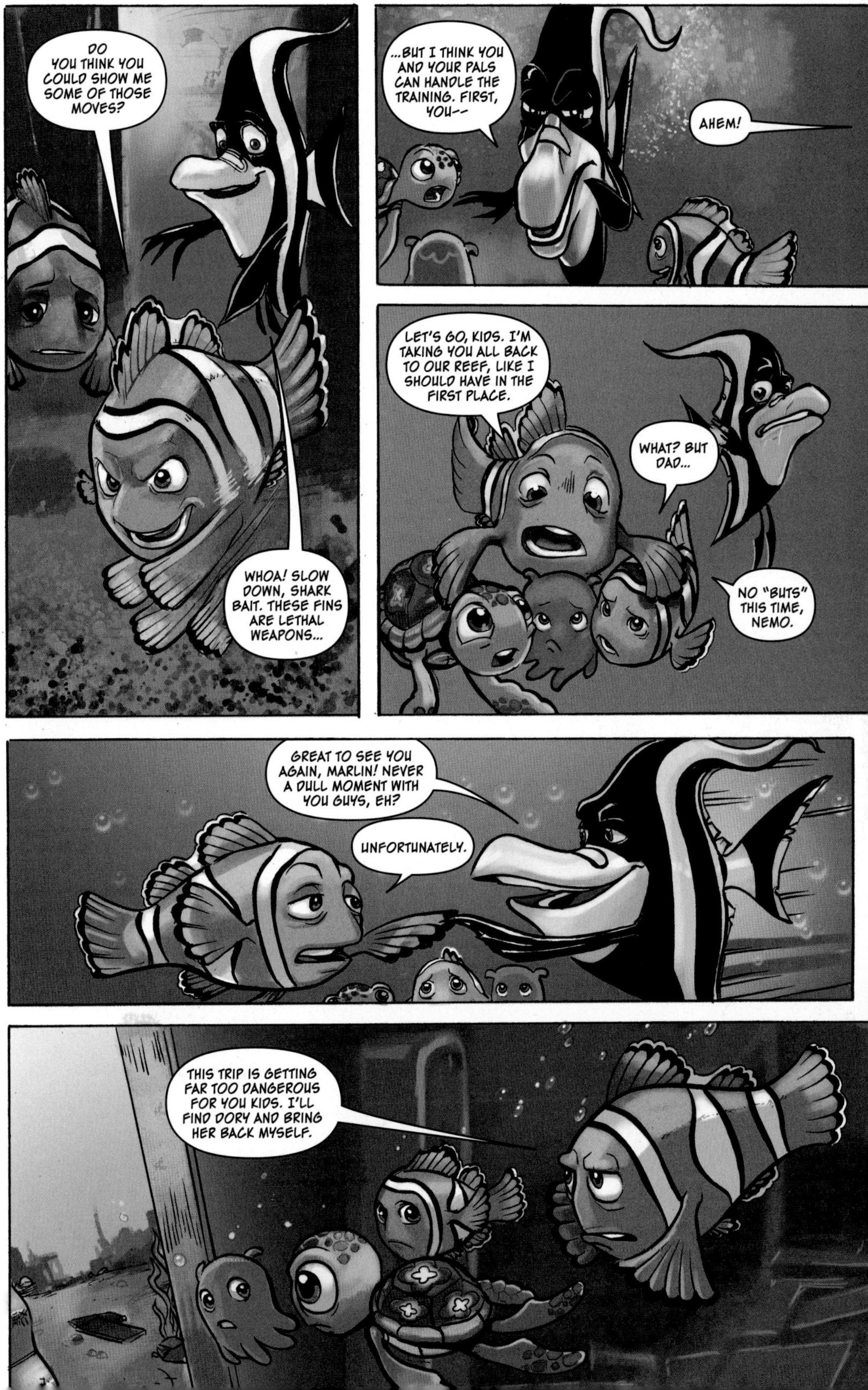
DO YOU THINK YOU COULD SHOW ME SOME OF THOSE MOVES?
WHOA! SLOW DOWN, SHARK BAIT. THESE FINS ARE LETHAL WEAPONS...
...BUT I THINK YOU AND YOUR PALS CAN HANDLE THE TRAINING. FIRST, YOU--
AHEM!
LET'S GO, KIDS. I'M TAKING YOU ALL BACK TO OUR REEF, LIKE I SHOULD HAVE IN THE FIRST PLACE.
WHAT? BUT DAD...
NO "BUTS" THIS TIME, NEMO.
GREAT TO SEE YOU AGAIN, MARLIN! NEVER A DULL MOMENT WITH YOU GUYS, EH?
UNFORTUNATELY.
THIS TRIP IS GETTING FAR TOO DANGEROUS FOR YOU KIDS. I'LL FIND DORY AND BRING HER BACK MYSELF.

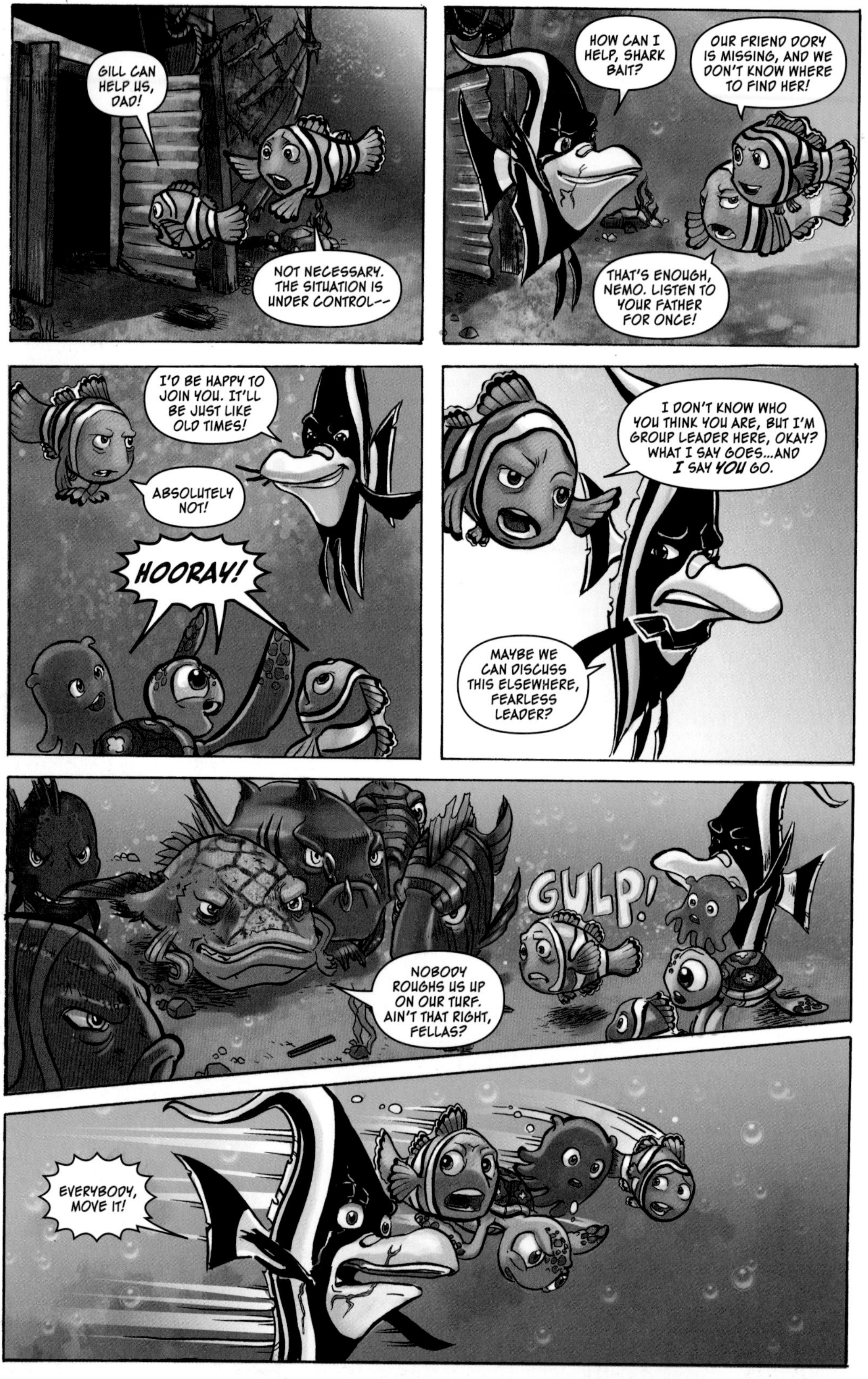
GILL CAN HELP US, DAD!
NOT NECESSARY. THE SITUATION IS UNDER CONTROL--
HOW CAN I HELP, SHARK BAIT?
OUR FRIEND DORY IS MISSING, AND WE DON'T KNOW WHERE TO FIND HER!
THAT'S ENOUGH, NEMO. LISTEN TO YOUR FATHER FOR ONCE!
I'D BE HAPPY TO JOIN YOU. IT'LL BE JUST LIKE OLD TIMES!
ABSOLUTELY NOT!
HOORAY!
I DON'T KNOW WHO YOU THINK YOU ARE, BUT I'M GROUP LEADER HERE, OKAY? WHAT I SAY GOES...AND I SAY YOU GO.
MAYBE WE CAN DISCUSS THIS ELSEWHERE, FEARLESS LEADER?
GULP!
NOBODY ROUGHS US UP ON OUR TURF. AIN'T THAT RIGHT, FELLAS?
EVERYBODY, MOVE IT!

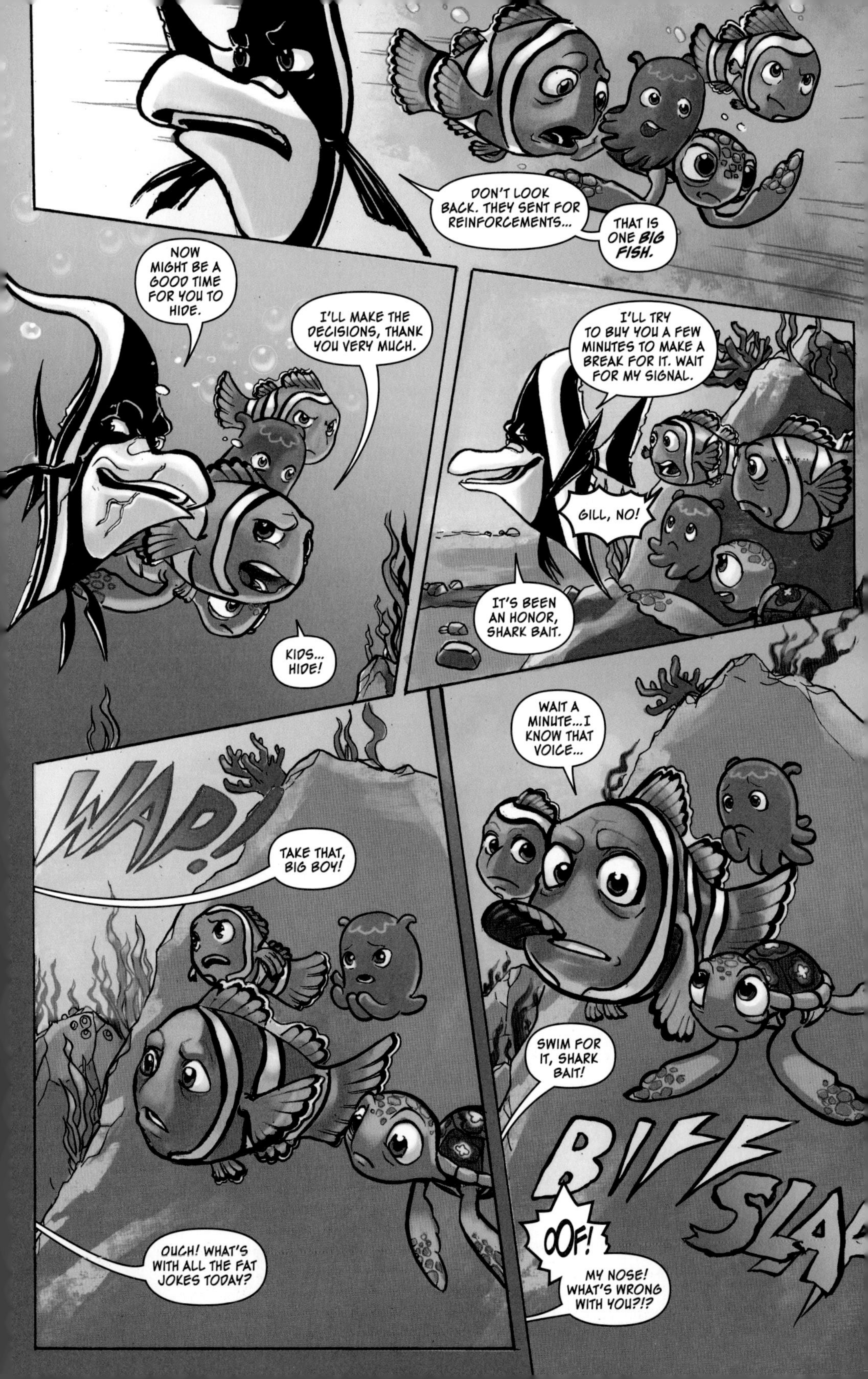
DON'T LOOK BACK. THEY SENT FOR REINFORCEMENTS...
THAT IS ONE *BIG FISH.*
NOW MIGHT BE A GOOD TIME FOR YOU TO HIDE.
I'LL MAKE THE DECISIONS, THANK YOU VERY MUCH.
KIDS... HIDE!
I'LL TRY TO BUY YOU A FEW MINUTES TO MAKE A BREAK FOR IT. WAIT FOR MY SIGNAL.
GILL, NO!
IT'S BEEN AN HONOR, SHARK BAIT.
WAP!
TAKE THAT, BIG BOY!
OUCH! WHAT'S WITH ALL THE FAT JOKES TODAY?
WAIT A MINUTE...I KNOW THAT VOICE...
SWIM FOR IT, SHARK BAIT!
BIFF
OOF!
MY NOSE! WHAT'S WRONG WITH YOU?!?

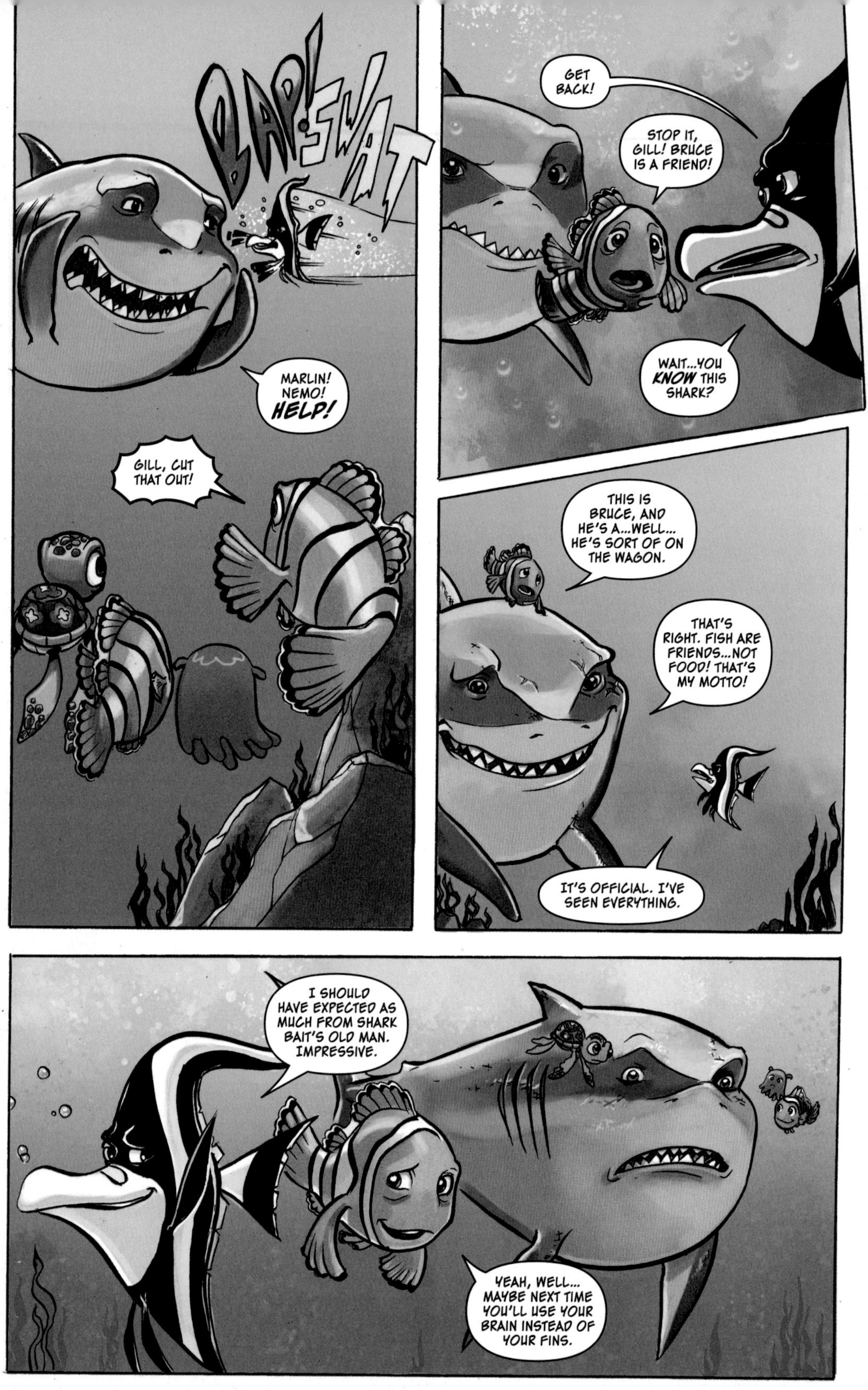
BAP! SWAT
MARLIN! NEMO! HELP!
GILL, CUT THAT OUT!
GET BACK!
STOP IT, GILL! BRUCE IS A FRIEND!
WAIT...YOU KNOW THIS SHARK?
THIS IS BRUCE, AND HE'S A...WELL... HE'S SORT OF ON THE WAGON.
THAT'S RIGHT. FISH ARE FRIENDS...NOT FOOD! THAT'S MY MOTTO!
IT'S OFFICIAL. I'VE SEEN EVERYTHING.
I SHOULD HAVE EXPECTED AS MUCH FROM SHARK BAIT'S OLD MAN. IMPRESSIVE.
YEAH, WELL... MAYBE NEXT TIME YOU'LL USE YOUR BRAIN INSTEAD OF YOUR FINS.

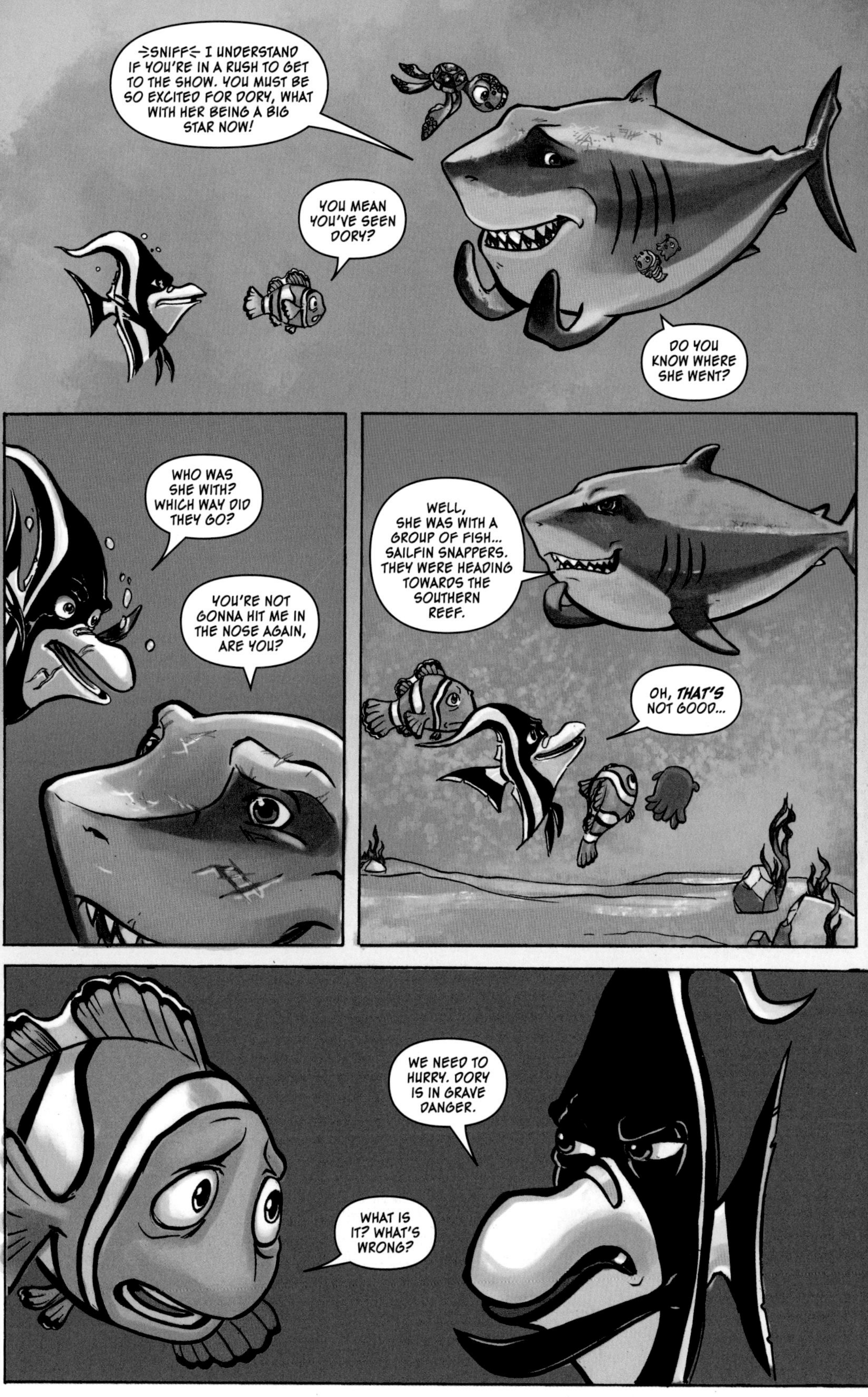

=SNIFF= I UNDERSTAND IF YOU'RE IN A RUSH TO GET TO THE SHOW. YOU MUST BE SO EXCITED FOR DORY, WHAT WITH HER BEING A BIG STAR NOW!
YOU MEAN YOU'VE SEEN DORY?
DO YOU KNOW WHERE SHE WENT?
WHO WAS SHE WITH? WHICH WAY DID THEY GO?
YOU'RE NOT GONNA HIT ME IN THE NOSE AGAIN, ARE YOU?
WELL, SHE WAS WITH A GROUP OF FISH... SAILFIN SNAPPERS. THEY WERE HEADING TOWARDS THE SOUTHERN REEF.
OH, THAT'S NOT GOOD...
WE NEED TO HURRY. DORY IS IN GRAVE DANGER.
WHAT IS IT? WHAT'S WRONG?

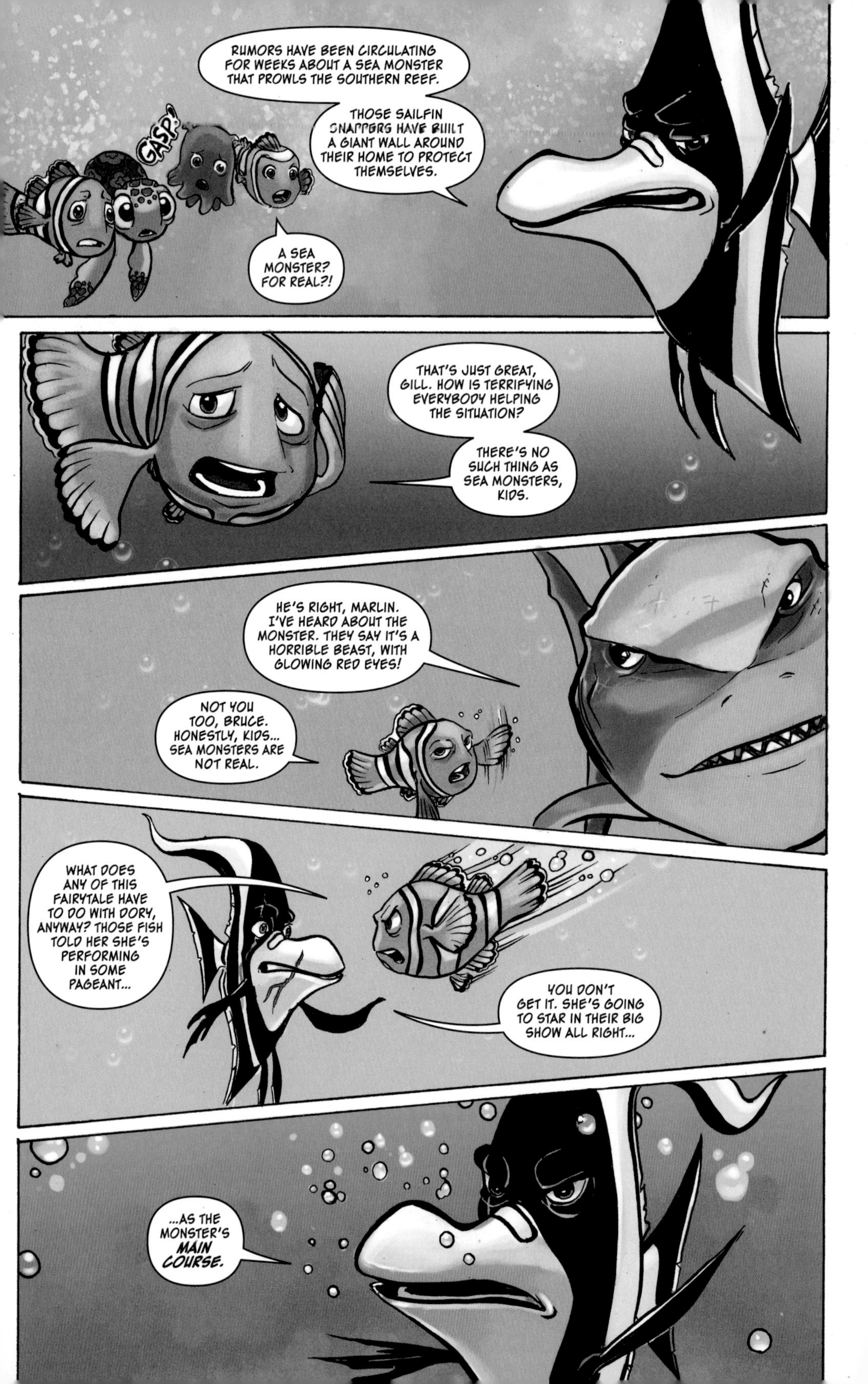

RUMORS HAVE BEEN CIRCULATING FOR WEEKS ABOUT A SEA MONSTER THAT PROWLS THE SOUTHERN REEF.
THOSE SAILFIN SNAPPERS HAVE BUILT A GIANT WALL AROUND THEIR HOME TO PROTECT THEMSELVES.
GASP!
A SEA MONSTER? FOR REAL?!
THAT'S JUST GREAT, GILL. HOW IS TERRIFYING EVERYBODY HELPING THE SITUATION?
THERE'S NO SUCH THING AS SEA MONSTERS, KIDS.
HE'S RIGHT, MARLIN. I'VE HEARD ABOUT THE MONSTER. THEY SAY IT'S A HORRIBLE BEAST, WITH GLOWING RED EYES!
NOT YOU TOO, BRUCE. HONESTLY, KIDS... SEA MONSTERS ARE NOT REAL.
WHAT DOES ANY OF THIS FAIRYTALE HAVE TO DO WITH DORY, ANYWAY? THOSE FISH TOLD HER SHE'S PERFORMING IN SOME PAGEANT...
YOU DON'T GET IT. SHE'S GOING TO STAR IN THEIR BIG SHOW ALL RIGHT...
...AS THE MONSTER'S ***MAIN COURSE.***

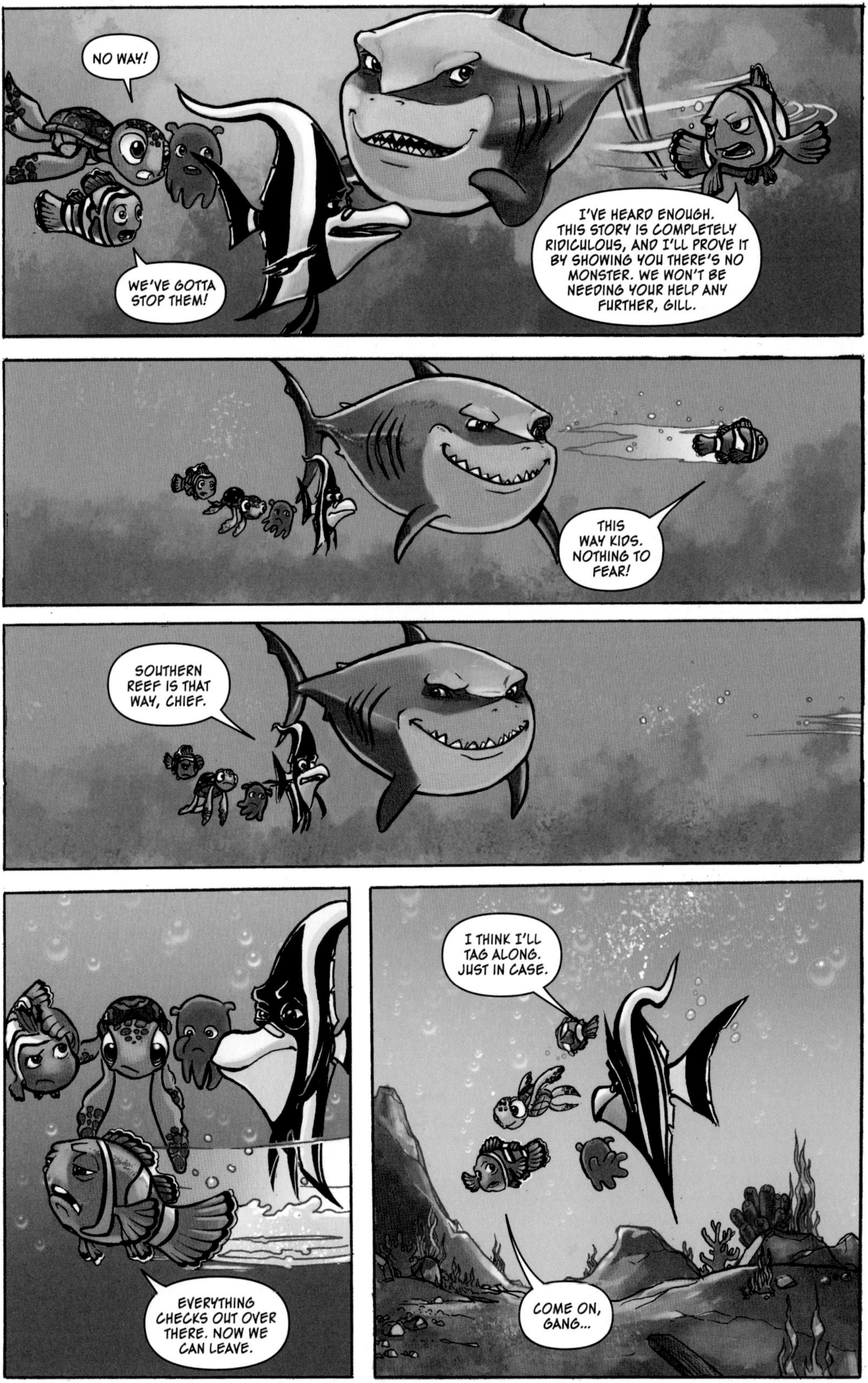
NO WAY!
WE'VE GOTTA STOP THEM!
I'VE HEARD ENOUGH. THIS STORY IS COMPLETELY RIDICULOUS, AND I'LL PROVE IT BY SHOWING YOU THERE'S NO MONSTER. WE WON'T BE NEEDING YOUR HELP ANY FURTHER, GILL.
THIS WAY KIDS. NOTHING TO FEAR!
SOUTHERN REEF IS THAT WAY, CHIEF.
EVERYTHING CHECKS OUT OVER THERE. NOW WE CAN LEAVE.
I THINK I'LL TAG ALONG. JUST IN CASE.
COME ON, GANG...

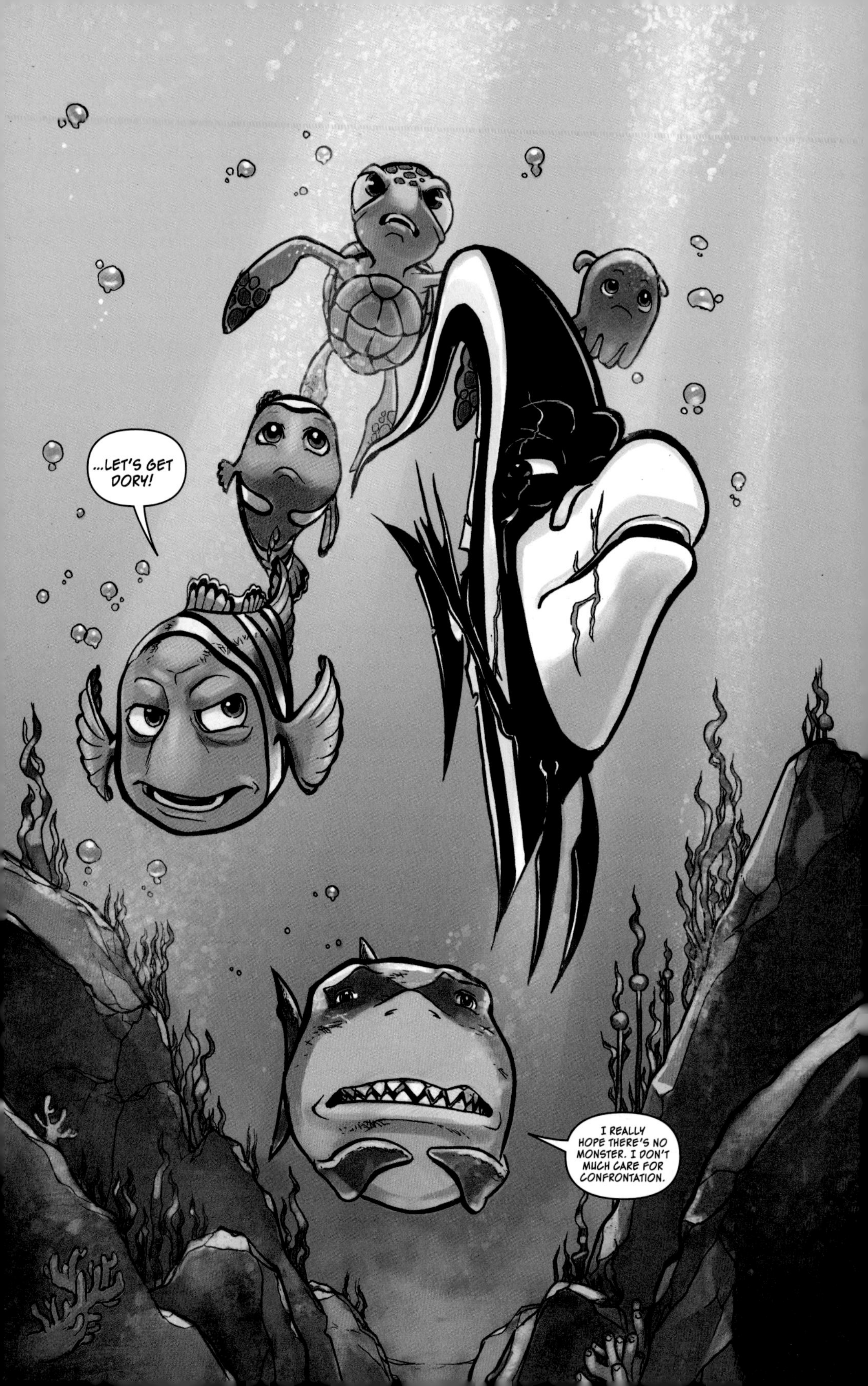
...LET'S GET DORY!
I REALLY HOPE THERE'S NO MONSTER. I DON'T MUCH CARE FOR CONFRONTATION.

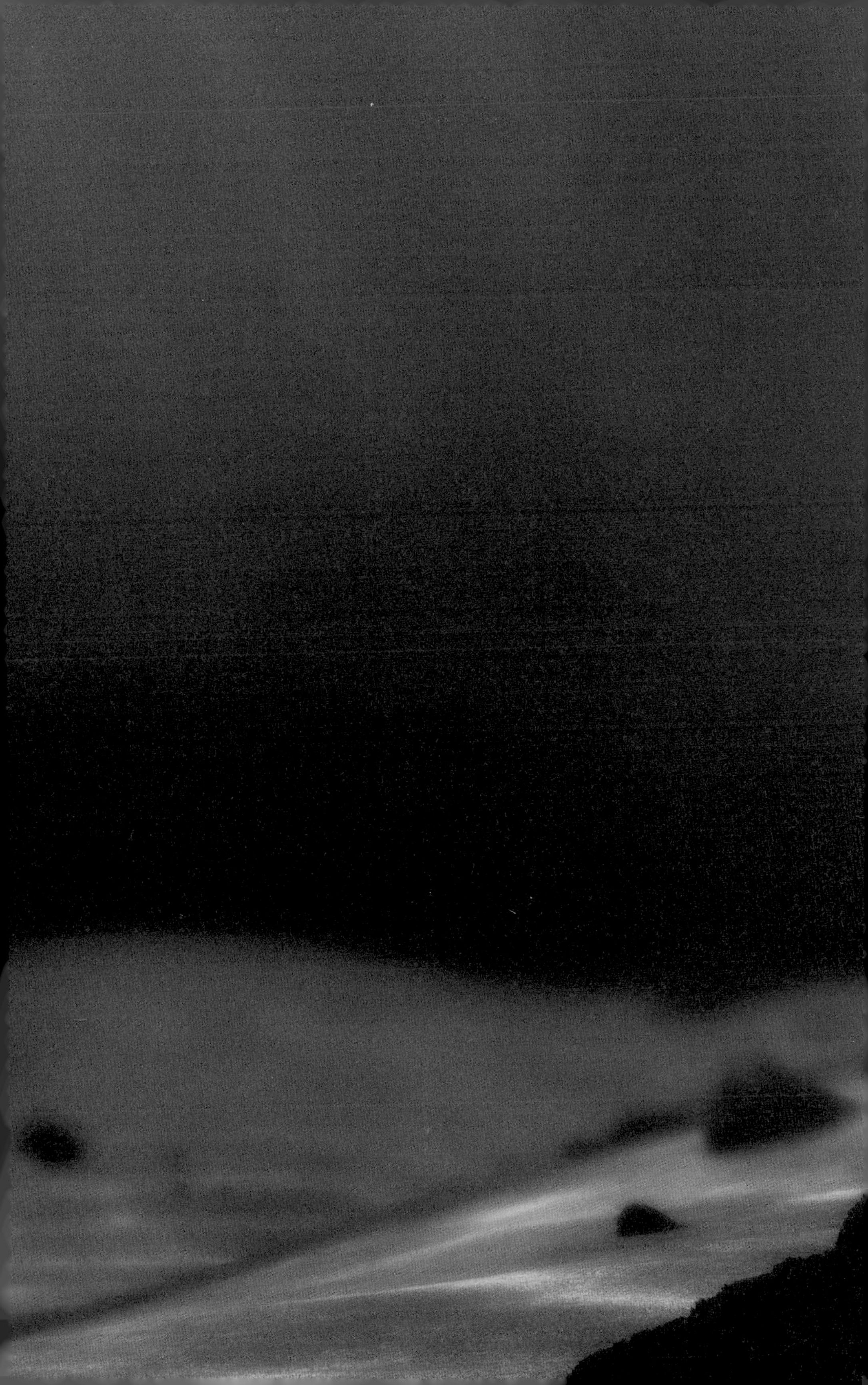

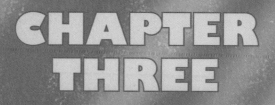

# CHAPTER THREE

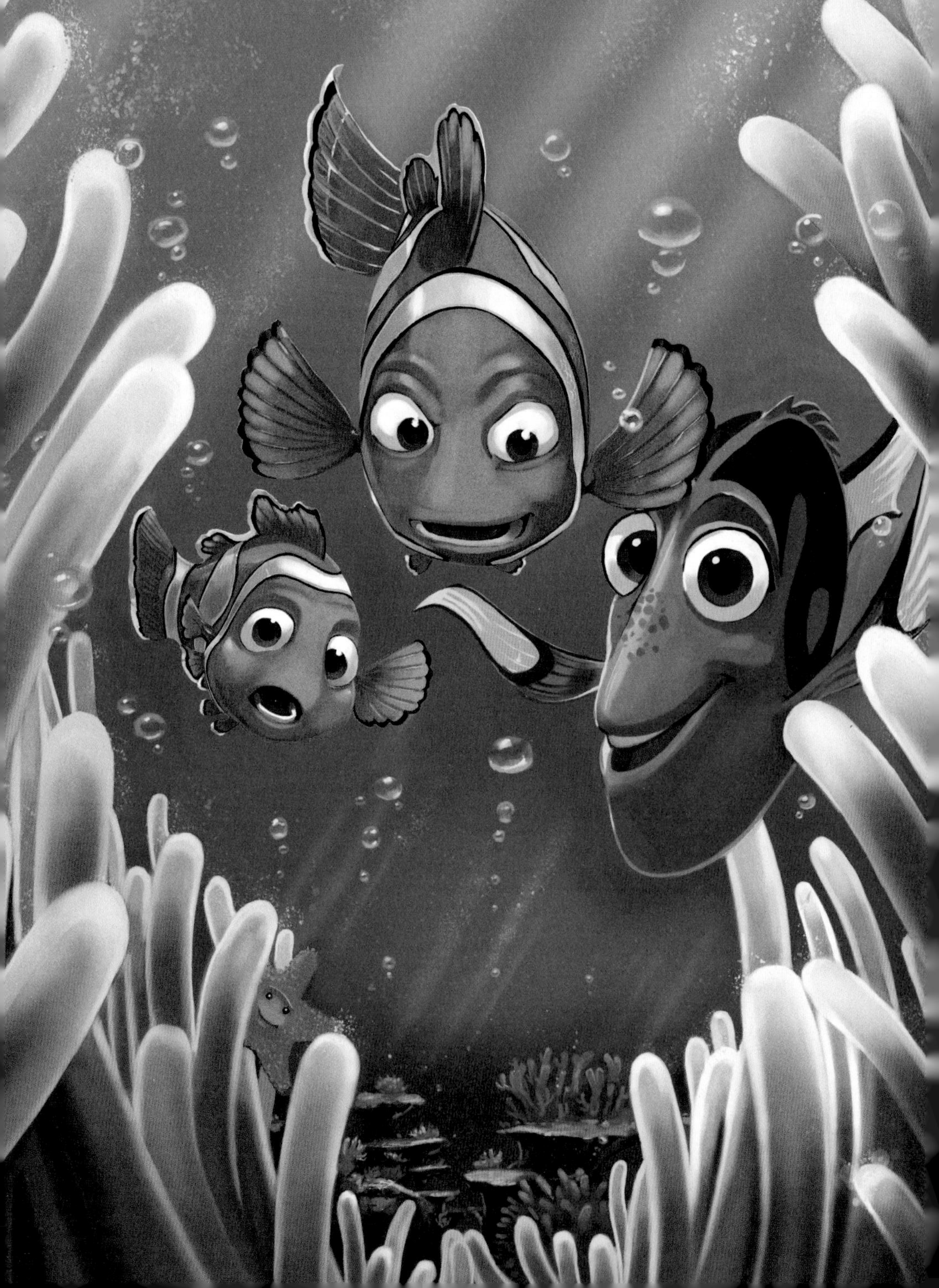

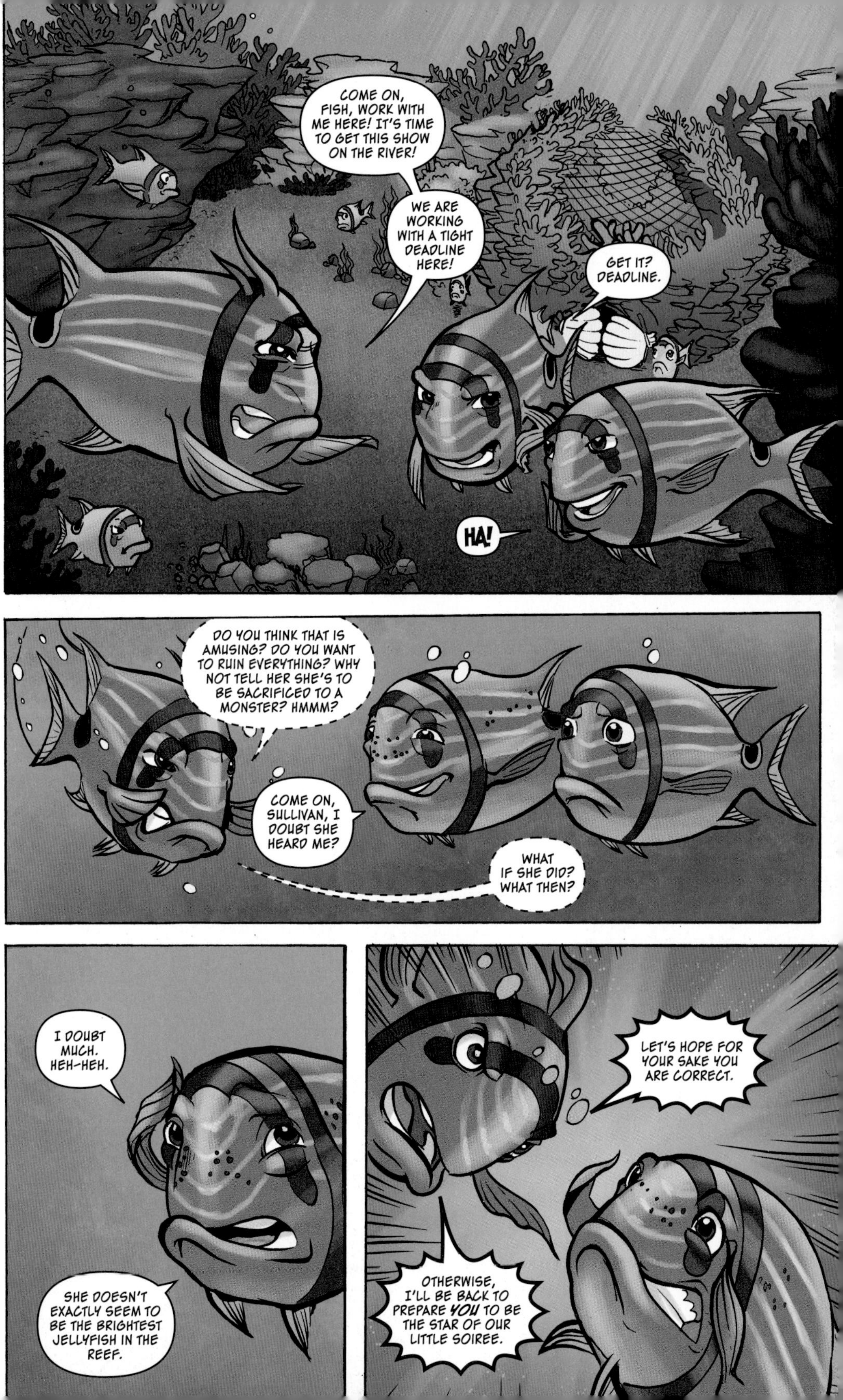
COME ON, FISH, WORK WITH ME HERE! IT'S TIME TO GET THIS SHOW ON THE RIVER!
WE ARE WORKING WITH A TIGHT DEADLINE HERE!
GET IT? DEADLINE.
HA!
DO YOU THINK THAT IS AMUSING? DO YOU WANT TO RUIN EVERYTHING? WHY NOT TELL HER SHE'S TO BE SACRIFICED TO A MONSTER? HMMM?
COME ON, SULLIVAN, I DOUBT SHE HEARD ME?
WHAT IF SHE DID? WHAT THEN?
I DOUBT MUCH. HEH-HEH.
SHE DOESN'T EXACTLY SEEM TO BE THE BRIGHTEST JELLYFISH IN THE REEF.
LET'S HOPE FOR YOUR SAKE YOU ARE CORRECT.
OTHERWISE, I'LL BE BACK TO PREPARE *YOU* TO BE THE STAR OF OUR LITTLE SOIREE.

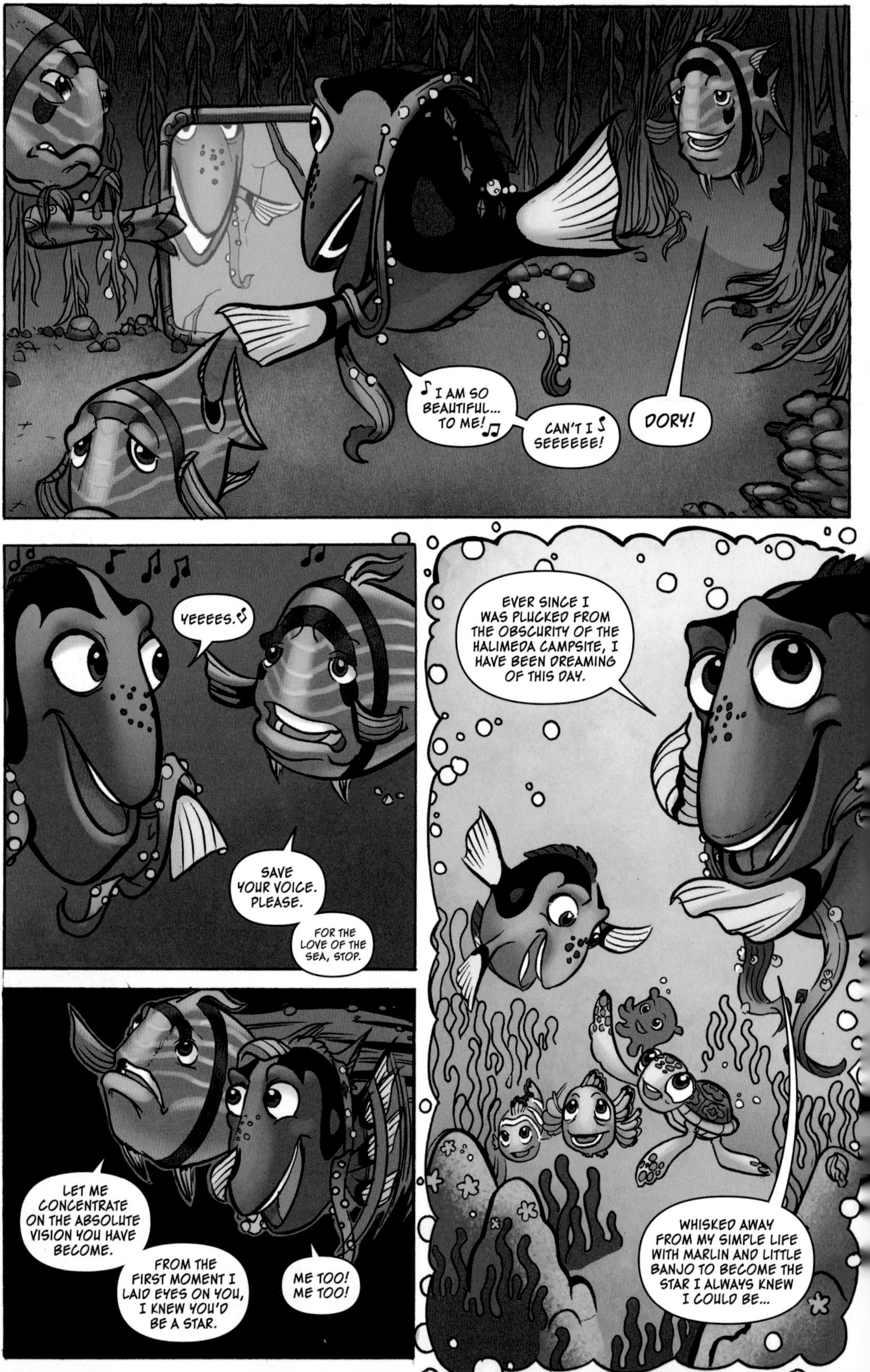
I AM SO BEAUTIFUL... TO ME!
CAN'T I SEEEEEE!
DORY!
YEEEES.
SAVE YOUR VOICE. PLEASE.
FOR THE LOVE OF THE SEA, STOP.
LET ME CONCENTRATE ON THE ABSOLUTE VISION YOU HAVE BECOME.
FROM THE FIRST MOMENT I LAID EYES ON YOU, I KNEW YOU'D BE A STAR.
ME TOO! ME TOO!
EVER SINCE I WAS PLUCKED FROM THE OBSCURITY OF THE HALIMEDA CAMPSITE, I HAVE BEEN DREAMING OF THIS DAY.
WHISKED AWAY FROM MY SIMPLE LIFE WITH MARLIN AND LITTLE BANJO TO BECOME THE STAR I ALWAYS KNEW I COULD BE...

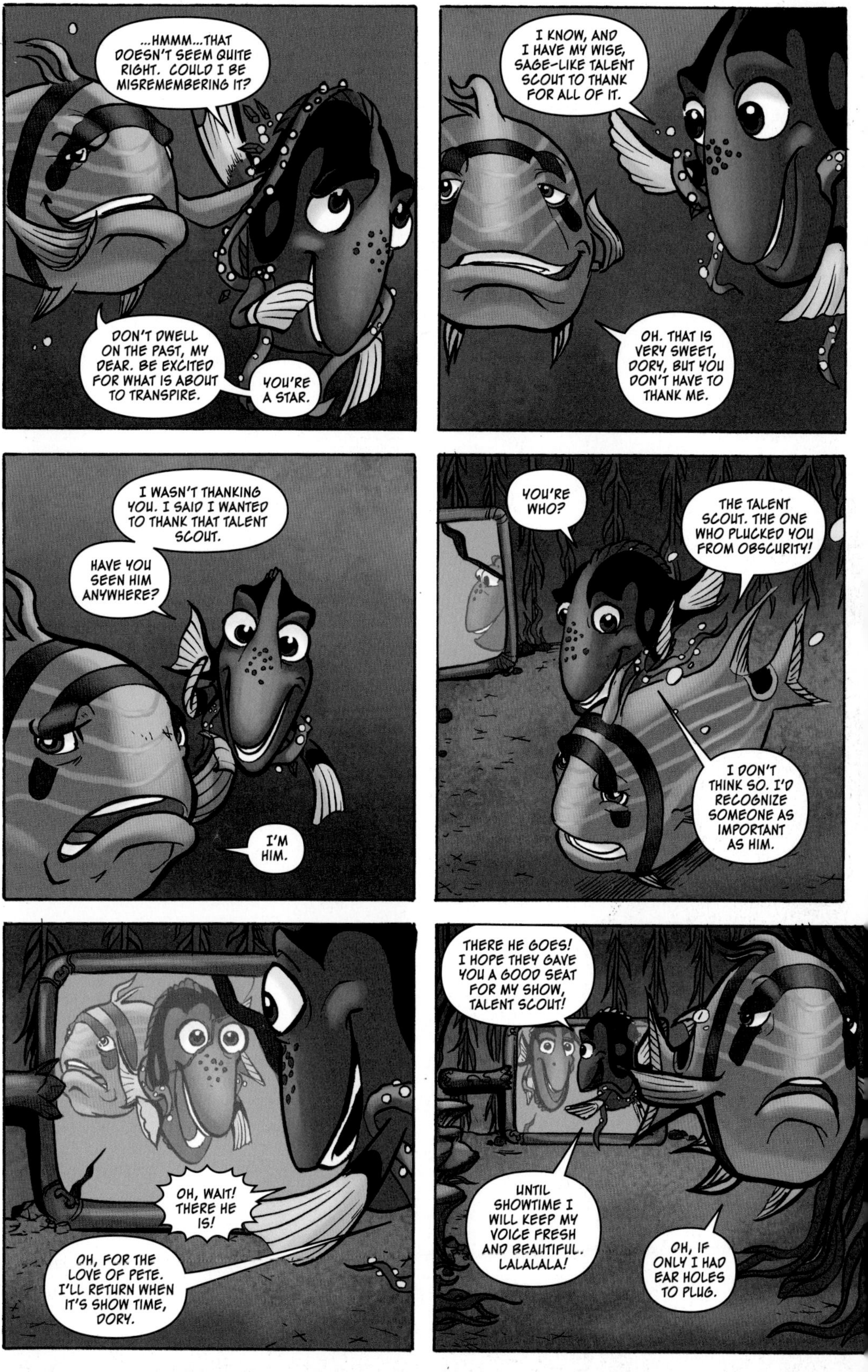
...HMMM...THAT DOESN'T SEEM QUITE RIGHT. COULD I BE MISREMEMBERING IT?
DON'T DWELL ON THE PAST, MY DEAR. BE EXCITED FOR WHAT IS ABOUT TO TRANSPIRE.
YOU'RE A STAR.
I KNOW, AND I HAVE MY WISE, SAGE-LIKE TALENT SCOUT TO THANK FOR ALL OF IT.
OH. THAT IS VERY SWEET, DORY, BUT YOU DON'T HAVE TO THANK ME.
I WASN'T THANKING YOU. I SAID I WANTED TO THANK THAT TALENT SCOUT.
HAVE YOU SEEN HIM ANYWHERE?
I'M HIM.
YOU'RE WHO?
THE TALENT SCOUT. THE ONE WHO PLUCKED YOU FROM OBSCURITY!
I DON'T THINK SO. I'D RECOGNIZE SOMEONE AS IMPORTANT AS HIM.
OH, WAIT! THERE HE IS!
OH, FOR THE LOVE OF PETE. I'LL RETURN WHEN IT'S SHOW TIME, DORY.
THERE HE GOES! I HOPE THEY GAVE YOU A GOOD SEAT FOR MY SHOW, TALENT SCOUT!
UNTIL SHOWTIME I WILL KEEP MY VOICE FRESH AND BEAUTIFUL. LALALALA!
OH, IF ONLY I HAD EAR HOLES TO PLUG.

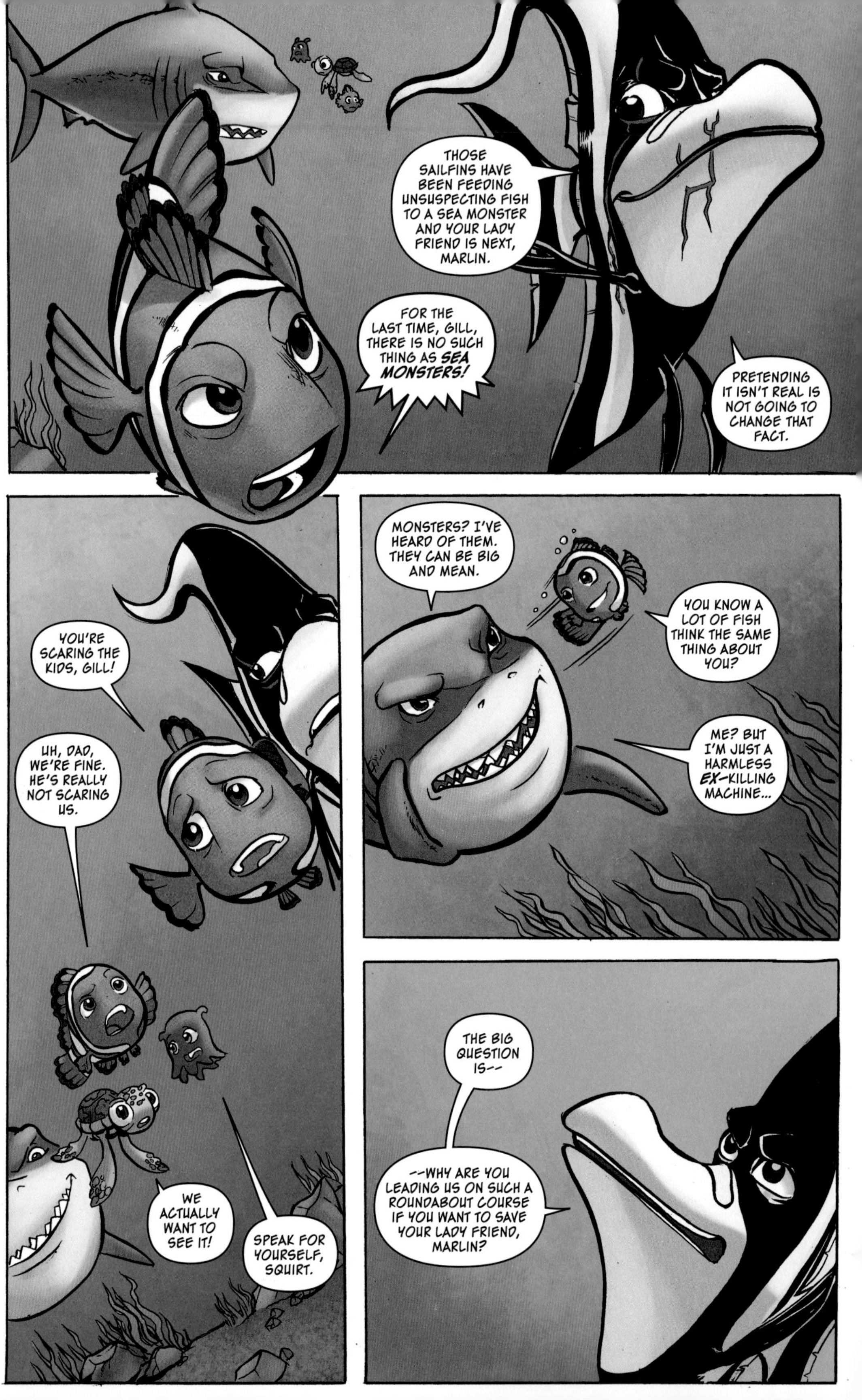
THOSE SAILFINS HAVE BEEN FEEDING UNSUSPECTING FISH TO A SEA MONSTER AND YOUR LADY FRIEND IS NEXT, MARLIN.
FOR THE LAST TIME, GILL, THERE IS NO SUCH THING AS ***SEA MONSTERS!***
PRETENDING IT ISN'T REAL IS NOT GOING TO CHANGE THAT FACT.
YOU'RE SCARING THE KIDS, GILL!
UH, DAD, WE'RE FINE. HE'S REALLY NOT SCARING US.
WE ACTUALLY WANT TO SEE IT!
SPEAK FOR YOURSELF, SQUIRT.
MONSTERS? I'VE HEARD OF THEM. THEY CAN BE BIG AND MEAN.
YOU KNOW A LOT OF FISH THINK THE SAME THING ABOUT YOU?
ME? BUT I'M JUST A HARMLESS ***EX***--KILLING MACHINE...
THE BIG QUESTION IS--
--WHY ARE YOU LEADING US ON SUCH A ROUNDABOUT COURSE IF YOU WANT TO SAVE YOUR LADY FRIEND, MARLIN?

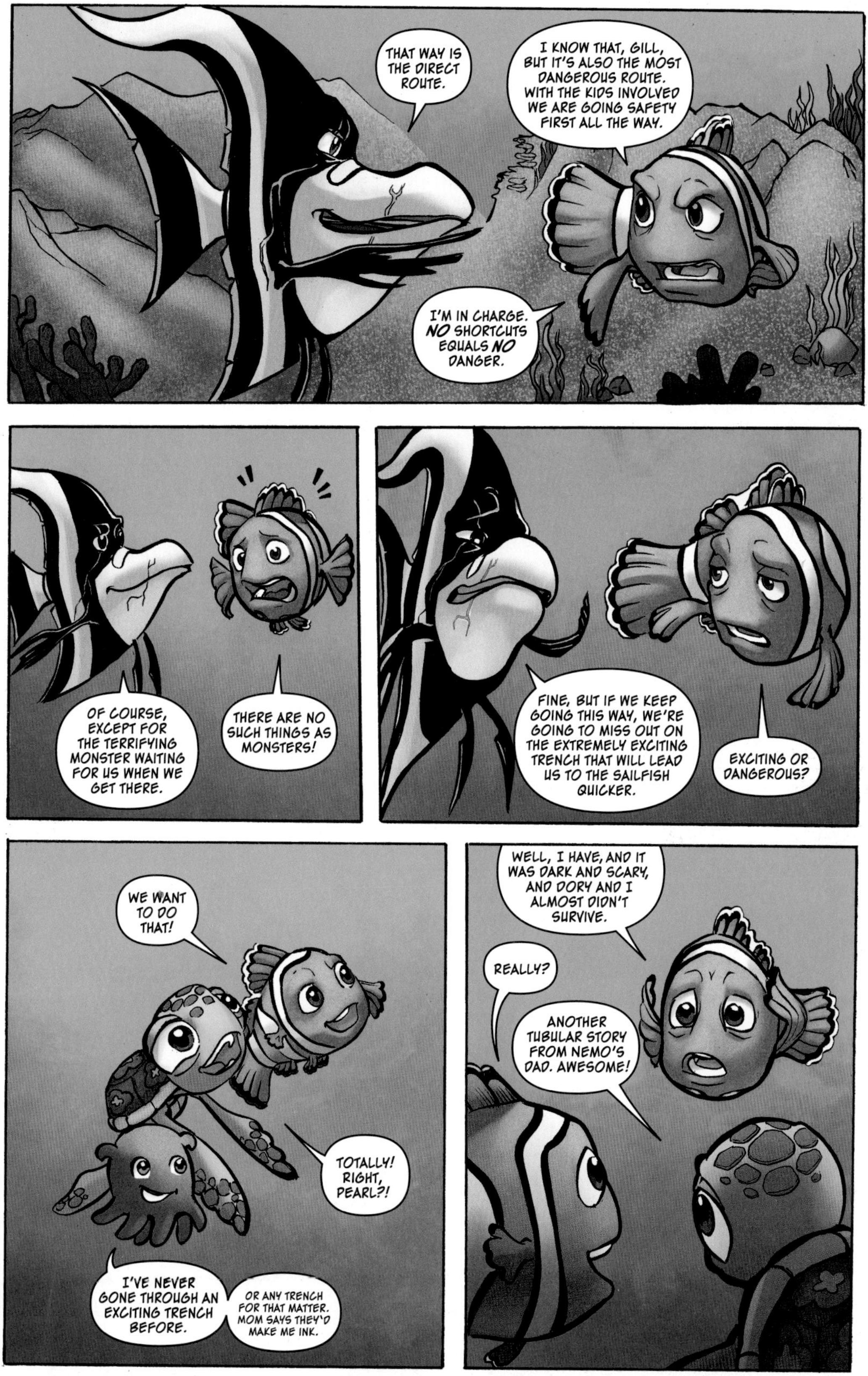
THAT WAY IS THE DIRECT ROUTE.
I KNOW THAT, GILL, BUT IT'S ALSO THE MOST DANGEROUS ROUTE. WITH THE KIDS INVOLVED WE ARE GOING SAFETY FIRST ALL THE WAY.
I'M IN CHARGE. NO SHORTCUTS EQUALS NO DANGER.
OF COURSE, EXCEPT FOR THE TERRIFYING MONSTER WAITING FOR US WHEN WE GET THERE.
THERE ARE NO SUCH THINGS AS MONSTERS!
FINE, BUT IF WE KEEP GOING THIS WAY, WE'RE GOING TO MISS OUT ON THE EXTREMELY EXCITING TRENCH THAT WILL LEAD US TO THE SAILFISH QUICKER.
EXCITING OR DANGEROUS?
WE WANT TO DO THAT!
TOTALLY! RIGHT, PEARL?!
I'VE NEVER GONE THROUGH AN EXCITING TRENCH BEFORE.
OR ANY TRENCH FOR THAT MATTER. MOM SAYS THEY'D MAKE ME INK.
WELL, I HAVE, AND IT WAS DARK AND SCARY, AND DORY AND I ALMOST DIDN'T SURVIVE.
REALLY?
ANOTHER TUBULAR STORY FROM NEMO'S DAD. AWESOME!

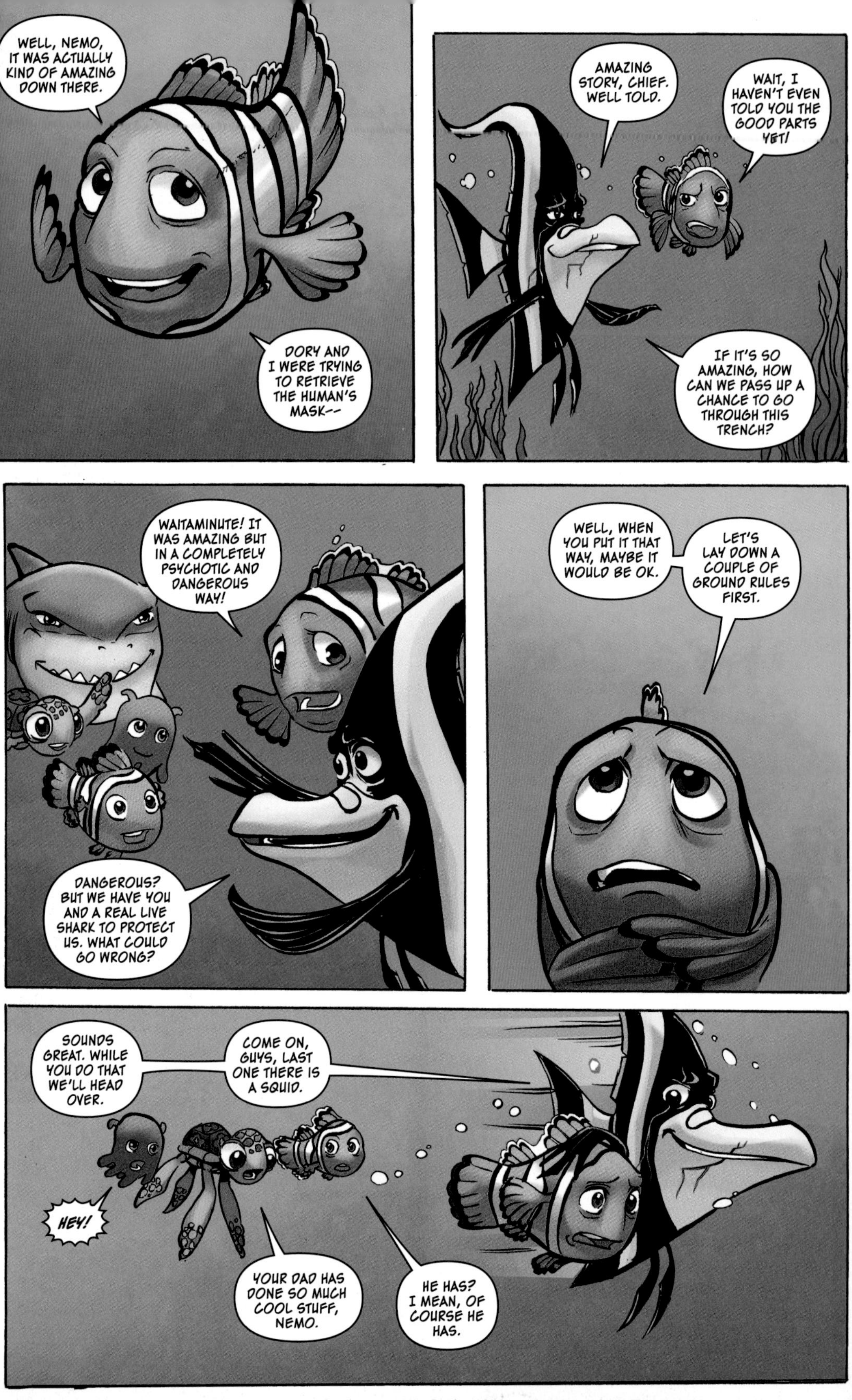
WELL, NEMO, IT WAS ACTUALLY KIND OF AMAZING DOWN THERE.
DORY AND I WERE TRYING TO RETRIEVE THE HUMAN'S MASK--
AMAZING STORY, CHIEF. WELL TOLD.
WAIT, I HAVEN'T EVEN TOLD YOU THE GOOD PARTS YET!
IF IT'S SO AMAZING, HOW CAN WE PASS UP A CHANCE TO GO THROUGH THIS TRENCH?
WAITAMINUTE! IT WAS AMAZING BUT IN A COMPLETELY PSYCHOTIC AND DANGEROUS WAY!
DANGEROUS? BUT WE HAVE YOU AND A REAL LIVE SHARK TO PROTECT US. WHAT COULD GO WRONG?
WELL, WHEN YOU PUT IT THAT WAY, MAYBE IT WOULD BE OK.
LET'S LAY DOWN A COUPLE OF GROUND RULES FIRST.
SOUNDS GREAT. WHILE YOU DO THAT WE'LL HEAD OVER.
COME ON, GUYS, LAST ONE THERE IS A SQUID.
HEY!
YOUR DAD HAS DONE SO MUCH COOL STUFF, NEMO.
HE HAS? I MEAN, OF COURSE HE HAS.

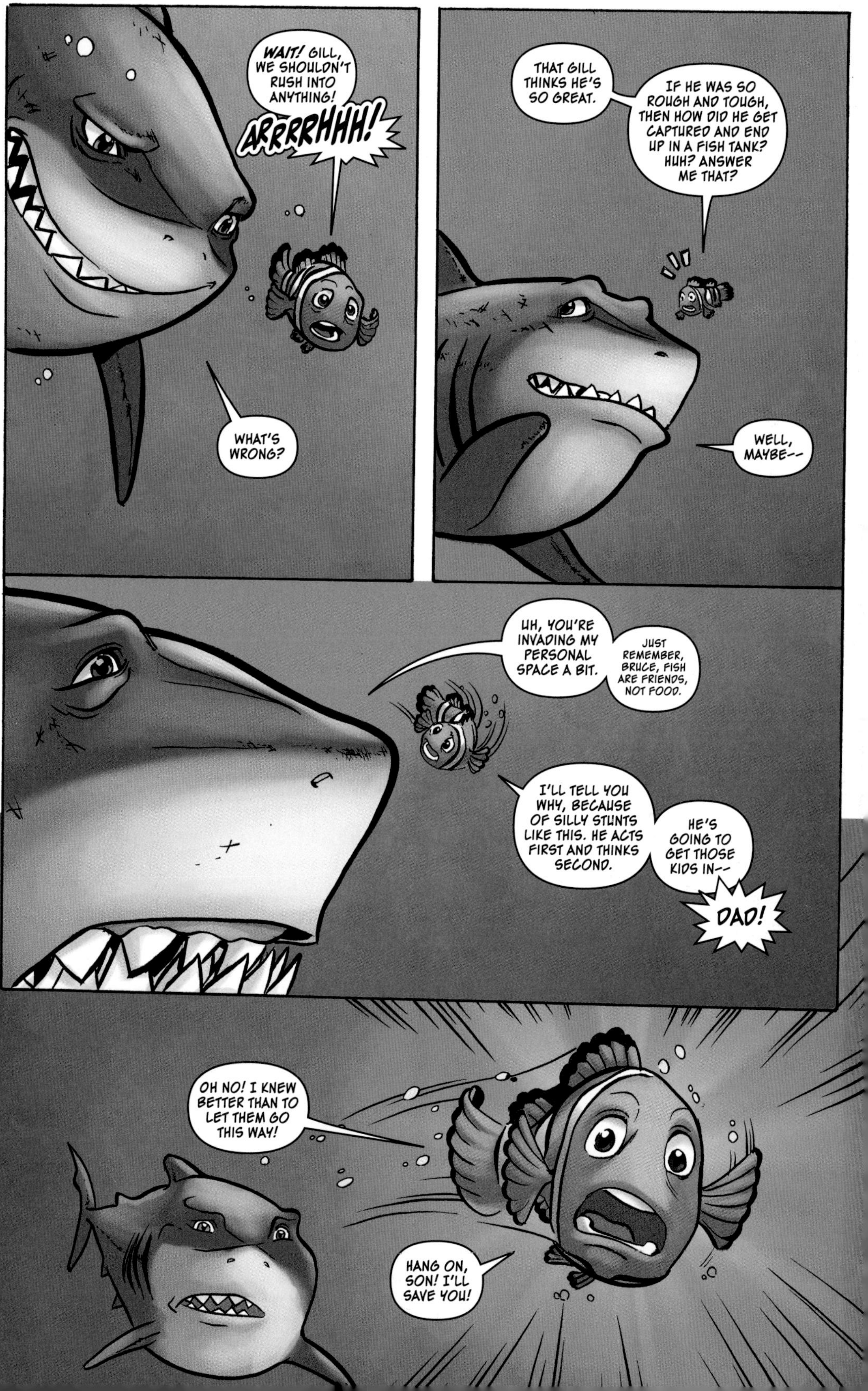
WAIT! GILL, WE SHOULDN'T RUSH INTO ANYTHING!
ARRRRHHH!
WHAT'S WRONG?
THAT GILL THINKS HE'S SO GREAT.
IF HE WAS SO ROUGH AND TOUGH, THEN HOW DID HE GET CAPTURED AND END UP IN A FISH TANK? HUH? ANSWER ME THAT?
WELL, MAYBE--
UH, YOU'RE INVADING MY PERSONAL SPACE A BIT.
JUST REMEMBER, BRUCE, FISH ARE FRIENDS, NOT FOOD.
I'LL TELL YOU WHY, BECAUSE OF SILLY STUNTS LIKE THIS. HE ACTS FIRST AND THINKS SECOND.
HE'S GOING TO GET THOSE KIDS IN--
DAD!
OH NO! I KNEW BETTER THAN TO LET THEM GO THIS WAY!
HANG ON, SON! I'LL SAVE YOU!

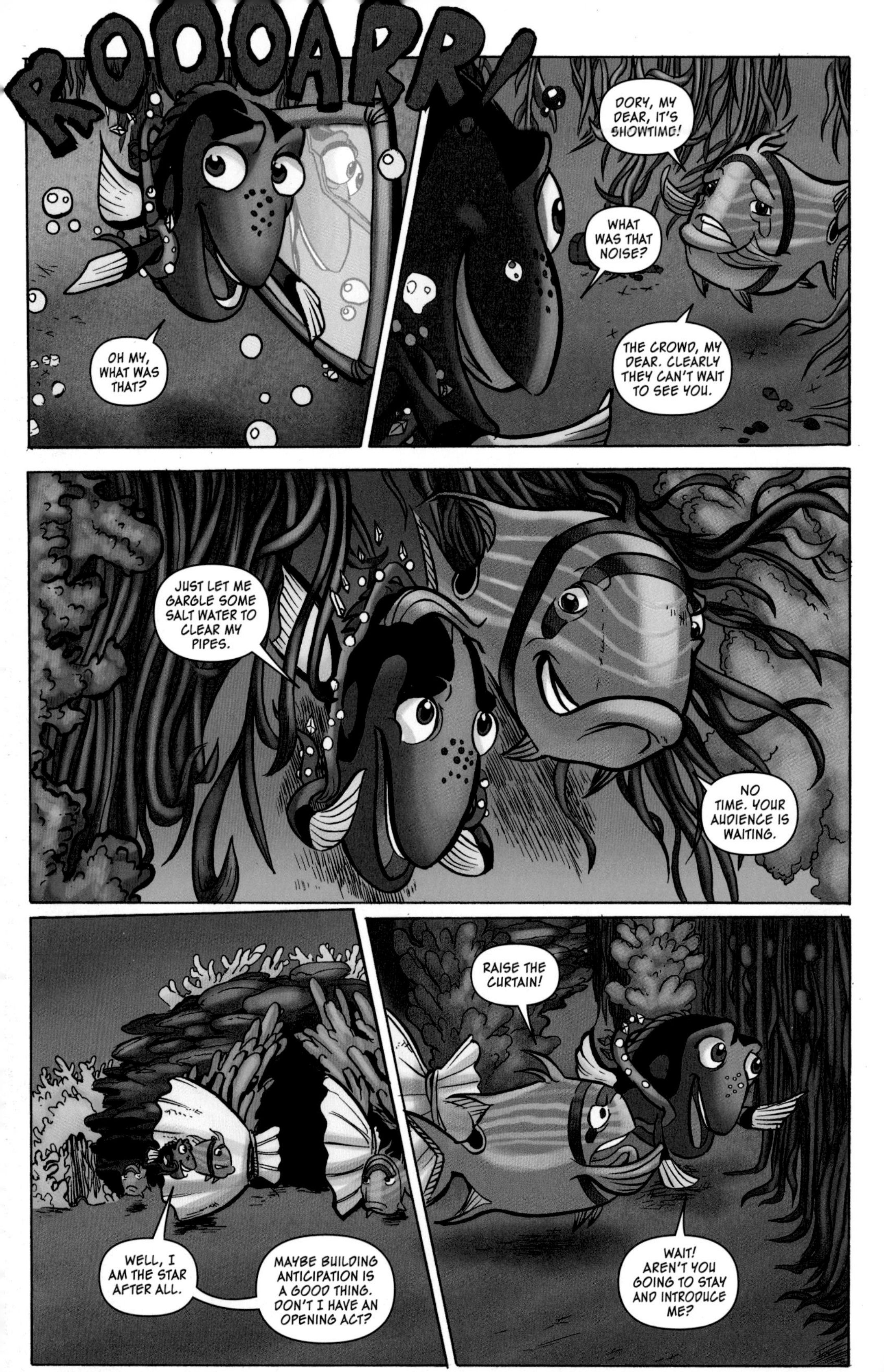
ROOOARR!
OH MY, WHAT WAS THAT?
DORY, MY DEAR, IT'S SHOWTIME!
WHAT WAS THAT NOISE?
THE CROWD, MY DEAR. CLEARLY THEY CAN'T WAIT TO SEE YOU.
JUST LET ME GARGLE SOME SALT WATER TO CLEAR MY PIPES.
NO TIME. YOUR AUDIENCE IS WAITING.
WELL, I AM THE STAR AFTER ALL.
MAYBE BUILDING ANTICIPATION IS A GOOD THING. DON'T I HAVE AN OPENING ACT?
RAISE THE CURTAIN!
WAIT! AREN'T YOU GOING TO STAY AND INTRODUCE ME?

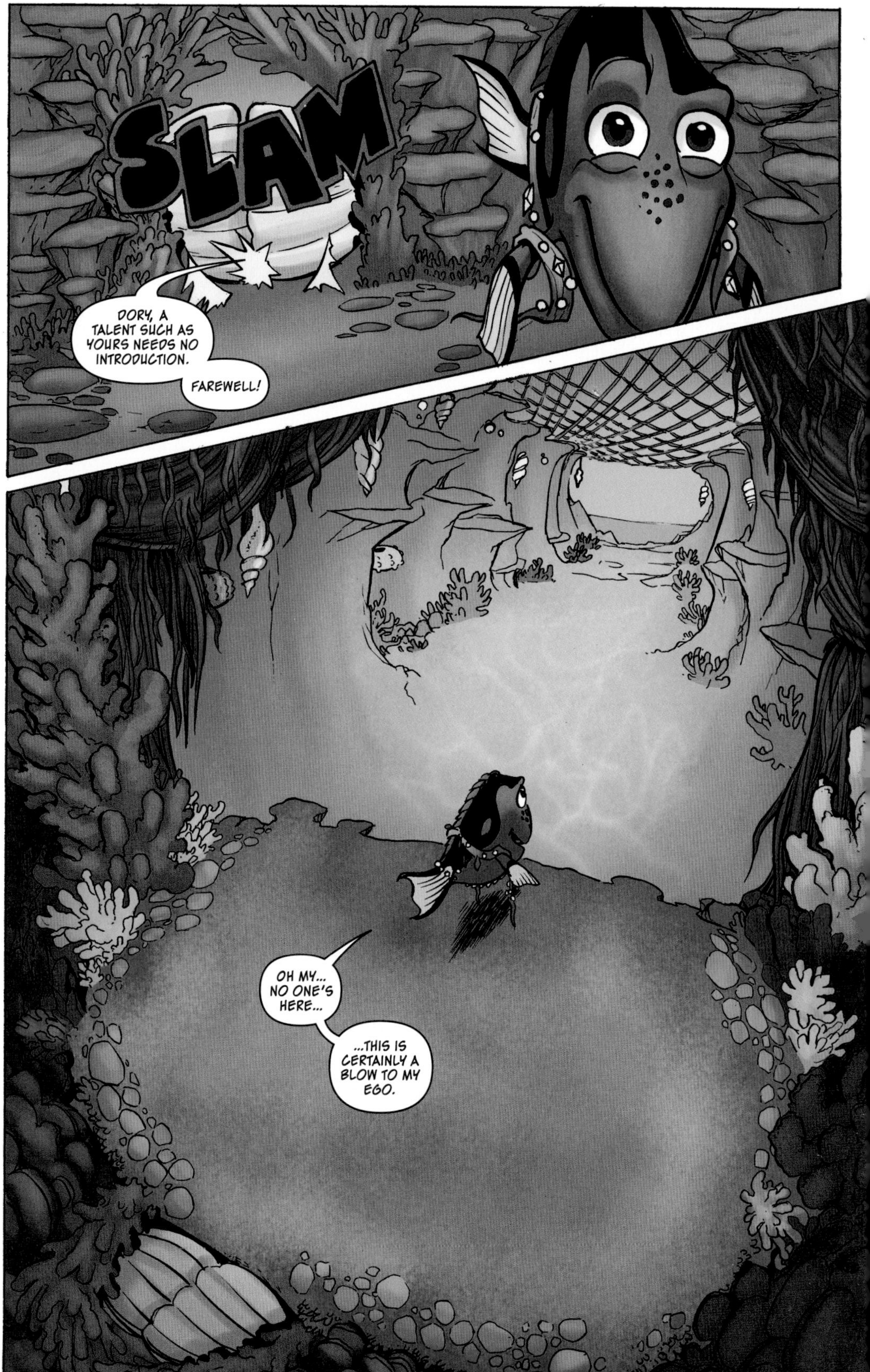
SLAM
DORY, A TALENT SUCH AS YOURS NEEDS NO INTRODUCTION.
FAREWELL!
OH MY... NO ONE'S HERE...
...THIS IS CERTAINLY A BLOW TO MY EGO.

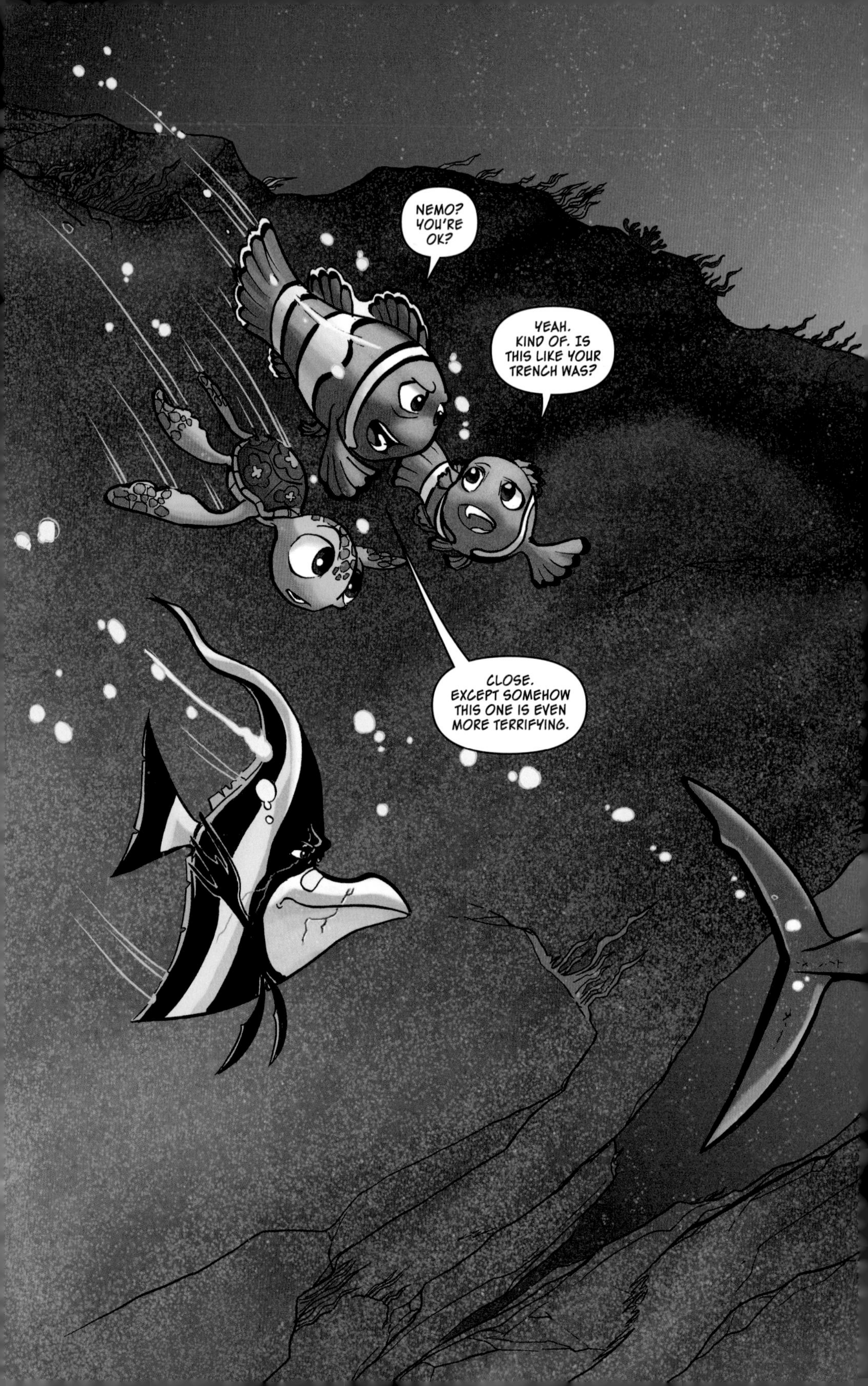
NEMO? YOU'RE OK?
YEAH. KIND OF. IS THIS LIKE YOUR TRENCH WAS?
CLOSE. EXCEPT SOMEHOW THIS ONE IS EVEN MORE TERRIFYING.

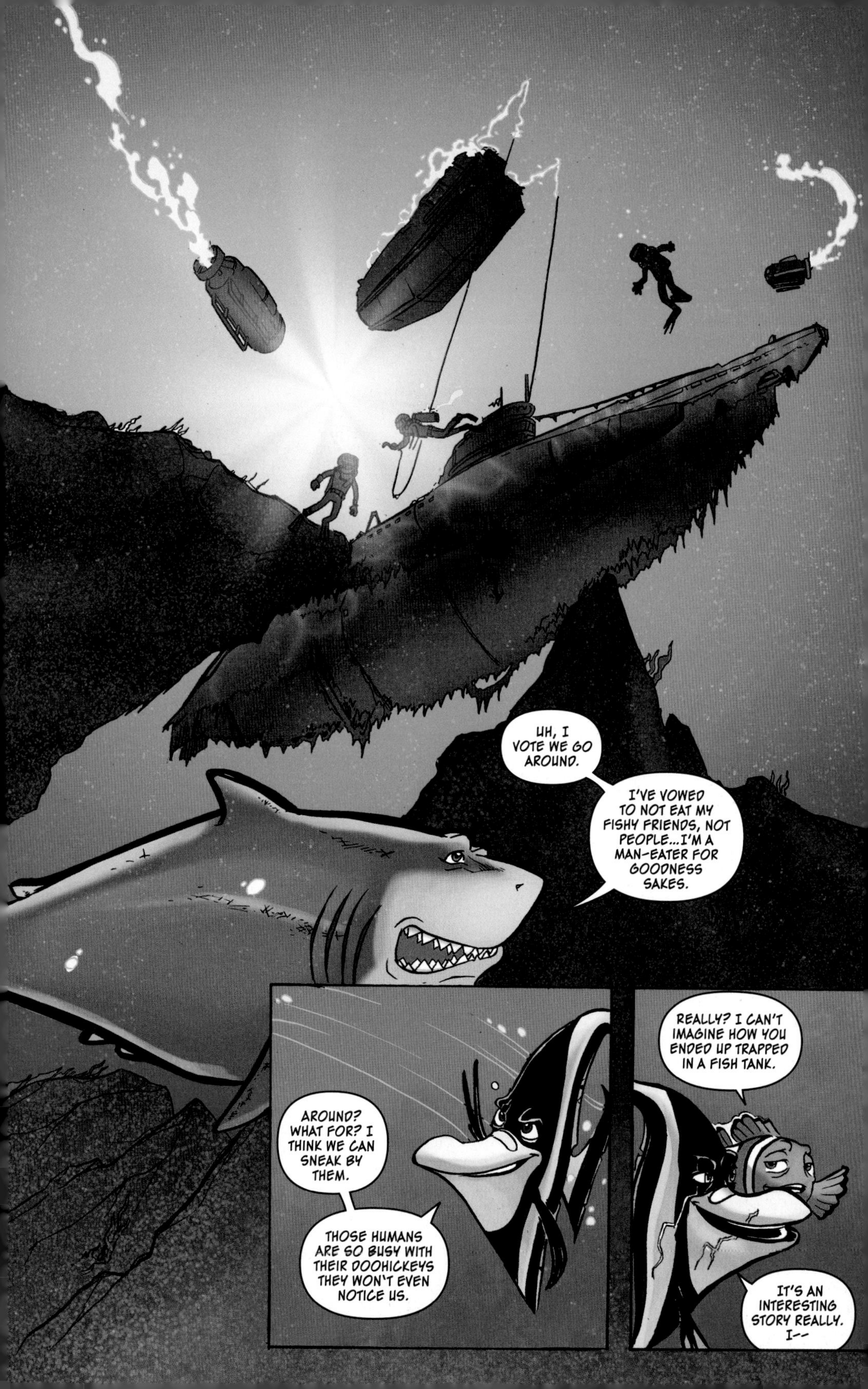
UH, I VOTE WE GO AROUND.
I'VE VOWED TO NOT EAT MY FISHY FRIENDS, NOT PEOPLE...I'M A MAN-EATER FOR GOODNESS SAKES.
AROUND? WHAT FOR? I THINK WE CAN SNEAK BY THEM.
THOSE HUMANS ARE SO BUSY WITH THEIR DOOHICKEYS THEY WON'T EVEN NOTICE US.
REALLY? I CAN'T IMAGINE HOW YOU ENDED UP TRAPPED IN A FISH TANK.
IT'S AN INTERESTING STORY REALLY. I--

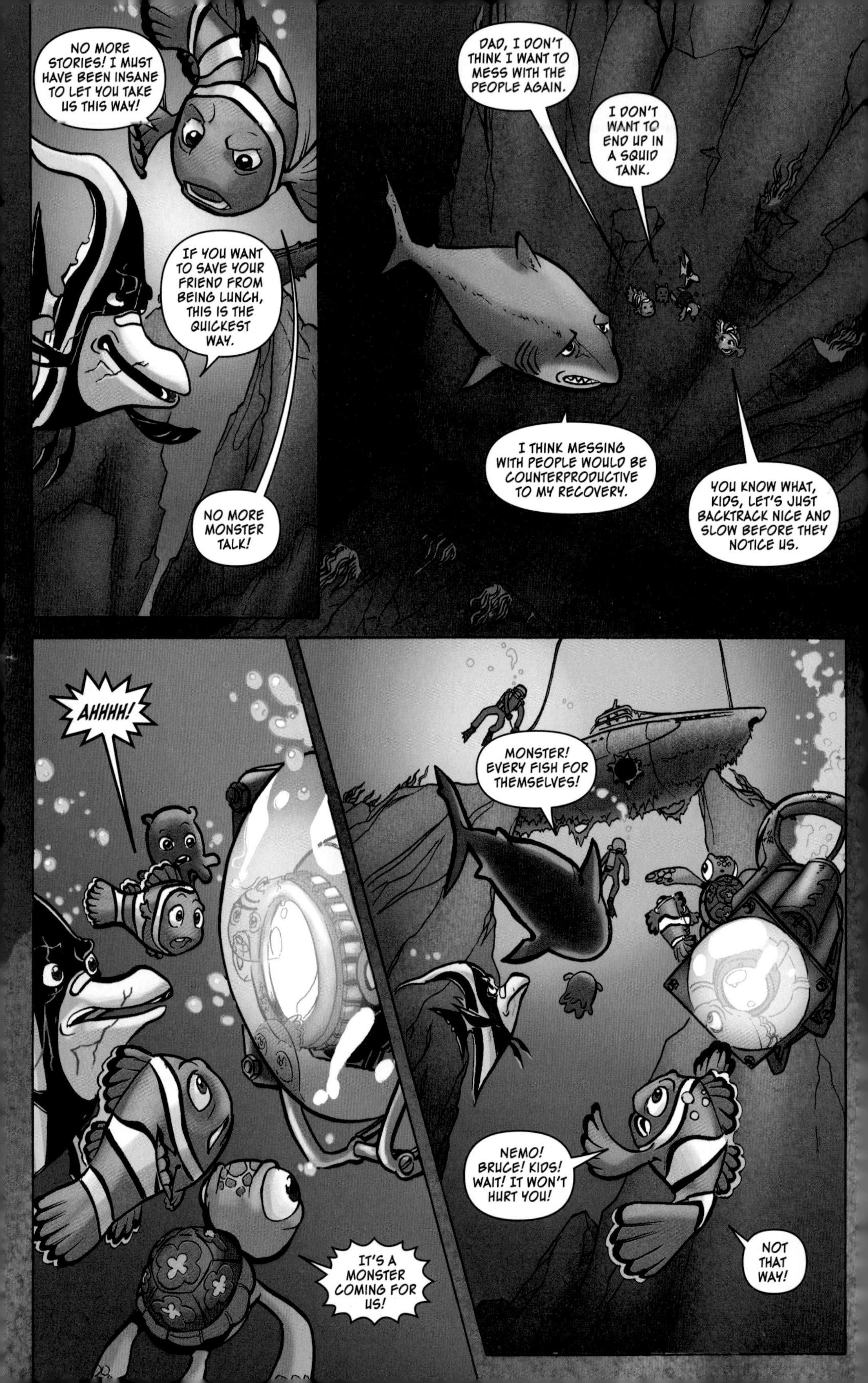
NO MORE STORIES! I MUST HAVE BEEN INSANE TO LET YOU TAKE US THIS WAY!
IF YOU WANT TO SAVE YOUR FRIEND FROM BEING LUNCH, THIS IS THE QUICKEST WAY.
NO MORE MONSTER TALK!
DAD, I DON'T THINK I WANT TO MESS WITH THE PEOPLE AGAIN.
I DON'T WANT TO END UP IN A SQUID TANK.
I THINK MESSING WITH PEOPLE WOULD BE COUNTERPRODUCTIVE TO MY RECOVERY.
YOU KNOW WHAT, KIDS, LET'S JUST BACKTRACK NICE AND SLOW BEFORE THEY NOTICE US.
AHHHH!
IT'S A MONSTER COMING FOR US!
MONSTER! EVERY FISH FOR THEMSELVES!
NEMO! BRUCE! KIDS! WAIT! IT WON'T HURT YOU!
NOT THAT WAY!

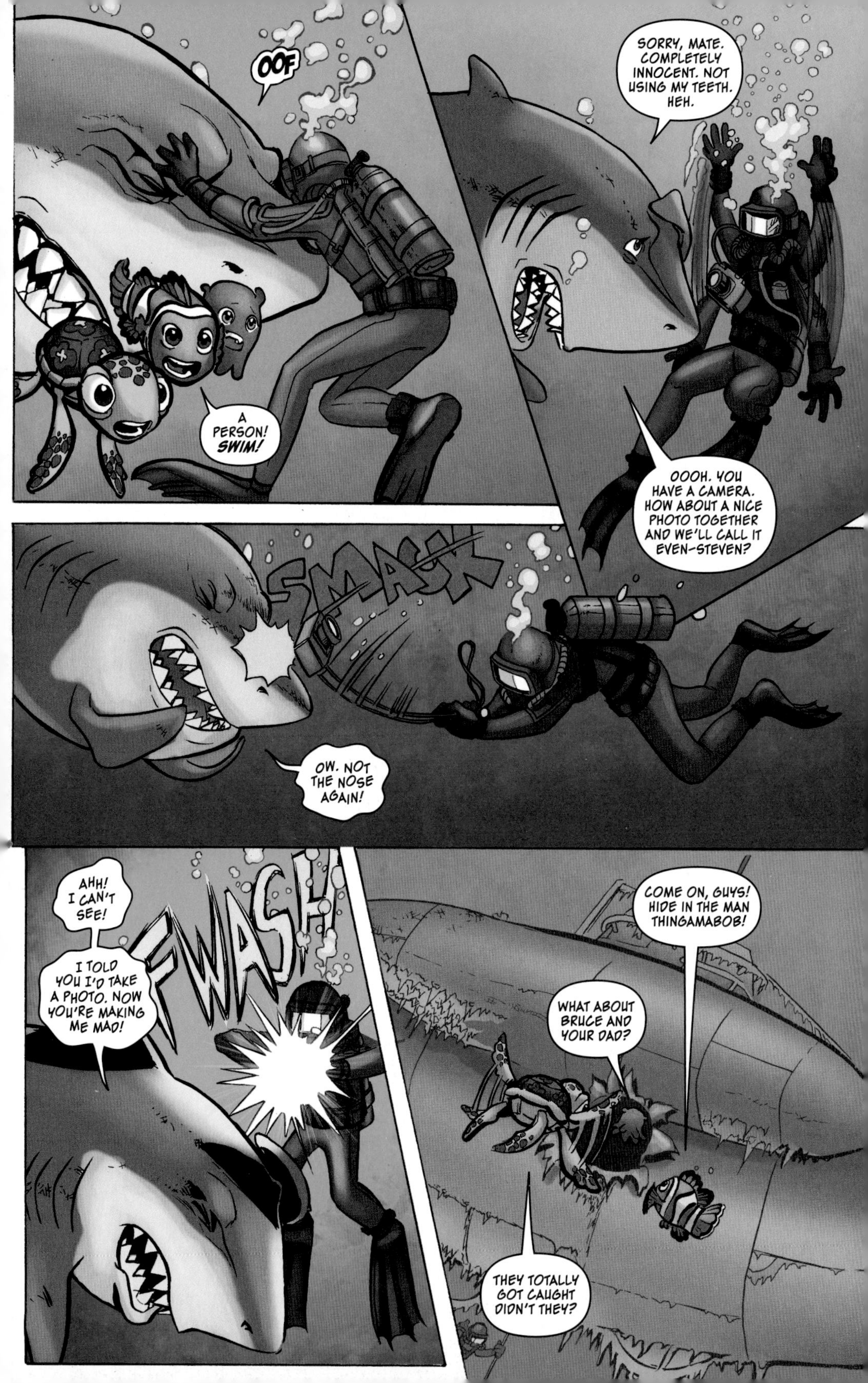
OOF
A PERSON! SWIM!
SORRY, MATE. COMPLETELY INNOCENT. NOT USING MY TEETH. HEH.
OOOH. YOU HAVE A CAMERA. HOW ABOUT A NICE PHOTO TOGETHER AND WE'LL CALL IT EVEN-STEVEN?
SMACK
OW. NOT THE NOSE AGAIN!
AHH! I CAN'T SEE!
FWASH
I TOLD YOU I'D TAKE A PHOTO. NOW YOU'RE MAKING ME MAD!
COME ON, GUYS! HIDE IN THE MAN THINGAMABOB!
WHAT ABOUT BRUCE AND YOUR DAD?
THEY TOTALLY GOT CAUGHT DIDN'T THEY?

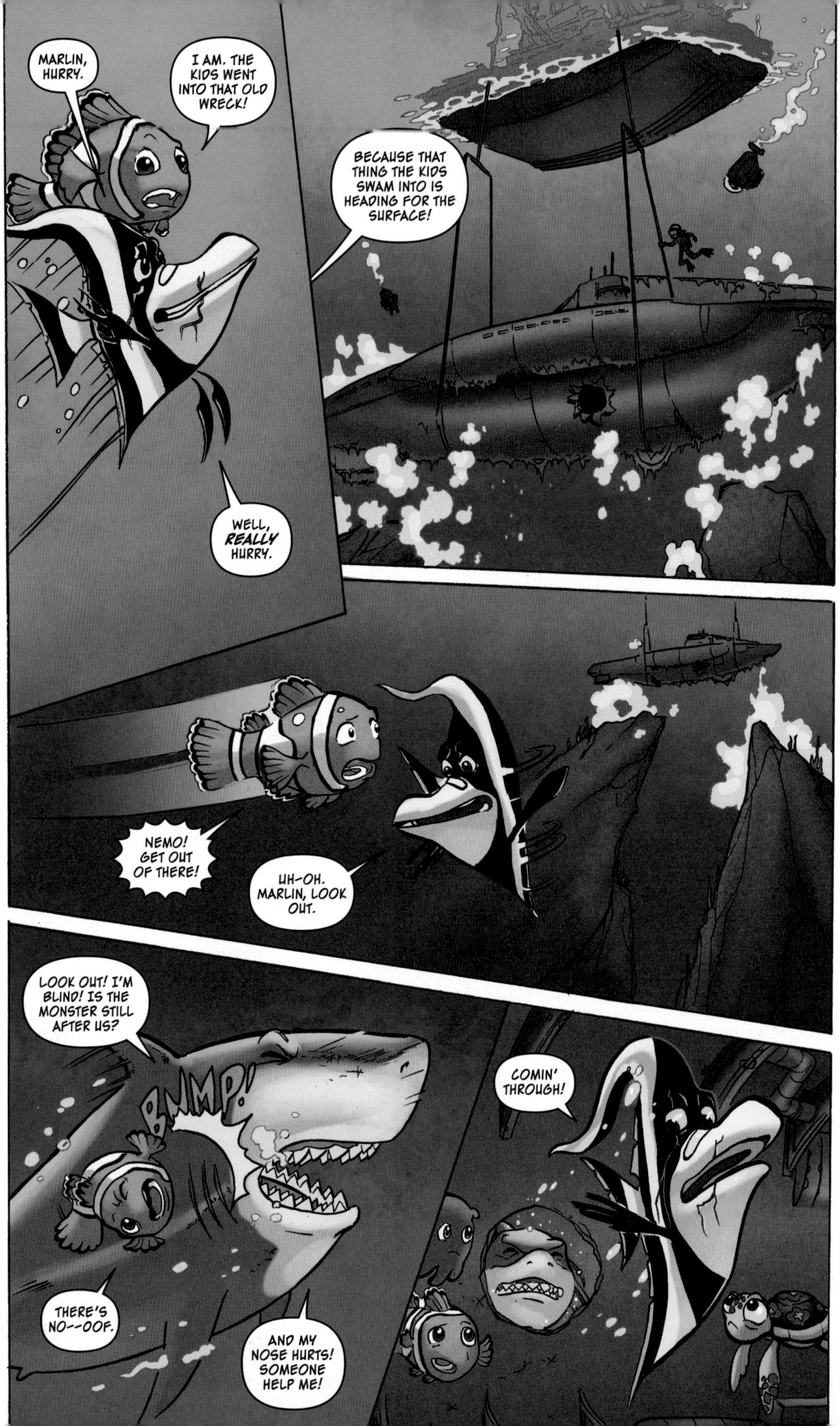
MARLIN, HURRY.
I AM. THE KIDS WENT INTO THAT OLD WRECK!
BECAUSE THAT THING THE KIDS SWAM INTO IS HEADING FOR THE SURFACE!
WELL, *REALLY* HURRY.
NEMO! GET OUT OF THERE!
UH-OH. MARLIN, LOOK OUT.
LOOK OUT! I'M BLIND! IS THE MONSTER STILL AFTER US?
BUMP!
THERE'S NO--OOF.
AND MY NOSE HURTS! SOMEONE HELP ME!
COMIN' THROUGH!

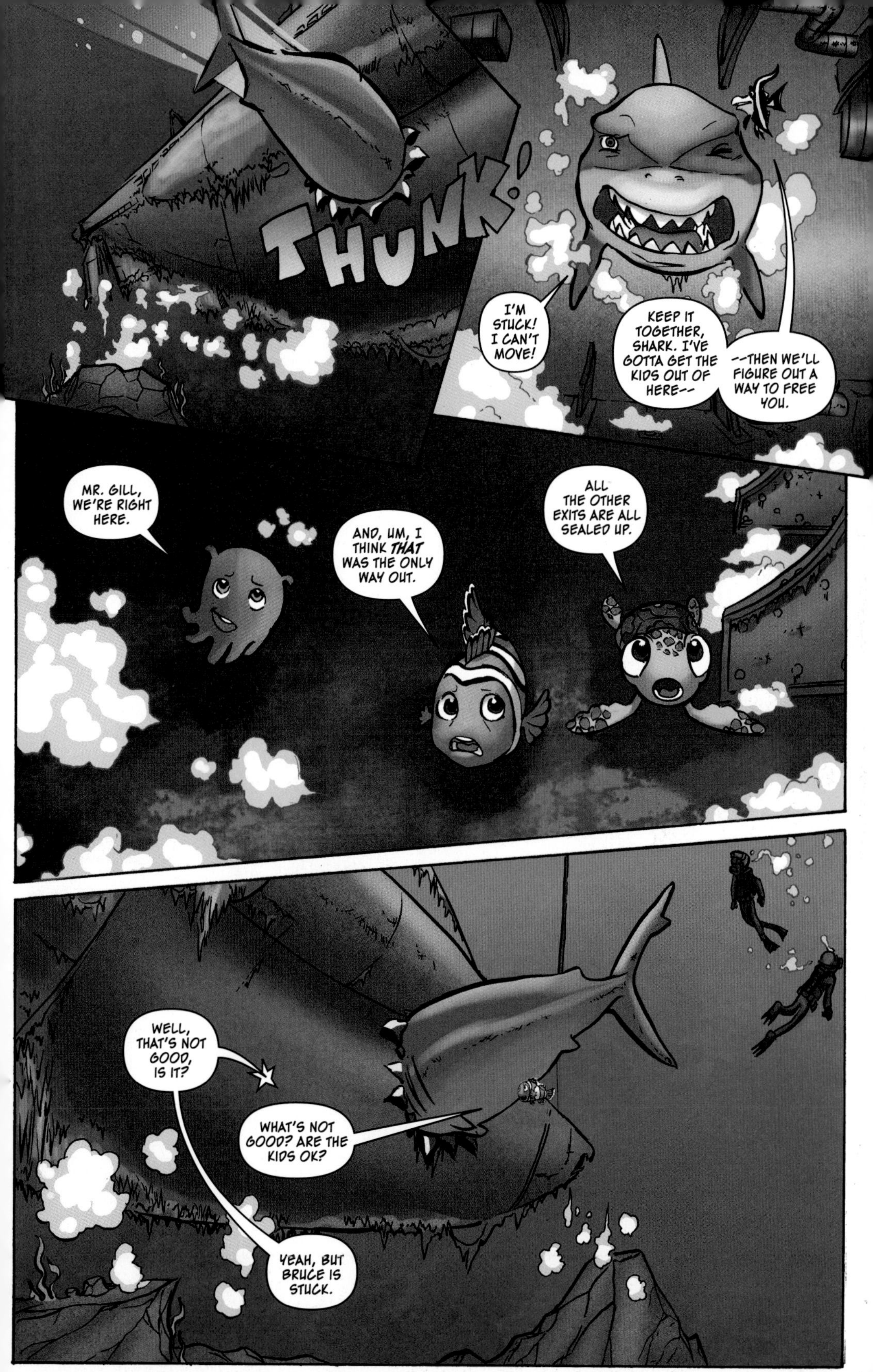
THUNK!
I'M STUCK! I CAN'T MOVE!
KEEP IT TOGETHER, SHARK. I'VE GOTTA GET THE KIDS OUT OF HERE--
--THEN WE'LL FIGURE OUT A WAY TO FREE YOU.
MR. GILL, WE'RE RIGHT HERE.
AND, UM, I THINK THAT WAS THE ONLY WAY OUT.
ALL THE OTHER EXITS ARE ALL SEALED UP.
WELL, THAT'S NOT GOOD, IS IT?
WHAT'S NOT GOOD? ARE THE KIDS OK?
YEAH, BUT BRUCE IS STUCK.

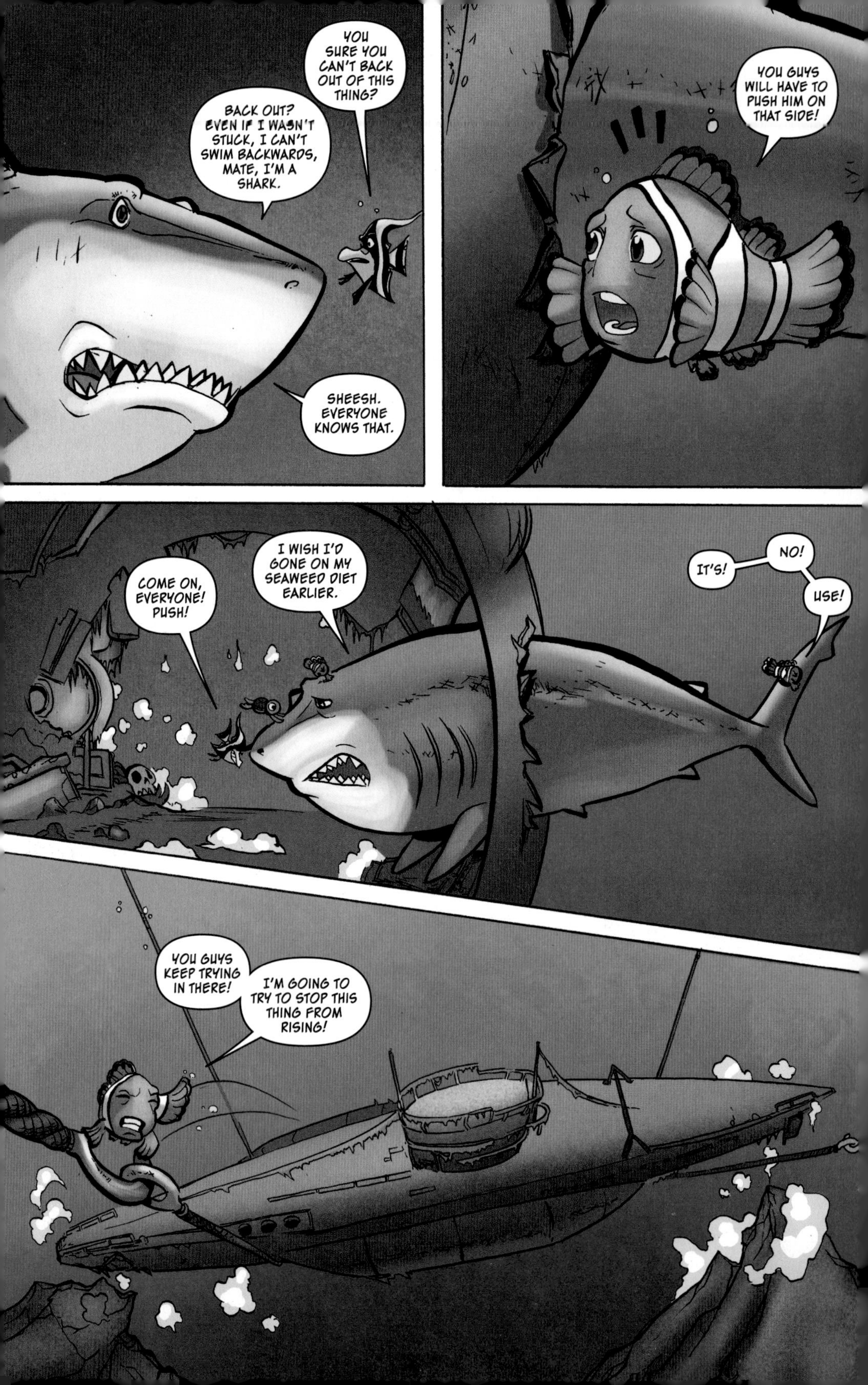
YOU SURE YOU CAN'T BACK OUT OF THIS THING?
BACK OUT? EVEN IF I WASN'T STUCK, I CAN'T SWIM BACKWARDS, MATE, I'M A SHARK.
SHEESH. EVERYONE KNOWS THAT.
YOU GUYS WILL HAVE TO PUSH HIM ON THAT SIDE!
COME ON, EVERYONE! PUSH!
I WISH I'D GONE ON MY SEAWEED DIET EARLIER.
IT'S!
NO!
USE!
YOU GUYS KEEP TRYING IN THERE!
I'M GOING TO TRY TO STOP THIS THING FROM RISING!

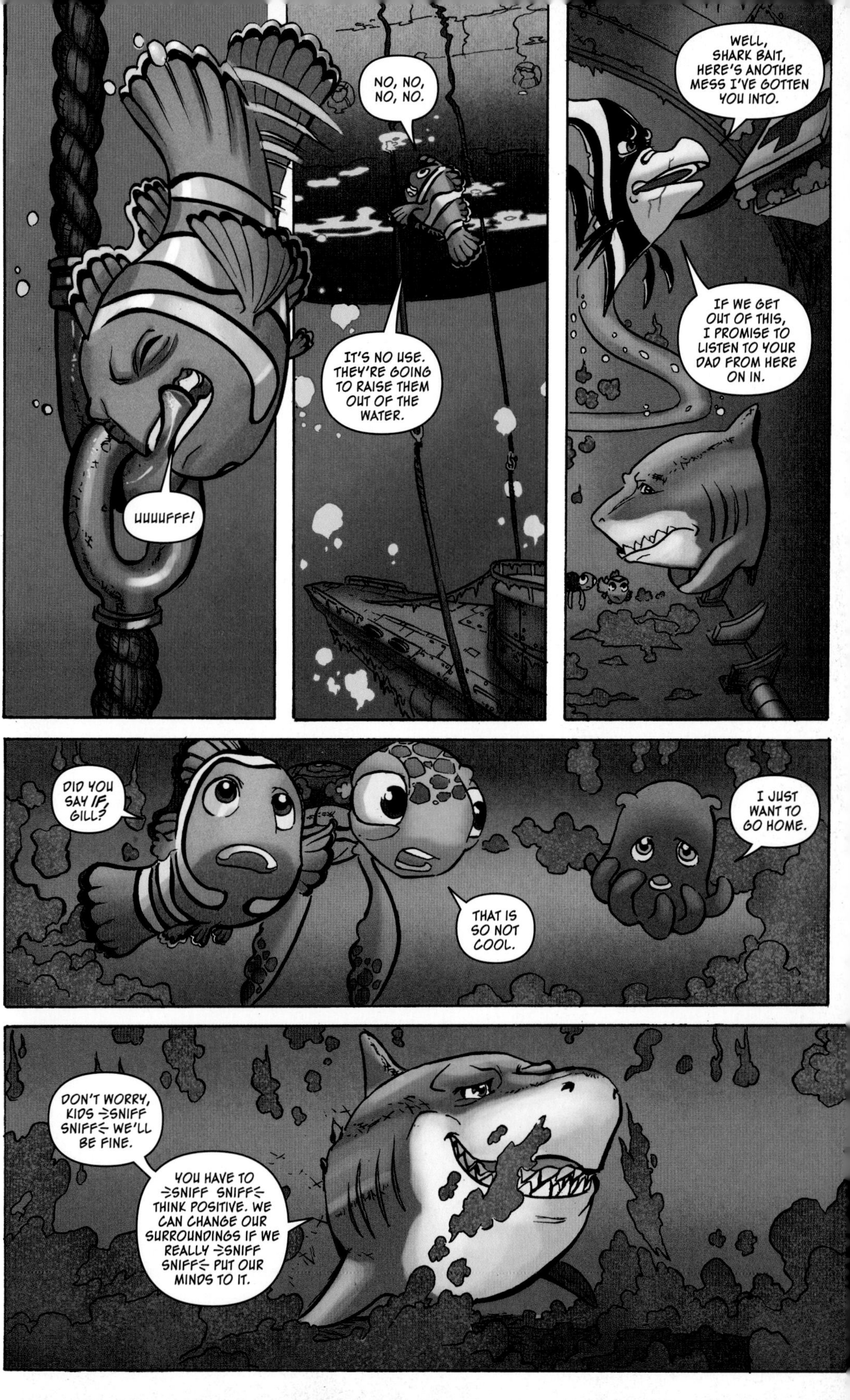
UUUUFFF!
NO, NO, NO, NO.
IT'S NO USE. THEY'RE GOING TO RAISE THEM OUT OF THE WATER.
WELL, SHARK BAIT, HERE'S ANOTHER MESS I'VE GOTTEN YOU INTO.
IF WE GET OUT OF THIS, I PROMISE TO LISTEN TO YOUR DAD FROM HERE ON IN.
DID YOU SAY *IF*, GILL?
THAT IS SO NOT COOL.
I JUST WANT TO GO HOME.
DON'T WORRY, KIDS ⋑SNIFF SNIFF⋐ WE'LL BE FINE.
YOU HAVE TO ⋑SNIFF SNIFF⋐ THINK POSITIVE. WE CAN CHANGE OUR SURROUNDINGS IF WE REALLY ⋑SNIFF SNIFF⋐ PUT OUR MINDS TO IT.

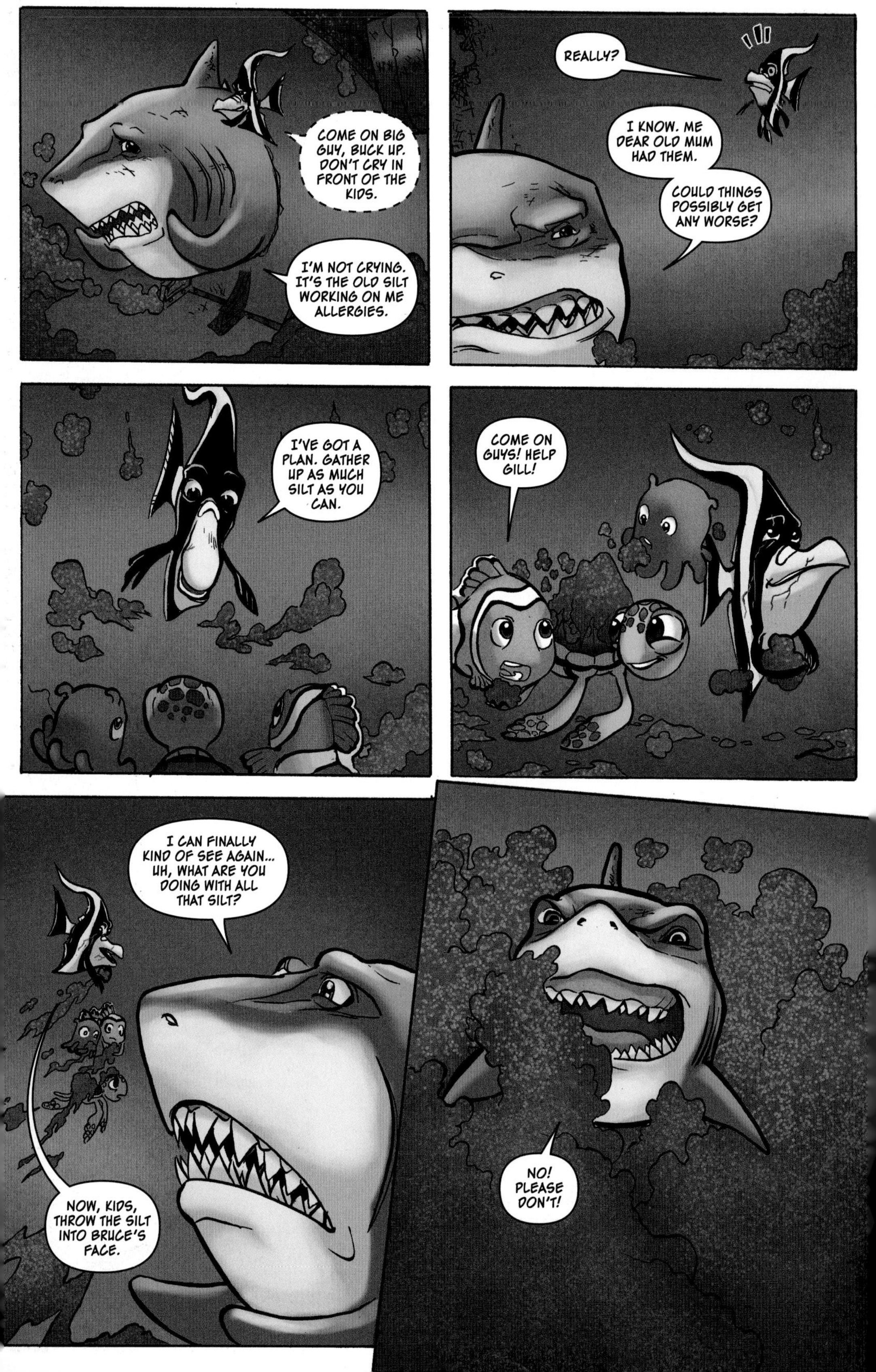
COME ON BIG GUY, BUCK UP. DON'T CRY IN FRONT OF THE KIDS.
I'M NOT CRYING. IT'S THE OLD SILT WORKING ON ME ALLERGIES.
REALLY?
I KNOW. ME DEAR OLD MUM HAD THEM.
COULD THINGS POSSIBLY GET ANY WORSE?
I'VE GOT A PLAN. GATHER UP AS MUCH SILT AS YOU CAN.
COME ON GUYS! HELP GILL!
I CAN FINALLY KIND OF SEE AGAIN... UH, WHAT ARE YOU DOING WITH ALL THAT SILT?
NOW, KIDS, THROW THE SILT INTO BRUCE'S FACE.
NO! PLEASE DON'T!

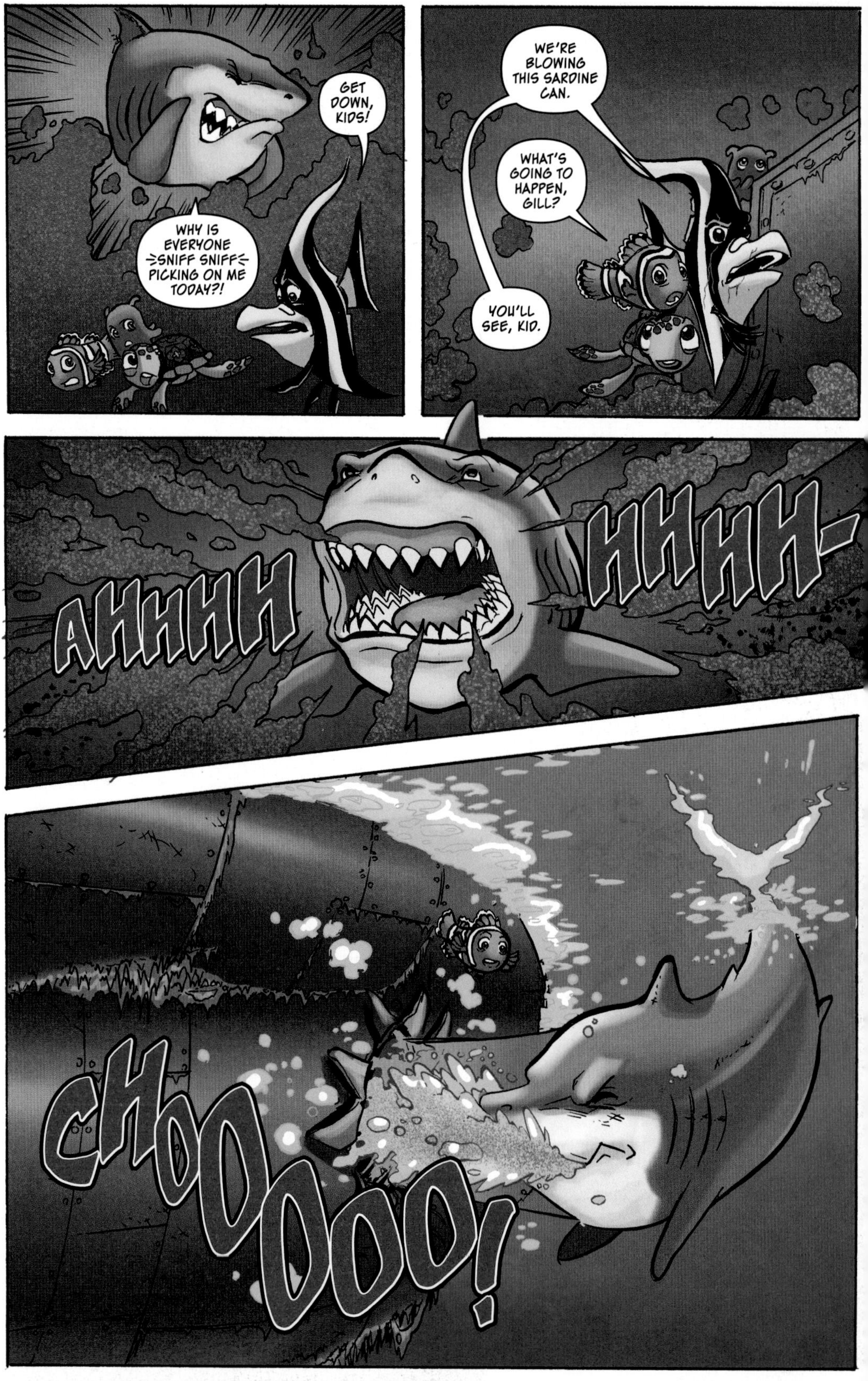
GET DOWN, KIDS!
WHY IS EVERYONE =SNIFF SNIFF= PICKING ON ME TODAY?!
WE'RE BLOWING THIS SARDINE CAN.
WHAT'S GOING TO HAPPEN, GILL?
YOU'LL SEE, KID.
AHHHH HHHH-
CHOOOOOO!

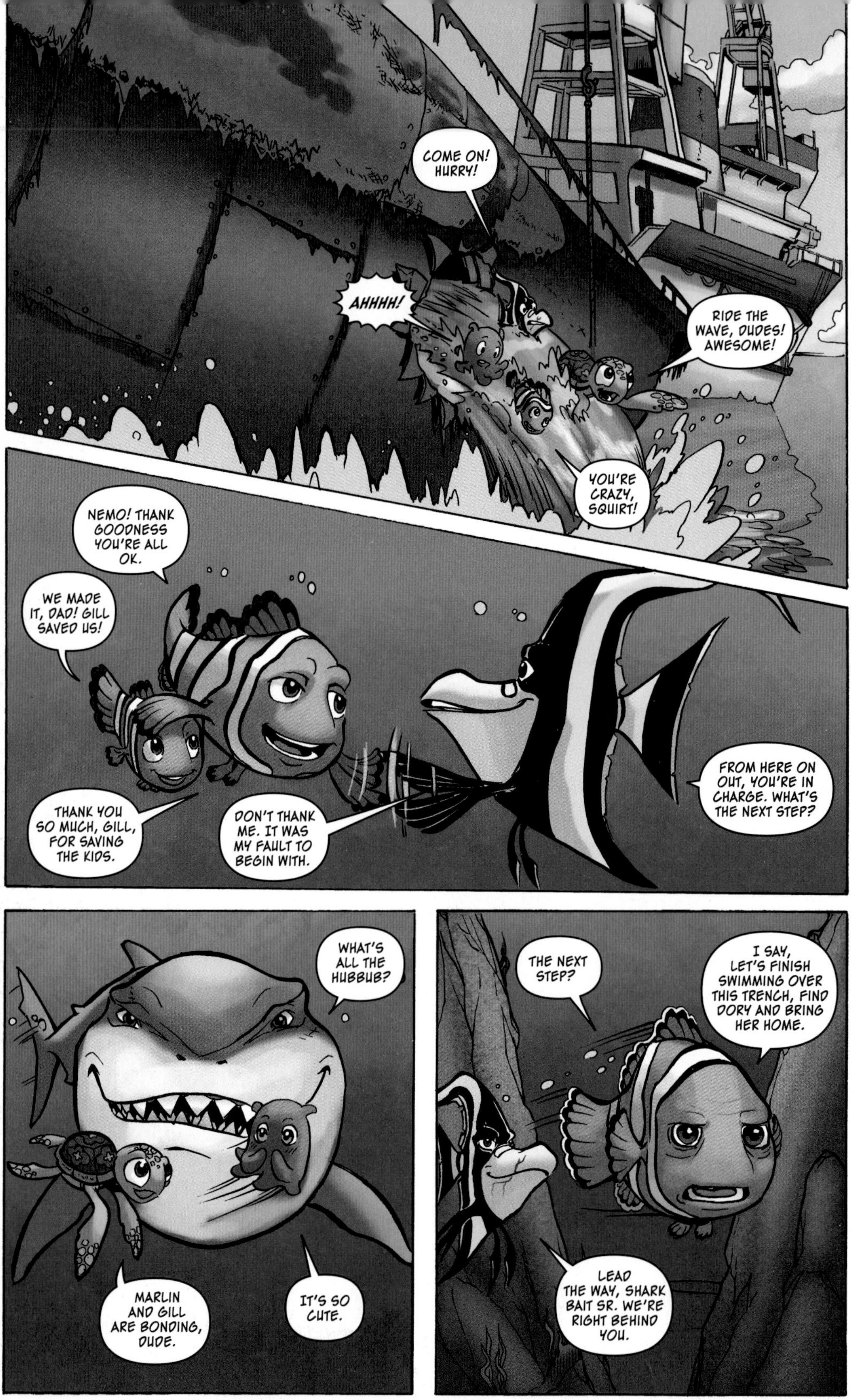
COME ON! HURRY!
AHHHH!
RIDE THE WAVE, DUDES! AWESOME!
YOU'RE CRAZY, SQUIRT!
NEMO! THANK GOODNESS YOU'RE ALL OK.
WE MADE IT, DAD! GILL SAVED US!
THANK YOU SO MUCH, GILL, FOR SAVING THE KIDS.
DON'T THANK ME. IT WAS MY FAULT TO BEGIN WITH.
FROM HERE ON OUT, YOU'RE IN CHARGE. WHAT'S THE NEXT STEP?
WHAT'S ALL THE HUBBUB?
MARLIN AND GILL ARE BONDING, DUDE.
IT'S SO CUTE.
THE NEXT STEP?
I SAY, LET'S FINISH SWIMMING OVER THIS TRENCH, FIND DORY AND BRING HER HOME.
LEAD THE WAY, SHARK BAIT SR. WE'RE RIGHT BEHIND YOU.

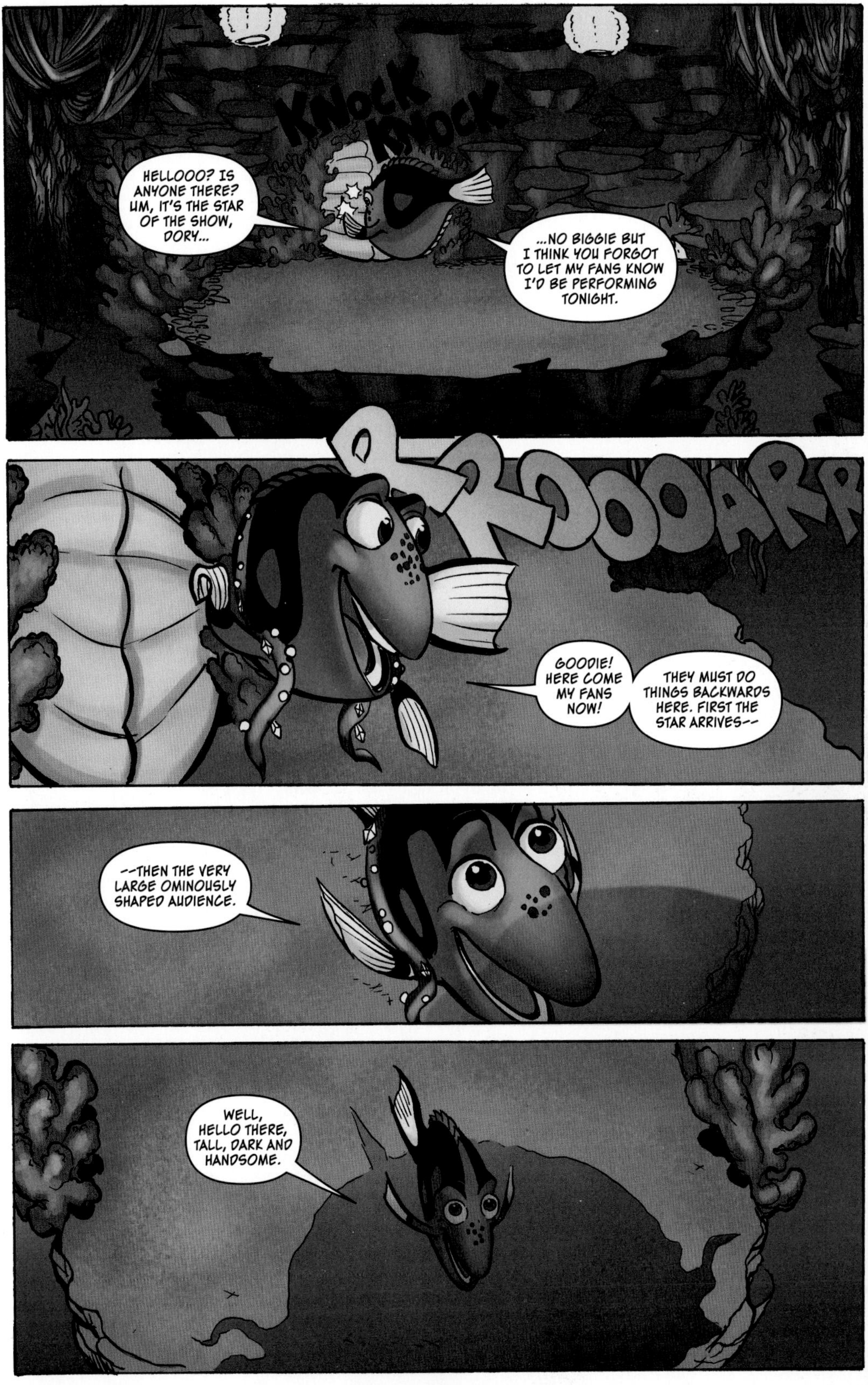
KNOCK KNOCK
HELLOOO? IS ANYONE THERE? UM, IT'S THE STAR OF THE SHOW, DORY...
...NO BIGGIE BUT I THINK YOU FORGOT TO LET MY FANS KNOW I'D BE PERFORMING TONIGHT.
RROOOARR
GOODIE! HERE COME MY FANS NOW!
THEY MUST DO THINGS BACKWARDS HERE. FIRST THE STAR ARRIVES--
--THEN THE VERY LARGE OMINOUSLY SHAPED AUDIENCE.
WELL, HELLO THERE, TALL, DARK AND HANDSOME.

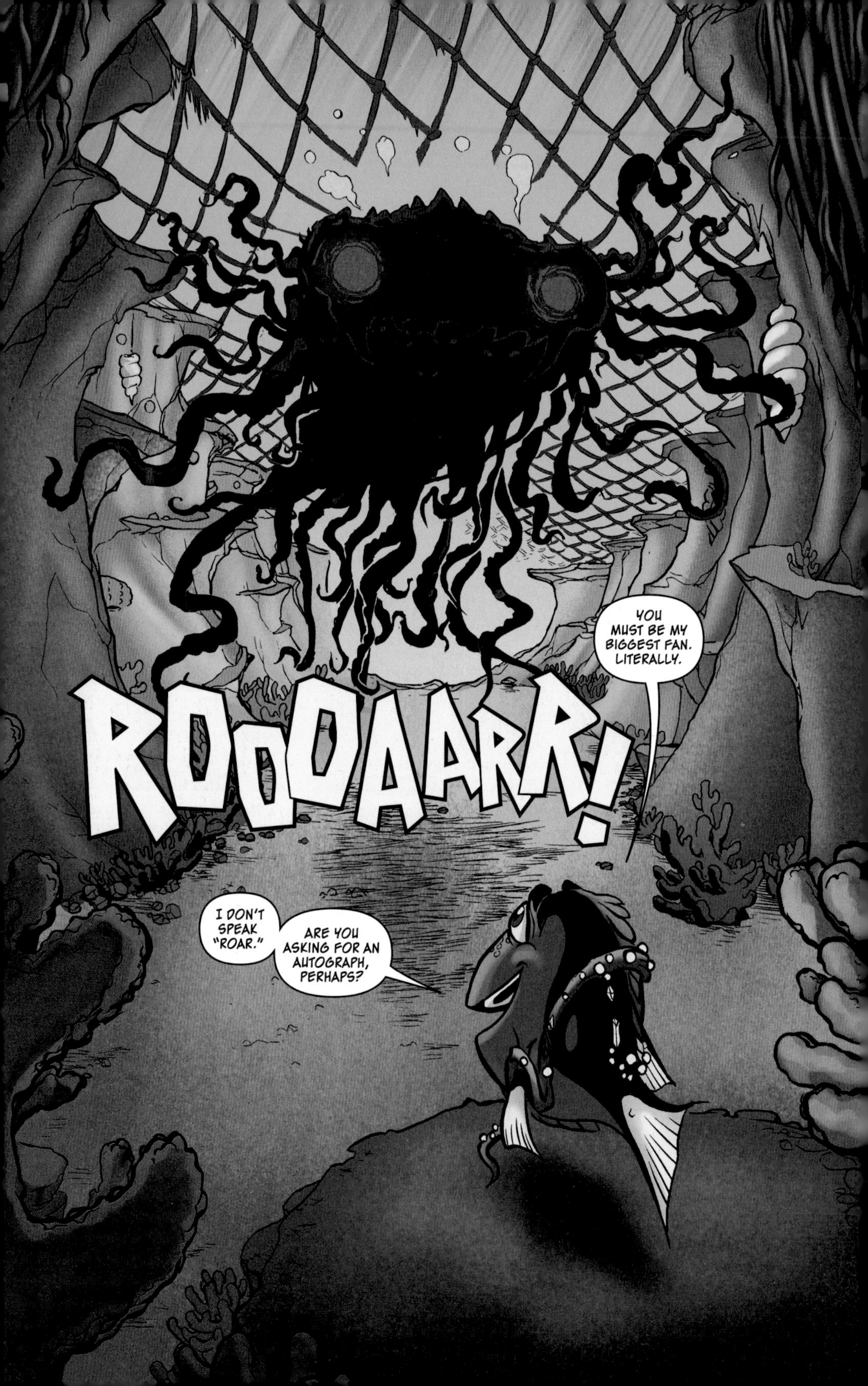
ROOOAARR!
YOU MUST BE MY BIGGEST FAN. LITERALLY.
I DON'T SPEAK "ROAR."
ARE YOU ASKING FOR AN AUTOGRAPH, PERHAPS?

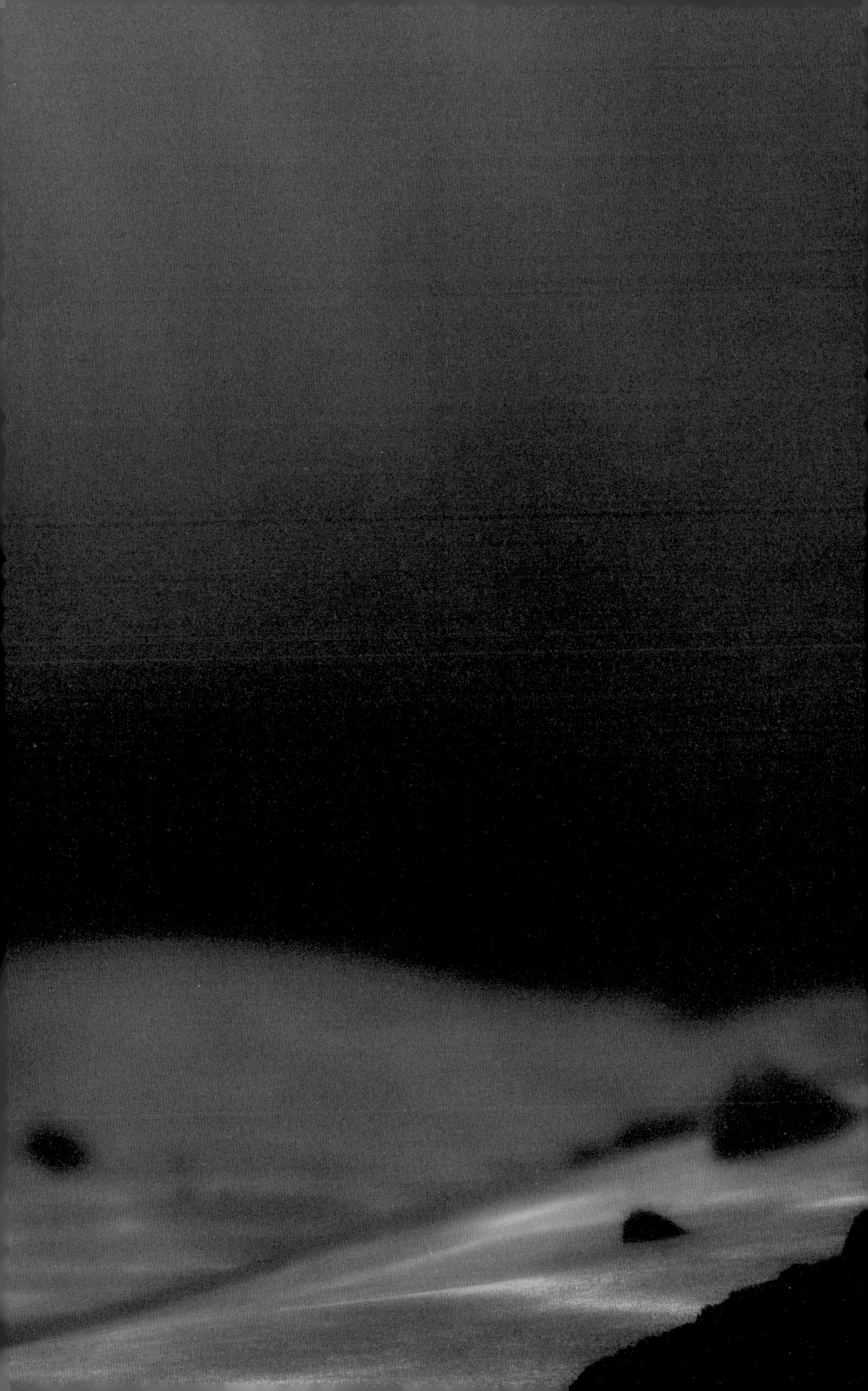

# CHAPTER FOUR

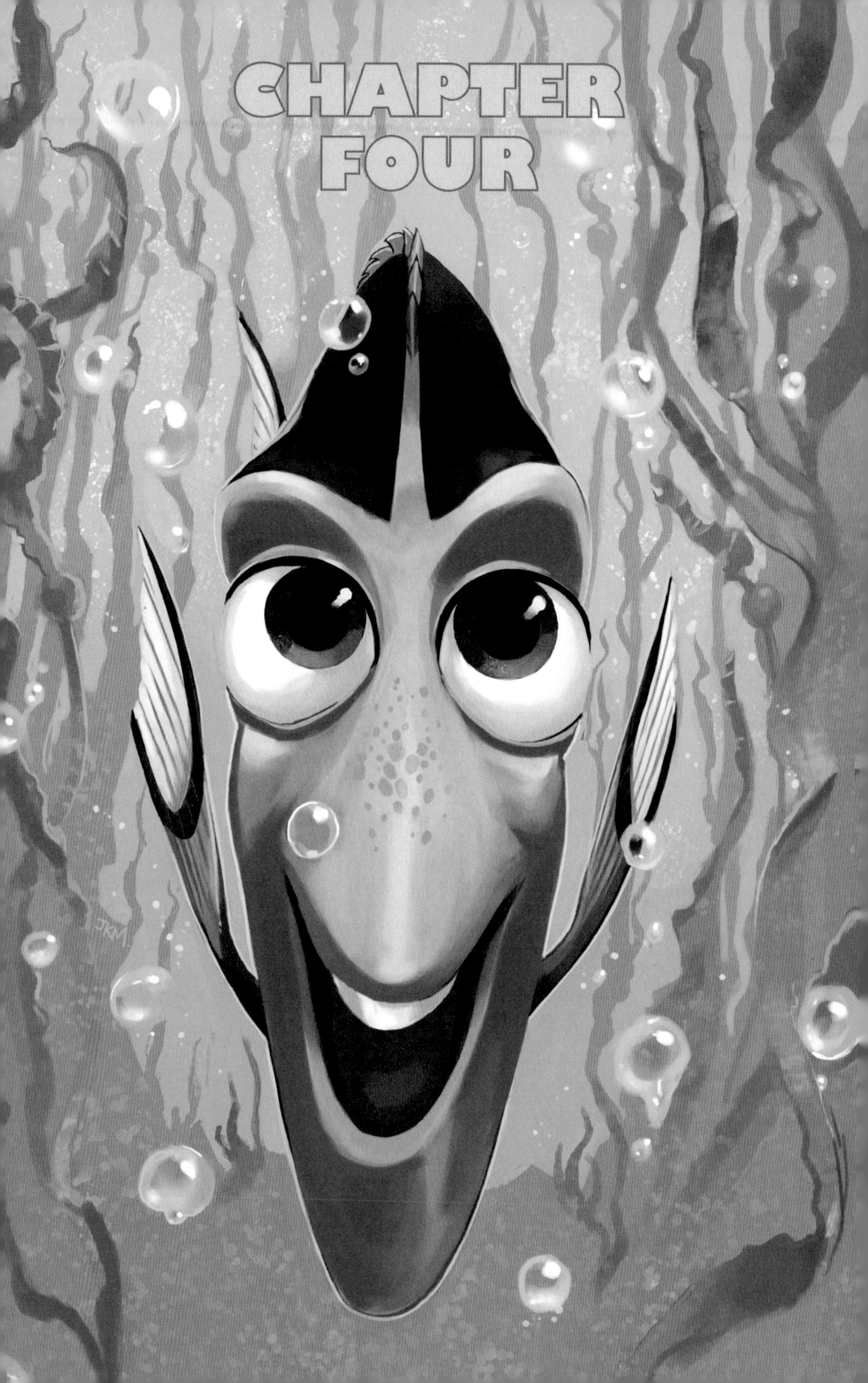
JKM

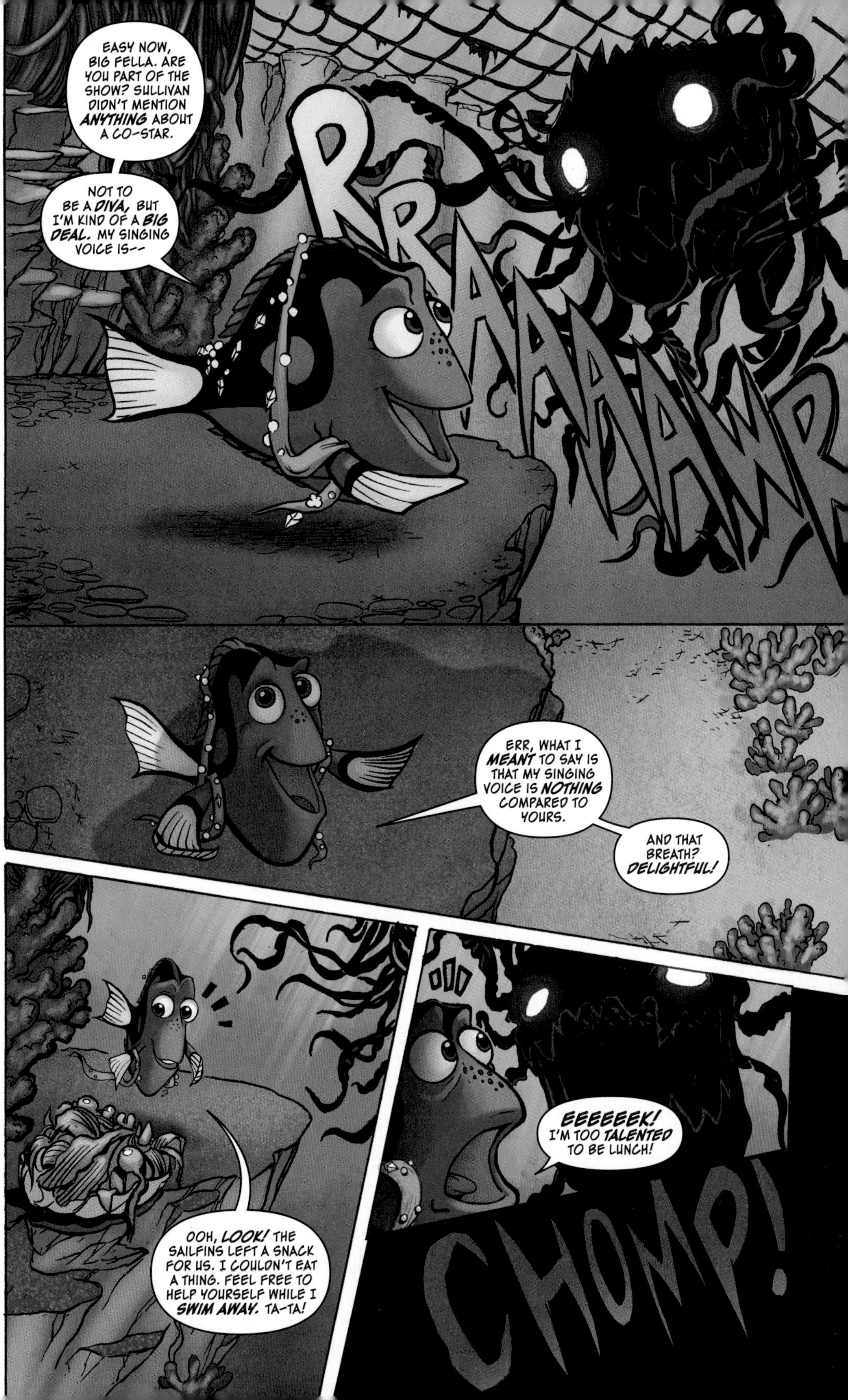
EASY NOW, BIG FELLA. ARE YOU PART OF THE SHOW? SULLIVAN DIDN'T MENTION ANYTHING ABOUT A CO-STAR.
NOT TO BE A DIVA, BUT I'M KIND OF A BIG DEAL. MY SINGING VOICE IS--
RRAAAAAWR
ERR, WHAT I MEANT TO SAY IS THAT MY SINGING VOICE IS NOTHING COMPARED TO YOURS.
AND THAT BREATH? DELIGHTFUL!
OOH, LOOK! THE SAILFINS LEFT A SNACK FOR US. I COULDN'T EAT A THING. FEEL FREE TO HELP YOURSELF WHILE I SWIM AWAY. TA-TA!
EEEEEEK! I'M TOO TALENTED TO BE LUNCH!
CHOMP!

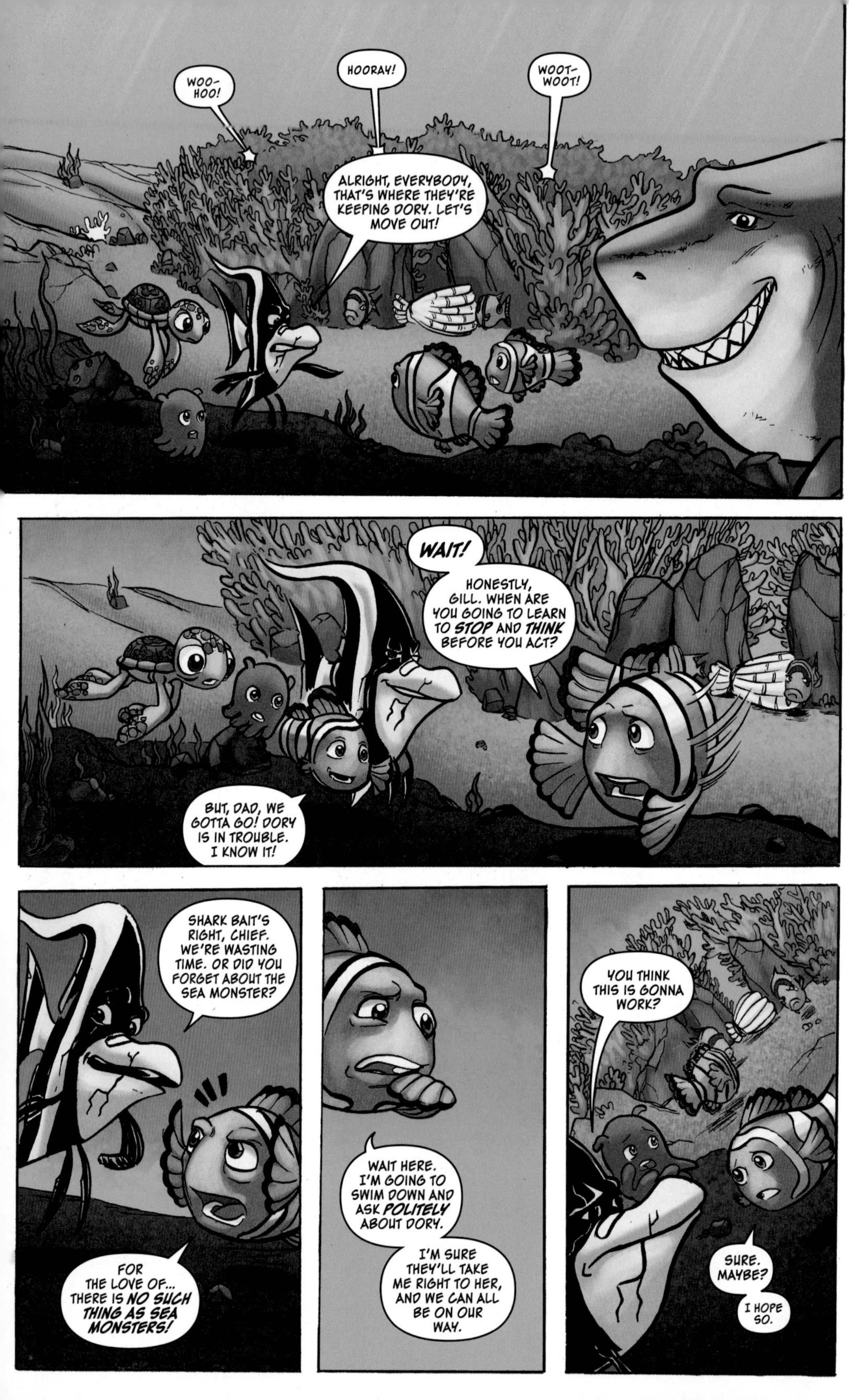
WOO-HOO!
HOORAY!
WOOT-WOOT!
ALRIGHT, EVERYBODY, THAT'S WHERE THEY'RE KEEPING DORY. LET'S MOVE OUT!
WAIT!
HONESTLY, GILL. WHEN ARE YOU GOING TO LEARN TO STOP AND THINK BEFORE YOU ACT?
BUT, DAD, WE GOTTA GO! DORY IS IN TROUBLE. I KNOW IT!
SHARK BAIT'S RIGHT, CHIEF. WE'RE WASTING TIME. OR DID YOU FORGET ABOUT THE SEA MONSTER?
FOR THE LOVE OF... THERE IS NO SUCH THING AS SEA MONSTERS!
WAIT HERE. I'M GOING TO SWIM DOWN AND ASK POLITELY ABOUT DORY.
I'M SURE THEY'LL TAKE ME RIGHT TO HER, AND WE CAN ALL BE ON OUR WAY.
YOU THINK THIS IS GONNA WORK?
SURE. MAYBE?
I HOPE SO.

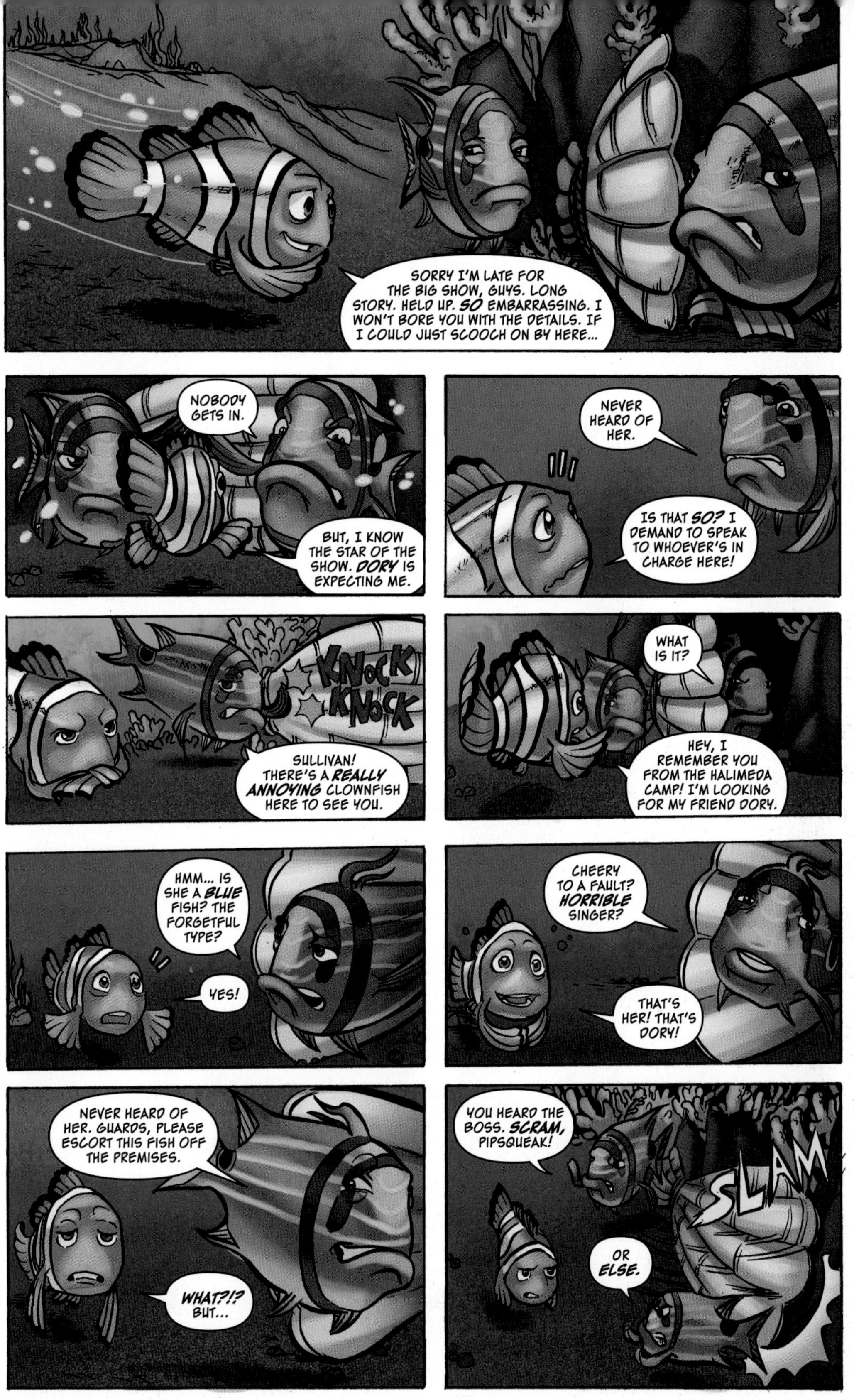
SORRY I'M LATE FOR THE BIG SHOW, GUYS. LONG STORY. HELD UP. SO EMBARRASSING. I WON'T BORE YOU WITH THE DETAILS. IF I COULD JUST SCOOCH ON BY HERE...
NOBODY GETS IN.
BUT, I KNOW THE STAR OF THE SHOW. DORY IS EXPECTING ME.
NEVER HEARD OF HER.
IS THAT SO? I DEMAND TO SPEAK TO WHOEVER'S IN CHARGE HERE!
KNOCK KNOCK
SULLIVAN! THERE'S A REALLY ANNOYING CLOWNFISH HERE TO SEE YOU.
WHAT IS IT?
HEY, I REMEMBER YOU FROM THE HALIMEDA CAMP! I'M LOOKING FOR MY FRIEND DORY.
HMM... IS SHE A BLUE FISH? THE FORGETFUL TYPE?
YES!
CHEERY TO A FAULT? HORRIBLE SINGER?
THAT'S HER! THAT'S DORY!
NEVER HEARD OF HER. GUARDS, PLEASE ESCORT THIS FISH OFF THE PREMISES.
WHAT?!? BUT...
YOU HEARD THE BOSS. SCRAM, PIPSQUEAK!
SLAM
OR ELSE.

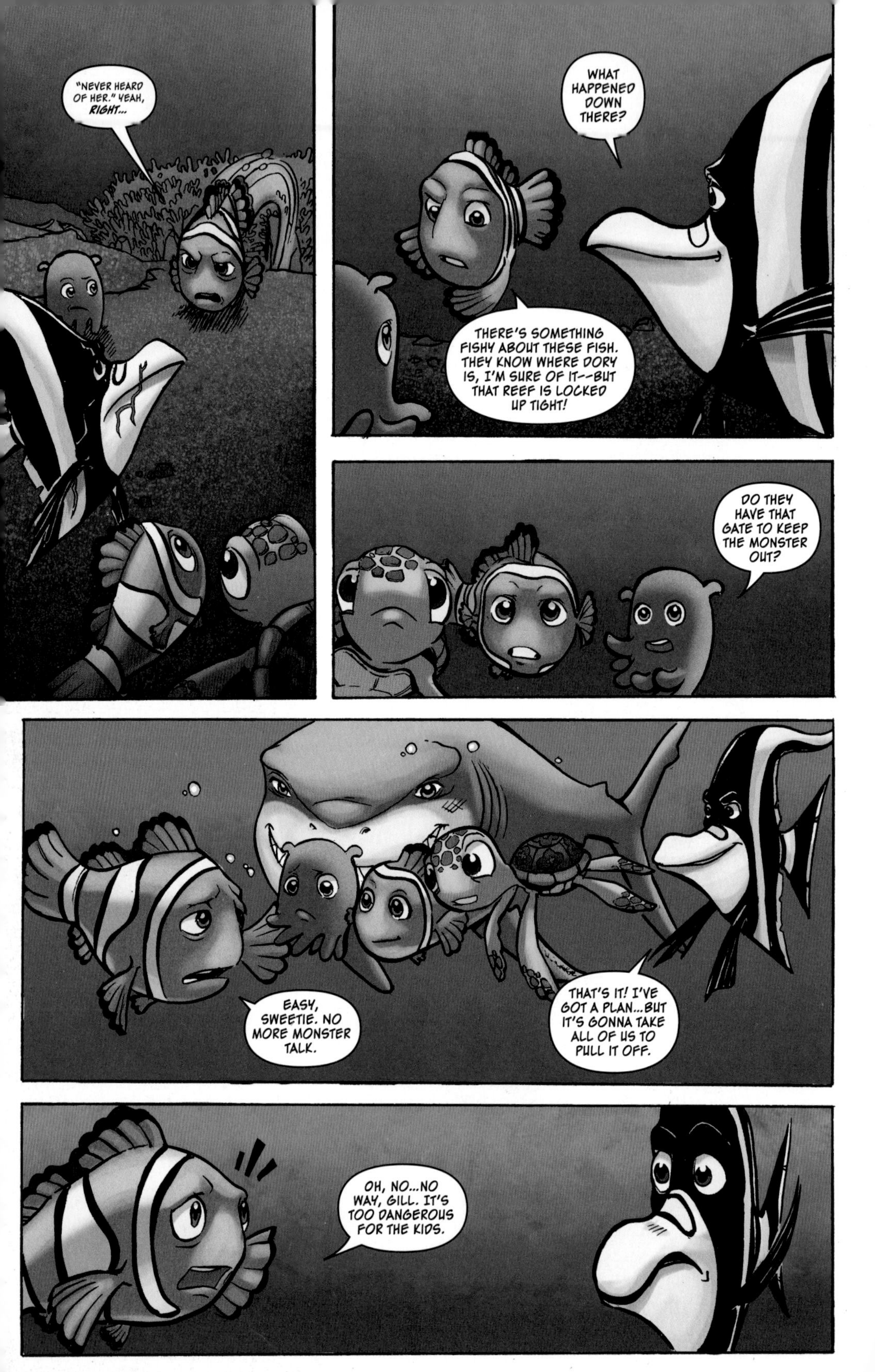
"NEVER HEARD OF HER." YEAH, RIGHT...
WHAT HAPPENED DOWN THERE?
THERE'S SOMETHING FISHY ABOUT THESE FISH. THEY KNOW WHERE DORY IS, I'M SURE OF IT--BUT THAT REEF IS LOCKED UP TIGHT!
DO THEY HAVE THAT GATE TO KEEP THE MONSTER OUT?
EASY, SWEETIE. NO MORE MONSTER TALK.
THAT'S IT! I'VE GOT A PLAN...BUT IT'S GONNA TAKE ALL OF US TO PULL IT OFF.
!!
OH, NO...NO WAY, GILL. IT'S TOO DANGEROUS FOR THE KIDS.

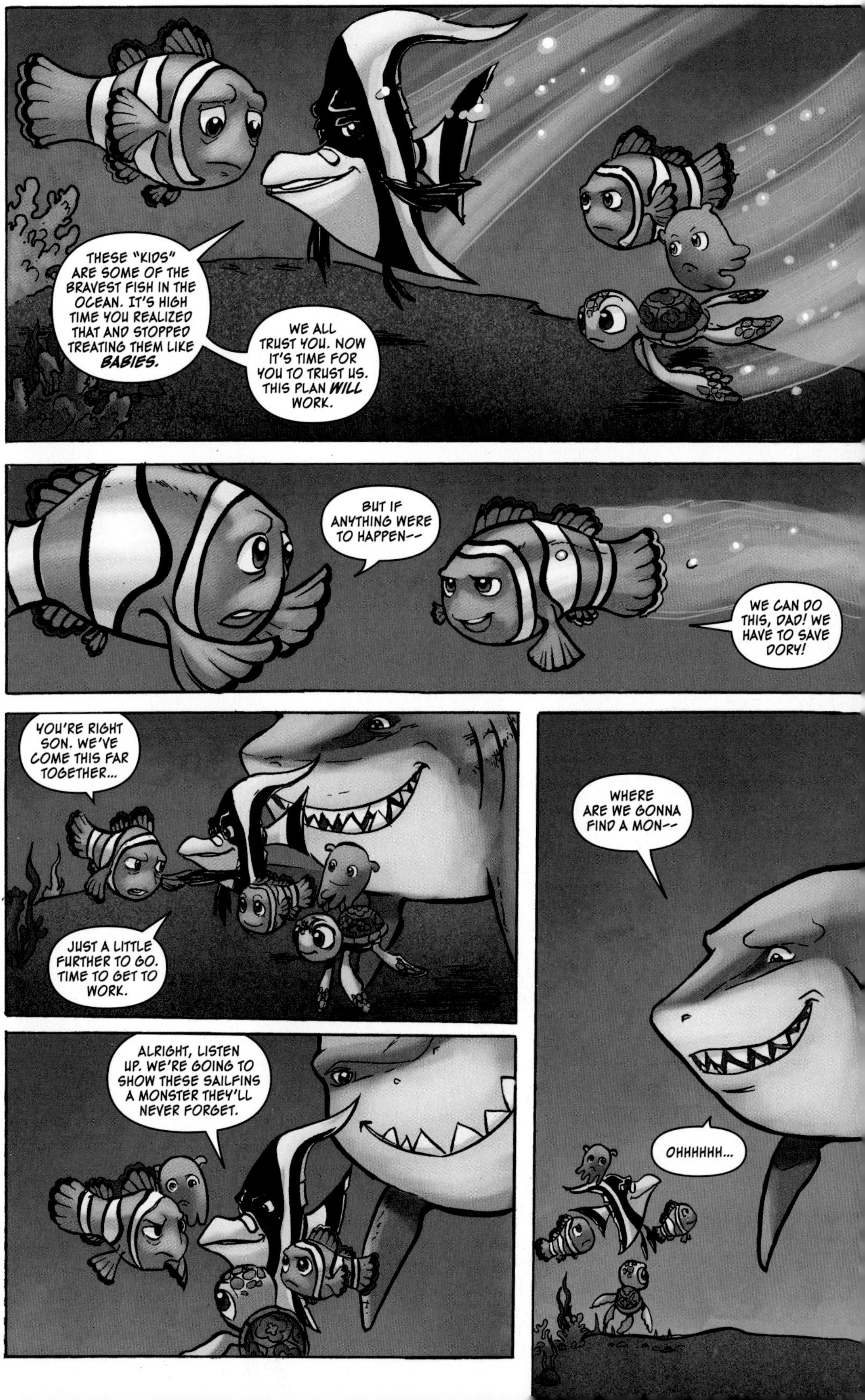
THESE "KIDS" ARE SOME OF THE BRAVEST FISH IN THE OCEAN. IT'S HIGH TIME YOU REALIZED THAT AND STOPPED TREATING THEM LIKE BABIES.
WE ALL TRUST YOU. NOW IT'S TIME FOR YOU TO TRUST US. THIS PLAN WILL WORK.
BUT IF ANYTHING WERE TO HAPPEN--
WE CAN DO THIS, DAD! WE HAVE TO SAVE DORY!
YOU'RE RIGHT SON. WE'VE COME THIS FAR TOGETHER...
JUST A LITTLE FURTHER TO GO. TIME TO GET TO WORK.
ALRIGHT, LISTEN UP. WE'RE GOING TO SHOW THESE SAILFINS A MONSTER THEY'LL NEVER FORGET.
WHERE ARE WE GONNA FIND A MON--
OHHHHHH...

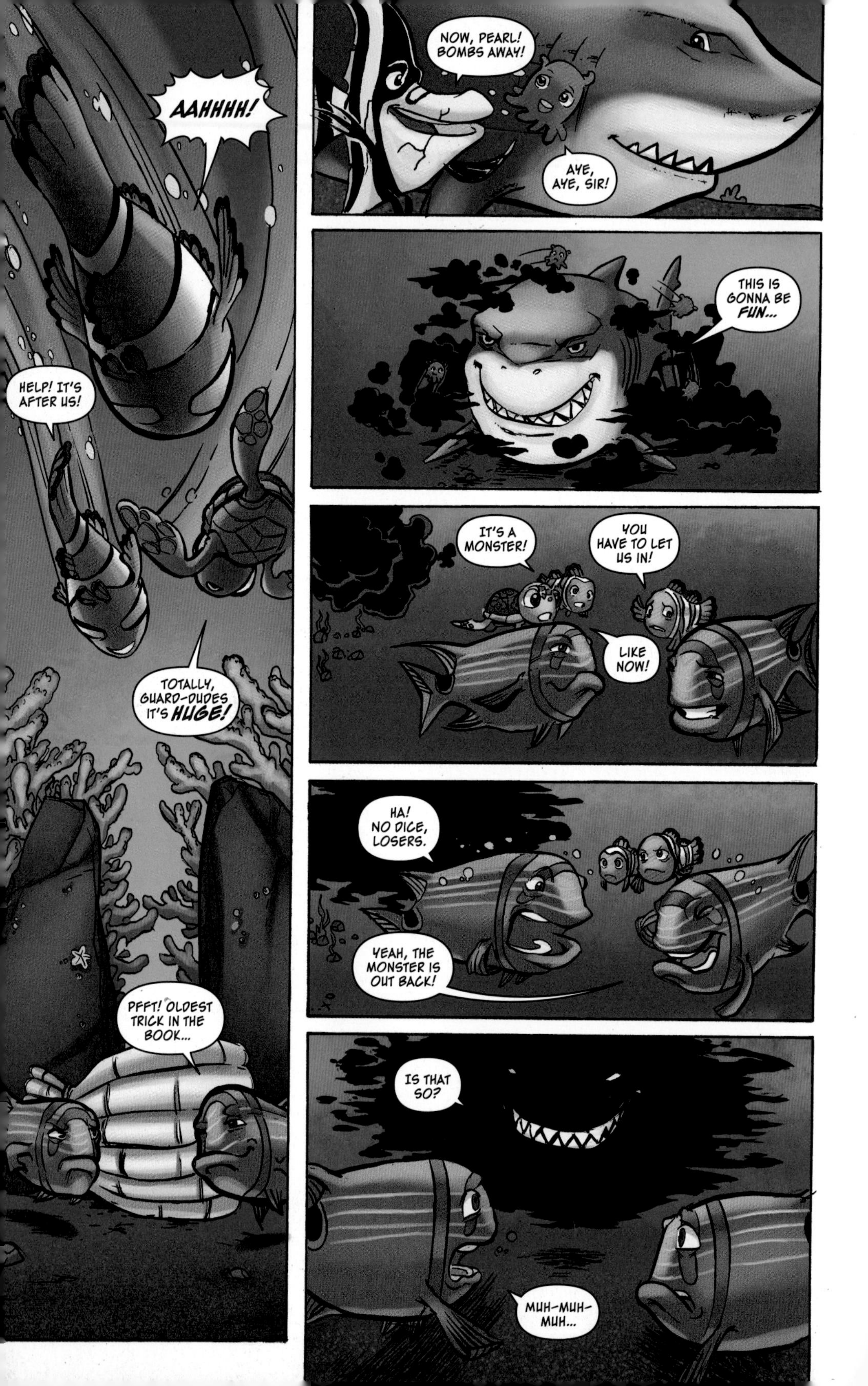
AAHHHH!
HELP! IT'S AFTER US!
TOTALLY, GUARD-DUDES IT'S HUGE!
PFFT! OLDEST TRICK IN THE BOOK...
NOW, PEARL! BOMBS AWAY!
AYE, AYE, SIR!
THIS IS GONNA BE FUN...
IT'S A MONSTER!
YOU HAVE TO LET US IN!
LIKE NOW!
HA! NO DICE, LOSERS.
YEAH, THE MONSTER IS OUT BACK!
IS THAT SO?
MUH-MUH-MUH...

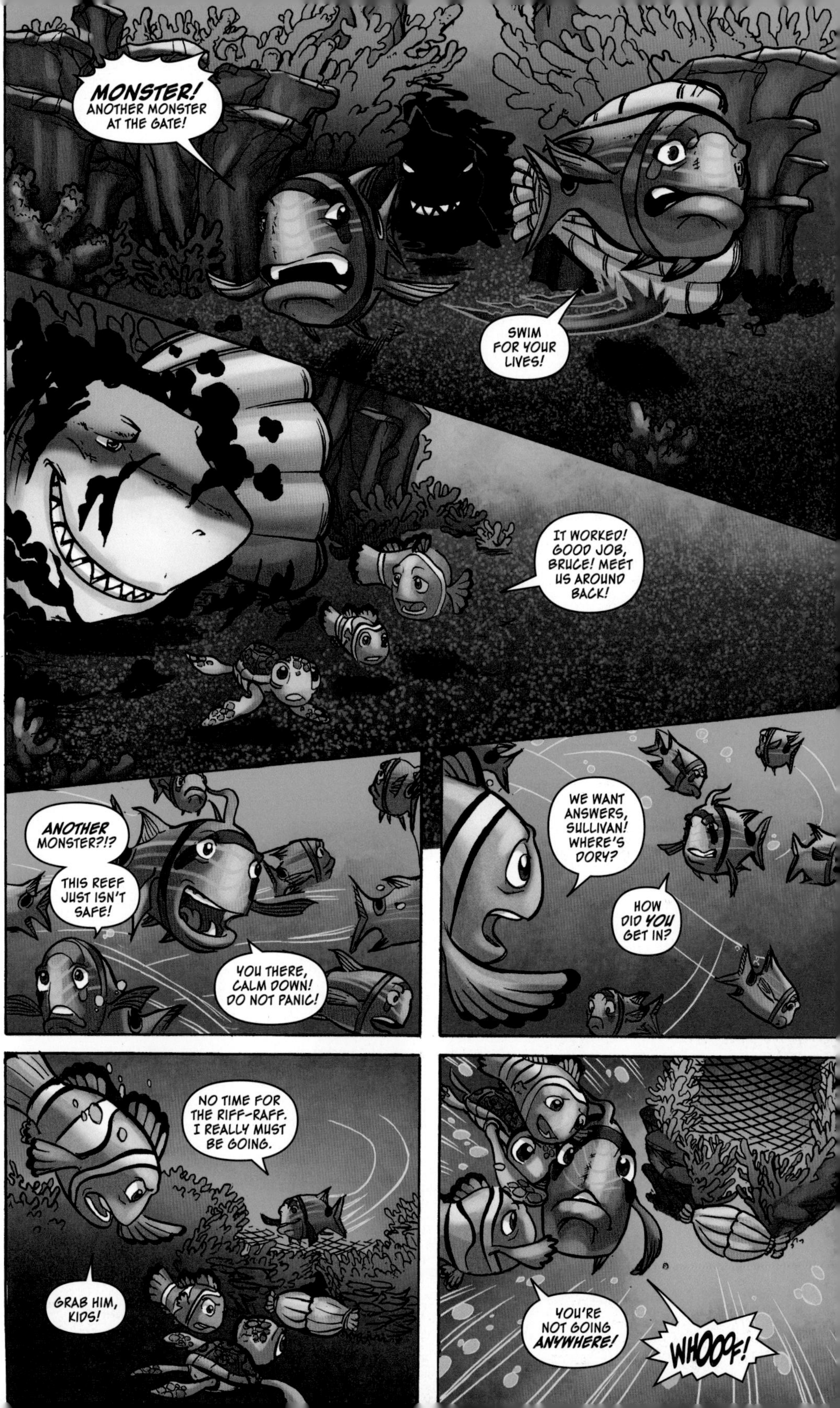
MONSTER! ANOTHER MONSTER AT THE GATE!
SWIM FOR YOUR LIVES!
IT WORKED! GOOD JOB, BRUCE! MEET US AROUND BACK!
ANOTHER MONSTER?!?
THIS REEF JUST ISN'T SAFE!
YOU THERE, CALM DOWN! DO NOT PANIC!
WE WANT ANSWERS, SULLIVAN! WHERE'S DORY?
HOW DID YOU GET IN?
NO TIME FOR THE RIFF-RAFF. I REALLY MUST BE GOING.
GRAB HIM, KIDS!
YOU'RE NOT GOING ANYWHERE!
WHOOF!

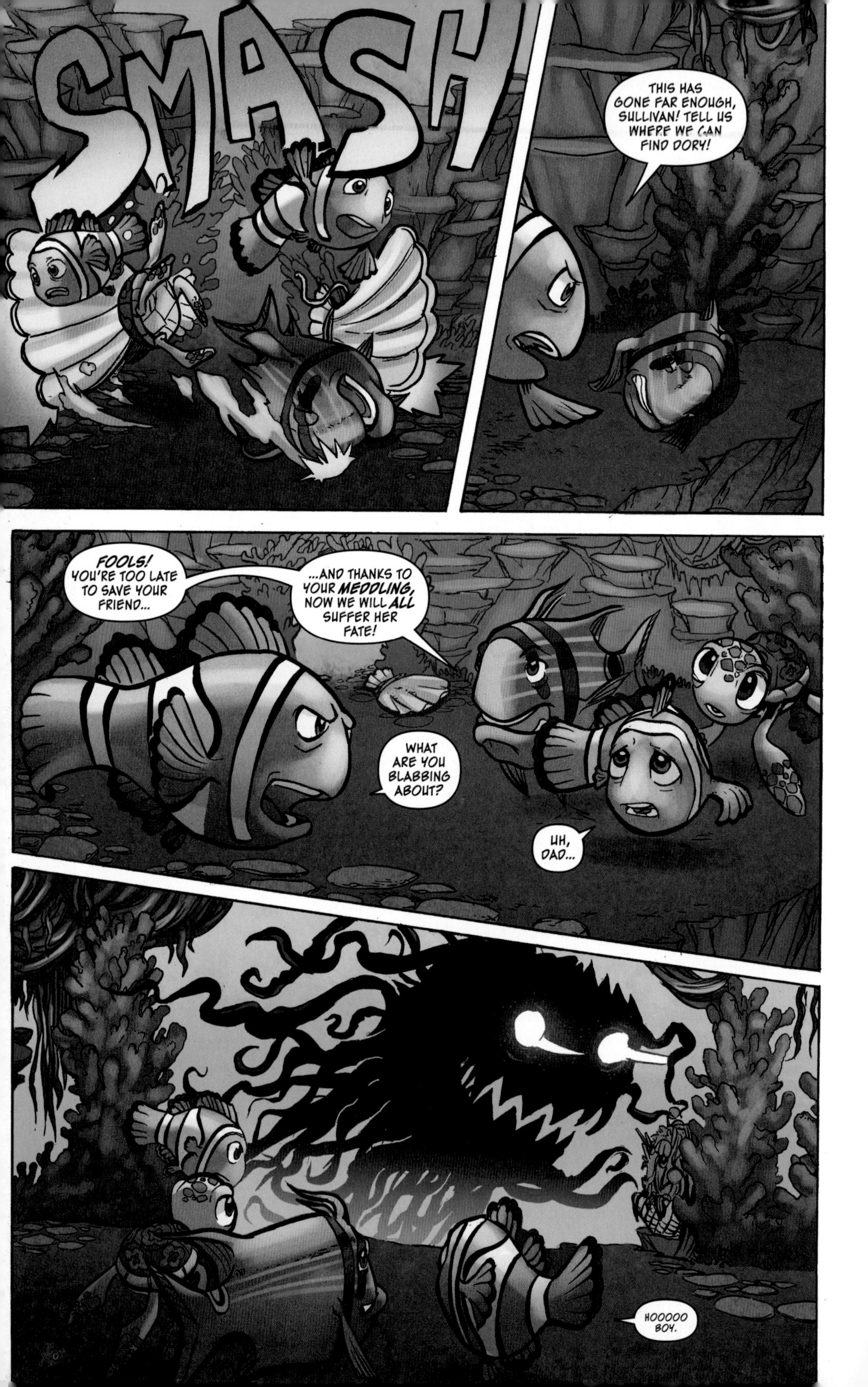
SMASH
THIS HAS GONE FAR ENOUGH, SULLIVAN! TELL US WHERE WE CAN FIND DORY!
FOOLS! YOU'RE TOO LATE TO SAVE YOUR FRIEND...
...AND THANKS TO YOUR MEDDLING, NOW WE WILL ALL SUFFER HER FATE!
WHAT ARE YOU BLABBING ABOUT?
UH, DAD...
HOOOOO BOY.

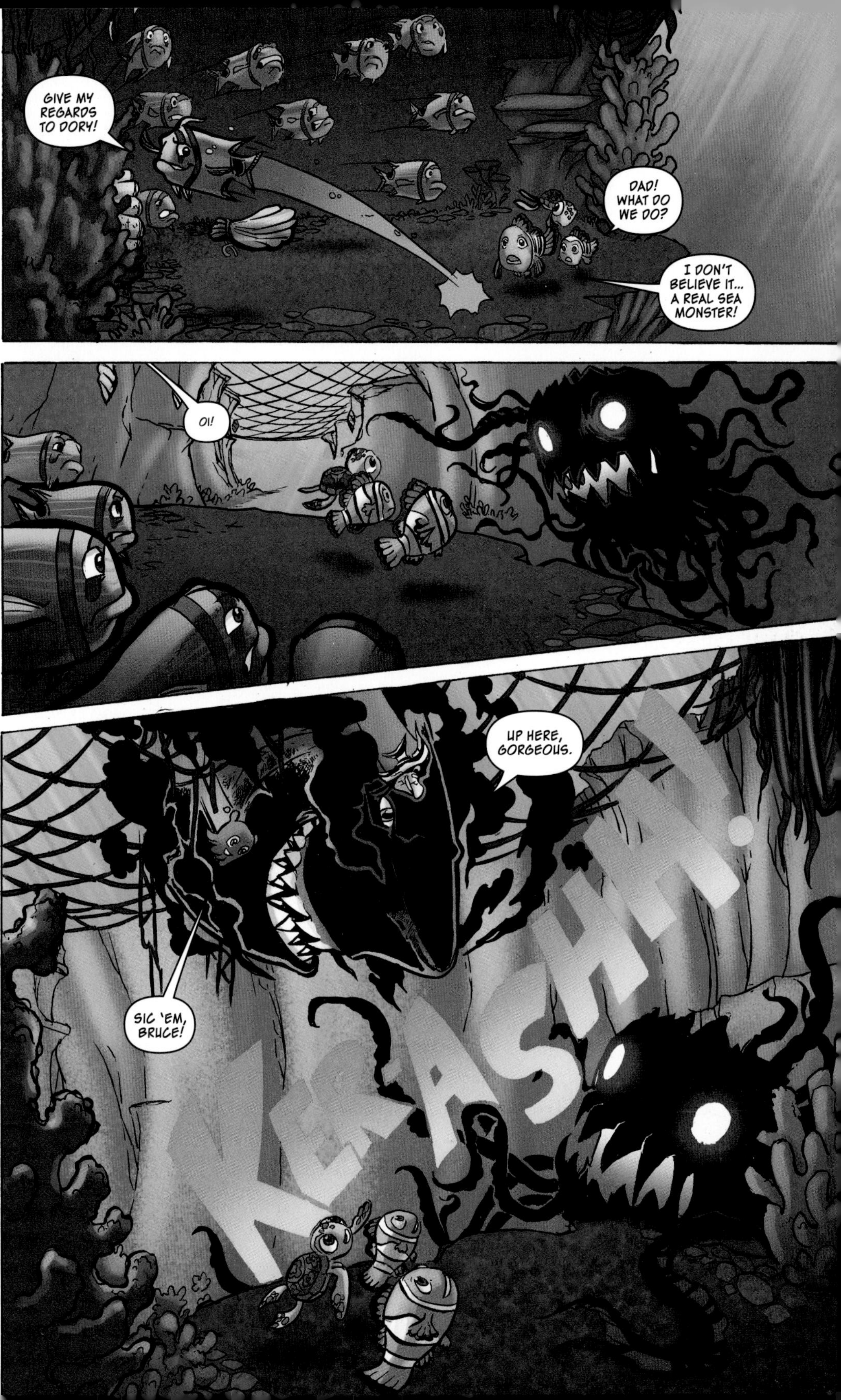
GIVE MY REGARDS TO DORY!
DAD! WHAT DO WE DO?
I DON'T BELIEVE IT... A REAL SEA MONSTER!
OI!
UP HERE, GORGEOUS.
SIC 'EM, BRUCE!
KER-ASHH!

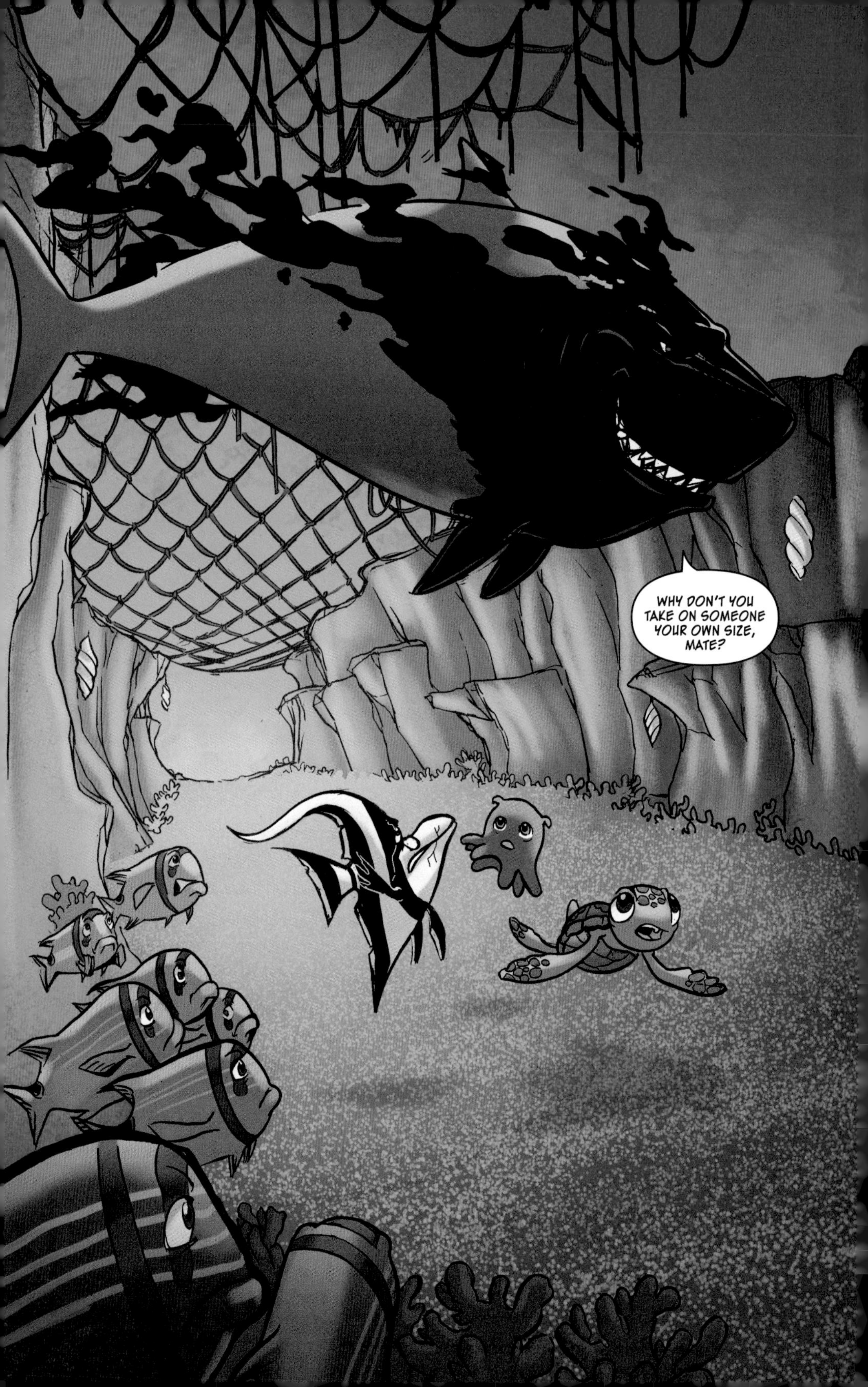
WHY DON'T YOU TAKE ON SOMEONE YOUR OWN SIZE, MATE?

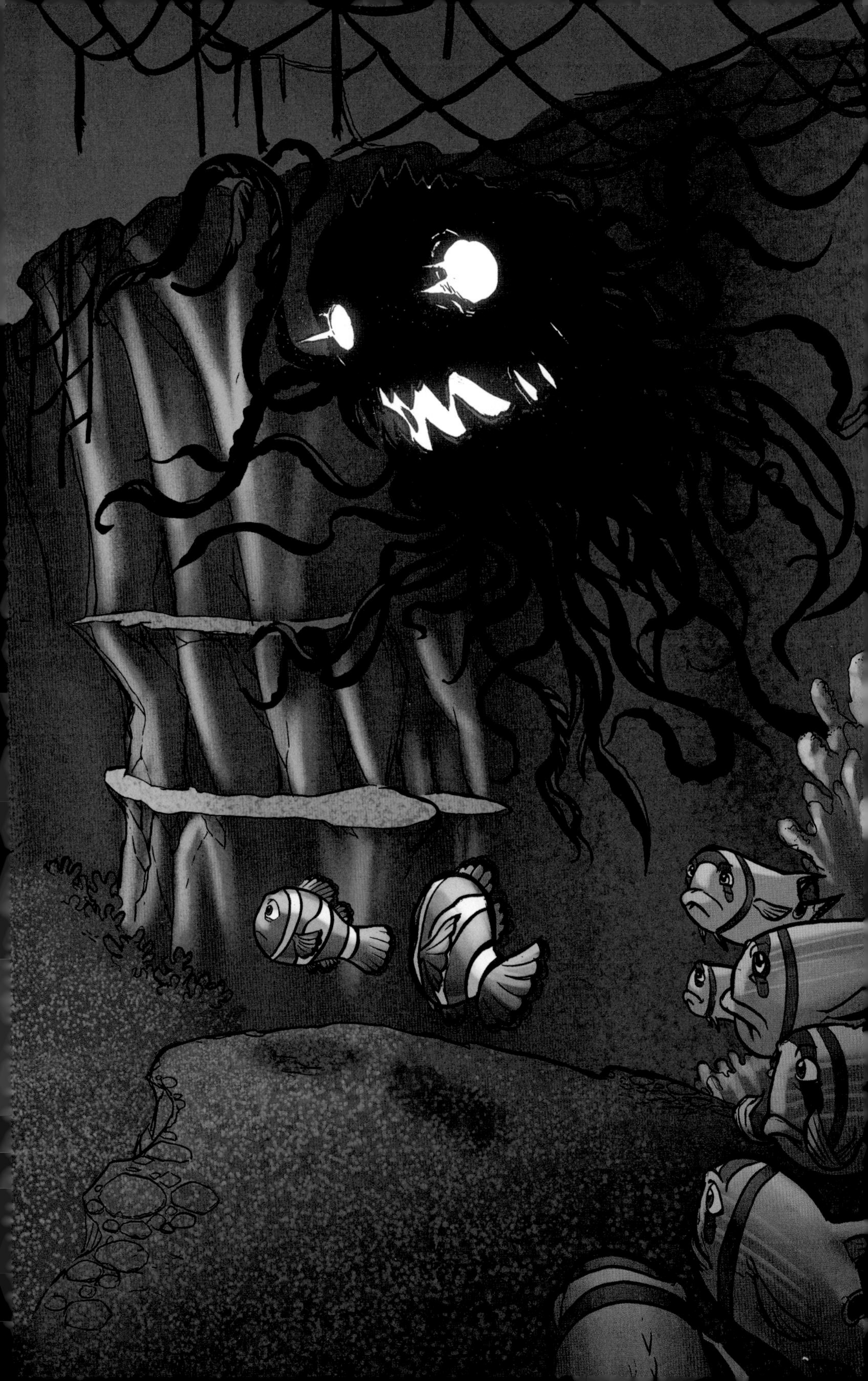

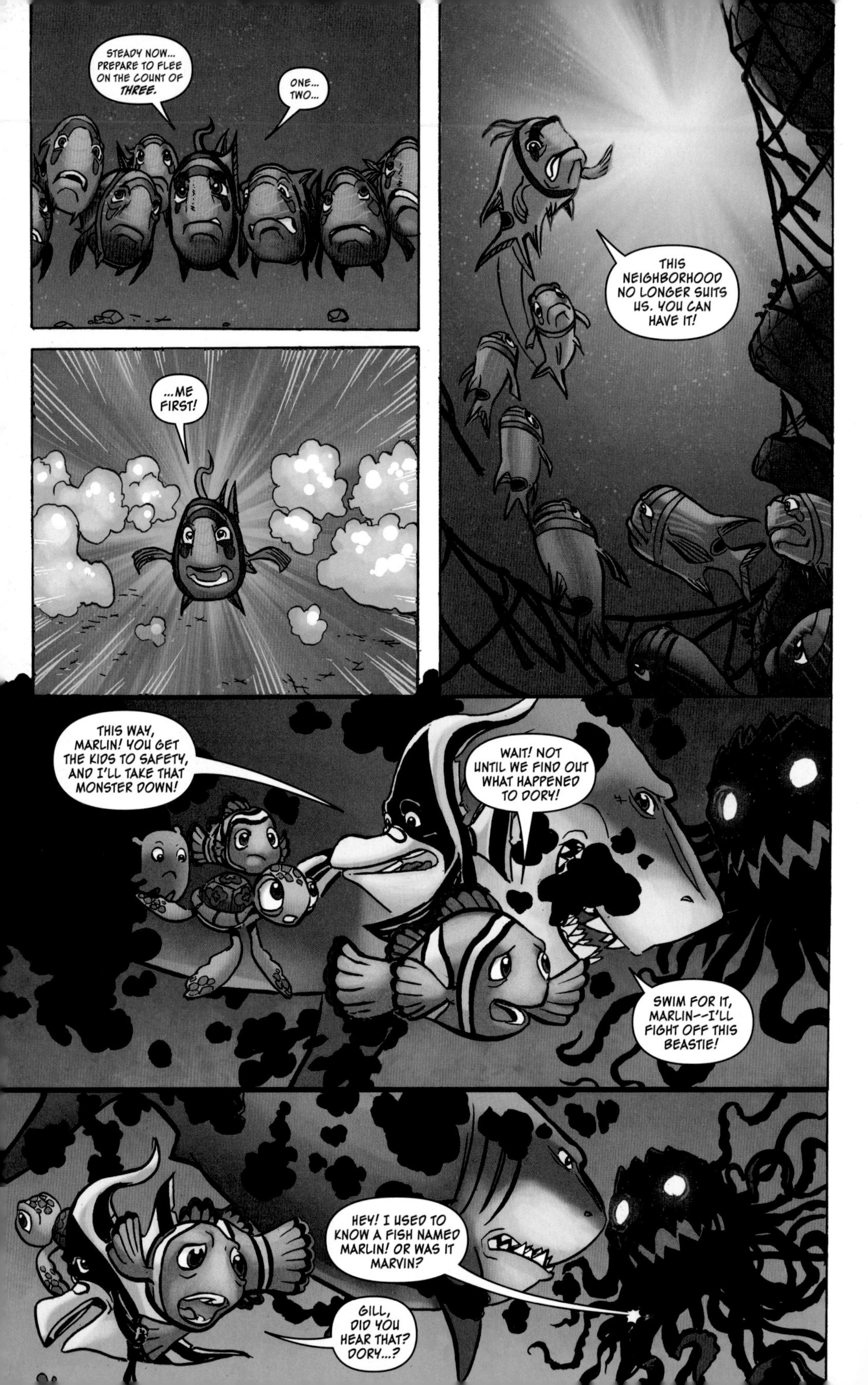
STEADY NOW... PREPARE TO FLEE ON THE COUNT OF *THREE.*
ONE... TWO...
...ME FIRST!
THIS NEIGHBORHOOD NO LONGER SUITS US. YOU CAN HAVE IT!
THIS WAY, MARLIN! YOU GET THE KIDS TO SAFETY, AND I'LL TAKE THAT MONSTER DOWN!
WAIT! NOT UNTIL WE FIND OUT WHAT HAPPENED TO DORY!
SWIM FOR IT, MARLIN--I'LL FIGHT OFF THIS BEASTIE!
HEY! I USED TO KNOW A FISH NAMED MARLIN! OR WAS IT MARVIN?
GILL, DID YOU HEAR THAT? DORY...?

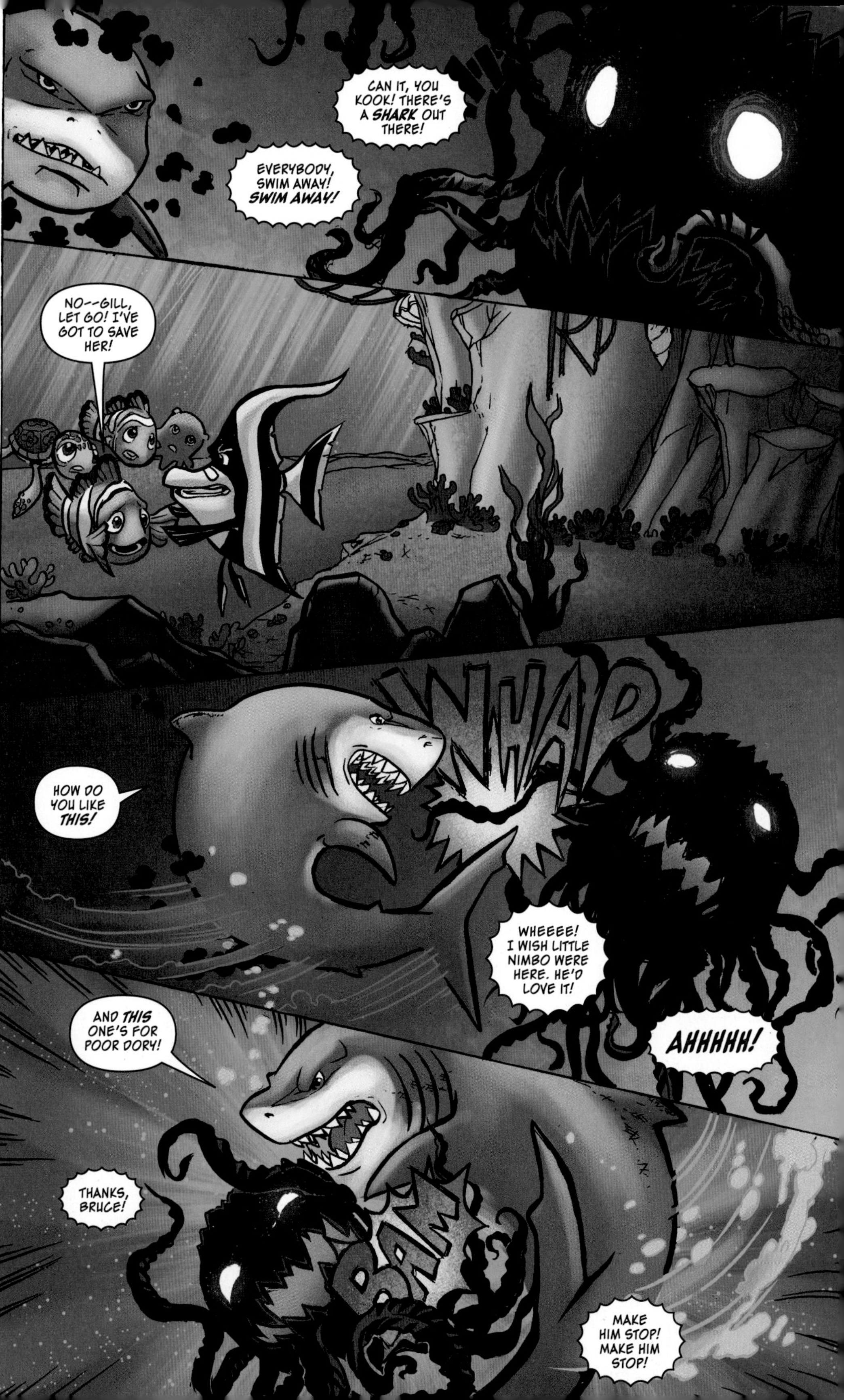
CAN IT, YOU KOOK! THERE'S A SHARK OUT THERE!
EVERYBODY, SWIM AWAY! SWIM AWAY!
NO--GILL, LET GO! I'VE GOT TO SAVE HER!
WHAP
HOW DO YOU LIKE THIS!
WHEEEE! I WISH LITTLE NIMBO WERE HERE. HE'D LOVE IT!
AND THIS ONE'S FOR POOR DORY!
AHHHHH!
THANKS, BRUCE!
BAM
MAKE HIM STOP! MAKE HIM STOP!

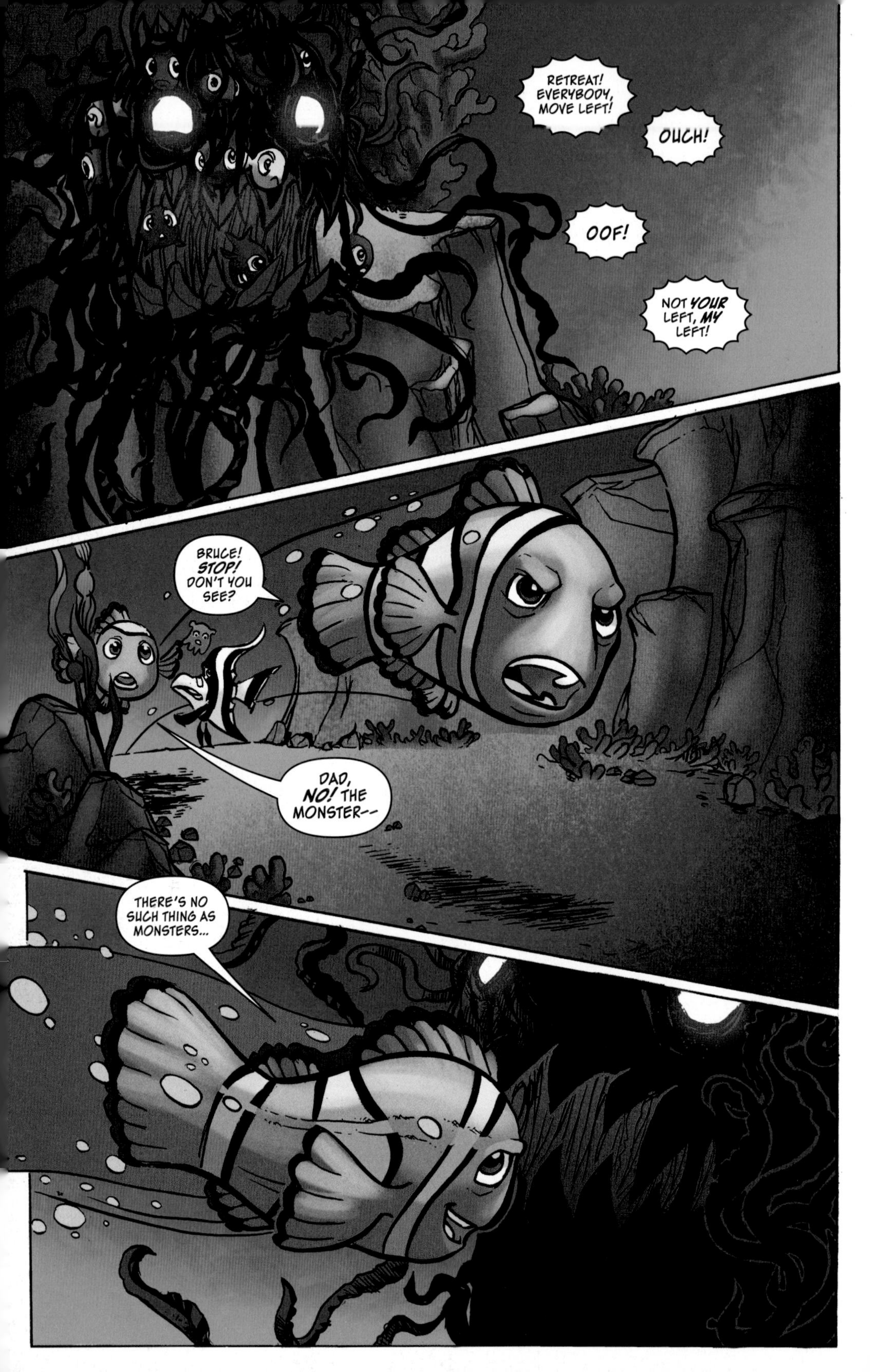
RETREAT! EVERYBODY, MOVE LEFT!
OUCH!
OOF!
NOT YOUR LEFT, MY LEFT!
BRUCE! STOP! DON'T YOU SEE?
DAD, NO! THE MONSTER--
THERE'S NO SUCH THING AS MONSTERS...

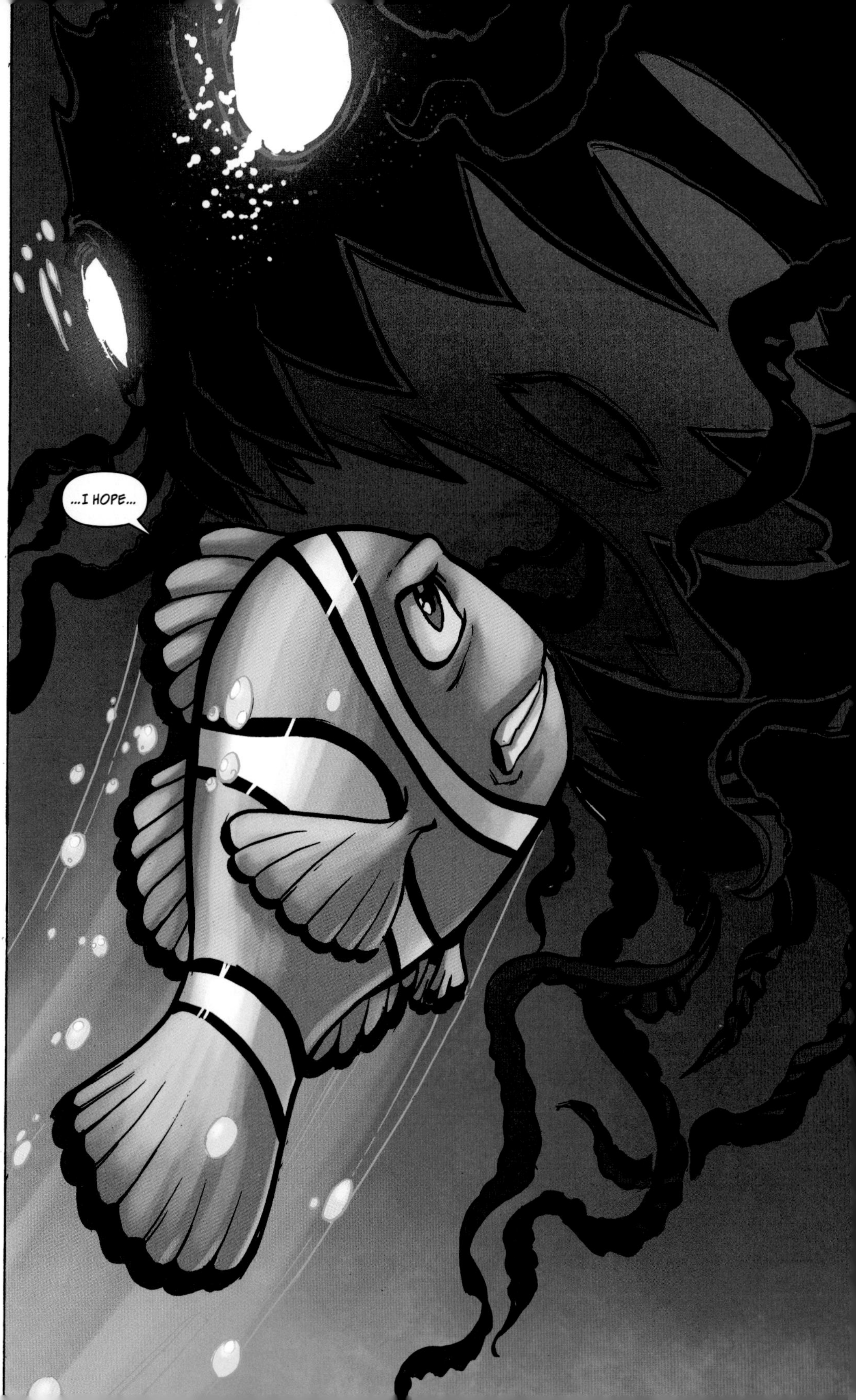
...I HOPE...

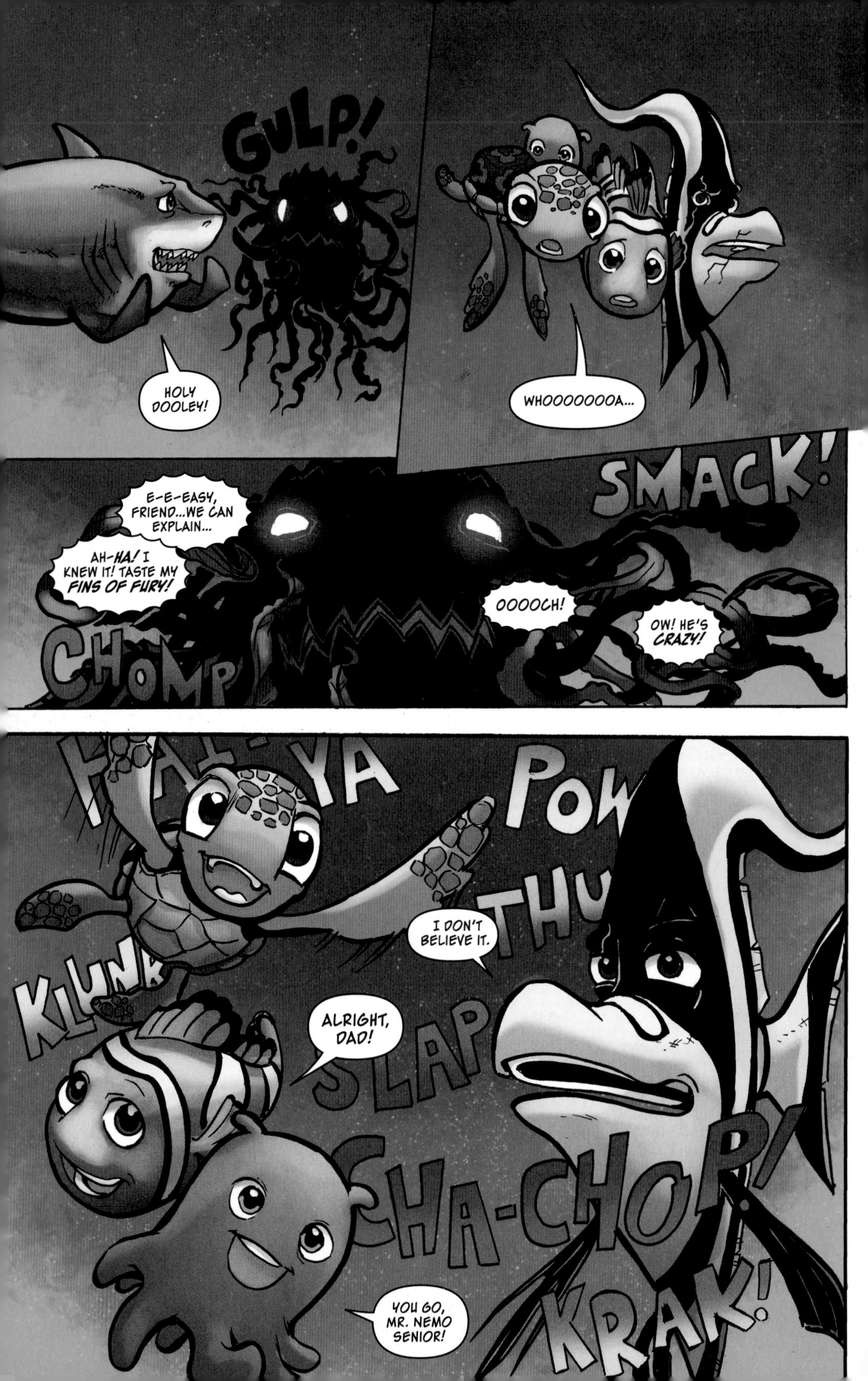
GULP!
HOLY DOOLEY!
WHOOOOOOOA...
SMACK!
E-E-EASY, FRIEND...WE CAN EXPLAIN...
AH-HA! I KNEW IT! TASTE MY FINS OF FURY!
OOOOCH!
OW! HE'S CRAZY!
CHOMP
YA
POW
THU
I DON'T BELIEVE IT.
KLUNK
ALRIGHT, DAD!
SLAP
CHA-CHOP!
YOU GO, MR. NEMO SENIOR!
KRAK!

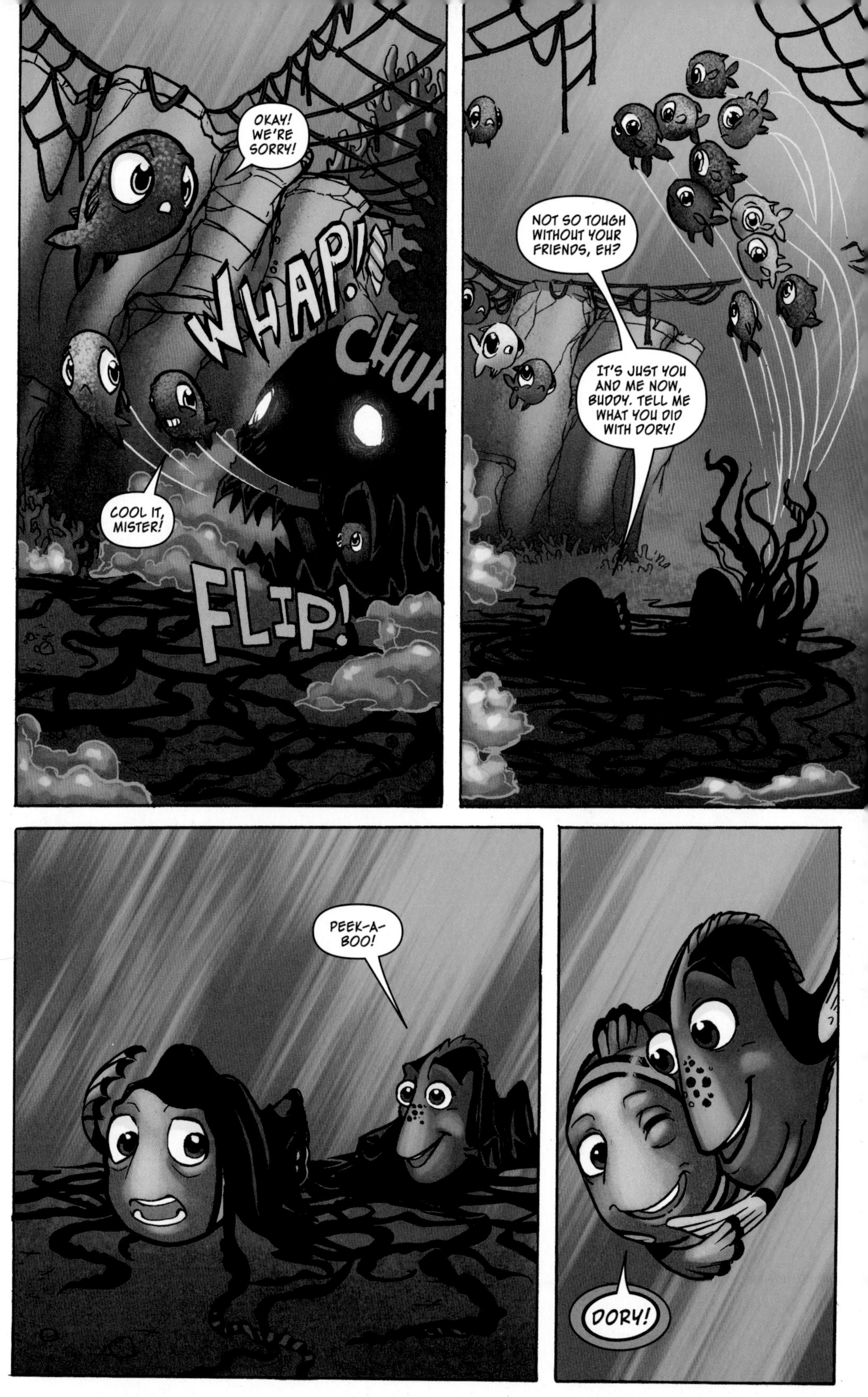
OKAY! WE'RE SORRY!
WHAP!
CHUK
COOL IT, MISTER!
FLIP!
NOT SO TOUGH WITHOUT YOUR FRIENDS, EH?
IT'S JUST YOU AND ME NOW, BUDDY. TELL ME WHAT YOU DID WITH DORY!
PEEK-A-BOO!
DORY!

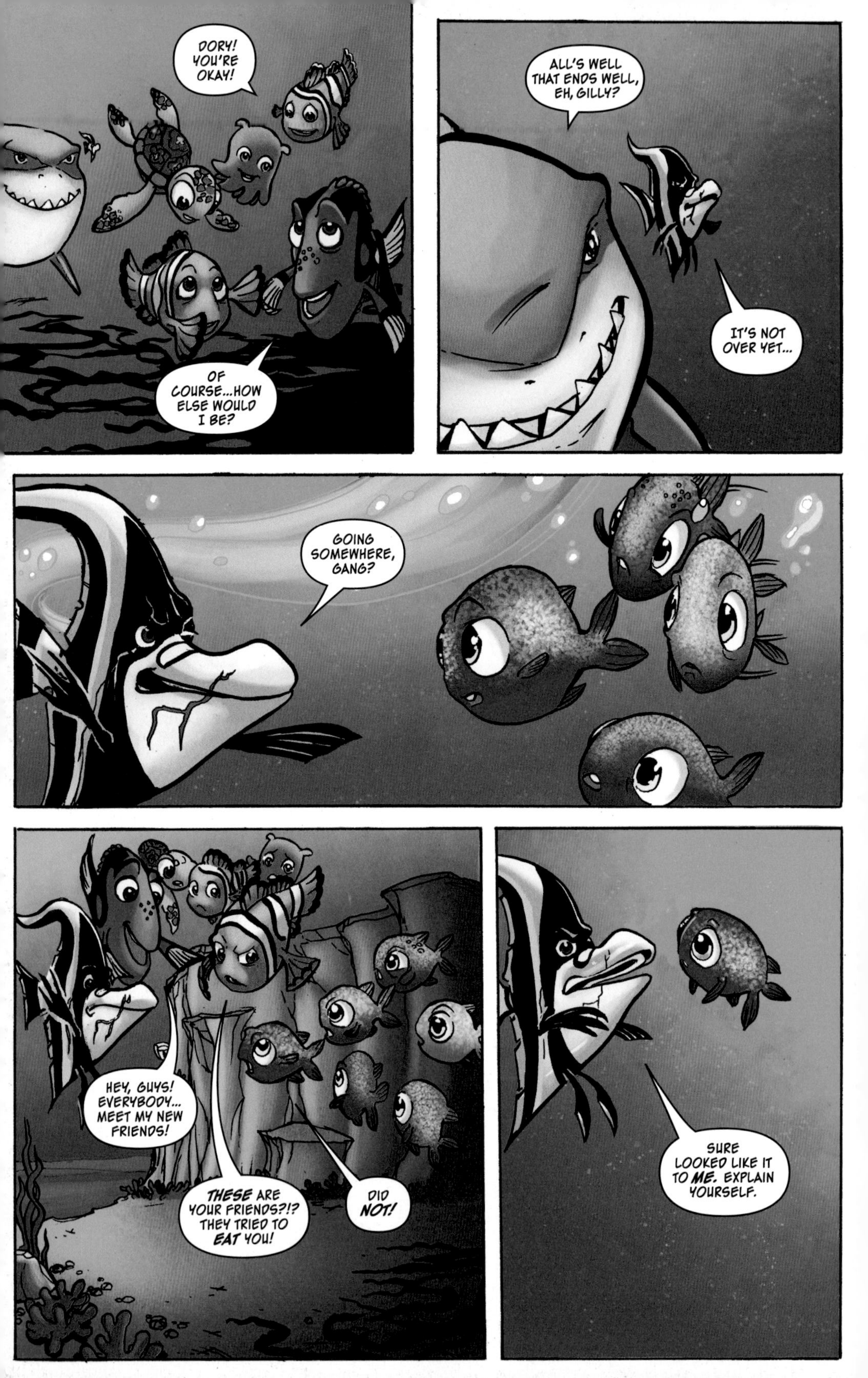
DORY! YOU'RE OKAY!
OF COURSE...HOW ELSE WOULD I BE?
ALL'S WELL THAT ENDS WELL, EH, GILLY?
IT'S NOT OVER YET...
GOING SOMEWHERE, GANG?
HEY, GUYS! EVERYBODY... MEET MY NEW FRIENDS!
THESE ARE YOUR FRIENDS?!? THEY TRIED TO EAT YOU!
DID NOT!
SURE LOOKED LIKE IT TO ME. EXPLAIN YOURSELF.

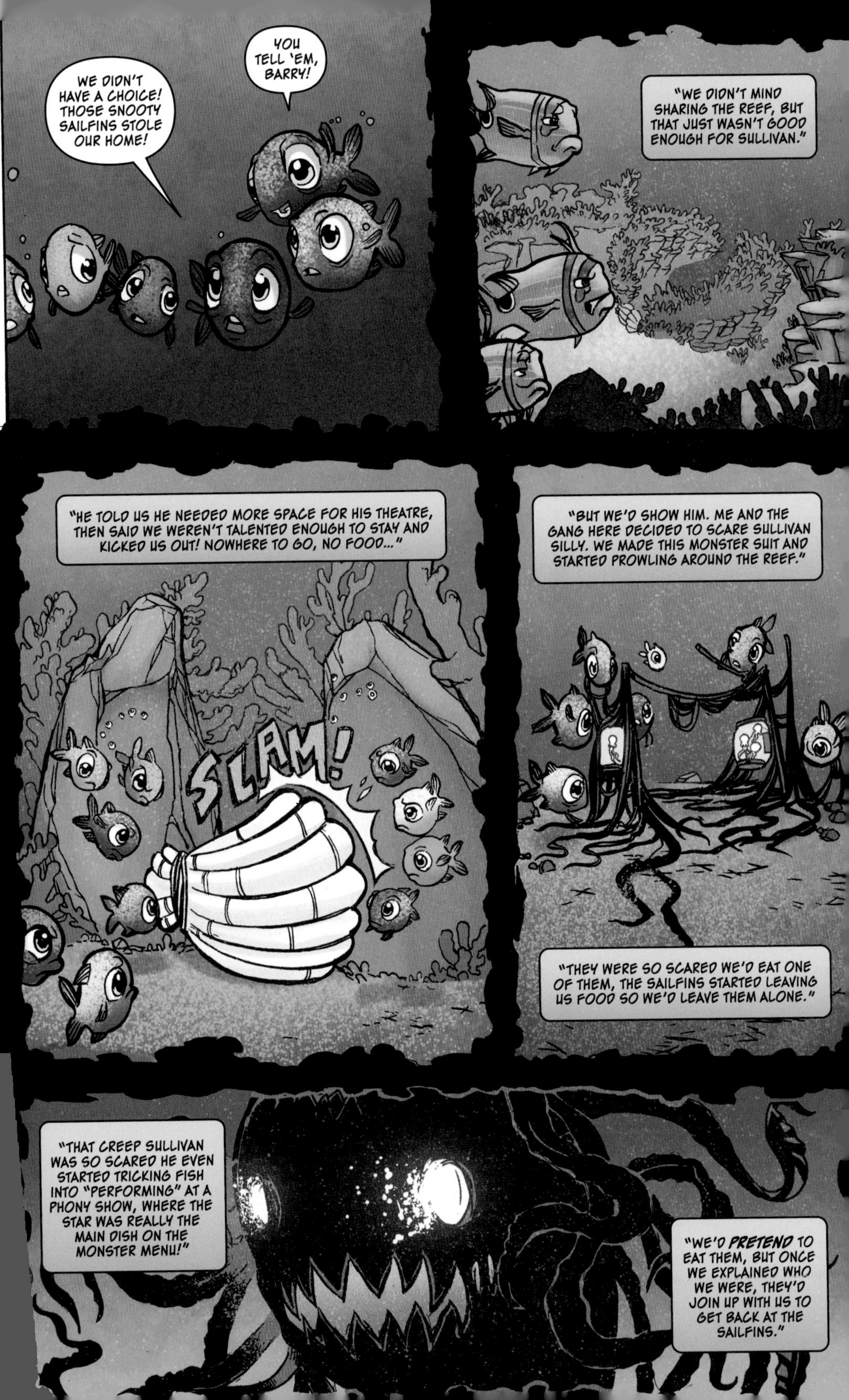
WE DIDN'T HAVE A CHOICE! THOSE SNOOTY SAILFINS STOLE OUR HOME!
YOU TELL 'EM, BARRY!
"WE DIDN'T MIND SHARING THE REEF, BUT THAT JUST WASN'T GOOD ENOUGH FOR SULLIVAN."
"HE TOLD US HE NEEDED MORE SPACE FOR HIS THEATRE, THEN SAID WE WEREN'T TALENTED ENOUGH TO STAY AND KICKED US OUT! NOWHERE TO GO, NO FOOD..."
SLAM!
"BUT WE'D SHOW HIM. ME AND THE GANG HERE DECIDED TO SCARE SULLIVAN SILLY. WE MADE THIS MONSTER SUIT AND STARTED PROWLING AROUND THE REEF."
"THEY WERE SO SCARED WE'D EAT ONE OF THEM, THE SAILFINS STARTED LEAVING US FOOD SO WE'D LEAVE THEM ALONE."
"THAT CREEP SULLIVAN WAS SO SCARED HE EVEN STARTED TRICKING FISH INTO "PERFORMING" AT A PHONY SHOW, WHERE THE STAR WAS REALLY THE MAIN DISH ON THE MONSTER MENU!"
"WE'D **PRETEND** TO EAT THEM, BUT ONCE WE EXPLAINED WHO WE WERE, THEY'D JOIN UP WITH US TO GET BACK AT THE SAILFINS."

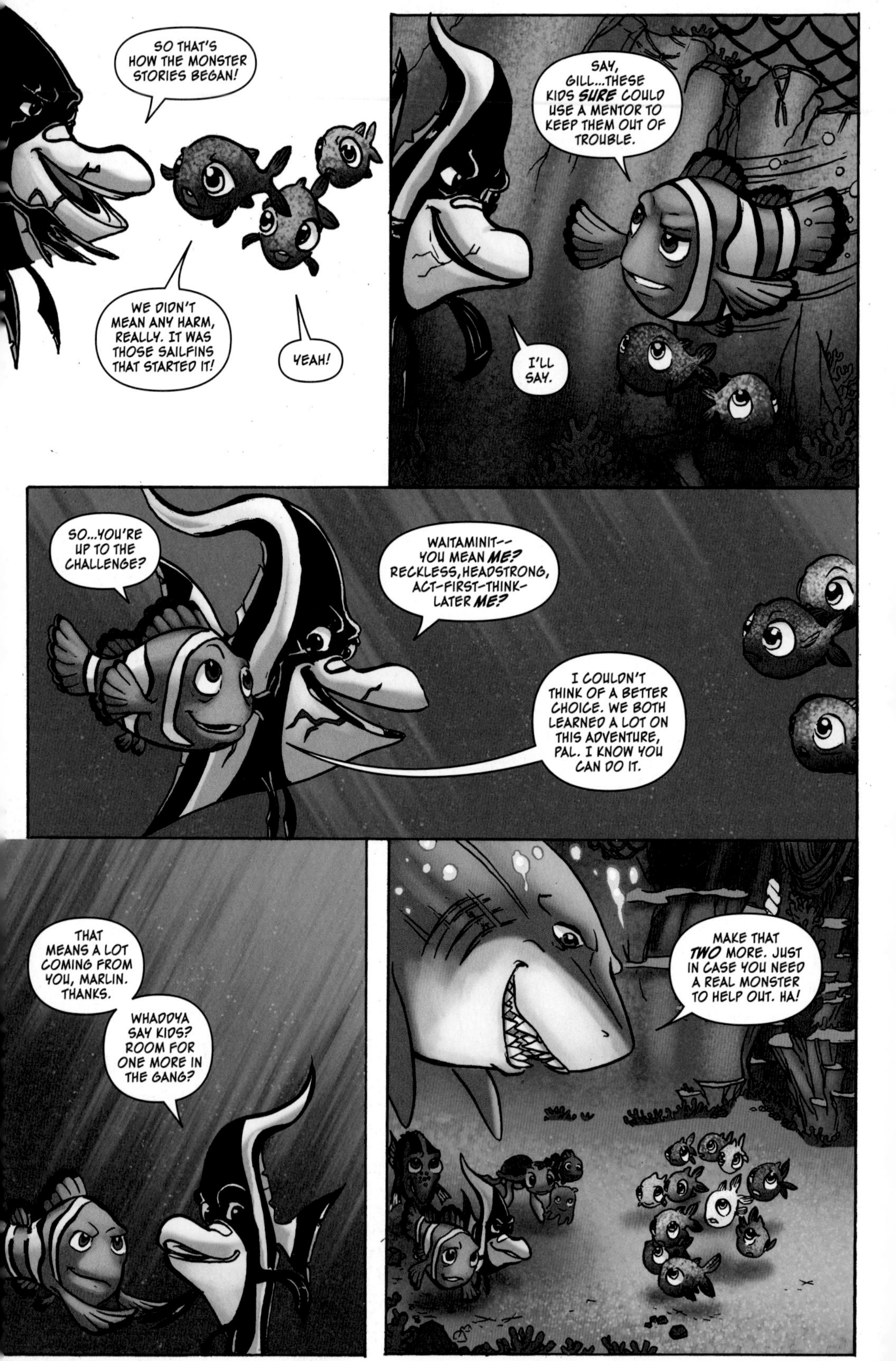
SO THAT'S HOW THE MONSTER STORIES BEGAN!
WE DIDN'T MEAN ANY HARM, REALLY. IT WAS THOSE SAILFINS THAT STARTED IT!
YEAH!
SAY, GILL...THESE KIDS SURE COULD USE A MENTOR TO KEEP THEM OUT OF TROUBLE.
I'LL SAY.
SO...YOU'RE UP TO THE CHALLENGE?
WAITAMINIT-- YOU MEAN ME? RECKLESS, HEADSTRONG, ACT-FIRST-THINK-LATER ME?
I COULDN'T THINK OF A BETTER CHOICE. WE BOTH LEARNED A LOT ON THIS ADVENTURE, PAL. I KNOW YOU CAN DO IT.
THAT MEANS A LOT COMING FROM YOU, MARLIN. THANKS.
WHADDYA SAY KIDS? ROOM FOR ONE MORE IN THE GANG?
MAKE THAT TWO MORE. JUST IN CASE YOU NEED A REAL MONSTER TO HELP OUT. HA!

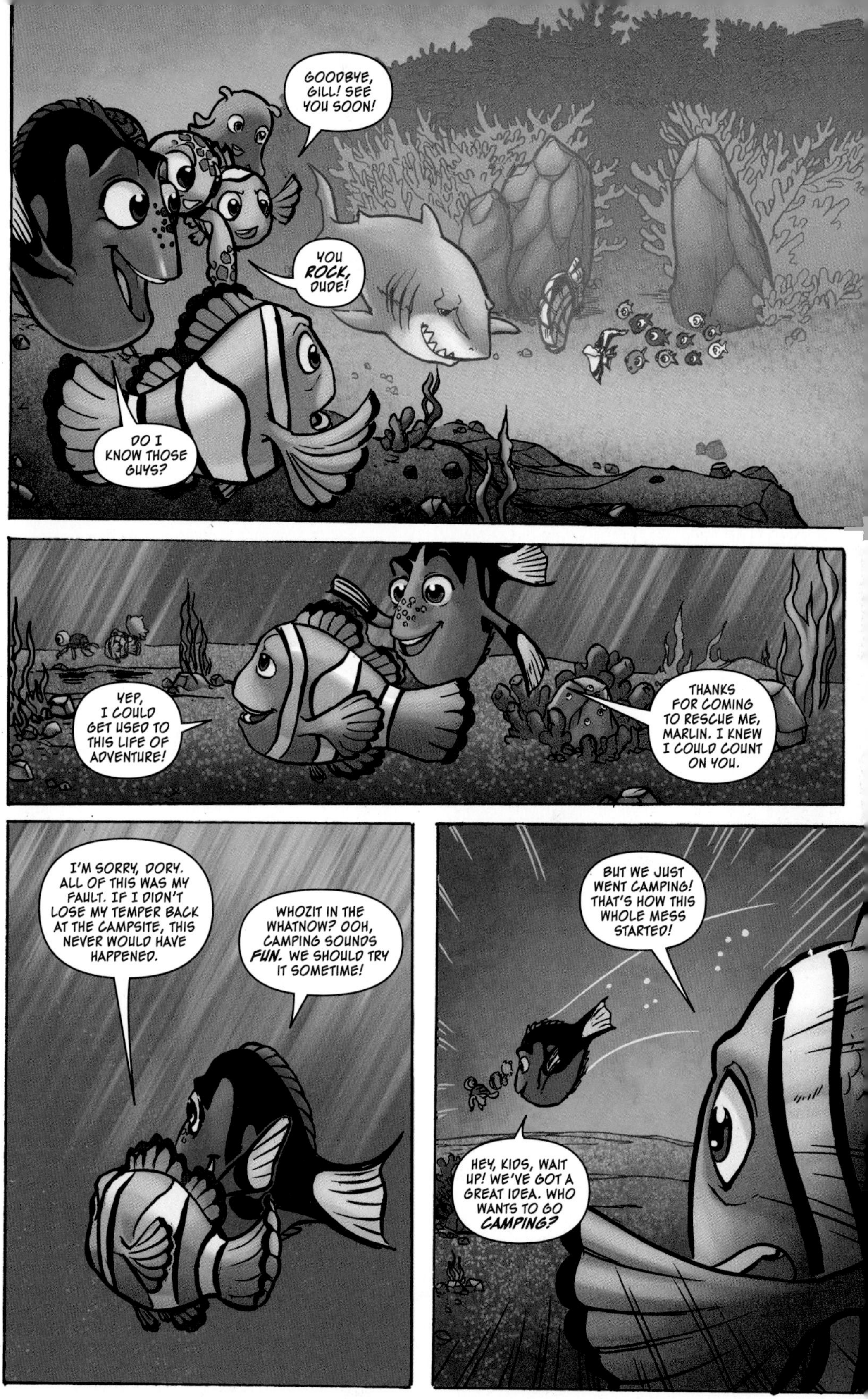
GOODBYE, GILL! SEE YOU SOON!
YOU ROCK, DUDE!
DO I KNOW THOSE GUYS?
YEP, I COULD GET USED TO THIS LIFE OF ADVENTURE!
THANKS FOR COMING TO RESCUE ME, MARLIN. I KNEW I COULD COUNT ON YOU.
I'M SORRY, DORY. ALL OF THIS WAS MY FAULT. IF I DIDN'T LOSE MY TEMPER BACK AT THE CAMPSITE, THIS NEVER WOULD HAVE HAPPENED.
WHOZIT IN THE WHATNOW? OOH, CAMPING SOUNDS FUN. WE SHOULD TRY IT SOMETIME!
BUT WE JUST WENT CAMPING! THAT'S HOW THIS WHOLE MESS STARTED!
HEY, KIDS, WAIT UP! WE'VE GOT A GREAT IDEA. WHO WANTS TO GO CAMPING?

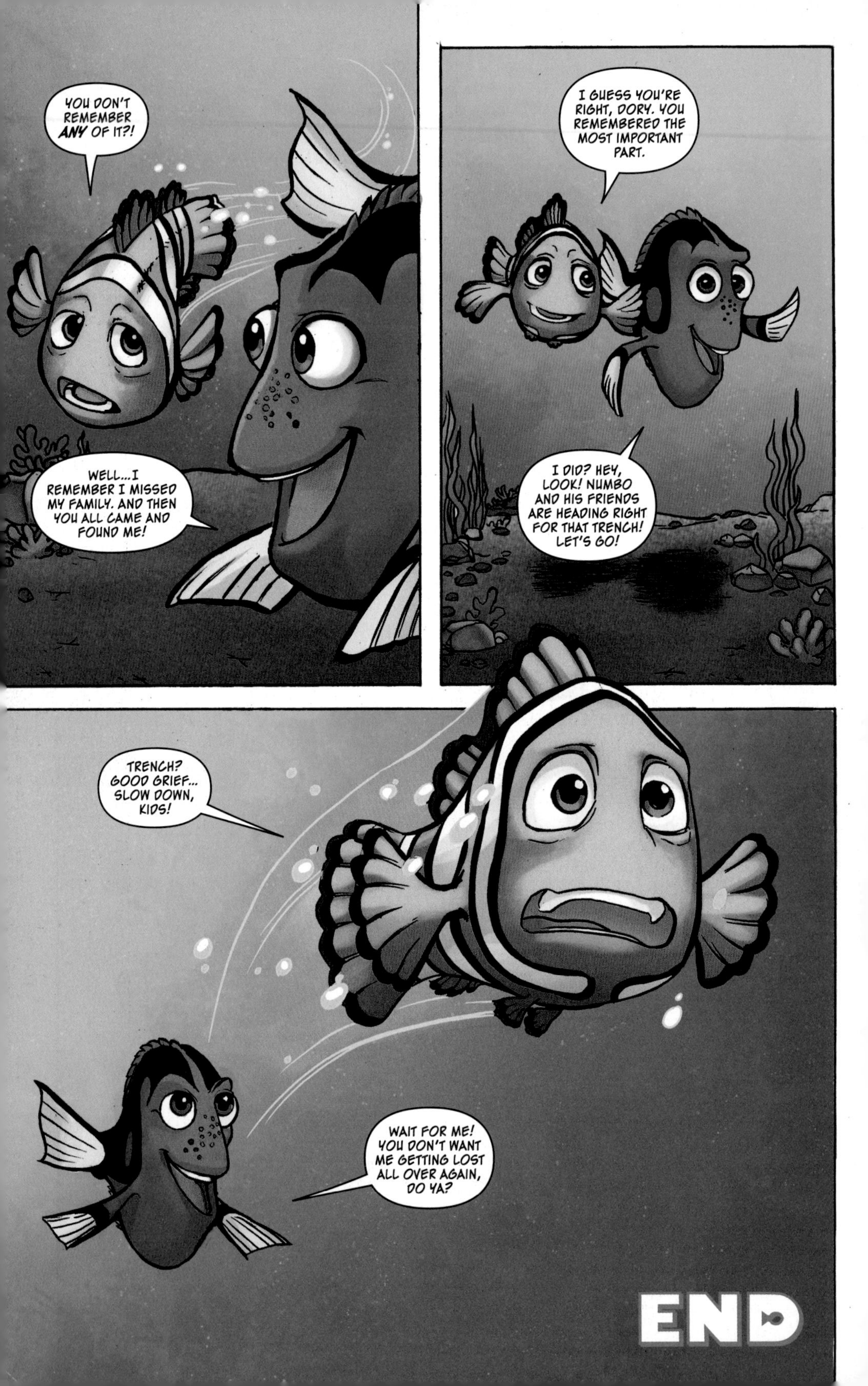
YOU DON'T REMEMBER ANY OF IT?!
WELL...I REMEMBER I MISSED MY FAMILY. AND THEN YOU ALL CAME AND FOUND ME!
I GUESS YOU'RE RIGHT, DORY. YOU REMEMBERED THE MOST IMPORTANT PART.
I DID? HEY, LOOK! NUMBO AND HIS FRIENDS ARE HEADING RIGHT FOR THAT TRENCH! LET'S GO!
TRENCH? GOOD GRIEF... SLOW DOWN, KIDS!
WAIT FOR ME! YOU DON'T WANT ME GETTING LOST ALL OVER AGAIN, DO YA?
END

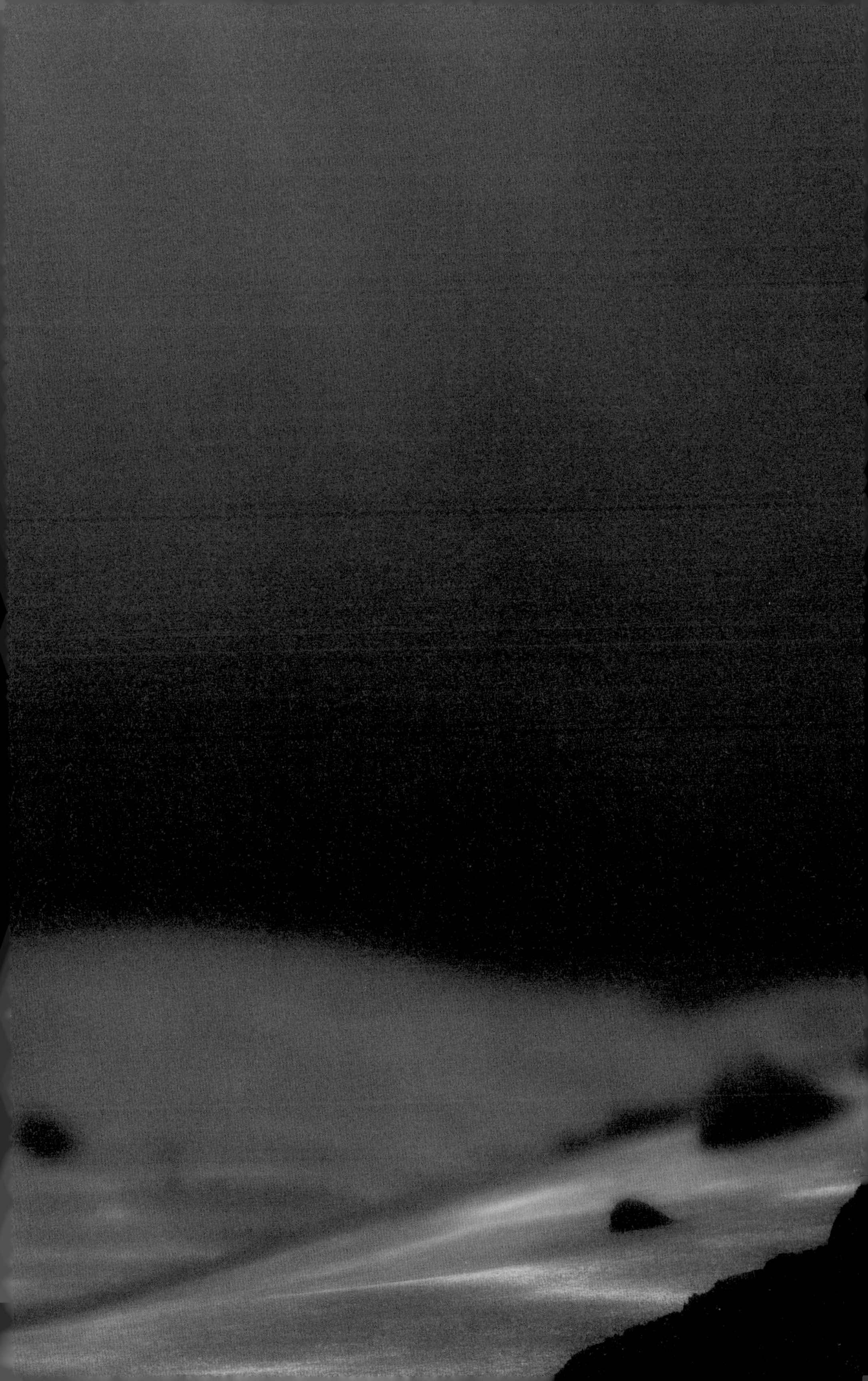

# LOOKING FOR MORE FUN WITH YOUR FAVORITE CHARACTERS?

CHECK OUT THESE EXCLUSIVE PREVIEWS OF OTHER GREAT TITLES NOW AVAILABLE FROM

BOOM KIDS!

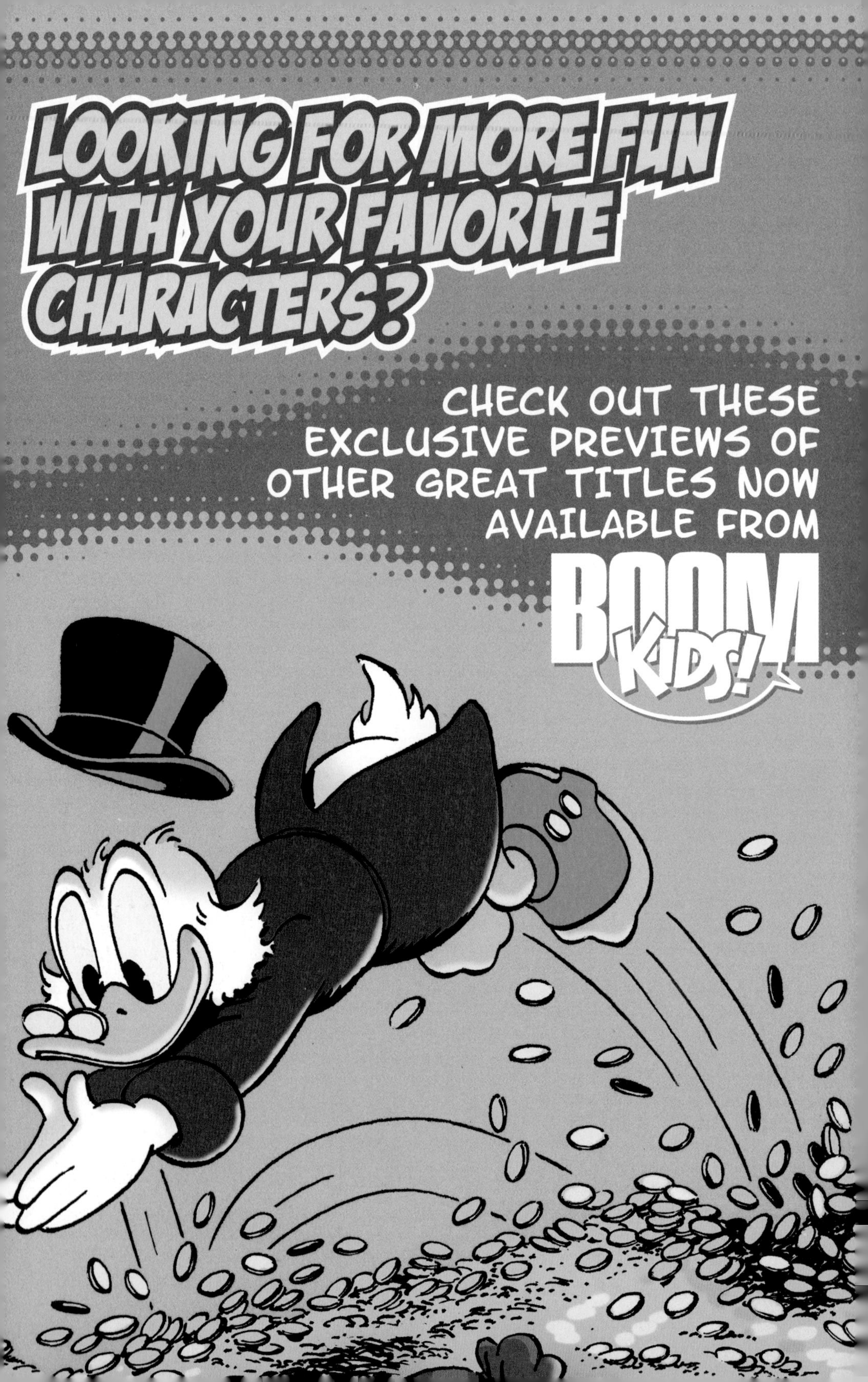

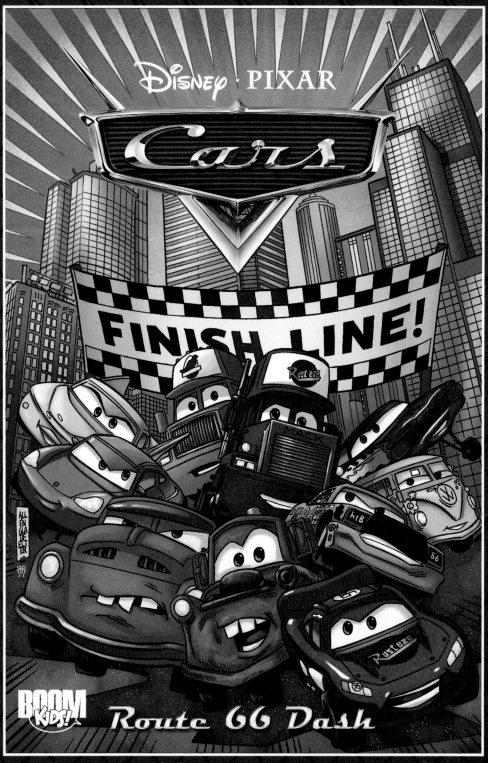

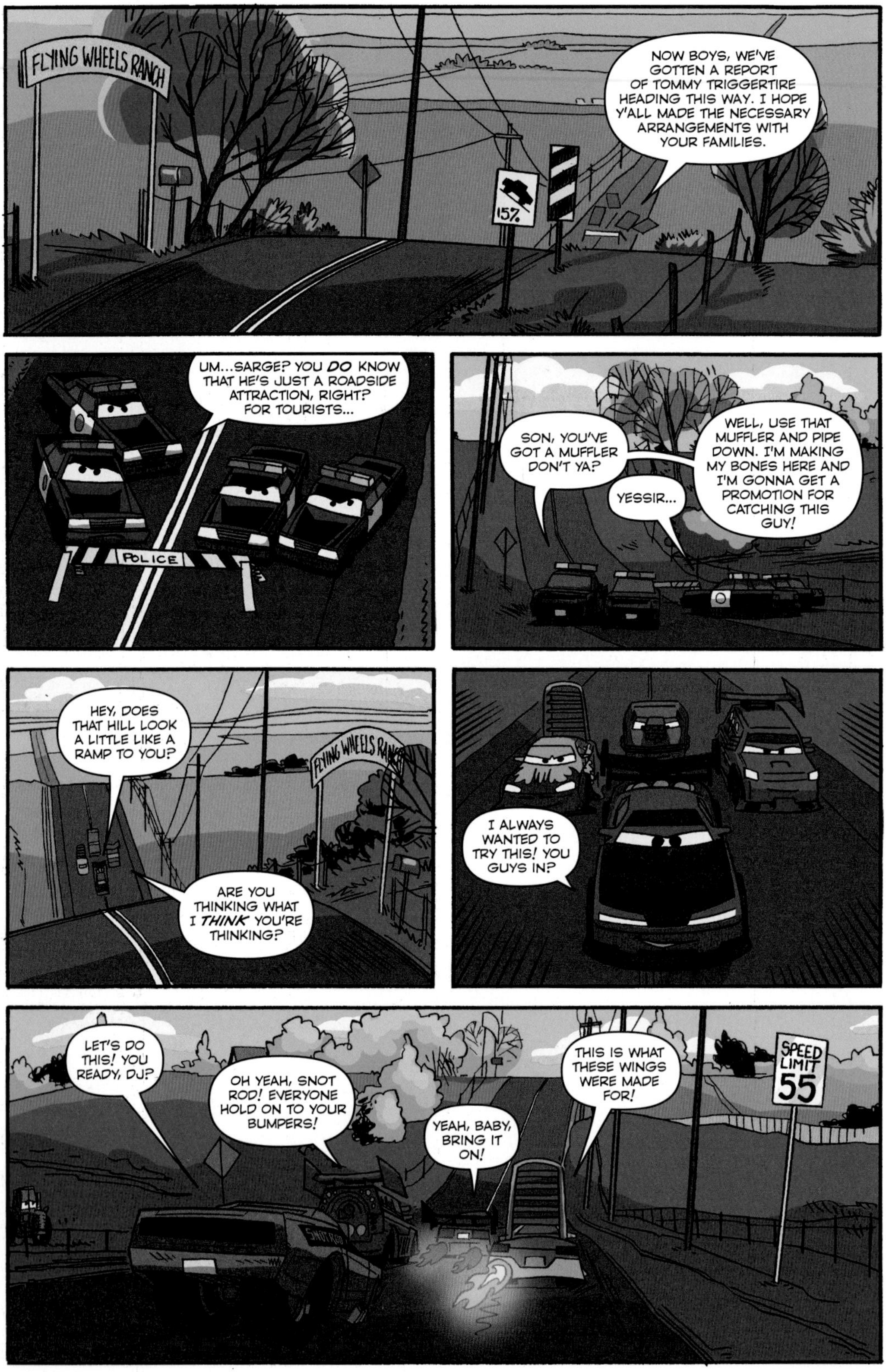
FLYING WHEELS RANCH
15%
NOW BOYS, WE'VE GOTTEN A REPORT OF TOMMY TRIGGERTIRE HEADING THIS WAY. I HOPE Y'ALL MADE THE NECESSARY ARRANGEMENTS WITH YOUR FAMILIES.
UM...SARGE? YOU *DO* KNOW THAT HE'S JUST A ROADSIDE ATTRACTION, RIGHT? FOR TOURISTS...
POLICE
SON, YOU'VE GOT A MUFFLER DON'T YA?
YESSIR...
WELL, USE THAT MUFFLER AND PIPE DOWN. I'M MAKING MY BONES HERE AND I'M GONNA GET A PROMOTION FOR CATCHING THIS GUY!
HEY, DOES THAT HILL LOOK A LITTLE LIKE A RAMP TO YOU?
FLYING WHEELS RANCH
ARE YOU THINKING WHAT I *THINK* YOU'RE THINKING?
I ALWAYS WANTED TO TRY THIS! YOU GUYS IN?
LET'S DO THIS! YOU READY, DJ?
OH YEAH, SNOT ROD! EVERYONE HOLD ON TO YOUR BUMPERS!
YEAH, BABY, BRING IT ON!
THIS IS WHAT THESE WINGS WERE MADE FOR!
SPEED LIMIT 55

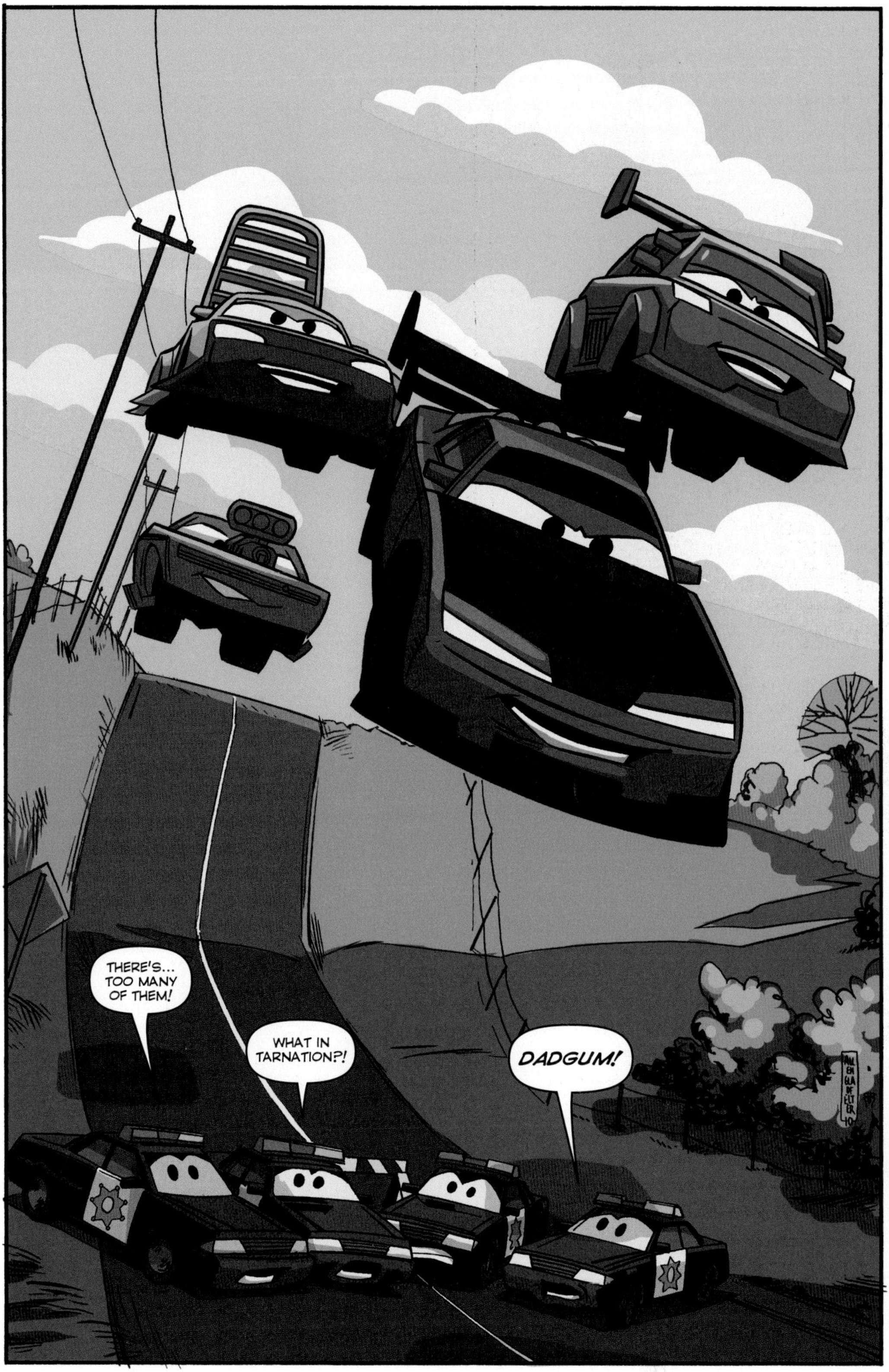
THERE'S... TOO MANY OF THEM!
WHAT IN TARNATION?!
DADGUM!

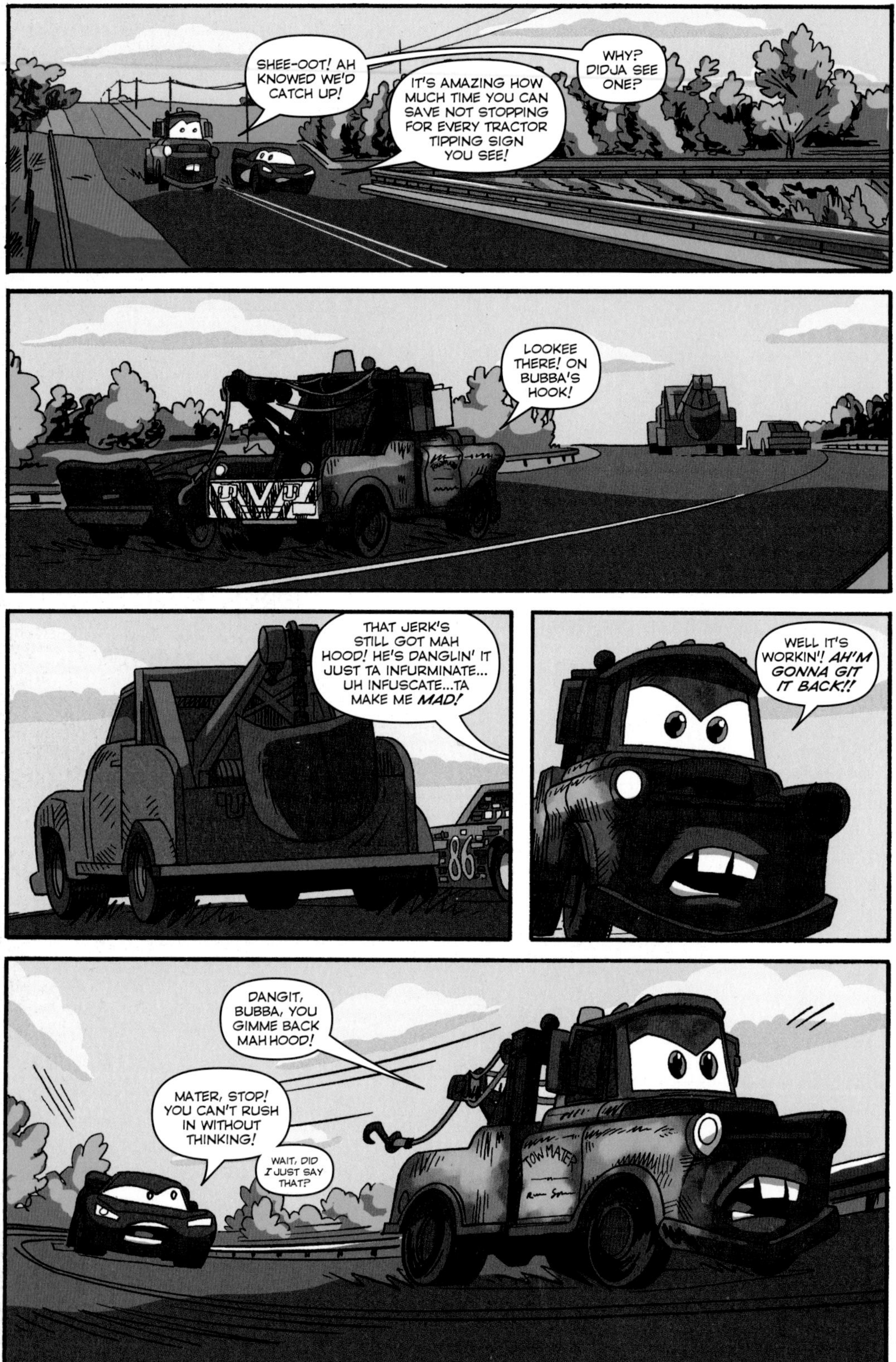
SHEE-OOT! AH KNOWED WE'D CATCH UP!
IT'S AMAZING HOW MUCH TIME YOU CAN SAVE NOT STOPPING FOR EVERY TRACTOR TIPPING SIGN YOU SEE!
WHY? DIDJA SEE ONE?
LOOKEE THERE! ON BUBBA'S HOOK!
THAT JERK'S STILL GOT MAH HOOD! HE'S DANGLIN' IT JUST TA INFURMINATE... UH INFUSCATE...TA MAKE ME MAD!
86
WELL IT'S WORKIN'! AH'M GONNA GIT IT BACK!!
DANGIT, BUBBA, YOU GIMME BACK MAH HOOD!
MATER, STOP! YOU CAN'T RUSH IN WITHOUT THINKING!
WAIT, DID I JUST SAY THAT?
TOW MATER

DISNEY · PIXAR

# WALL·E

## OUT THERE

A brand-new story set before the hit film! When a mysterious spaceship crash-lands on Earth, WALL•E makes a new friend...but can the adventurous pair triumph over the robot's tyrannical boss, BULL•E?

WALL•E: OUT THERE
DIAMOND CODE: MAY100900
SC $9.99 ISBN 9781608865680

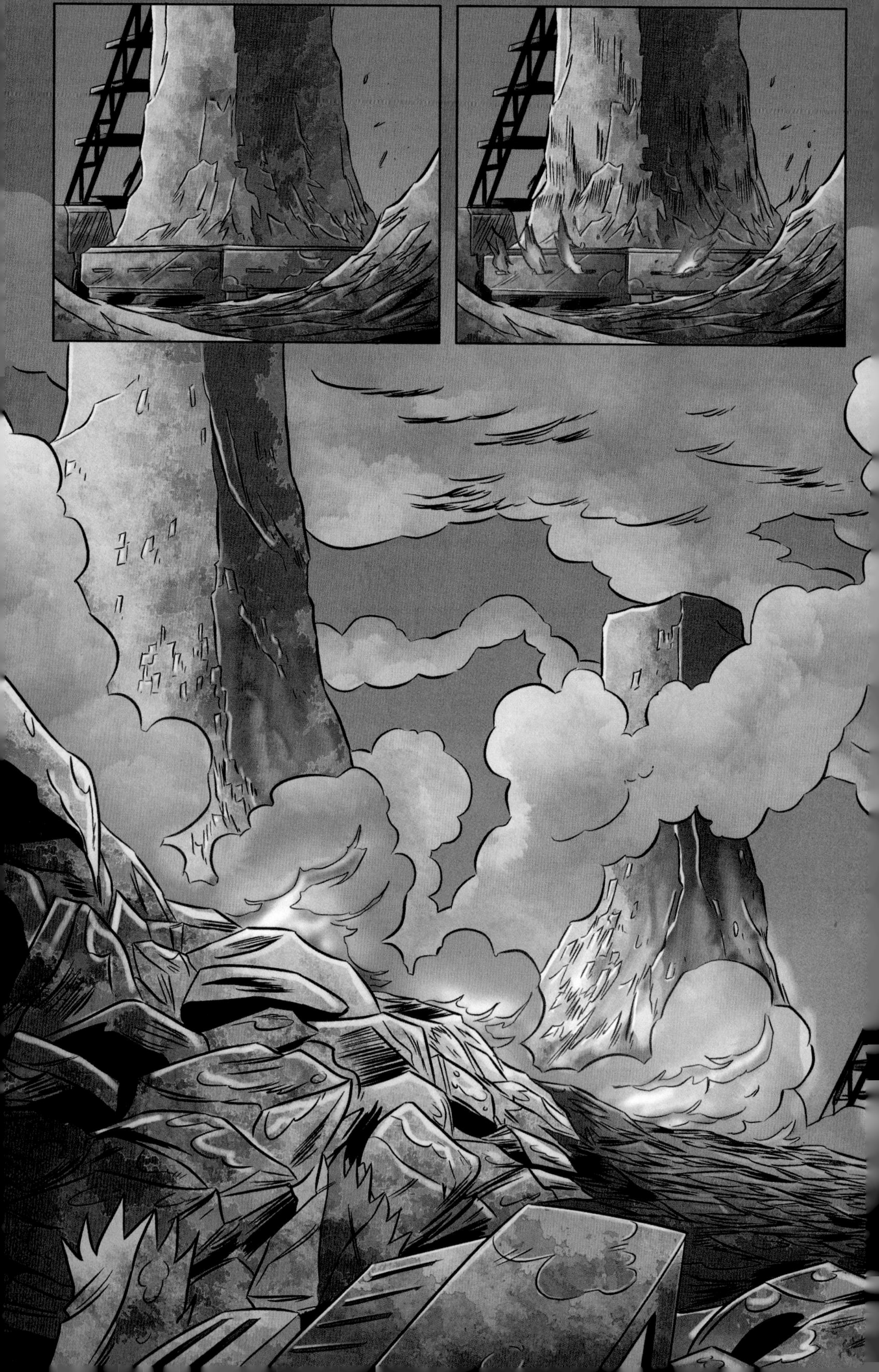

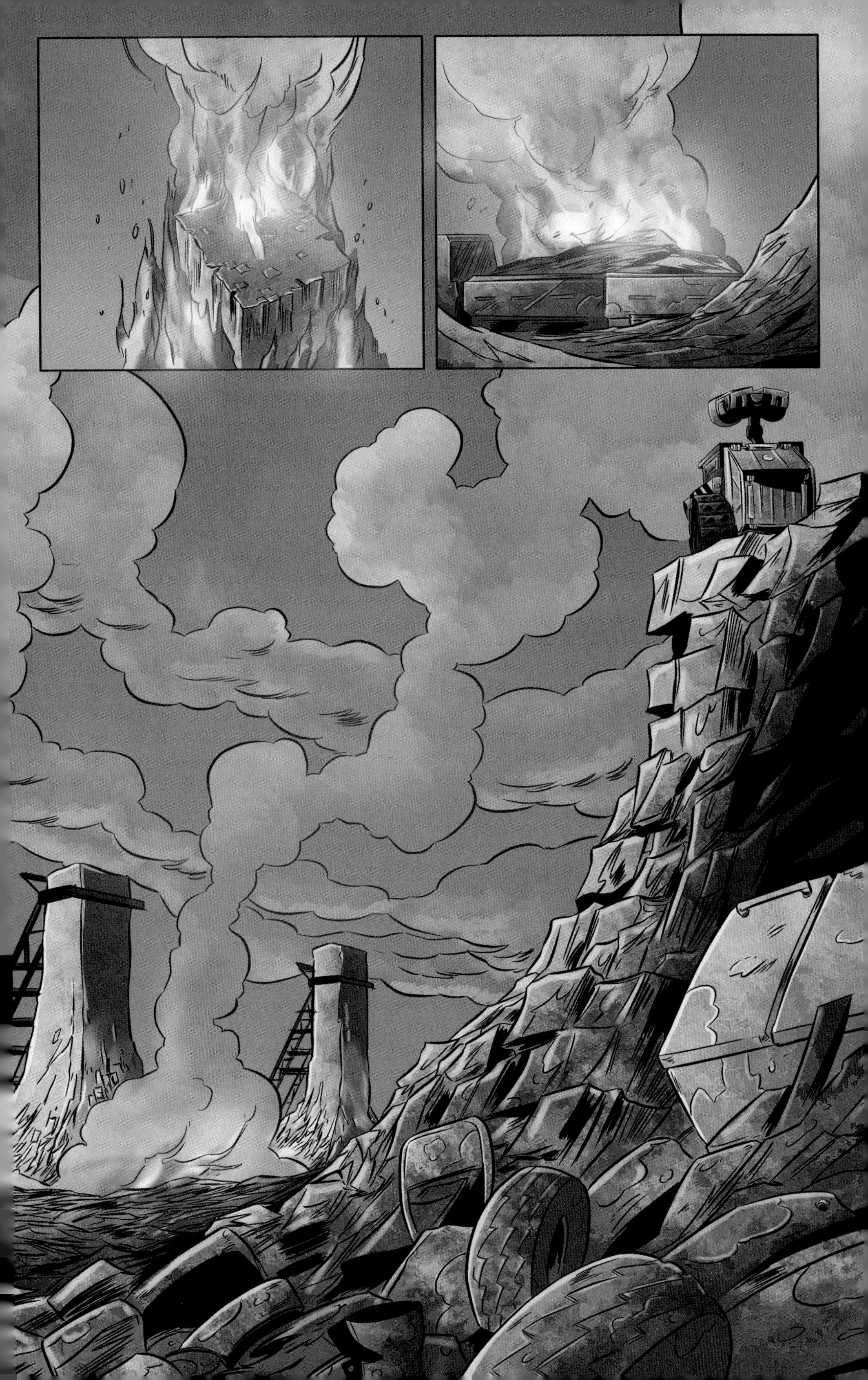

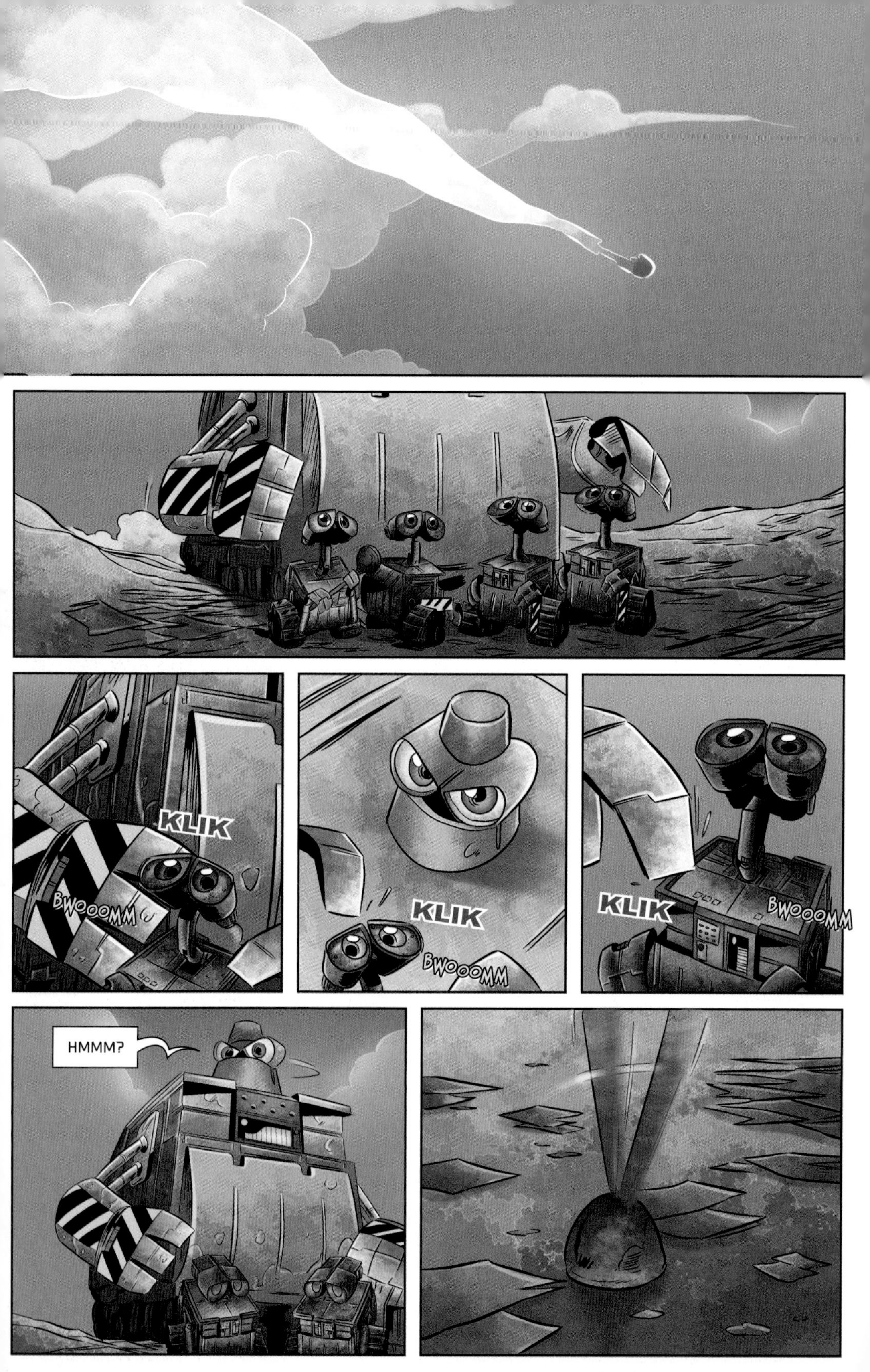
KLIK
BWOOOMM
KLIK
BWOOOMM
KLIK
BWOOOMM
HMMM?

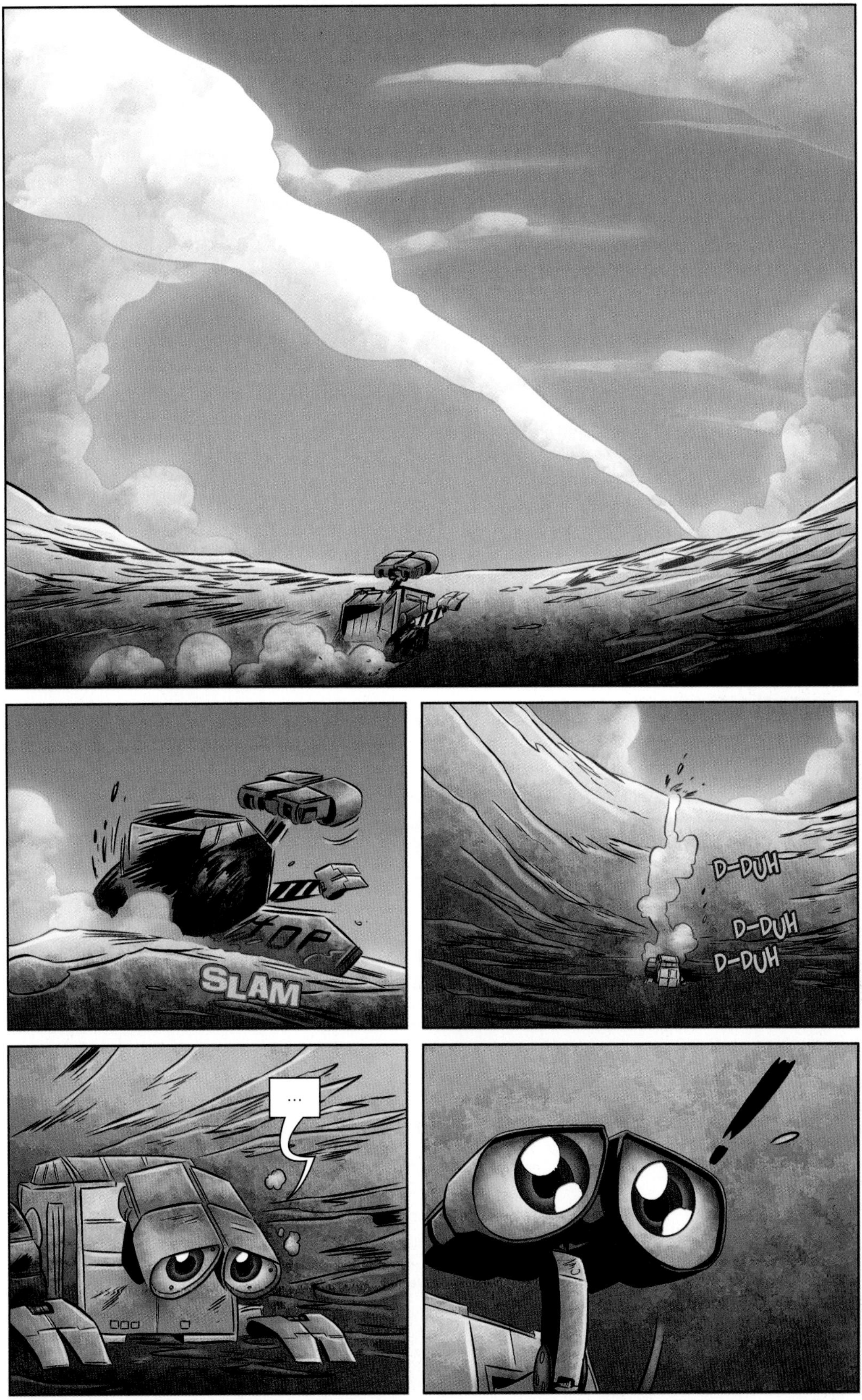
SLAM
D-DUH
D-DUH
D-DUH
...
!

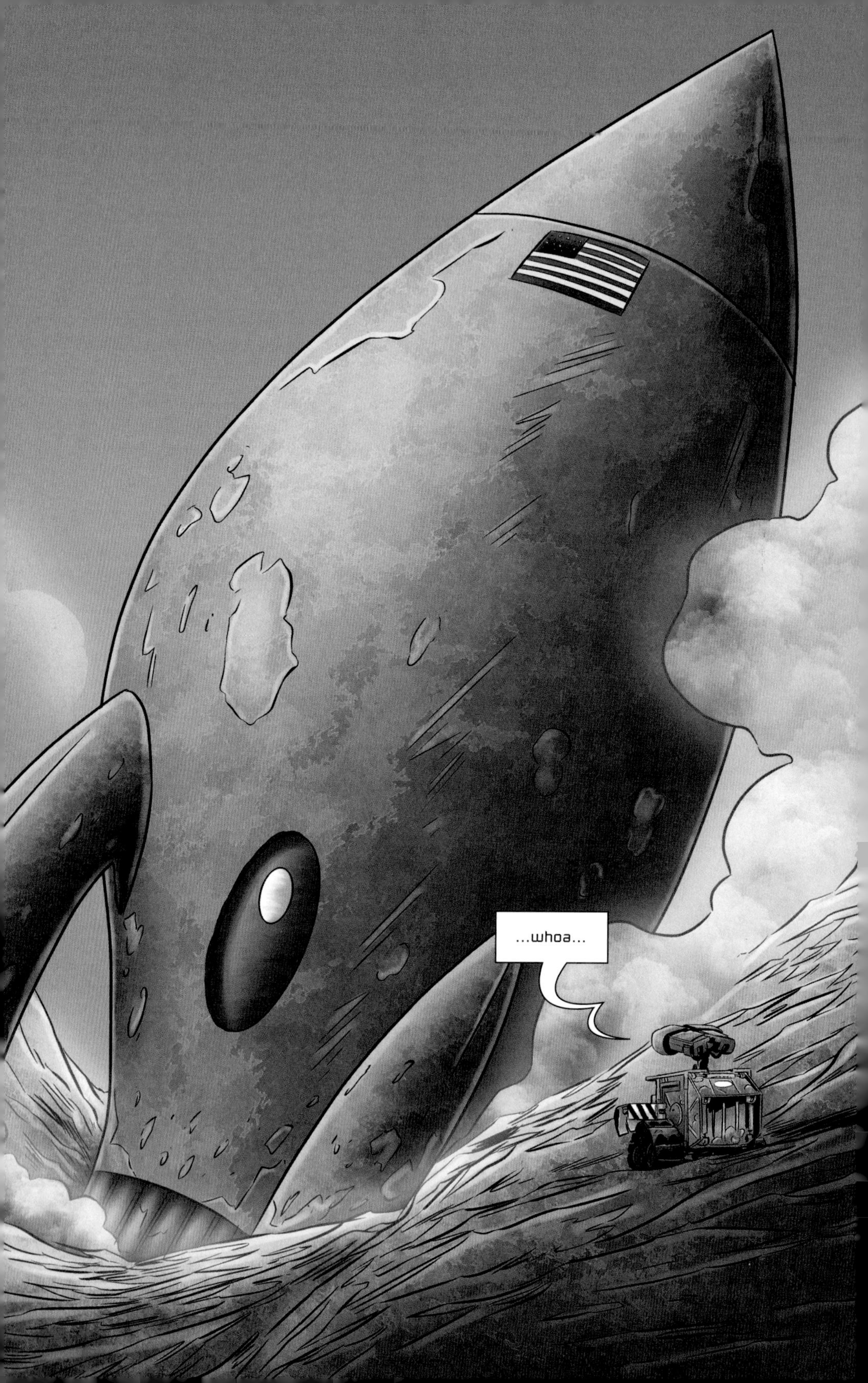
...whoa...

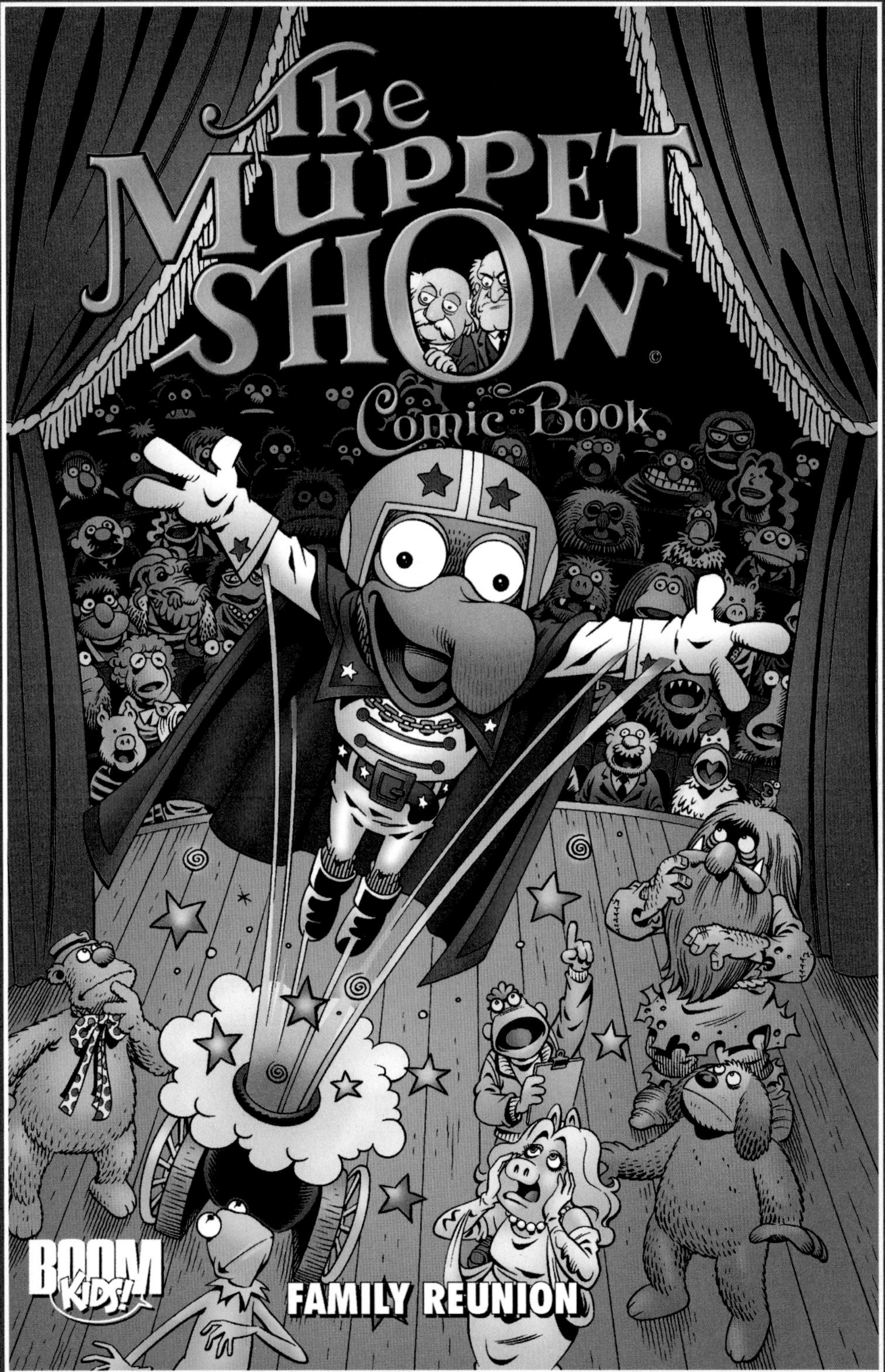

The MUPPET SHOW
©
Comic Book
BOOM KIDS!
FAMILY REUNION

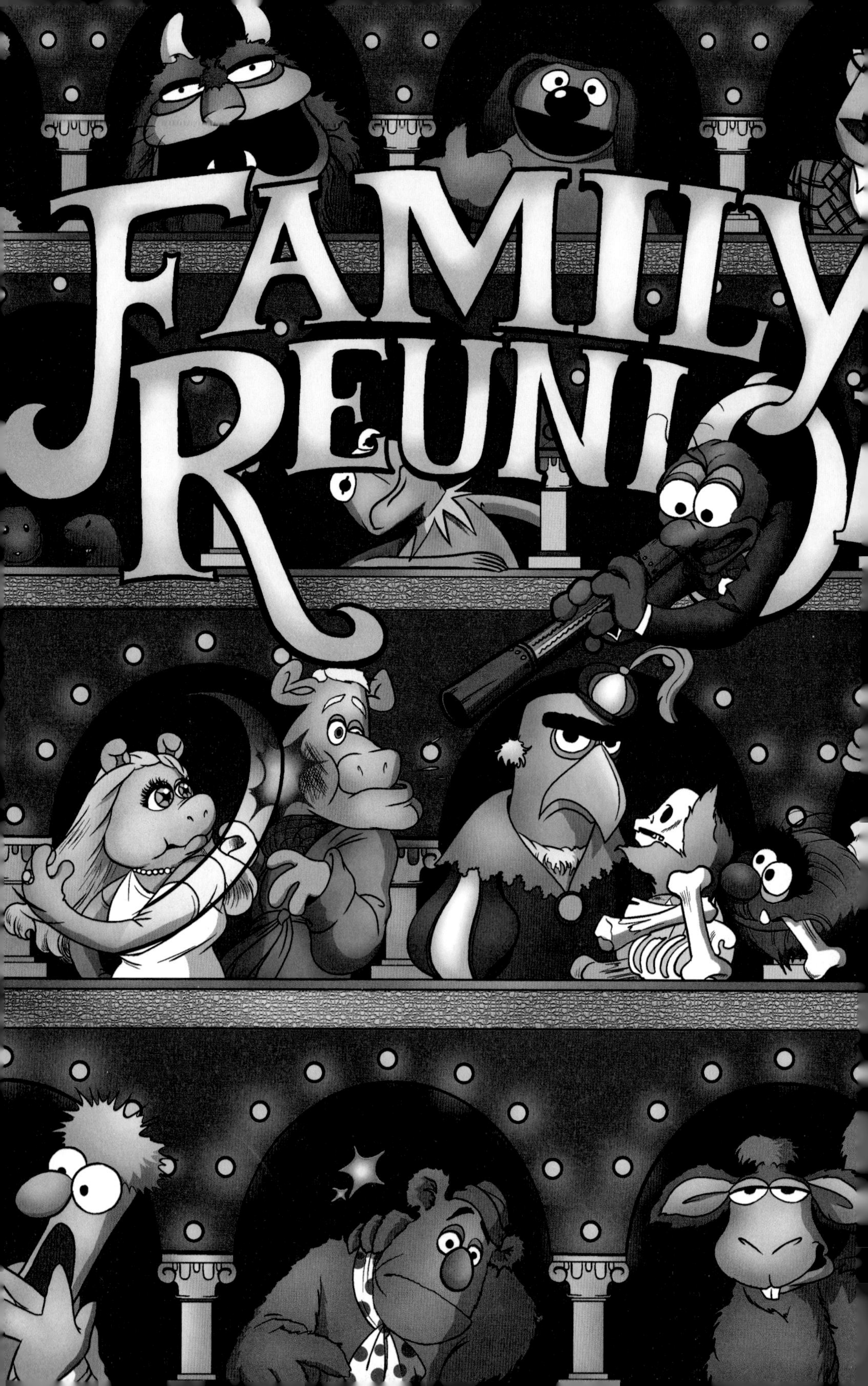
FAMILY
REUNI

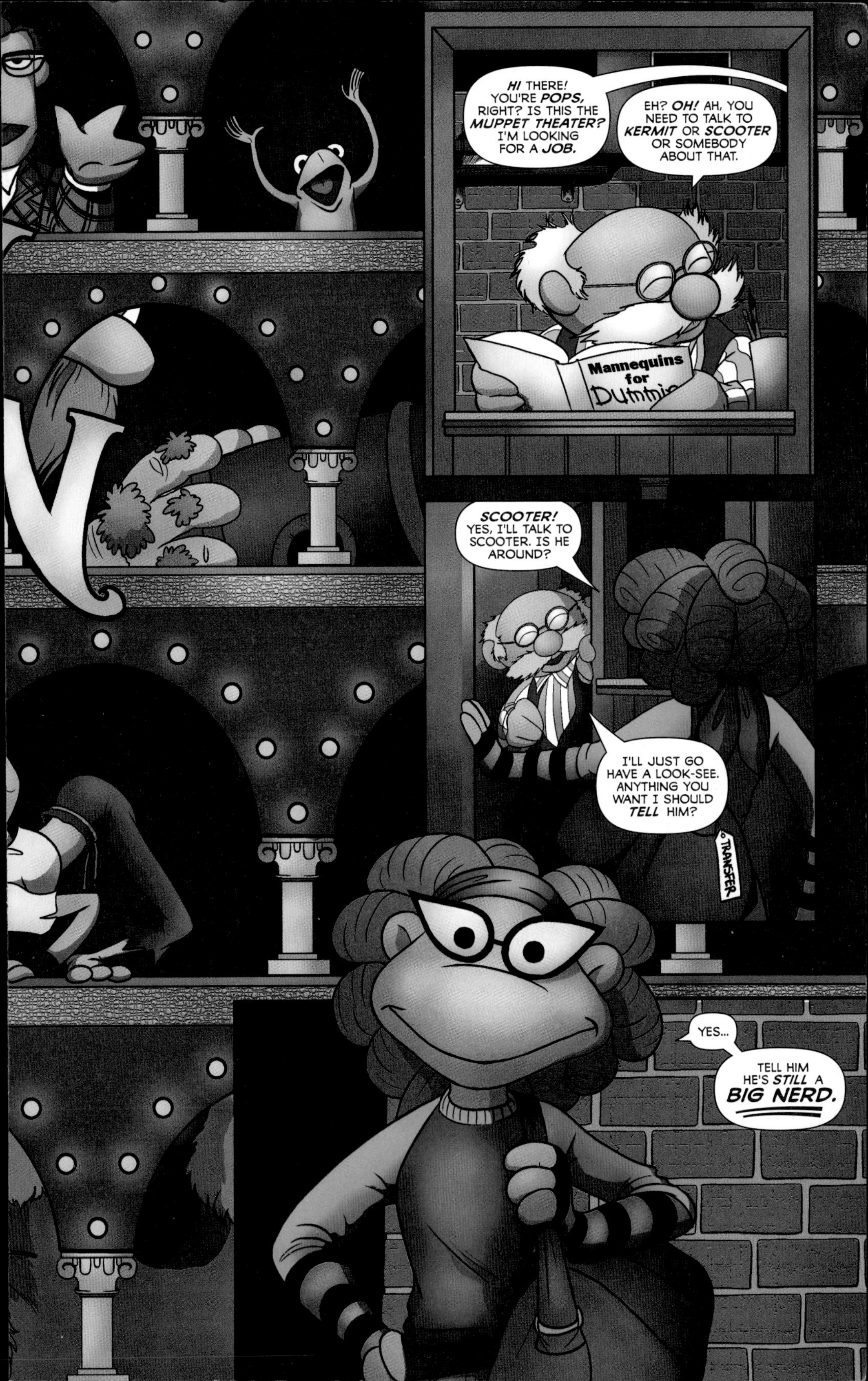
HI THERE! YOU'RE POPS, RIGHT? IS THIS THE MUPPET THEATER? I'M LOOKING FOR A JOB.
EH? OH! AH, YOU NEED TO TALK TO KERMIT OR SCOOTER OR SOMEBODY ABOUT THAT.
Mannequins for Dummie
SCOOTER! YES, I'LL TALK TO SCOOTER. IS HE AROUND?
I'LL JUST GO HAVE A LOOK-SEE. ANYTHING YOU WANT I SHOULD TELL HIM?
TRANSFER
YES...
TELL HIM HE'S STILL A BIG NERD.

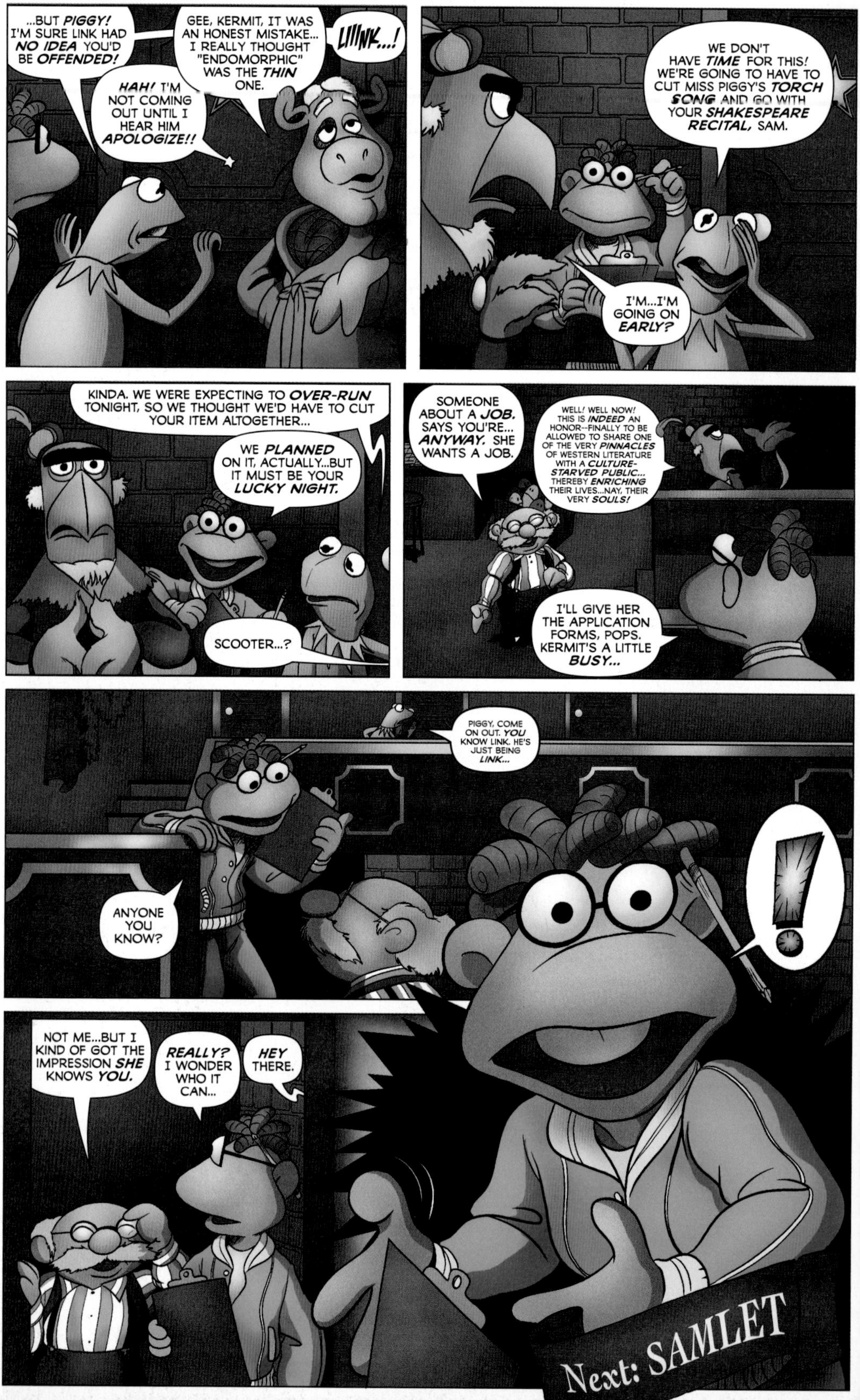
...BUT PIGGY! I'M SURE LINK HAD NO IDEA YOU'D BE OFFENDED!
GEE, KERMIT, IT WAS AN HONEST MISTAKE... I REALLY THOUGHT "ENDOMORPHIC" WAS THE THIN ONE.
LIIINK...!
HAH! I'M NOT COMING OUT UNTIL I HEAR HIM APOLOGIZE!!
WE DON'T HAVE TIME FOR THIS! WE'RE GOING TO HAVE TO CUT MISS PIGGY'S TORCH SONG AND GO WITH YOUR SHAKESPEARE RECITAL, SAM.
I'M...I'M GOING ON EARLY?
KINDA. WE WERE EXPECTING TO OVER-RUN TONIGHT, SO WE THOUGHT WE'D HAVE TO CUT YOUR ITEM ALTOGETHER...
WE PLANNED ON IT, ACTUALLY...BUT IT MUST BE YOUR LUCKY NIGHT.
SCOOTER...?
SOMEONE ABOUT A JOB. SAYS YOU'RE... ANYWAY. SHE WANTS A JOB.
WELL! WELL NOW! THIS IS INDEED AN HONOR--FINALLY TO BE ALLOWED TO SHARE ONE OF THE VERY PINNACLES OF WESTERN LITERATURE WITH A CULTURE-STARVED PUBLIC... THEREBY ENRICHING THEIR LIVES...NAY, THEIR VERY SOULS!
I'LL GIVE HER THE APPLICATION FORMS, POPS. KERMIT'S A LITTLE BUSY...
PIGGY, COME ON OUT. YOU KNOW LINK. HE'S JUST BEING LINK...
ANYONE YOU KNOW?
!
NOT ME...BUT I KIND OF GOT THE IMPRESSION SHE KNOWS YOU.
REALLY? I WONDER WHO IT CAN...
HEY THERE.
Next: SAMLET

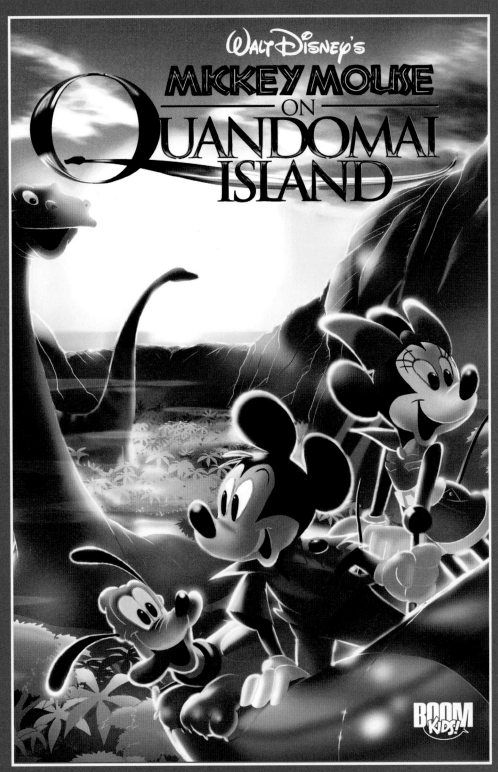

When their ship sinks in a storm, Mickey Mouse, Minnie, Goofy and the gang find themselves marooned on the mysterious Quandomai Island, where dinosaurs still roam the earth, and nothing is as it seems!

MICKEY MOUSE ON QUANDOMAI ISLAND
DIAMOND CODE: SEP100907
SC $9.99 ISBN 9781608865994

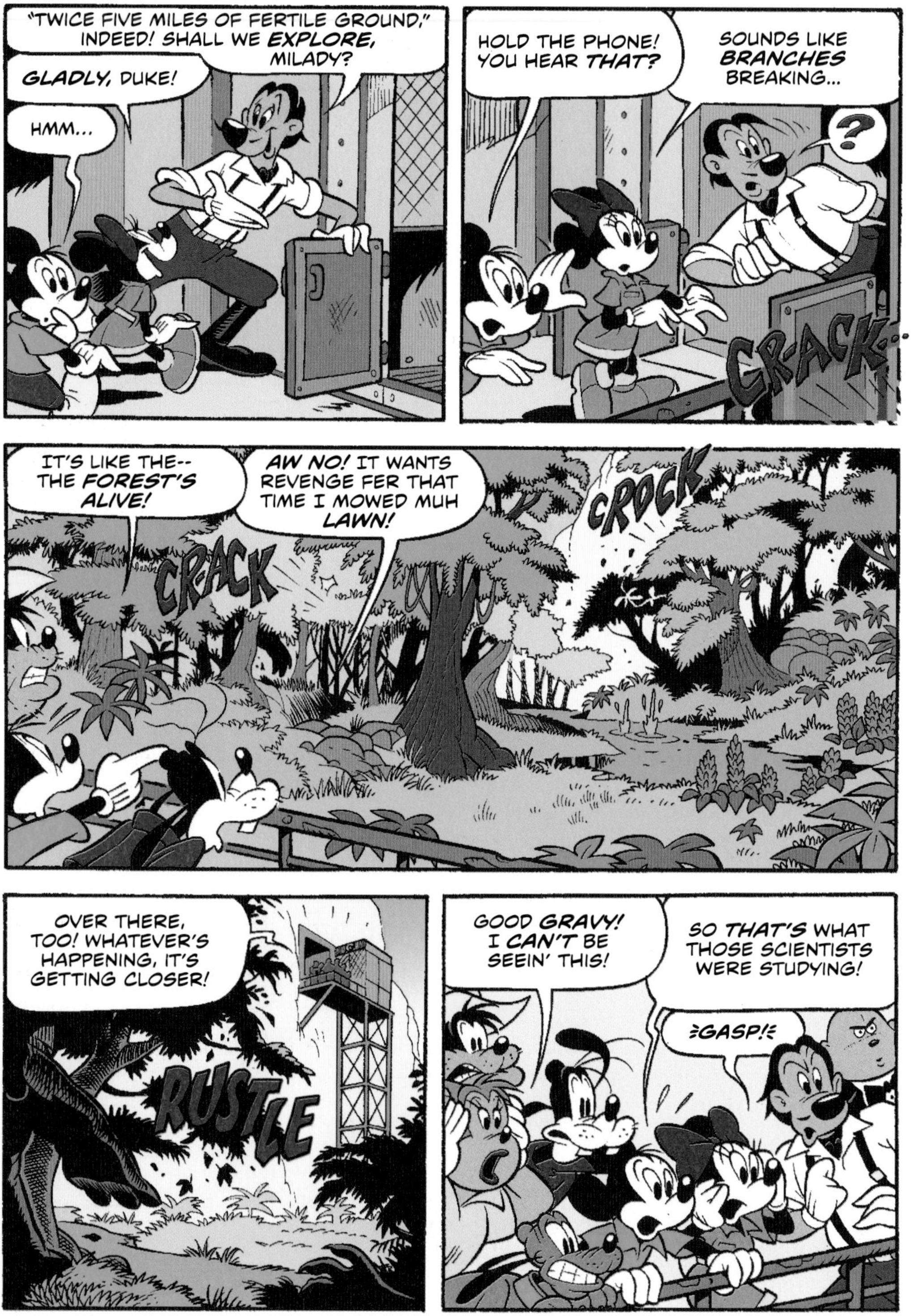
"TWICE FIVE MILES OF FERTILE GROUND," INDEED! SHALL WE EXPLORE, MILADY?
GLADLY, DUKE!
HMM...
HOLD THE PHONE! YOU HEAR THAT?
SOUNDS LIKE BRANCHES BREAKING...
?
CR-ACK...
IT'S LIKE THE-- THE FOREST'S ALIVE!
AW NO! IT WANTS REVENGE FER THAT TIME I MOWED MUH LAWN!
CROCK
CR-ACK
OVER THERE, TOO! WHATEVER'S HAPPENING, IT'S GETTING CLOSER!
RUSTLE
GOOD GRAVY! I CAN'T BE SEEIN' THIS!
SO THAT'S WHAT THOSE SCIENTISTS WERE STUDYING!
GASP!

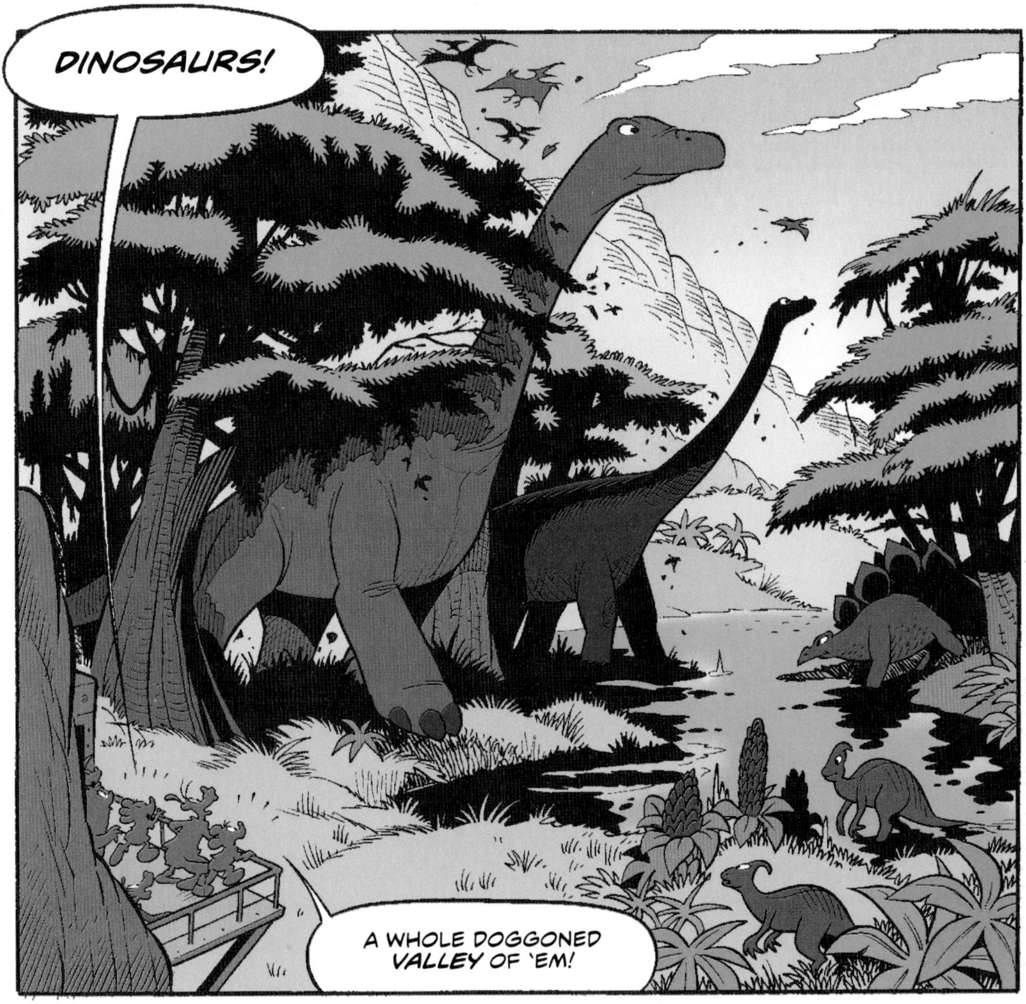
DINOSAURS!
A WHOLE DOGGONED VALLEY OF 'EM!

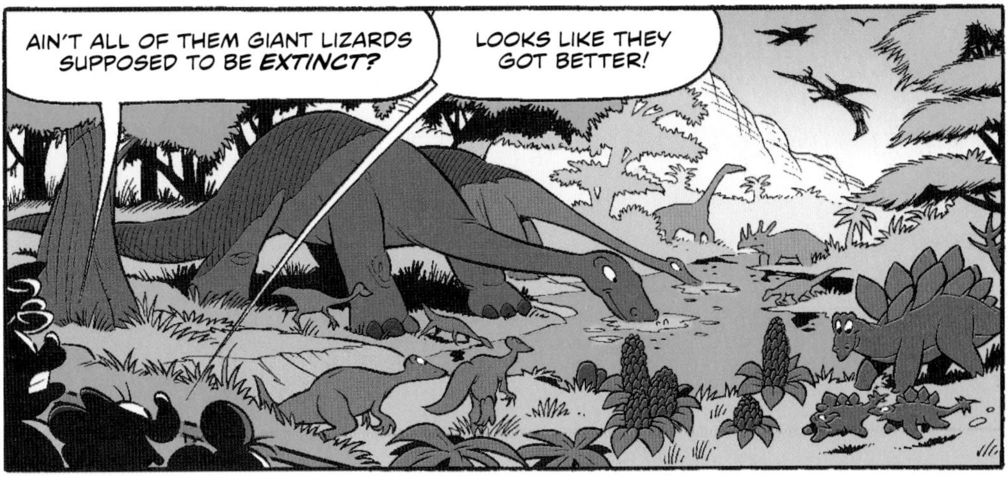
AIN'T ALL OF THEM GIANT LIZARDS SUPPOSED TO BE EXTINCT?
LOOKS LIKE THEY GOT BETTER!

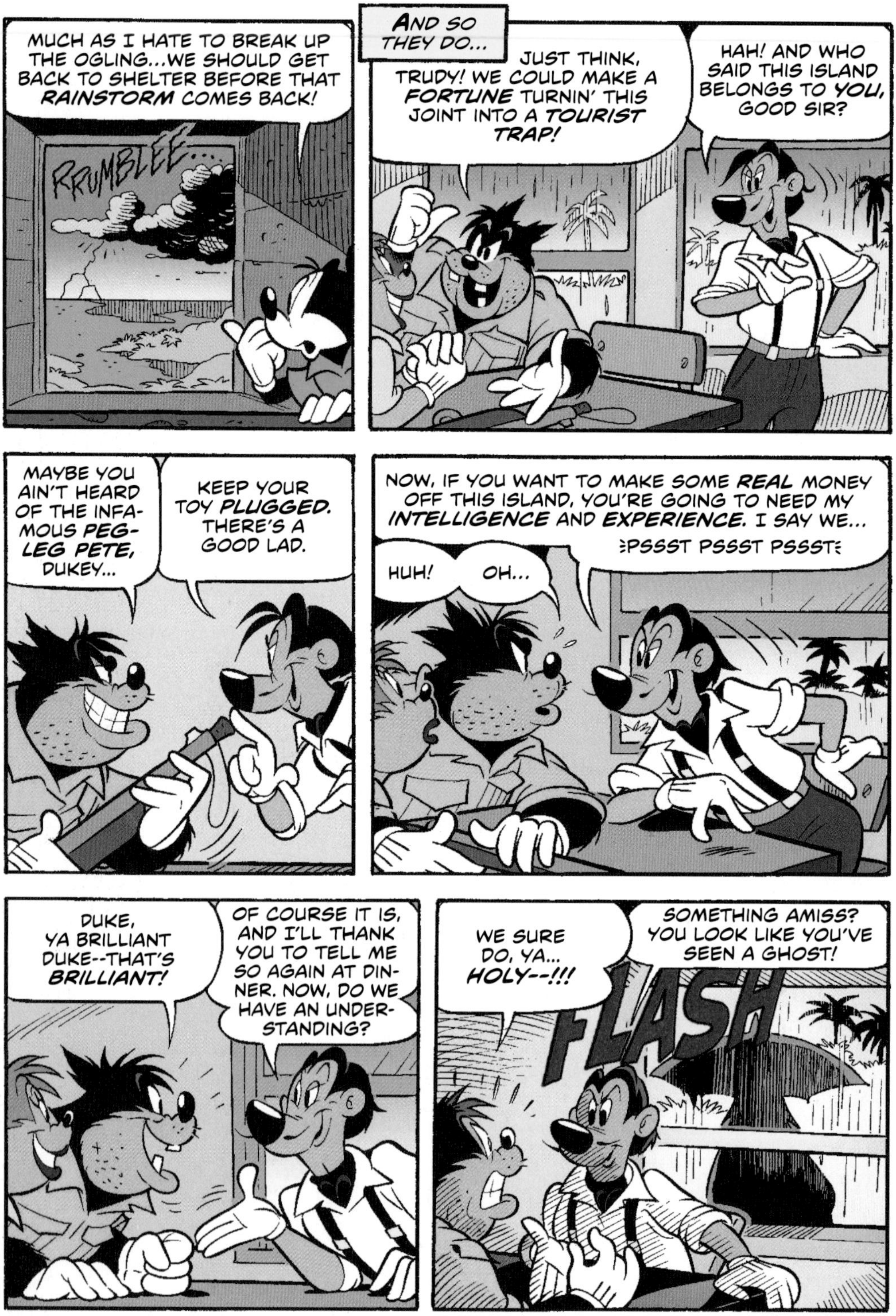
MUCH AS I HATE TO BREAK UP THE OGLING...WE SHOULD GET BACK TO SHELTER BEFORE THAT RAINSTORM COMES BACK!
RRUMBLEE...
AND SO THEY DO...
JUST THINK, TRUDY! WE COULD MAKE A FORTUNE TURNIN' THIS JOINT INTO A TOURIST TRAP!
HAH! AND WHO SAID THIS ISLAND BELONGS TO YOU, GOOD SIR?
MAYBE YOU AIN'T HEARD OF THE INFAMOUS PEG-LEG PETE, DUKEY...
KEEP YOUR TOY PLUGGED. THERE'S A GOOD LAD.
NOW, IF YOU WANT TO MAKE SOME REAL MONEY OFF THIS ISLAND, YOU'RE GOING TO NEED MY INTELLIGENCE AND EXPERIENCE. I SAY WE...
PSSST PSSST PSSST
HUH!
OH...
DUKE, YA BRILLIANT DUKE--THAT'S BRILLIANT!
OF COURSE IT IS, AND I'LL THANK YOU TO TELL ME SO AGAIN AT DINNER. NOW, DO WE HAVE AN UNDERSTANDING?
WE SURE DO, YA... HOLY--!!!
FLASH
SOMETHING AMISS? YOU LOOK LIKE YOU'VE SEEN A GHOST!

Someone is stealing comedy props from the other employees,
making it hard for them to harvest the laughter they need to
power Monstropolis...and all evidence points to Sulley's best
friend, Mike Wazowski!

MONSTERS, INC.: LAUGH FACTORY
DIAMOND CODE: OCT090801
SC $9.99 ISBN 9781608865086
HC $24.99 ISBN 9781608865338

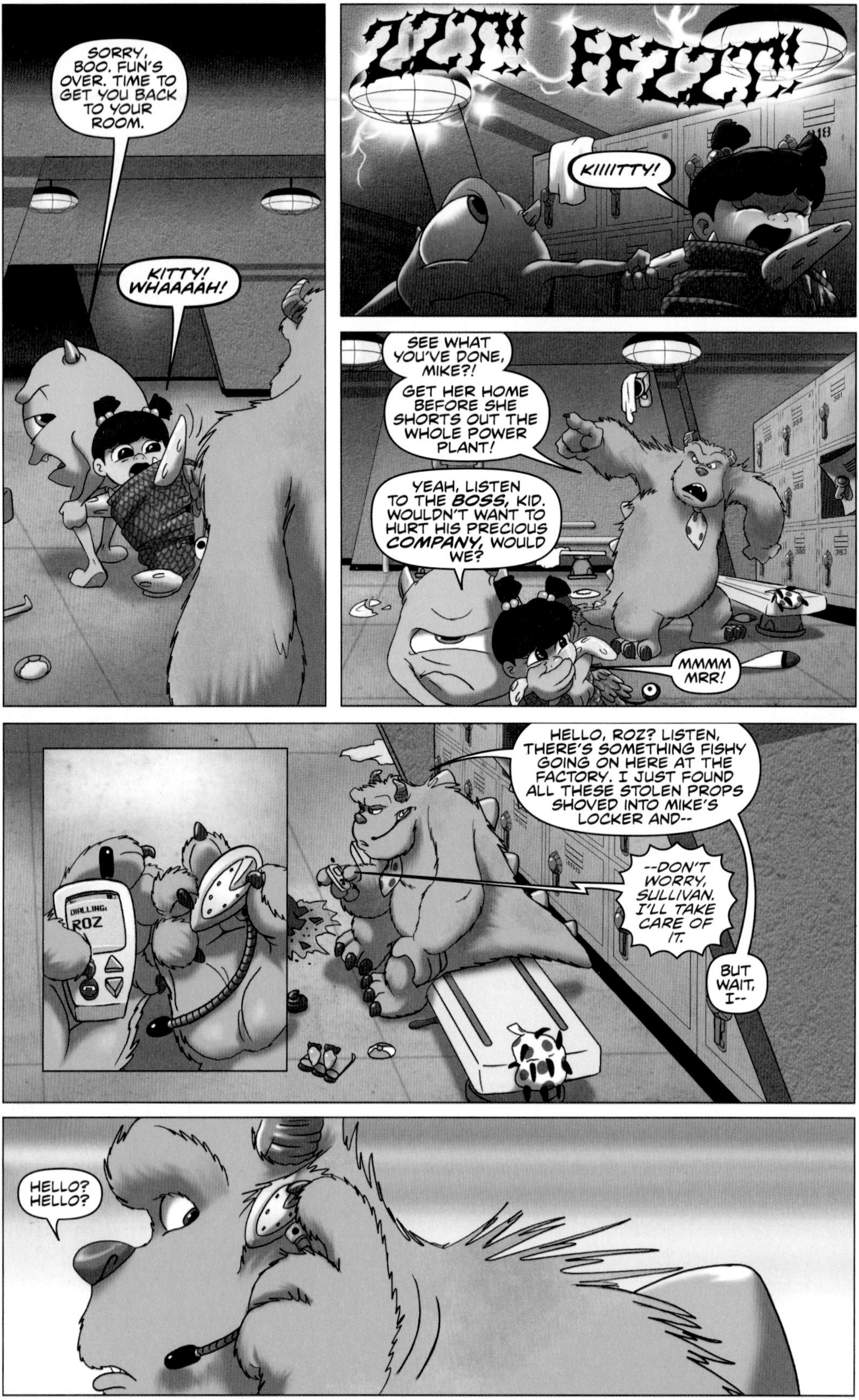
SORRY, BOO. FUN'S OVER. TIME TO GET YOU BACK TO YOUR ROOM.
KITTY! WHAAAAAH!
ZZZT!! FFZZZT!!
KIIIITTY!
SEE WHAT YOU'VE DONE, MIKE?!
GET HER HOME BEFORE SHE SHORTS OUT THE WHOLE POWER PLANT!
YEAH, LISTEN TO THE BOSS, KID. WOULDN'T WANT TO HURT HIS PRECIOUS COMPANY, WOULD WE?
MMMM MRR!
DIALLING: ROZ
HELLO, ROZ? LISTEN, THERE'S SOMETHING FISHY GOING ON HERE AT THE FACTORY. I JUST FOUND ALL THESE STOLEN PROPS SHOVED INTO MIKE'S LOCKER AND--
--DON'T WORRY, SULLIVAN. I'LL TAKE CARE OF IT.
BUT WAIT, I--
HELLO? HELLO?

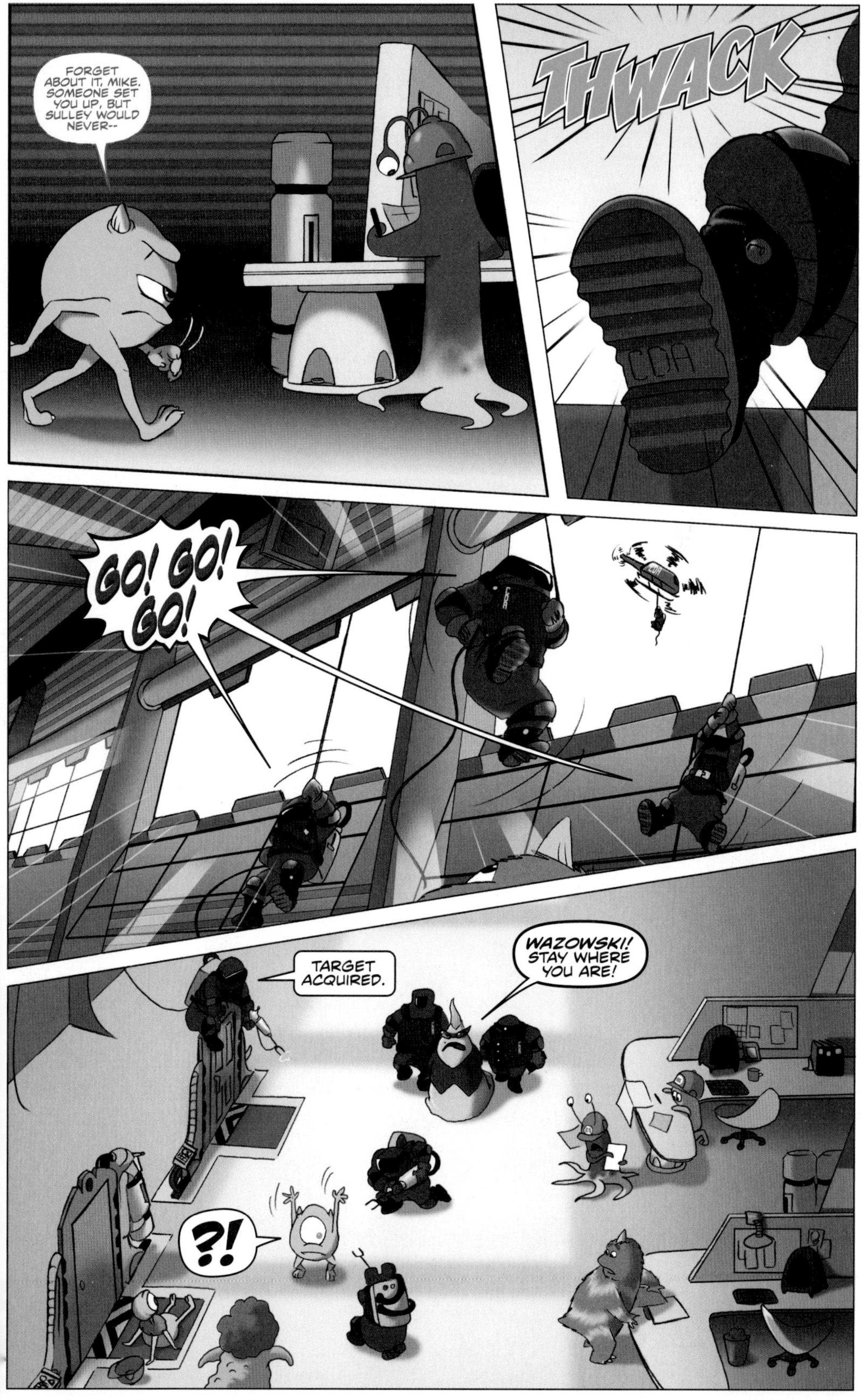
FORGET ABOUT IT, MIKE. SOMEONE SET YOU UP, BUT SULLEY WOULD NEVER--
THWACK
CDA
GO! GO! GO!
TARGET ACQUIRED.
WAZOWSKI! STAY WHERE YOU ARE!
?!

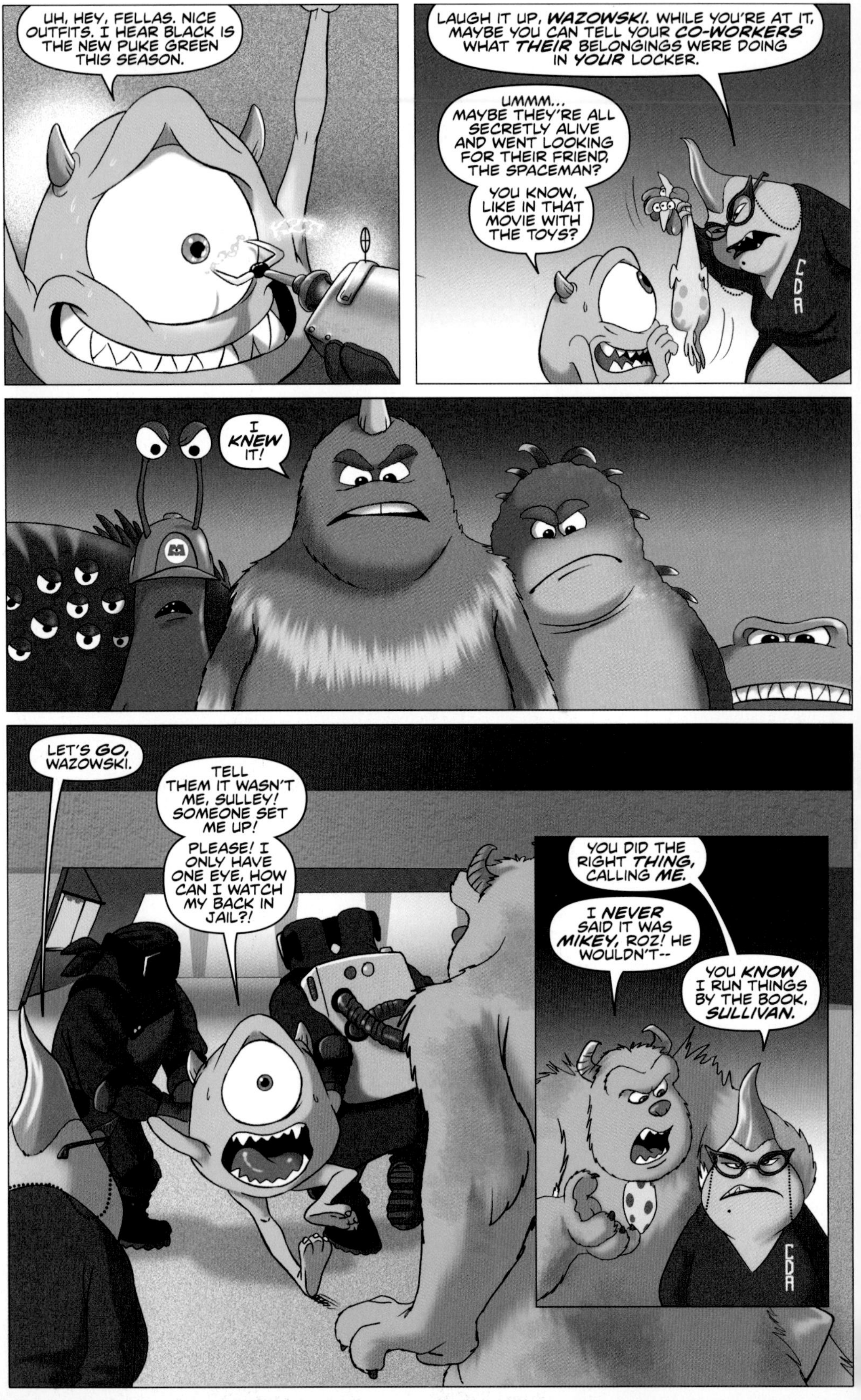
UH, HEY, FELLAS. NICE OUTFITS. I HEAR BLACK IS THE NEW PUKE GREEN THIS SEASON.
LAUGH IT UP, WAZOWSKI. WHILE YOU'RE AT IT, MAYBE YOU CAN TELL YOUR CO-WORKERS WHAT THEIR BELONGINGS WERE DOING IN YOUR LOCKER.
UMMM... MAYBE THEY'RE ALL SECRETLY ALIVE AND WENT LOOKING FOR THEIR FRIEND, THE SPACEMAN?
YOU KNOW, LIKE IN THAT MOVIE WITH THE TOYS?
CDA
I KNEW IT!
LET'S GO, WAZOWSKI.
TELL THEM IT WASN'T ME, SULLEY! SOMEONE SET ME UP!
PLEASE! I ONLY HAVE ONE EYE, HOW CAN I WATCH MY BACK IN JAIL?!
YOU DID THE RIGHT THING, CALLING ME.
I NEVER SAID IT WAS MIKEY, ROZ! HE WOULDN'T--
YOU KNOW I RUN THINGS BY THE BOOK, SULLIVAN.
CDA

# GRAPHIC NOVELS AVAILABLE NOW!

BOOM KIDS!

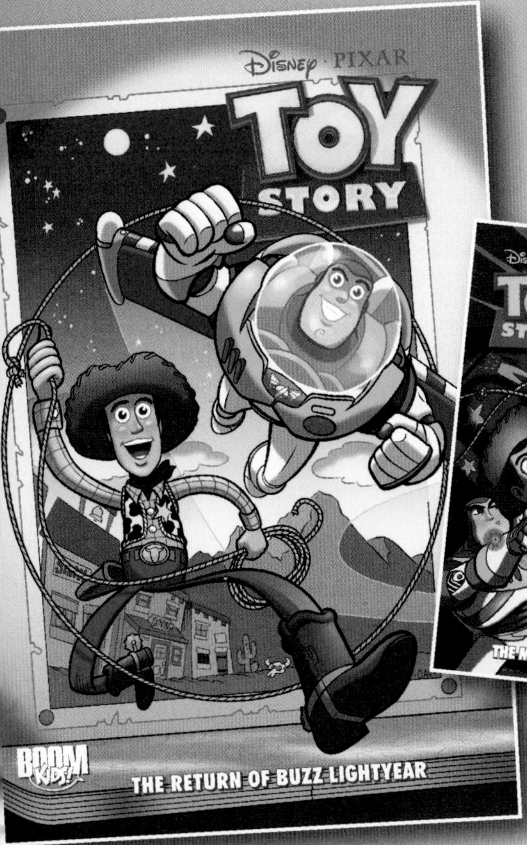

DISNEY · PIXAR
TOY STORY
BOOM KIDS!
THE RETURN OF BUZZ LIGHTYEAR


**TOY STORY: THE RETURN OF BUZZ LIGHTYEAR**

When Andy is given a surprise gift, no one is more surprised than the toys in his room...it's a second Buzz Lightyear! The stage is set for a Star Command showdown when only one Buzz can stay!

SC $9.99 ISBN 9781608865574
HC $24.99 ISBN 9781608865581

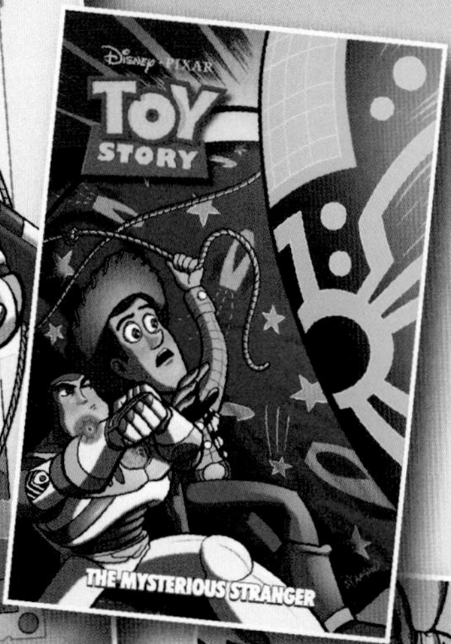

DISNEY · PIXAR
TOY STORY
THE MYSTERIOUS STRANGER


**TOY STORY: THE MYSTERIOUS STRANGER**

Andy has a new addition to his room–a circuit-laden egg. Is this new gizmo a friend or foe? This adventure kicks off the first of four self-contained stories featuring all your favorite characters from the TOY STORY movies – Woody, Buzz and the gang!

SC $9.99 ISBN 9781934506912
HC $24.99 ISBN 9781608865239

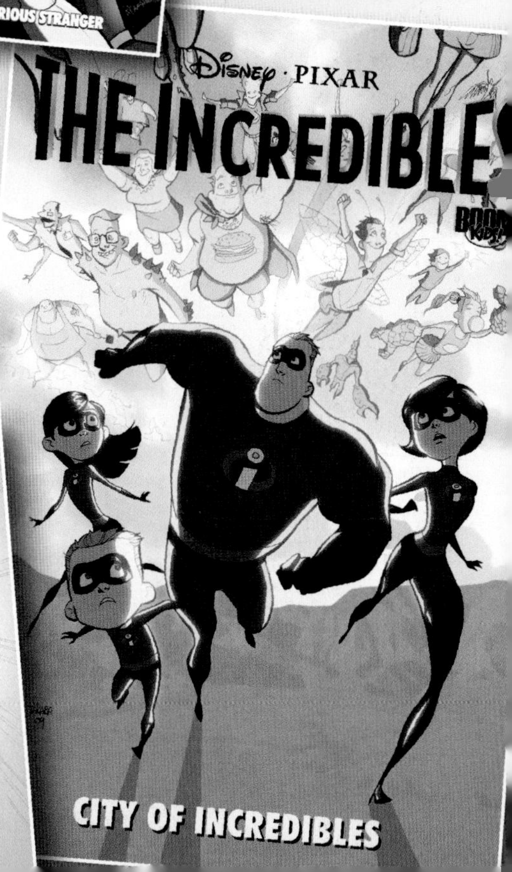

DISNEY · PIXAR
THE INCREDIBLES
BOOM KIDS!
CITY OF INCREDIBLES


**THE INCREDIBLES: CITY OF INCREDIBLES**

Baby Jack-Jack, everyone's favorite super-powered toddler, battles...a nasty cold! Hopefully the rest of the Parr family can stay healthy, because the henchmen of super villains are rapidly starting to exhibit superpowers!

SC $9.99 ISBN 9781608865031
HC $24.99 ISBN 9781608865291

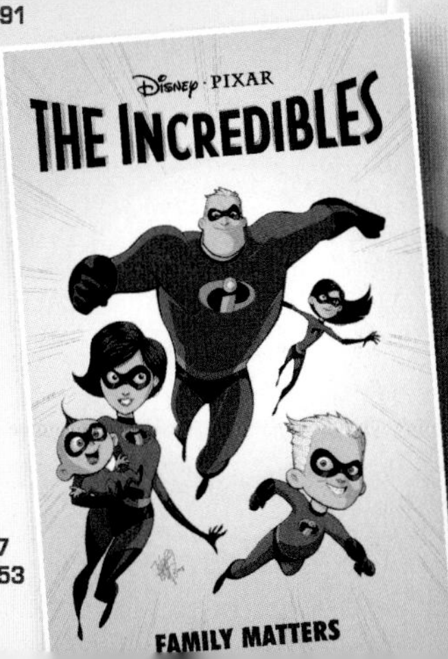

DISNEY · PIXAR
THE INCREDIBLES
FAMILY MATTERS


**THE INCREDIBLES: FAMILY MATTERS**

Acclaimed scribe Mark Waid has written the perfect INCREDIBLES story! What happens when Mr. Incredible's super-abilities start to wane...and how long can he keep his powerlessness a secret from his wife and kids?

SC $9.99 ISBN 9781934506837
HC $24.99 ISBN 9781608865253

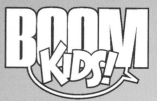

## WALL•E: RECHARGE

Before WALL•E becomes the hardworking robot we know and love, he lets the few remaining robots take care of the trash compacting while he collects interesting junk. But when these robots start breaking down, WALL•E must adjust his priorities...or else Earth is doomed!

SC $9.99 ISBN 9781608865123
HC $24.99 ISBN 9781608865543

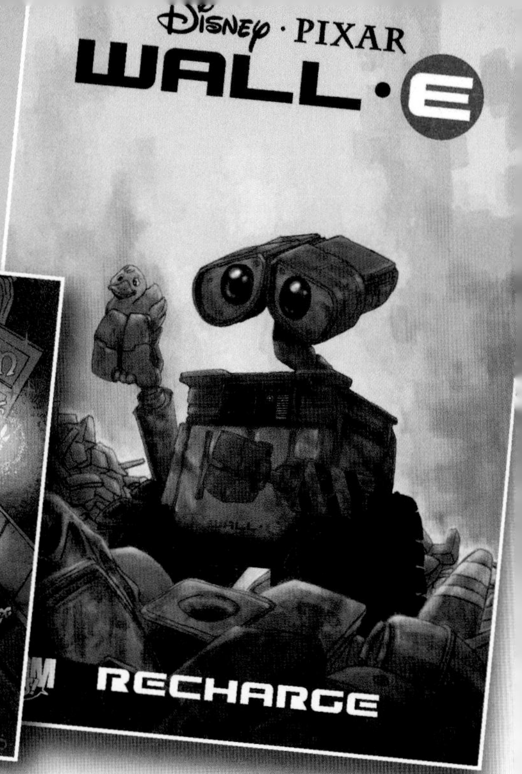
Disney · PIXAR
WALL·E
RECHARGE

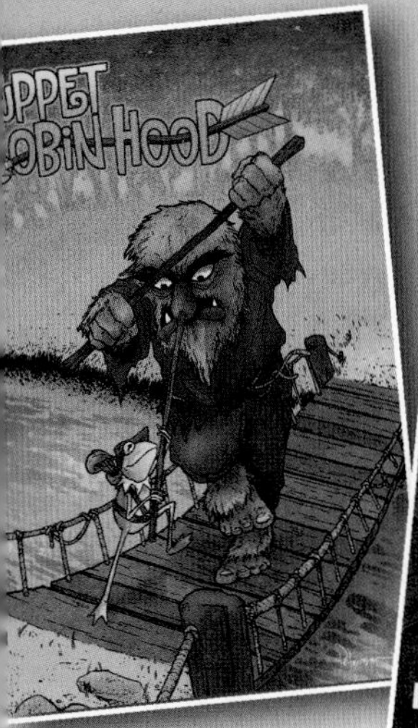

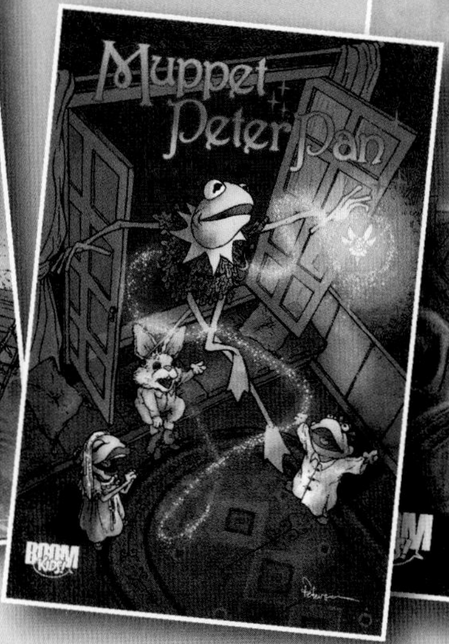
Muppet
Peter Pan

## MUPPET ROBIN HOOD

The Muppets tell the Robin Hood legend for laughs, and it's the reader who will be merry! Robin Hood (Kermit the Frog) joins with the Merry Men, Sherwood Forest's infamous gang of misfit outlaws, to take on the Sheriff of Nottingham (Sam the Eagle)!

SC $9.99 ISBN 9781934506790
HC $24.99 ISBN 9781608865260

## MUPPET PETER PAN

When Peter Pan (Kermit) whisks Wendy (Janice) and her brothers to Neverswamp, the adventure begins! With Captain Hook (Gonzo) out for revenge for the loss of his hand, can even the magic of Piggytink (Miss Piggy) save Wendy and her brothers?

SC $9.99 ISBN 9781608865079
HC $24.99 ISBN 9781608865314

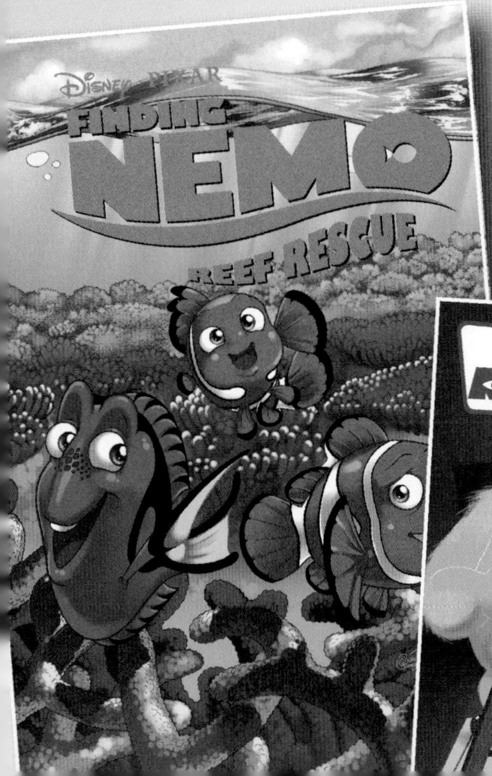
FINDING
NEMO
REEF RESCUE

## FINDING NEMO: REEF RESCUE

Nemo, Dory and Marlin have become local heroes, and are recruited to embark on an all-new adventure in this exciting collection! The reef is mysteriously dying and no one knows why. So Nemo and his friends must travel the great blue sea to save their home!

SC $9.99 ISBN 9781934506882
HC $24.99 ISBN 9781608865246

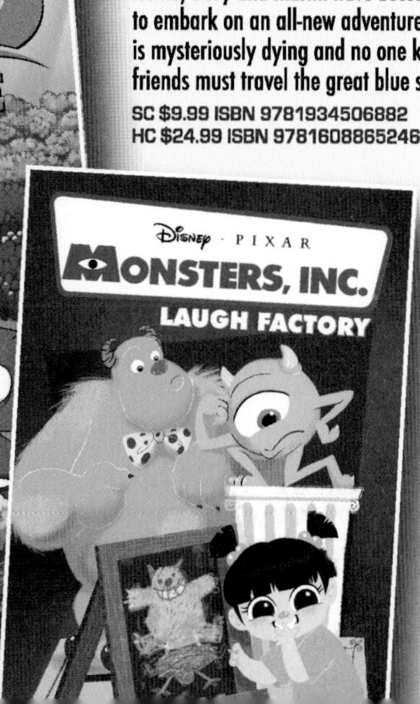
Disney · PIXAR
MONSTERS, INC.
LAUGH FACTORY

## MONSTERS, INC.: LAUGH FACTORY

Someone is stealing comedy props from the other employees, making it difficult for them to harvest the laughter they need to power Monstropolis...and all evidence points to Sulley's best friend Mike Wazowski!

SC $9.99 ISBN 9781608865086
HC $24.99 ISBN 9781608865338

## DISNEY'S HERO SQUAD: ULTRAHEROES VOL. 1: SAVE THE WORLD

It's an all-star cast of your favorite Disney characters, as you have never seen them before. Join Donald Duck, Goofy, Daisy, and even Mickey himself as they defend the fate of the planet as the one and only Ultraheroes!

SC $9.99 ISBN 9781608865437
HC $24.99 ISBN 9781608865529

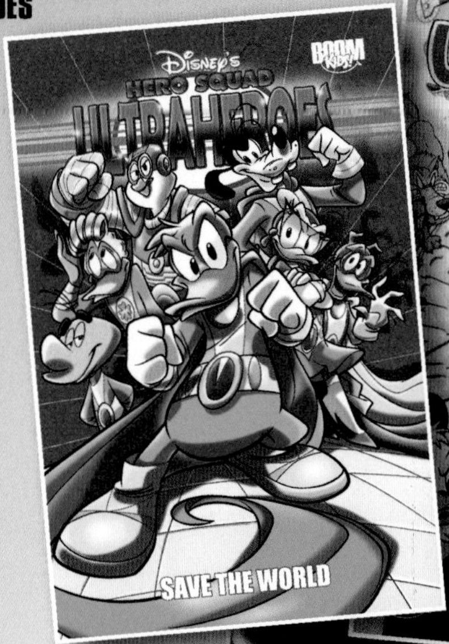
Disney's
HERO SQUAD
ULTRAHEROES
BOOM KIDS!
SAVE THE WORLD

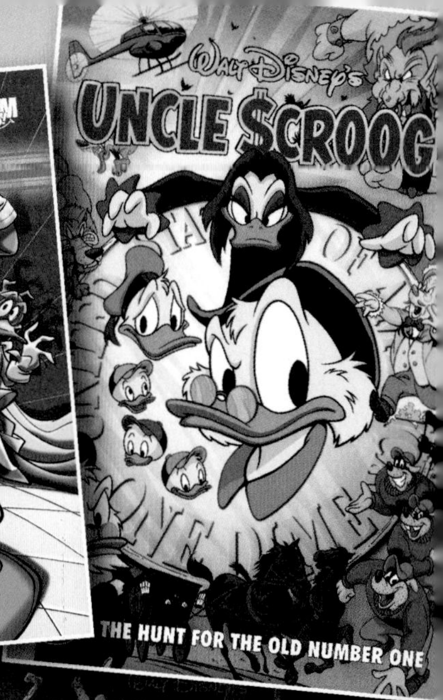
Walt Disney's
UNCLE $CROOGE
THE HUNT FOR THE OLD NUMBER ONE

## UNCLE SCROOGE: THE HUNT FOR THE OLD NUMBER ONE

Join Donald Duck's favorite penny-pinching Uncle Scrooge as he, Donald himself and Huey, Dewey, and Louie embark on a globe-spanning trek to recover treasure and save Scrooge's "number one dime" from the treacherous Magica De Spell.

SC $9.99 ISBN 9781608865475
HC $24.99 ISBN 9781608865536

## WIZARDS OF MICKEY VOL. 1: MOUSE MAGIC

Your favorite Disney characters star in this magical fantasy epic! Student of the great wizard Nereus, Mickey allies himself with Donald and teammate Goofy, in a quest to find a magical crown that will give him mastery over all spells!

SC $9.99 ISBN 9781608865413
HC $24.99 ISBN 9781608865505

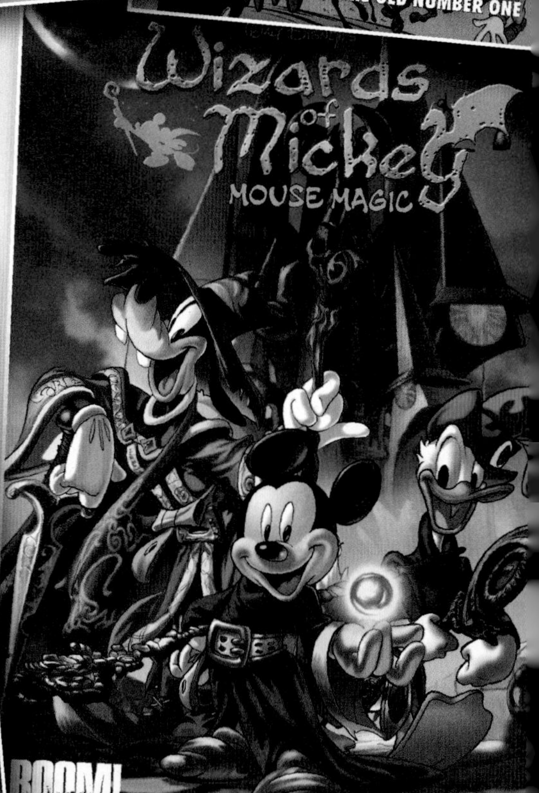
Wizards of Mickey
MOUSE MAGIC
BOOM! STUDIOS

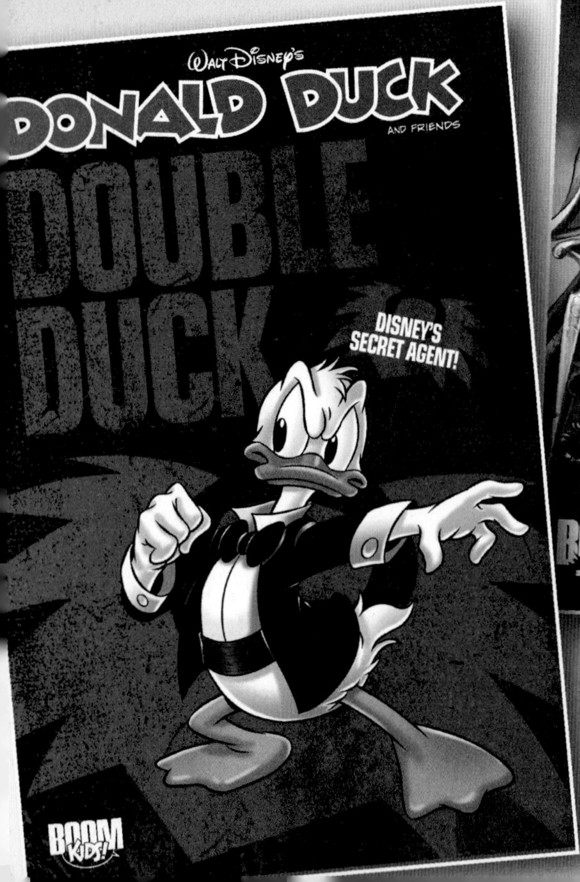
Walt Disney's
DONALD DUCK
AND FRIENDS
DOUBLE DUCK
DISNEY'S SECRET AGENT!
BOOM KIDS!

## DONALD DUCK AND FRIENDS: DOUBLE DUCK VOL. 1

Donald Duck as a secret agent? Villainous fiends beware as the world of super sleuthing and espionage will never be the same! This is Donald Duck like you've never seen him!

SC $9.99 ISBN 9781608865451
HC $24.99 ISBN 9781608865512

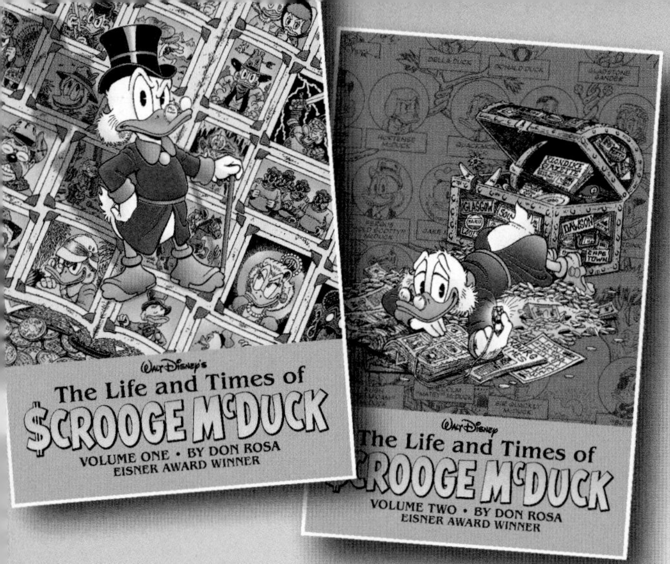

## THE LIFE AND TIMES OF SCROOGE McDUCK VOL. 1

BOOM Kids! proudly collects the first half of THE LIFE AND TIMES OF SCROOGE MCDUCK in a gorgeous hardcover collection — featuring smyth sewn binding, a gold-on-gold foil-stamped case wrap, and a bookmark ribbon! These stories, written and drawn by legendary cartoonist Don Rosa, chronicle Scrooge McDuck's fascinating life.
HC $24.99 ISBN 9781608865383

## THE LIFE AND TIMES OF SCROOGE McDUCK VOL. 2

BOOM Kids! proudly presents volume two of THE LIFE AND TIMES OF SCROOGE MCDUCK in a gorgeous hardcover collection in a beautiful, deluxe package featuring smyth sewn binding and a foil-stamped case wrap! These stories, written and drawn by legendary cartoonist Don Rosa, chronicle Scrooge McDuck's fascinating life.
HC $24.99 ISBN 9781608865420

## MICKEY MOUSE CLASSICS: MOUSE TAILS

See Mickey Mouse as he was meant to be seen! Solving mysteries, fighting off pirates, and generally saving the day! These classic stories comprise a "Greatest Hits" series for the mouse, including a story produced by seminal Disney creator Carl Barks!
HC $24.99 ISBN 9781608865390

## DONALD DUCK CLASSICS: QUACK UP

Whether it's finding gold, journeying to the Klondike, or fighting ghosts, Donald will always have the help of his much more prepared nephews — Huey, Dewey, and Louie — by his side. Featuring some of the best Donald Duck stories Carl Barks ever produced!
HC $24.99 ISBN 9781608865406

## WALT DISNEY'S VALENTINE'S CLASSICS

Love is in the air for Mickey Mouse, Donald Duck and the rest of the gang. But will Cupid's arrows cause happiness or heartache? Find out in this collection of classic stories featuring work by Carl Barks, Floyd Gottfredson, Daan Jippes, Romano Scarpa and Al Taliaferro.
HC $24.99 ISBN 9781608865499

## WALT DISNEY'S CHRISTMAS CLASSICS

BOOM Kids! has raided the Disney publishing archives and searched every nook and cranny to find the best and the greatest Christmas stories from Disney's vast comic book publishing history for this "best of" compilation.
HC $24.99 ISBN 9781608865482

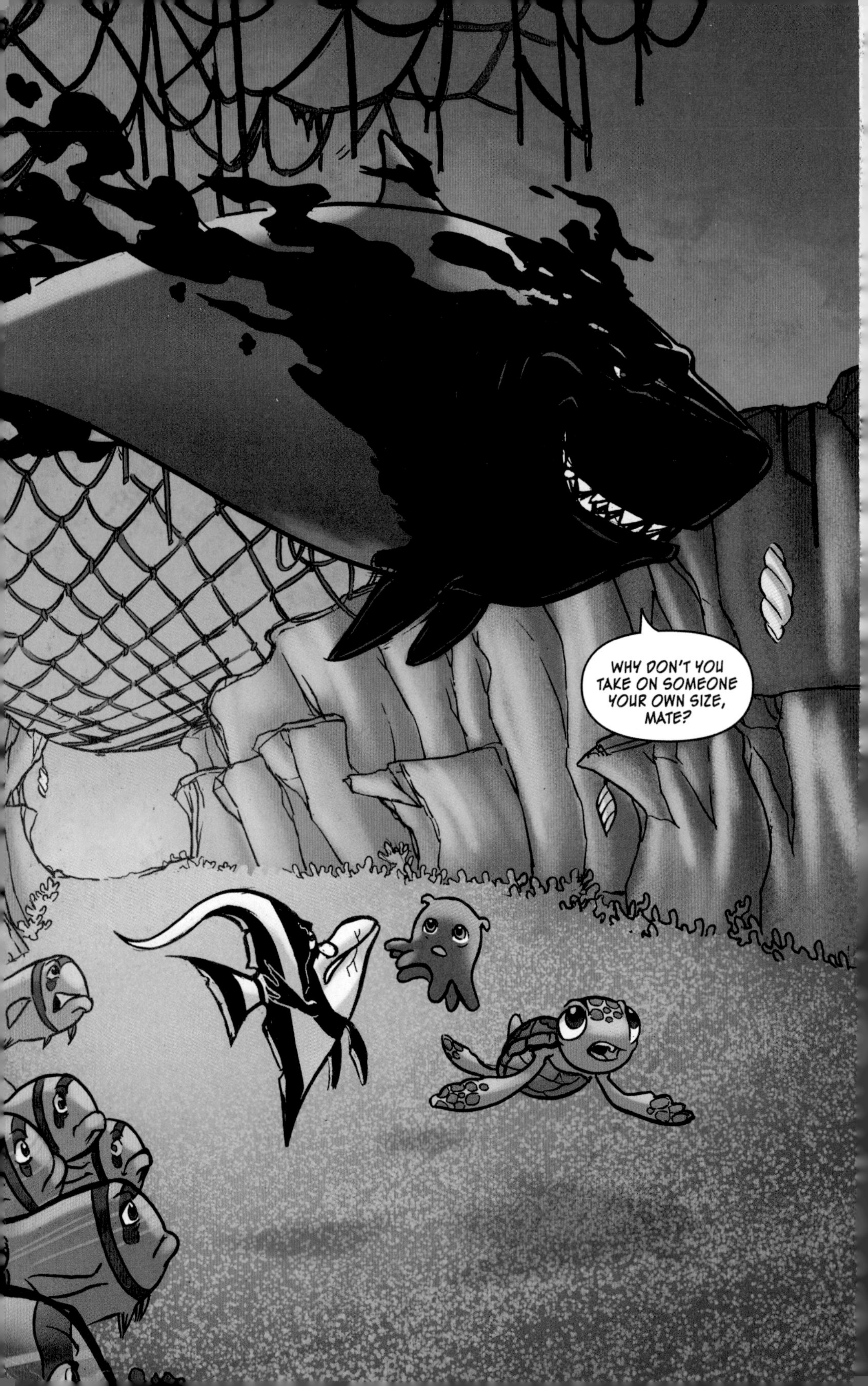
WHY DON'T YOU TAKE ON SOMEONE YOUR OWN SIZE, MATE?